F

ANCIENT ECHOES

ANCIENT ECHOES

ROBERT HOLDSTOCK

Copyright © Robert Holdstock 1996
All rights reserved

The right of Robert Holdstock to be identified as the author of this
work has been asserted him in accordance with the
Copyright, Designs and Patents Act 1988.

First published in Great Britain in 1996 by
Voyager
An imprint of Harper Collins *Publishers*

This edition published in Great Britain in 2009 by
Gollancz
An imprint of the Orion Publishing Group
Orion House, 5 Upper St Martin's Lane, London WC2H 9EA
An Hachette UK company

1 3 5 7 9 10 8 6 4 2

A CIP catalogue record for this book is available
from the British Library

ISBN 978 0 575 08418 6

Typeset at The Spartan Press Ltd,
Lymington, Hants

Printed and bound in the UK by
CPI Mackays, Chatham ME5 8TD

The Orion Publishing Group's policy is to use papers that
are natural, renewable and recyclable products and made
from wood grown in sustainable forests. The logging and
manufacturing processes are expected to conform to the
environmental regulations of the country of origin.

www.robertholdstock.com
www.orionbooks.co.uk

Contents

Between the idea
And the reality
Between the motion
And the act
Falls the Shadow
            For Thine is the Kingdom

T. S. Eliot: *The Hollow Men*

Woe to the bloody city!
It is all full of lies and predation.
Its prey departeth not!

Book of Nahum, 3: 1

PROLOGUE

The City

The man who had spent his life dowsing for lost cities eventually came to Exburgh, drawn by the shadow of ancient *Glanum*, a place of sanctuaries and sacred groves which had suddenly become visible to him among the office blocks and churches of the modern age.

For the next fourteen years, John Garth prowled the board-walks around each site, supervising the excavations with little more than a murmured word and gentle encouragement. To his own eyes, as the flint walls, the fallen trees and the forgotten shrines were exposed, the buried town of Glanum grew above him and around him, engaging all his senses as its ghosts seeped up from the excavation.

He took photographs and made sketches, but his gaze was as often in the middle distance, above the foundations, as on the cold remains below. A tall man, he wore his long, greying hair in a ponytail, below a wide-brimmed, black oilskin hat which helped to hide the deep and ugly scar between his eyes. Rain or shine, he dressed in boots, jeans and a long, olive-green raincoat. His eyes weakening as he approached the last years of his forties, he now wore gold-rimmed glasses. He had stopped smoking cigarettes, but regularly indulged in the luxury of a half-corona. The students and assistants who worked on the dig, scattered across the town, referred to him as the Sixties Kid, an affectionate nickname that amused him.

On a stifling, hot summer's day, he crouched on the muddy boards around the edge of what had been named the 'Hercules pit' and surveyed the shattered signs of the temple that were slowly coming to light. An archaeologist from Cambridge was supervising the site, which was being extensively photographed; and a detailed drawing was being made as four students with trowels and brushes did their gentle work in the dry clay, below the lines of white labels that tagged the levels.

As with everything that was emerging from Glanum, nothing was right about what Garth could see. The attribution to 'Hercules' was for convenience, based on little more than fragments of statue – muscular and male – and the base of what was unmistakably a granite phallic column. And yet there were clear intrusions of a second shrine, fragments of vast, carved stone vessels more familiar from the Minoan culture. And a mud-brick wall, almost *inserted* into the limestone of the Hercules shrine, suggesting either an earlier or an eccentric addition to this part of the city.

Nothing was right, and Garth was not surprised. Like the bones of prehistoric men, the bones of ancient cities could be mixed, mingled and confused in the grave. Garth, though, was entertaining another possibility, one that had little to do with the compression of time.

And then, as he tried to smell, see and hear the true life of this strange place, his mind drifting through the ghostly walls, there was a shout from below.

'There's something here!'

Drawn back to reality, Garth stood and strode quickly round the boardwalk.

There's something here!

How many times in his long life had he heard those words? It was a phrase he never tired of hearing.

He slipped down the ladder to the lower level of the pit and crossed to the flash of colour that one of the students had revealed. She was kneeling, sitting back, shaking her head as she stared at the wall.

'What have we got?'

'Two masks,' she said, using the brush as a pointer, outlining the faces. 'Pecked out of the mudbrick, I think, thinly

2

plastered and painted. The colour is very strong, though the plaster's loosening.' She seemed uncomfortable. 'There's something not right about them.'

'Not right?'

'They make me nervous. I don't want to work on them any more. If you don't mind.'

'I don't mind,' Garth said, and took the brush from her.

Gently, then, over the next two hours, he revealed the faces, one decorated in black and white, the other in whorls and stripes of green. The eyes of both had been gouged out and the mouths gaped. The green mask had a 'female' feel to its shape.

'Well, well. Hello again . . .'

Eventually, he couldn't resist the impulse: he reached out with both hands, one to each mask, and touched the dead eyes.

It was nearly three o'clock in the afternoon.

For the first time in ages, he felt a city shift below him . . .

PART ONE

Shadows in Stone

I

Ten minutes before the end of the class, the unmistakable and pungent aroma of dense, dank forest began to emanate from Jack Chatwin.

It was a bright day and he was sitting by the open window, staring vacantly out across the playing fields. The room was filled with the sweet smell of newly-cut grass, coming off the sun-warmed football pitch. The class was drowsy with warmth and the dullness of the lesson, which was on the subject of Language, Literature and the Representation of the Primitive. Miss Pierce paced up and down, reading from Golding's *The Inheritors*, punctuating her reading with sharp, critical points that a few of the pupils were lazily noting, their enthusiasm for the dissection no match for their enjoyment of the book itself.

The sudden, alien smell of musty woodland made Angela Harris look up sharply from her notes. She was sitting behind Jack and her first thought was that the school's drains had flooded; but she caught the faint illumination around her friend and leaned forward sharply.

'He's shimmering!' she hissed to the girl sitting next to her. 'It's happening again.'

Instinctively, she glanced at the classroom clock. *Ten minutes to three*. She scrawled the time on her pad then again leaned close to Jack.

Around the boy's wavy brown hair, a ripple of strange light had formed. It was so thin it might have been a film of moisture, but Angela could see flashing greens and reds, and something white in that faint halo, moving left to right then back. There was the faintest sound of shouting, so distant it might have been a child playing across the fields, but it was coming from Jack Chatwin, who sat still and silent at his desk!

The wildwood blew at her, and she breathed the other world, drawn to it, drawn to Jack through the almost ecstatic nature of her curiosity.

Deborah had slipped from her chair and tip-toed to the front of the class, halting the intense reading from Golding, drawing Miss Pierce's attention to the boy.

'He's shimmering.'

'Are you sure? Then fetch Mr Keeble.'

As Deborah went for the headmaster, the teacher opened the resources cupboard, where a video camera was set up and ready to run. She pulled the camera and its trolley into the room, focused it carefully on Jack in full close-up and set it recording.

Around the silent, dreaming boy, the rest of the class had drawn back, shuffling on their chairs, delighted at the break in routine and fascinated by the odd phenomenon. Angela had reached out her hand and was trying to touch the *shimmering*. As she brushed Jack's hair the boy moaned, then raised his voice in a cry that was more akin to pain than pleasure.

'Move away from him, Angela,' Miss Pierce said quietly, and the girl drew back her hand.

'I was just seeing if I could feel it,' she said.

'I don't want him disturbed.'

'It's very close,' Angela murmured. 'They're very frightened. Several people. I can hear them shouting . . .'

Miss Pierce frowned at that, but again insisted, 'Move away for the moment.'

The headteacher came quickly, quietly into the room and walked over to the boy, leaning down to stare at the film of light. He sniffed the air. He carried the reek of pipe-tobacco about him, but he still wrinkled his nose at the scent of rotting forest.

'Has he said anything? Do we know where the hell he is now?'

Miss Pierce was touching absorbent paper discs to the skin of Jack's neck and cheeks, where the *shimmering* was most visible and moisture was forming. 'Use the trigger word,' she whispered, putting the discs into a sterile bottle.

After a second, Keeble agreed. He spoke slowly, steadily. 'Tell me about the hunters. Jack? Tell me about the hunters.'

'Greyface,' Jack said. He was almost inaudible, the word, which he kept repeating, no more than a breath.

'Tell me about the hunters. Jack? Tell me about the hunters.'

'Greyface,' Jack said, aloud this time. He became agitated, looking away from the window and into the class, a watery, frightened gaze that swept past teachers and pupils alike. 'Greenface is lost. She's sinking . . . in the river . . . too deep, too fast. . . Greyface swimming down for her. Hitting the rocks, bruising, bleeding. The stone beast is close. The bull is close. It's so cold . . .'

'Where are they, Jack? Can you tell me where they are?'

'Running . . . hunters being hunted . . . so far to travel . . . Greenface is drowning . . .'

'Is it our world, Jack?'

'Not our world.'

'Can you tell which world it is?'

'Far away place. Very far away. But closer now. Running closer . . .' He began to gasp for breath, half choking, hands flapping at the air. Around him, no one moved. The video camera whirred.

A second later, before Keeble could continue to speak to him, or act, Jack flung himself to his feet with a howling cry, followed by a long, loud inhalation. He stood rigidly, eyes staring, his head tilted up. As he sucked in breath it was as if he had surfaced from water and was struggling again for life.

The moment of drowning had passed. Greenface was alive. And Jack fell into the headteacher's waiting arms, a limp figure still shuddering with the aftershock of the encounter.

2

Camera and tape-recorder running, his pulse connected to an oscillograph, Jack sat in the technician's room of the physics lab. The headmaster leaned against one of the benches, Angela next to him, her notebook ready, her gaze intense and curious as she waited for the session to begin. Opposite Jack sat a psychologist from Exburgh's General Hospital, a woman who was fascinated by the paranormal and who had agreed to be on call should the *shimmering* effect occur again. He was to call her Ruth. Jack was slightly intimidated by the fierceness of her blue eyes and the sharp authority in her voice, but she spoke reassuringly, now, calming him as she explained what she was doing, how she wished to proceed.

It was not a lie-detector, she pointed out as she finished taping electrodes to his wrist and temples. She was simply looking to see where the memory of his encounter was sharpest, and where his own imagination might be filling in gaps in perceived detail.

The chemical samples from his skin had already been passed to the hospital's forensic section to see if there were traces of the sort of chemicals – terpenes, esters – that would be found in a dank wildwood.

Jack was impatient to get on with the 'debriefing'. It was nearly five, now, and he wanted to earn some money. His friend Simon and the others would be waiting outside; and his parents would want him home by seven. They'd already called to agree the session and for it to proceed without them. Neither could get away from work. Finally, Ruth said, 'Now. I want you to describe what you saw, how you saw it, every detail that is familiar to you from this encounter. Don't worry about repeating yourself. Just say it as you felt it, and saw it.

'Begin now, please.'

Angela looked over at him and smiled, giving him a supportive thumbs-up.

They're like humans, but they're not human. The man is tall and very fast on his feet; his face is painted grey, his hair looks silver and he wears a thick, black headband with animal teeth stitched into it. He carries a heavy leather pack, and two long spears. He has a foul cloak made out of scalps and feathers, mostly black, some coppery, so that they gleam in the twilight. It's a twilight world. The sun seems so big, the sky so red. It's not always like that, I just don't think they come close when the day is hottest. But I've seen blue sky, and the tall towers, but just in glimpses. In the dreams it's always twilight.

Greenface is tall too. Her face is covered in lines and circles of green marks, running up from her chin, over her mouth and fanning out on each side. Her eyes are really dark. Her hair is long and shining black. She ties it to a brooch on her shoulder when she's running. Sometimes she ties it into strands with blue glass beads. She glitters with amber and green stones, very polished and shiny. She carries two long pipes which she uses to shoot darts when the strange-looking creatures attack them. She plays them too, and Greyface does a twirling dance with his eyes closed. The tunes aren't very interesting. Sometimes, at the end of the twilight, she goes and crouches by rivers and lakes and watches the flocks of waterbirds. I think she's crying.

Greyface lopes through the woods like a wolf. He's a good hunter. He only ever seems really afraid when he sees the tall, stone towers, or hears the creatures. They don't have horses or carts or anything like that, just running all the time. Sometimes there are sounds like machines coming and going, a deep vibrating noise, and the running people are very wary.

I don't know who's following them, who's chasing them,

but they're running for their lives. They're looking for a gate made of ivory, I think, and Greenface sometimes gets upset. She doesn't think they'll get there before the hunters hunt them down. Greyface keeps shouting at her, encouraging her to run. She finds paths and escape routes, but she's very sad.

There's something else:

I think they did something terrible. A long way away – very far away – in a city. They did something that means they can never go back. The people from the city are following them. It's the city people, I think, who build the watching towers which frighten the runners.

That's just a feeling.

I saw them really clearly this time. They were in a thick wood, very hot, very humid. There was something behind them, running on hindlegs, but so big it was getting caught in the undergrowth. There was a lot of briar with small, red flowers on it. Greyface was hacking his way through it with a big, stone blade with a heavy wooden handle.

Then suddenly they'd slipped down a bank and over the edge of a rocky cliff, falling quite a way into a narrow gorge. They splashed into the water and sank a long way down before surfacing. Rubble and dirt were falling after them from the precipice and a piece of stone hit Greenface and she started to sink again. She was choking. I could feel her beginning to swallow water, then Greyface had swum down and grabbed her. The river was running very fast, surging over sharp rocks, but he hauled them both to a ledge, turned her face down and she started to be sick, then breathed in, gasping for breath. He went back into the water and rescued the pack. For a moment I thought I was drowning. I was so close, so *inside* them both. And then it was like falling asleep again. It always ends with me falling asleep.

He shrugged to indicate he'd finished. But Ruth was fascinated.

'I want to hear more!'

3

He had been five years old when the bull-runners first smashed through the walls of space-time and plundered his inner eye.

He was on a hillside, looking out over scattered woods, downland and fields golden with late summer wheat, hazy in the strong sun. Behind him, in the shade of tall trees on the knoll, his father sat cross-legged and contemplative, staring into the distance, while his mother read a fat book, lazily turning the pages.

The remains of the picnic were scattered on the white cloth, where two finches darted in to feed.

Jack suddenly wanted to run down the hill, arms wide like a plane, until the wind took him and lifted him, to float out across the fragrant land. It was a dream he often experienced, though he was usually hunched up, arms round his legs, skimming the tree tops, turning sharp angles, circling above and around his home. Now he wanted to run. He could hear running, the sound of gasping breath. His legs felt compelled to move as the sound of people running came pounding close behind him.

He glanced back in fright, just as the shadow-shapes leaped across him, making him cry out. In the trees behind his parents, an enormous red-faced bull bellowed; he glimpsed the spread of its horns, the wet glistening around its mouth.

If he was aware of his father's cry of alarm, he later forgot it. Suddenly he was running – running down the hill – then towards the sandstone cliff, to the overhang, where deep shadows on the sun-baked red rock suggested shelter, safety.

The tall, dark man in his swirling cloak was ahead of him, the woman in her leopard skins and flayed leathers running at his shoulder, her green face grimacing with fear.

On he ran, towards the cliff, above the wide, parched land, descending fast, his legs threatening to give way.

He started to scream. An animal's breath was hot and hoarse behind him, bellowing suddenly as the ground thundered beneath its hooves.

The bull-runners had fled into the shadows against the rock wall. Jack stumbled, rolling towards the precipice – falling heavily down the hill until strong arms grabbed him, halted his uncontrollable tumble. Breathless, he gazed at the sky. His father's ruddy face loomed close.

'What are you doing? You'll hurt yourself, you silly boy! What was all that screaming?'

He didn't know what to say. He watched a floating cloud, felt the warm drops of sweat from his father's face on his own.

'The running people. Running before the bull. Red cliffs . . .'

'You've been daydreaming,' the strong man said. 'Come on. It's a long way back to the knoll.'

He stood, hauled up by his father. He heard his mother's voice, distantly, and his father shouted, 'He's fine. Just acting on impulse. Get the heart massage machine ready for me, though.'

He grinned down at the wheezing boy. 'You certainly run fast!'

'Bull-runners. Running from the bull.'

They began the hot walk up the hill.

His story about two running people was put down to a blossoming imagination. His cousin Roland was much the same, an older lad who delighted in constructing wild tales, usually concerned with the grotesque murders of the Victorian Age, from Burke and Hare to the Ripper, but often with that abiding obsession of the young: buried treasure.

Jack liked Roland's company, he liked the stories, he liked the hidden camps in his cousin's huge family garden in Devon, a tract of land that opened onto fields, and the river shore. He especially liked fantasizing about building a raft and floating away down the wide river and out to sea.

It was here, two years after the incident known in the family as 'running-down-the-hill', that Jack glimpsed the two hunted people for the second time. He was sitting with Roland on the upturned rowing boat that belonged to Roland's family. It was a cool autumn day, heavily overcast and showery and the river was grey and choppy.

They'd been sitting in silence for a while, caught in that restless *ennui* that comes from being aspiringly adventurous, but constrained by the conditions of the weather. They certainly didn't want to go up to the house, where the parents and grandparents would be talking endlessly about things the boys had no interest in. They wanted to go exploring, but Jack had to leave in thirty minutes for the return drive to Exburgh.

With a shift in the wind came the smell of fire and the sound of flames, huge flames, like a forest burning . . .

The man and the woman were suddenly stumbling towards him, the wood behind them brilliant with the conflagration. Both of the bull-runners were coughing violently, the woman crying out in her distress. She was carrying a flaming torch, which she cast aside, throwing it into Jack's face, it seemed. They ran past him, smoke streaming from the fire that burned them, brushing at their smouldering clothes. Jack heard the roar of an animal beyond the wall of fire, the shaking of the earth as it ran towards him. In terror, he turned and ran after the hunters, the heat making him sweat, the smoke making him gag. The land gave way to water, an angled drop down rocks, and he scrambled down to the cool river, where Grey-face and Greenface were already immersed and swimming strongly in the current. As he followed them in, splashing helplessly as the river swept him round and down towards the sheer sides of a gorge, he looked back and saw the swaying shape of an immense horned animal, standing on the rocks above the water.

Behind it, white stone towers gleamed! The ruins of a castle, he imagined, reaching right to the river, half fallen into the river itself.

This was all he glimpsed before the current tugged him down and he felt water in his lungs . . .

And was suddenly being dragged up by the hair, pulled to the shore amidst screaming voices and confusion.

Roland was half crying, half shouting.

'He just suddenly ran into the water! I couldn't stop him. He shouted, "It's burning!" and ran into the water. But I can't swim! I can't swim!'

A soothing voice calmed the boy. Then Jack's father's voice, '*Was* something burning, Roland?'

'No. I *did* smell woodsmoke, just briefly, but there wasn't a fire. He just ran away from the shore. He was splashing so hard, but he was in deep water in no time. I can't swim. I'm sorry . . .'

'It's OK, Roland. You did the right thing, fetching us as quickly as you did. Everything's all right. Jack's OK, now. Aren't you, Jack?'

Jack sat up, shivering. It was beginning to rain again. He stared at the ring of solemn, adult faces. Their expressions seemed to demand an explanation.

'I thought there was a fire. I followed the running people, the bull-runners. I think they'd started it – the fire – to stop the beast – but they got caught in it . . .'

'The runners, again,' his father said, shaking his head and looking away in exasperation.

His mother said something sharp to her husband, then helped Jack up and placed a heavy towel around his shoulders. He huddled inside it, shaken and confused, as he followed the procession back up the five wooden steps from the shoreline and through the long garden, to the welcome warmth of his grandparents' house.

After this incident, running-from-the-fire, Roland became very aggressive toward his cousin. The friendship that had been close and comfortable now became a distanced challenge, Roland always putting the younger boy down, stalking off on his own, seeking separate company.

Jack missed the older boy, partly for his sense of direction, his knack of always knowing what to do, what to suggest for fun; but mostly for his gruesome stories.

A year after running-from-the-fire, however, he met Angela, the daughter of friends of his own parents, and at once found a willing pair of ears for his own versions of the 'gruesome', discovering that he could satisfy his own imaginative craving by copying Roland, by evoking memories of Roland's tales, and by describing, in as much detail as possible, his odd, occasional visions of the bull-runners. He could see and remember in such fine detail the various exotic landscapes that the hunted couple inhabited as they ran from the immense, red-faced beast which pursued them, and from the furious men who followed that beast, that his descriptions were awe-inspiring.

'It's as if you've really been there!'

And in a very real way, Jack had.

Angela was a tidy girl, orderly in her habits, precise in her thinking. She hated sports, preferring to read books about the mind, astronomy and bizarre events; so-called past-lives, which were fashionable parapsychology when she was nine years old, absorbed her thoroughly. She believed in them totally, but was unwilling to accept anything other than a rational basis for the phenomenon. It might or might not be reincarnation, but if it *were*, then reincarnation could be explained!

Her games invariably consisted of 'projects', analyses of her friends and family for evidence of reincarnation; searches in chalk quarries or other fossil sites for unusual remains (evidence of time travel); speculative essays about life on other planets. It was natural that she should begin to study Jack, and although their friendship waned towards the end of their primary school years and into their first years at Exburgh's red-brick comprehensive, they eventually came to be in the same class and joined the same group – which they called a tribe, the fashion of the time.

Angela's interest in the phenomenon associated with Jack's encounters remained high, and it was she who coined the word '*shimmering*' for the film of other light that seemed to seep from Jack's skin when the bull-runners were close.

4

Jack had finally escaped from school.

The endless questions from Ruth, the 'retesting' with electrodes as he described running-from-the-fire, and Angela's long conversation with the psychologist afterwards had eaten up his spare time, and he was edgy and irritable as he met Simon and the others at the school gates.

'Come on. There's a lot to tell.'

'Don't do this,' Angela called to him, standing away from the rest of the tribe. Jack ignored her.

Simon Baines' parents always worked late, and his house, close to Jack's, was a perfect place to go to after school. He'd been nicknamed 'Mouse' – alone in the house, although 'Mouse' hardly described his stocky, slightly swaggering gait and long, unkempt hair. He knew where to find the key to the glass-fronted cabinet where the Scotch, gin, Cognac and liqueurs were kept. Each drink was rationed carefully so that the dip in quantity wasn't too obvious. Even so, lately there had been a questioning look in his father's eyes as he studied the depleted bottle of Southern Comfort.

Most evenings, when Simon opened his house to the tribe, they watched videos, or played *Elite*, a 3-D space game that ran on Simon's personal computer. He alone possessed such an extravagance; the computers at school were never made available for games. Jack was hopeless at *Elite*, which depended on lightning reflexes and a willingness to kill everything in sight. He preferred to watch the Baines' collection of banned horror videos, and especially the pirated copy of

Clockwork Orange which they kept poorly hidden in the drawer of their bedroom table.

They approached the house shortly after six, Angela trailing reluctantly behind. Jack's parents wanted him home by seven, so there was not a lot of time, but Simon led the way to the front door, then stood back to collect the fifty pence coins, the price of entrance.

'Don't do this,' Angela said again, standing at the bottom of the step. Jack shrugged her off, but felt his skin flush at her disapproving look. 'You're such a fool!'

'I have to tell the story. I saw it today. I have to tell it.'

'You'll make it up. It's all lies. I don't like you, Jack. You're cheating on Greenface.'

Simon gave Jack four of the six coins. 'If you're coming in,' he said to Angela, his face pinched with hostility and dislike, 'pay up. If you're not: eff off!'

Angela stared at him for a moment. 'You're disgusting,' she said coldly. Then with a sharp glance at Jack she turned quickly away, hunched in her black school jacket, arms folded.

Inside, Jennifer was clumsily rolling a joint. Simon swore. 'Not that! They always know how much they've got of that!'

But Jennifer moved away from him to the window and leaned out with her friend Deborah, laughing as they drew on the cigarette, blowing the smoke into the day.

'Don't worry, Mouse, we won't give you away in court.'

'We love your *body* too much.'

Laughter.

Simon's parents had supplied the cannabis – inadvertently. The boy knew where everything was hidden, and how to get it, and kept most of his knowledge to himself. But the girls were sharper than him. They'd worked out *just* where to look and had taken their cut while the boy had been collecting the Jack-tale fee at the front door.

'Come on. Come on.'

They went up to Simon's room, closed the curtains and turned on the green light.

Jack sat on a high stool, the green spotlight on his face. The boys in the tribe sat on the floor, the girls on the bed, all holding plastic cups of gin, all waiting for the story of Jack's Vision.

It was so easy.

Jack had noticed months ago how quickly the two girls, Jennifer and Deborah, changed from being threatening to so *gullible* when it came to engaging their imaginations in a little romance. He sensed there was an explanation, but also that as yet he was too inexperienced to understand it fully, and so he never confronted them at school, where they'd certainly cut him as dead as they always cut Mouse (who in any case seemed to ask for abuse, as if he somehow thrived on it). He just kept them at a distance, but fed them the fairytale on these after-school sessions, and happily took their money.

And it was especially easy today because they'd all *seen* the encounter, they'd seen the fuss, the filming, the arrival of the psychologist . . . All of them, now, accepted that Jack could glimpse a world in parallel to their own. And though they hadn't heard the question and answer session in the technician's room, they were up for the fantasy today more so than on any of the days when he'd lied, claiming to have encountered the hunters in order to boost his finances. He should have charged more!

After a while, he began to speak:

'Their journey has now taken them away from the snows and the mountains of Eriodor (*he'd made the name up; it was the best he could do: a touch of Tolkien*), the land of the redskull knights . . . now the hunters, who are the hunted, have come to a land where the earth is older, where the creatures of the past struggle among the sucking swamps, and crowded, stinking forest of the oldest times . . .'

And later:

'. . . I saw them making love, a time of naked joy in a place that is trying to kill them. But when they made love it was sensuous and sexy . . . it went on for several hours . . . They were aware that the Scorched Face, their guardian, watched them from the treeline, smiling at them in this time of passion . . .'

And so on. He knew what the group wanted. He could read their faces, every one of them, knew how to add sexual titillation for Deborah, Rex, romantic longing for Jennifer and Kate, quest adventure for Danny and Sandra, and the macho detail of fights that always made Simon lick his lips and narrow his eyes as he sat cross-legged by the far wall, playing with the coins that were his cut of any evening in the house.

What they *all* really wanted was the *weird*, and to achieve this he simply combined what he had glimpsed in those terrifying moments of day-dream with the elements of fantasy that had always intrigued him: dragons and dinosaurs, time-travelling princesses from ancient Egypt, trigger words like Avalon, Atlantis, Lavondyss, Middle-earth. He had invented a burning face which watched the runners and warned them, The Scorched Face, a primal elemental which he used to get them out of trouble when his plotting failed him. And a wolf which served the same purpose by assisting their shape-changing into animals. He mixed it, he fixed it, and they loved it.

He was a born storyteller. He could have made a fortune in ancient times. Now he was making ten or twelve pounds a week evoking ancient echoes.

'Greenface is carrying a child, I think. The wounds inflicted on her by the *Megatherium*, that giant creature, with its horned protuberances, gaping jaws and slashing claws, those wounds have healed, but she is still weak. She holds the stolen magic carefully at night. There is something in the obsidian flask that flows into her, and Greyface knows it. He's jealous, but the child is his, and there are dangers all around . . . He's trying to ensure that the pursuing Demon cannot find a way to enter the unborn child . . .'

He didn't want to handle the subject of childbirth. Besides, the Greenface in his vision wasn't at all pregnant! He'd got into deep water trying to please the Romantics. Next time there'd have to be a miscarriage during a fight with a sabre-tooth.

It was nearly seven o'clock. Jack stopped speaking and walked silently from the room. He hoped that Angela would be outside waiting for him by the gate, but she'd gone home, angry.

The money for his Jack-tale felt good in his pocket.

His mother was tearful with guilty concern when he got home (she'd not been able to leave a meeting to go to the school and support him). She hugged him and fussed him. Later, when his father asked to hear what had happened, he simply recounted the brief details of his real glimpse into the parallel world, and concisely described the questions that Ruth had asked him afterwards.

He'd been frightened for a while, certainly, then elated. And he was still revelling in the experience of the encounter with the bull-runners.

Right now, though, he just wanted to watch TV.

5

A week later, Garth came to Jack's house, climbing the hill from Exburgh slowly and steadily, walking in the middle of the road. It was evening, and the sun was setting behind the town. Garth was a dark shape against the glare from the west, his long coat flung back, his hands in his pockets. A trail of smoke drifted behind him as he chewed on the stub of a cigar.

Jack saw the man from the window of his room and went out to meet him, walking to the end of the path. He'd had a phone call from Angela about two hours before, saying that Garth wanted to speak to him. Angela's father had taken photographs of the new frescoes in the pit, and the girl, who'd been with him, was surprised at the similarity between the blinded mask-faces on the east wall, and the sketches of the bull-runners, Greyface and Greenface, that Jack had been occasionally drawing over the years. Her articulated surprise had provoked the dowser's curiosity.

Angela cycled slowly behind the man, trying to keep her balance on the mountain bike as she weaved a zig-zag across the road. When Garth emerged from the sun's glare he tossed the cigar to the road then kicked it to the kerb, where it dropped into a drain. He removed his hat and swept fingers through his loose, long hair, then grinned.

'Are you the boy who sees other worlds?' he asked as he came up to Jack.

'Yes. You're the man who dowses for buried cities. I came to the excavation with the school.'

Garth towered above the boy, reaching out a hand that

almost enclosed Jack's fingers. The pressure was gentle, the skin of the man's hand coarse and etched. The face that smiled down was deeply lined too, around the eyes especially, which glittered greyly, almost without feature. The smell of the cigar was fresh. There was a fleck of black paper on the man's thin upper lip, and as if conscious of Jack's gaze on it he picked it away. Garth hadn't shaved for a couple of days, and a salt and pepper stubble covered his chin and cheeks.

'How do you find them?' Jack asked nervously. 'The ruins. . .'

'I don't use hazel rods, if that's what you mean. Not two sticks. Not like a water diviner.'

'What *do* you use?'

The man seemed amused by the question. 'Emotion. Insight. Magnetism? Christ! I don't know. Luck? Smell? *Dreams*. Simple tools, really. All the tools of any hunter! I never really think about it.'

'How do you know when a city's there?'

'I feel it move away from me,' the tall man said. 'They're clever, but they're big. They can't hide that easily.'

Jack laughed at that. 'Cities can't move . . .'

'Depends what you mean by a city,' Garth said pointedly, then tapped a long finger on the boy's shoulder. 'I came to talk about you. If that's all right? I'm intrigued by these visions of yours. We'll talk about hidden cities later. Are your parents in?'

Rachel and David Chatwin came out to greet their son's guest, and the three of them talked for a while, mostly about the excavations, partly about the worry of living with a son whose dreaming occasionally turned dangerous. Jack's father had work to do and excused himself. His mother and Angela brought four garden chairs and a small table out to the front lawn so they could sit and stare down the elm-lined avenue to the sprawl of Exburgh. The river could be glimpsed between the Abbey and the shopping centre. A few barges drifted downriver to the locks at Ashford. The church spire of St

John's still caught the dying light. The breeze was warm and John Garth sipped a cold beer and ate a welcome supper of toasted cheese and grilled bacon. 'When things are turning up all the time, on the sites, I forget to eat.'

As Jack described his visions of the running couple and their bizarre landscape, he kept to the actual detail of what he'd experienced, not embroidering, aware that Angela was sitting, watching him with censorious intentness. She was clutching the slim file of notes she'd compiled on her friend and was nervous, her palms leaving moist prints on the red plastic binder.

'Greyface, in a cloak of scalps and feathers, and Greenface, bright with mother of pearl.' Garth repeated the words as he absorbed the image. He lit a cigar, then thought better of it, grinding the tip against the sole of his patterned boot. 'Any chance of another beer? I feel I need it.'

Jack's mother smiled and went quickly to the kitchen.

As Garth sipped from the bottle, still contemplative, Angela opened her file and spread it on the garden table. The sun had vanished but it was a bright twilight and Jack's colourful sketches of the bull-runners were clear against the lined paper.

Angela said, 'Jack has been sketching the running couple for seven years, now. These are a selection of his drawings. Mrs Chatwin has lots more, from Jack's infant years.'

Rachel agreed. 'I have dozens. Jack started to draw oddities from about the age of five, mostly these two people, and prehistoric beasts attacking them. We always thought he'd have a career in drawing comics. If you'd like to see them . . .'

'Please. I'm fascinated.'

When Rachel returned with the sheaf of childish paintings and crayon drawings, Garth turned the pages, studying each representation with great care. 'Greyface and Greenface,' he repeated, running his fingers gently over the crude, increasingly sophisticated pictures. 'This one looks like a mountain pass. And this . . . it's swamp, I would think. These look like Mangroves.'

Jack agreed. 'I never seem to see them in the same place. It's like I get a glimpse when their world comes close to ours, just a glimpse, and maybe years have passed in their world.'

'Where *is* their world, I wonder?'

Angela was prepared for this moment and said quickly, 'I have some suggestions.'

She pulled the file towards her, watching Garth nervously. 'I've been keeping a record of Jack's experience, as he describes it, and as I can witness it. I've listed a few possibilities – I can outline them for you, if you like.'

'Please!' Garth agreed. 'As I said, I'm fascinated.'

The girl drew a deep breath, pushed back her tumble of hair as she scanned the first page of the file, then began, suddenly seeming years older than her age of fifteen.

'The first, most rational explanation for what Jack is experiencing is temporal lobe hallucination. This is quite common, and can be brought about by tumour, dysfunction akin to epilepsy, drugs, alcohol abuse or physical trauma. Jack doesn't take drugs, as far as we know.'

She said this pointedly and Jack answered irritably, 'I don't do drugs!'

'Jack doesn't take drugs, as you've just heard. And he hasn't suffered physical trauma. A tumour would have long since shown itself or killed him, and so we're left with a possible dysfunction, an inherited trait.

'We really *shouldn't* dismiss temporal lobe epilepsy: people who suffer from it have extremely realistic encounters with the imaginary, especially its sounds and smells. However:

'When the encounter occurs with Jack, there is a physical, and witnessable phenomenon associated with it. We call it the *shimmering*. It's like a skim of oil on water, reflective and occasional, but it covers his skin. Smells come from it, and distant sounds. His body could produce the odours – a form of psychosomatic-controlled excretion – but it's hard to explain how the sense of *sound* could be coming from his *skin*.'

She turned the page and drew breath, again pushing her hair back from her face as she read quickly through the next set of notes.

Garth had been staring at her in increasing astonishment. Now he exchanged a long look with Jack, raising his eyebrows on an otherwise blank face. Jack smiled. The man looked back at Angela, then folded his arms and settled into his seat, awaiting the next instalment.

Angela went on, 'The second rational possibility is that Jack is simply daydreaming. Quite literally Day Dreaming. His unconscious mind, a hurly-burly of images, memories, fears and shadows, is slipping through to his conscious mind during his waking hours, rather than just during sleep. This is so common that it is hardly worth mentioning, except that it may be occurring far more powerfully in Jack.

'And there is research to show that the *dying* brain *creates* images from memory/imagination – these seem very real to people experiencing "near-death". Oxygen starvation seems to be the trigger, coupled with sensory input reduction. Jack's sensory input is certainly reduced during his "Visions", and his breathing is very shallow. Is he having mini-near-death experiences?'

Jack's mother Rachel looked horrified.

'Again,' Angela said emphatically. 'The *shimmering* is the phenomenon that puts these explanations into doubt.

'So now we come to the paranormal,' she said after taking a deep breath.

'Oh good,' said Garth, with a sidelong glance at the silent boy. 'I like the paranormal. I use it a great deal.'

'A parallel world!' Angela said, stabbing a slim finger at the first of four numbered notes. She looked at the older man thoughtfully. 'If quantum theory is correct, then the possibility that there are innumerable worlds running alongside ours, but existing in one of innumerable, inaccessible dimensions, is very strong. When the boundaries between such worlds come close, then a certain spillage might occur, like two rivers running very close to each other, and intermingling during a flood season . . .'

'I get the idea,' Garth said.

'The channel for interactive parallel worlds might be the physical fabric of the external world, or the non-physical fabric of the mind. Question, then: is Jack experiencing a parallel world through his own unconscious mind?'

'Hell of a question!' Garth muttered.

'And if so, where *is* that world? Is it Earth? Or is it an alien world, whose own dimensions are running very close to our own, linked to our own by a wormhole effect?

'Is it the past?' she continued. 'Is it the future? Or is it a totally *imagined* world that has been given reality by the mind imagining it?'

There were a few seconds of silence. Garth realized that Angela had finished her report and was watching him expectantly. 'I think I'll have that cigar, now,' he murmured, and fumbled for a half-corona, lighting up as he reached for the folder, turning it towards him, reading quickly, then checking back through the pages, lingering on each sketch, each paragraph of observation, glancing at the columns of dates.

'This is very impressive. What are the dates?'

'Jack's visions. His encounters with Greyface and Greenface. As near as I can get them.'

In the seven years Jack had known Angela, he'd had twenty encounters with the bull-runners, and her record was accurate. Before that, Rachel Chatwin's letters to her own mother were a fair indication of when the 'fits' had occurred. Rachel herself had experienced something strange, a frightening vision of being pursued by huge, red-furred wolves, during the birth of her son.

Angela stared across the table at Jack. 'I suppose it has to be from the past. If the faces are on the fresco, then you're picking up the ghosts of the hidden city.'

Without looking at her, still staring at the notes in her folder, Garth said, 'Who says all lost cities come from the past?'

Angela reacted with a pulled face of surprise. 'What?'

Garth patted the journal. 'May I borrow this? I'll take good care of it.'

'OK. But I want it back. Jack is my life's work, although he doesn't know it yet.'

'Thank you. I'd like to keep the other sketches, Rachel. If that's OK?'

Jack's mother was more than willing.

'Anything! If it helps us understand what's happening inside this strange head!' She ruffled Jack's brown hair and the boy pulled away in embarrassment.

Garth said, 'I'll look after them, I promise. I'll bring them back in a week or so.'

'What about Glanum?' Jack said. 'The excavation.'

'What about it?'

'You were going to tell me how you found it. Is it a Roman city?'

'There's some Roman in it, certainly. And some Greek. And Byzantine. And Celtic. Bronze Age, Persian . . . It's an odd place. You get the idea? It doesn't fit at all with what you might be expecting. As you'll find out when you come and visit.'

The man leaned across to Jack. 'What does the fifth of May 1965 mean to you?'

Jack almost laughed. 'It's when I was born.'

'I know. I just saw it on Angela's list of dates. Do you know what that date means to me?'

'No.'

'It's the day I dowsed Glanum for the first time.' He leaned close to Jack. 'Now ain't that peculiar?'

Jack was confused. Exburgh's hidden city hadn't come to light until nine years ago, in 1971, its discovery due to John Garth, who had been looking in the backstreets and on building sites for five years or more. The man talked in riddles. Garth stood and shrugged into his coat, fixing his hat and working the envelope of sketches into Angela's folder. He glanced at Jack, half amused. 'I said "dowsed" it. . . "sensed" it. Not "found" it. I was a long way away at the time – on your birthday. Thank you for the cheese, the bacon, and the beers, Rachel,' he said to Jack's mother. 'It was good to meet you. I expect I'll see you again. Angela? You're an inspiration. And now I'm to take you home.'

'I'd like to talk to Jack for a while . . .'

'I promised your father . . .'

Rachel said, 'I'll run her home. It's OK.'

Agreeing to that, Garth shook Jack's hand. 'Come down to the Hercules pit tomorrow. The excavation behind the shopping centre. I need you there. Can you get a morning off school? No?' He frowned. 'Then come after school. To the church. St John's. I'll be waiting for you. To give you a guided tour of a very ancient echo. Yes?'

'I'll be there. Thanks.'

'Don't let me down.'

Without being asked, Angela followed Jack up to his room. As he fussed with his computer – a very simple model compared to Simon's – she closed the door. He was conscious of his discarded clothes, the piles of superhero comics, the posters of his favourite Heavy Metal bands above his narrow bed. Was she looking round? She'd been here before. Oddly, he felt uncomfortable with her in his private space this time. He wondered – as he pretended to do things on the keyboard – whether she was feeling critical of the chaos she could see around her.

'Jack?'

'What?'

'I'd like to ask you a favour.' When he turned she was leaning against the door, arms crossed. She was biting her lip, watching him carefully. She walked over to him, still defensive, and lowered her gaze for a moment. Then she looked back at him and said firmly, 'Don't lie to me. Promise not to lie. To *me*.'

'I don't lie,' he muttered irritably, trying to turn away.

She reached for his arm. 'You lie all the time. But it's OK. I know you like telling the stories. I shouldn't have been so annoyed. They're good stories. I just want you to promise – *me* – promise me that you'll only tell *me* the *truth*.'

'Yeah. OK.'

'Promise it!'

'I *promise*,' he said, again irritably. He was shaking. The look in her large eyes was very earnest, but he could smell soap and her breath, which was warm and sweet. He was getting aroused, and he flushed as he realized it but was helpless to control his body, and he knew that he was beginning to show through the loose cotton trousers of his track suit. Angela aroused him. He'd heard through one of her friends that she'd like to be his girlfriend, but was as shy as Jack himself when it came to making such arrangements, something that amused the bolder members of the school's tribes. He'd also heard that she thought he lied too much for his own good. This recognition from her that it was all right to tell elaborate stories was almost an invitation.

He suddenly realized she was shaking, but not with nerves, with suppressed laughter. 'Is that where you keep your Heavy Metal?' she said, glancing quickly down, then went bright red, a hand to her mouth as she tried to control her amusement. 'I'm sorry,' she managed to say.

Jack twisted away, face burning, but she reached out and grabbed his arm again, stepping suddenly close, putting both arms round him. 'It's OK,' she said, and chanced a kiss, which was soft and nervous, very dry. 'It's OK, Jack. I really like you. The stories, that stuff you do, it's just like earning a living, isn't it? It's OK.'

'I know it is.' He licked his lips. He held her awkwardly, aware of the straining and longing below his waist. When they kissed for the second time it was soft and moist, the tentative then more adventurous probing of her tongue like a shock. She suddenly pushed against him and he tried to pull away, aware of the hardness of her breasts through her thin jumper. She tugged him back by the waistband of his track suit, breaking the kiss to whisper, 'Let me feel it. Don't pull back.'

Damn! His knees were shaking. *She'd* lost her shyness, *he* felt he was about to faint. He tightened his embrace, more for support than love, and Angela seemed to sink into him, kissing him again, a surprisingly confident hand suddenly reaching between their bodies to press against his groin.

He opened his eyes in delighted shock. She was already watching him as her fingers explored the Heavy Metal. And behind her, the door opened and his mother glanced in, made a profuse apology and backed out, but already the kiss was broken as each of them had leapt apart with the sudden surprise of the woman's voice.

Angela smiled mischievously. 'Don't tell me any lies,' she said as she ran quickly from the room. 'Remember – I'll be keeping my eye on you.'

6

John Garth was waiting for him on the steps of the greystone church, St John the Divine. He was pacing up and down, clearly impatient. Jack felt guilty for being late, but he had spent most of the day with Angela, either talking with her in the seclusion of the sports huts, or passing silly notes to her in class. He was basking in the excitement of the relationship that was now beginning to blossom. The touch and smell of her skin had become exquisitely sensuous.

Traffic shunted past, heading down the Church street to the ring road. It was cool in the shadow of the tower and Jack was glad to be out of the sun.

'What do you think is below us?' the dowser asked. Jack looked down, then around, at the wide flagstones, the cracked pavement by the road.

'The crypt?' he volunteered.

'The suicide gate through the city's curtain wall,' Garth corrected. 'Glanum was divided in two by a massive wall, several layers deep, labyrinthine. It separated the urban district, which had a gate to the outside, from the Sanctuary heart. The remains of the gate into the Sanctuary are below you.'

'How can you tell?'

'It's my job to tell. Come on.'

He led the way round St John's and through the narrow alley called Mourning Passage. They crossed High Street, passed through the crowds in Market Square to emerge onto Ickendon Way, a wide, busy road, now, but part of an ancient droving road. From here they walked briskly to the river. On the lawned bank, watching the barges and pleasure boats, Garth lit a cigar and pointed across to the recreation fields on the far side.

'The buried city crosses below the river and reaches its widest point. The urban area, with a single, towered gate opening to the north. Anything strike you as strange?'

'The city was built *across* the river?' Jack asked, frowning. 'It wouldn't be easy to defend.'

'Exactly,' the man said. 'It would be a stupid thing to do, wouldn't it? A weak design. You build along the bank, like at London, or Paris, and use natural wells. And you make sure you strongly defend an access way to the river itself.'

'Maybe the river changed its course. This could be the new course.'

'River's been flowing here for thousands of years.'

'Maybe there were water gates. Like in London.'

'Interesting idea. But I don't think so. Again: why make the main gate so close to two water gates? That's a concentration of weak points. It makes no sense. Does it?'

'No.'

'I'm glad you agree. Think hard about what we've just been saying. Come on.'

Garth, now, retraced their steps, working their way through Exburgh towards the Hercules excavation. Glanum, he explained as they walked, was shaped like a coffin, wide and single-gated at the head-end, the urban area with its forges, bakeries, potteries, leather-workers and discreet houses. The triple curtain wall, with its suicide passage, divided the coffin at the shoulders. The tapering body of the 'coffin', where the multitude of shrines were located, the actual heart of Glanum, lay substantially below Exburgh Castle hill.

As they walked up Abermyle Street, through Gogmagog Square and back towards the church, Garth defined the perimeter of the city, showing how the old walls were now below modern buildings, how nothing of the new in any way reflected the buried.

'It doesn't fit,' Garth said. 'Everything below you, everything to do with Glanum, is at the wrong angle. It's rare to encounter a hidden city like this, though they certainly exist. You usually get clues in the new town: Oldgate; Westgate; Oldwall street; Roman Way; Tower Green. You know the sort of thing. New towns are built on old towns and the shadows are there in the architecture.'

'But not here . . .'

'No. Not here. Because this is Glanum,' he added cryptically. 'The hidden city doesn't belong, Jack. What do you remember from the museum? What is it you *know* about Glanum?'

'That Glanum was obliterated on this site. Sometime in the third or fourth century AD. Between then and the first town of Exburgh, five hundred years later, this was just wildwood, wild country. The two histories don't connect.'

'What if there weren't two histories?'

'*Not* two histories? I don't get it.'

'What if Glanum was never here!'

'You mean – like a fake city? You're digging up a fake city?'

Garth was expressionless as they walked. He said only, 'Funny word: fake.'

Jack let Garth's words hang in his mind as they came to Westwell Passage and turned to walk along a cobbled way until they reached the excavation of the shrine to Hercules. And here, for the first time in the real world, he saw the blinded faces of the running hunters, the bull-runners.

And for a moment, as he gazed at them, time seemed to stop. The faces on the wall seemed to scream at him, but he could hear nothing. The gouged eyes seemed to weep as he watched them, but nothing had changed, only the pattern of shadow on the colour as the sun faded behind clouds.

He knew these people! They inhabited his dreams. Their violent retreat from the consequences of some terrible action was a sound of terror, and a fear of reprisal, and a stink of effort as they fled across the land that was ever-present in his life.

'Who blinded them?' he asked quietly.

'The person who painted them, I expect. Far away, in the past, or wherever. Your friend Angela might have a few suggestions. The blinding was part of the depiction. A curse, perhaps. Or a wish. Have you ever seen these faces before? In the town, I mean.'

'No.'

'Not in a church, somewhere? Or an old hall? Or the museum?'

'No. Only in visions.'

Jack understood the point of the question: if this savage painting of his dream-hunters was represented elsewhere in Exburgh, then he might have seen the faces, registered them subliminally, used them to inform his hallucinatory encounters with the running couple. But he could not recall seeing such faces in the churches, though there was an abundance of Green Men, gargoyles, and the stone faces of mediaeval peasants. And if his drawings of Greyface and Greenface had been taken from anything in the museum, then his school's head-teacher, Mr Keeble, would have recognized them: he'd been the museum's curator for years, before returning to the teaching profession. Besides, Jack instinctively *knew* that such exposure could never have happened. It simply didn't feel right. He couldn't articulate the particular feeling to the grey-haired man who now led him around the inner walls of what had once been a sanctuary, but the bull-runners were *real*. He wasn't hallucinating them; he wasn't daydreaming them, drawing on scenes from TV or comics, or film. He wasn't dreaming them at all! They were as real, when they appeared in his Vision, as the ancient plaster wall around the pit, with its fading colours, its frescoes depicting faces, figures and animals.

Greyface and Greenface were close enough to touch (almost). When they came to him, he was running *with* them, slipping from this world to theirs, aware of the textures of the earth, the gusting of the wind, the sounds and scents of the landscape they fought against.

They were not dreams. The bull-runners were a part of him. And even now he could feel them, hear them, but distantly, as if on the other side of a high wall, and as he realized this, so he realized that they had always been there, like a vague distraction, an ache, a murmuring in the ear, a part of his life that only occasionally concerned him when it became acute.

He realized that he was standing again by the mutilated faces of his dream, his hands reaching out to touch the thin paint, the grey, the green, the touches of red, feeling the moulded plaster below. Garth was standing behind him and he turned, squinting up at the man against the bright sky.

'It feels angry here. I'm frightened.'

'You've been drifting,' Garth said quietly. 'You've been standing there for thirty minutes . . .'

Jack was shocked. Seconds ago he'd been walking round the walls, listening as Garth suggested possible meanings in the various painted motifs of the place.

Seconds ago!

'I think I'll go home.'

'Stay,' the man said. 'I want to show you something else. This place has a grip on you. It has the same grip on me. I want you to enter more deeply . . . will you?'

The words were frightening. Jack tried to see the look in Garth's eyes, but there was just shadow below the brim of the hat, the faint waft of cigar smoke from the figure, the man standing on the rise of earth away from the wall, looking down at the shaking youth.

'I don't like it here,' Jack said loudly. 'I feel sick.'

'So do I. The place is alive. I know that now. That's why I want you to enter more deeply. Can you feel the bull-runners?'

'Yes.'

'Are they close?'

'No.'

'I want to be there when they next come. I want to see for myself . . .'

'But I already told you, I can't tell when they're going to come! It happens suddenly. I'll go home now, please.'

'Not yet.'

Garth stepped down and gripped Jack's shoulder, almost hauling him up to the level of earth, then propelling him to the ladder from the pit. His voice was a fierce whisper. 'Don't be afraid, boy. You have more control than you know. I was frightened at first, just like you. The fear passes – believe me. I want to show you where the shadows are. Stand in the shadows for a while and then go home. But come again. Come and help me out. There's a lot of digging to do, and I like the way you see things. Do you understand?'

'Do you see the bull-runners too?'

'If I did, I wouldn't need *you*. I'm not letting you go, Jack. This place is too alive and you're part of that life. If you want to know more, you've got to do what I say. Understand?'

Jack got the point. Garth released his grip and they walked the street at speed, the man's hand an occasional encouragement on his back, Jack almost stumbling at times. They crossed a road between complaining cars, walked over grass to the side of St John's, approached one of the flying buttresses, walking a straight line towards the sheer wall. Jack pulled back as they approached the dark stone, but Garth urged him on, until a moment later the man walked straight into the church, reeling back, holding his face.

Jack stood beside him, not knowing what to do. Garth fumbled in his pocket for a handkerchief, wiped at the blood that streamed from his nose.

'Damn and blast!'

He looked furiously up at the church. 'I'd forgotten this . . . this . . .' he bit back the expletive. 'This *thing* was in the way. Damn! Come on, we have to go round.'

He paced along the wall, occasionally glancing up, dabbing

at his nose. Jack followed behind, aware of the curious looks from the drivers on the Broadway, but now intrigued, his apprehension dissipated, perhaps by the odd impact of man on church, perhaps by being away from the excavation.

Garth was in his own world, it seemed. They entered the church, paced down the north aisle, and for a moment hesitated below a modern stained glass window that depicted the Garden of Eden and the dove released from the Ark, after the Flood.

'There's no way through,' Garth said. 'What about down here . . .'

'Why don't we just walk through Mourning Passage?'

The man stared at Jack for a second, then frowned, then smiled. He led the way back to the main doors, out and down the steps, and so to Mourning Passage, where he picked up speed again and followed an odd route until they came to the site of an excavation from four years ago, now preserved beneath a newly-built shopping centre, specifically, below the shoe shop.

The store was just closing, which would mean denying access to the ruins, but the store-manager knew John Garth and welcomed him in. He led the way to the rear of the shop and then down steps to the neon-lit room. An observation ramp ran all the way around the chamber; the remains of the shrine were now enclosed in glass.

Jack had been here two years ago and had been as little impressed then as he was now, finding no particular fascination in the exposed layers of red brick, the flint walls defining rooms and entrance ways, and the broken expanses of plaster with the faint impressions of goats, satyrs, bulls and sun discs.

To his surprise, Garth agreed. 'It's a shrine to Minerva: two a penny stuff. But it's all we could really get to, and that's the frustration, because just beyond the far wall it starts to get very interesting indeed!'

He moved round to a low door in the solid earth that bordered the excavation.

'As you'll have realized, if you're any good at orientation, a bloody great office block is built between us and the place where the heart of the city begins. The foundations have gone down through a part of it, but it's likely that most of what is really interesting is still there, just inaccessible. We can only get to a fragment of it. Older by far than Minerva and the dear, decaying Bacchus.' He used a key to open the low door, then reached in to switch on a light. Beyond the door was an earthy passage, just wide enough to accommodate them if they crawled on all fours along the wooden slats. Garth pushed Jack ahead of him. The tunnel was bright with fluorescence, opening after ten yards into a roughly hewn, claustrophobic chamber some ten feet across and four feet high. There were hints of colour, here, on a peculiarly organic-looking mass in one corner. As Jack grew accustomed to the earth and stone textures of the place, he realized he was looking at a small part of a massive carved structure, deeply embedded in the earth, protruding in this one place with a ripple of muscle and knobby excrescences, animal certainly, but shapeless because of the partial nature of its exposure.

'What the hell is it?' he asked, running his hand nervously over the cold stone until Garth reached to pull his probing fingers away, for fear, perhaps, that the boy would dislodge some of the flaking ochre that still adhered.

'Your guess is as good as mine,' the man said. 'The truth lies very deep, far down below the town above us. But we found bones here, human and animal, and signs that the shrines and sanctuaries continue ahead of you. Which is below the Castle – Castle Hill. The narrow end of the hidden city. The heart of Glanum. The shrines within the inner city form a channel into the heart. And my feeling is: the further they go in that direction, the older, the more primitive they get.'

The confined space seemed suddenly to shrink a little, and

Jack ducked, feeling the ceiling come down towards him. The ground vibrated.

They were coming back, closer than ever. He could hear their voices . . .

Garth's hand was on his shoulder, his voice concerned. 'Are you ill?'

'I can't breathe . . .'

They were almost on him, they were exhausted, terrified, running for their lives!

'Time to leave, then. You go first.'

Jack needed no second invitation. He crawled at full speed on his hands and knees away from the chamber to the glassed-off area where Roman murals played. He raced up the stairs to the shoe shop, bursting through the door – breathless as he plunged into the dense wood, running between the trees, weaving through the light wells, half blinded by the shafting glare of the sun as it broke through the canopy.

Greyface loped ahead of him, head turning as he sought the way through the tangles. He was shouting. *Come on. Come on. I can hear water!*

Jack could hardly breathe. His lungs were bursting with the humidity and the thickness of the forest air.

Come on!

He put on a burst of speed, struck against a tree and stumbled, then ran on, while behind him loud breathing made him cry out, and a hand reached for him, jerking him back, away from the figure of Greyface, away from the thin light, back on his haunches, dragging him, dragging him . . .

Onto the pavement!

Garth was standing over him, blood running freely from his nose, his face twisted with concern. The sound of traffic was loud and a man's voice was saying, 'What the hell's he up to? Running like that?'

'Easy. Easy,' Garth said and crouched by the trembling boy.

Jack sat up and watched a container truck slide past in a cloud of grey smoke. 'I was in the forest.'

'I know. I caught a hint of the smell as you ran through the shop.' He was crouching, now, quizzical. 'How close are they?'

Jack listened. The traffic growled along the Broadway, but he could hear them. He could hear Greyface shouting. *They were in terrible danger again, alive by the skins of their teeth, by the strength in their legs.*

'Close,' Jack whispered. 'Coming closer.'

7

Intrigued and fascinated by the city dowser though he was, the very proximity of the bull-runners, their constant shouting, the constant danger, the overspill of adrenalin from their hunted bodies into his own, pre-occupied Jack totally for a while.

They were close and coming closer, running through his dreams with moments of intense lucidity, before fading again into the distance. The odd reflectivity of his skin did not occur during these sleeping episodes, nor could Angela, occasionally sleeping over at the house and brought to Jack's room when the shouting started, hear or scent the otherworld as she had done that day in class.

During his waking hours the sound of the bull-runners was a constant breathless dash for safety, their running interspersed with fighting for survival, with swimming, with skirting the forests or the mountains where white towers shone, threatening them.

With his parents, he had two meetings with Ruth at the hospital where she worked. They reviewed the video footage and saw the shimmering of light, like a film of oil around his face as he was 'dreaming'; analysis of the film showed only normal wavelengths; there was nothing discreet or unusual in the glow.

The chemical pads from his skin showed traces of complex terpenes and plant esters, chemicals that were alien to the human excretory system, but familiar to marshland. Somehow, then, Jack's body had produced organic matter reflecting the landscape that he was hallucinating. Ruth was exercised in the extreme by this, almost wild in her excitement, and Jack agreed to have permanent swabs attached to his underarms, to be removed every day and posted to the hospital. He kept this up for a week, then because of the discomfort and inconvenience resorted to keeping a chemical record one day in seven.

Even so, he showed traces, on one occasion, of a polypeptide similar to that in the scent glands of a wolf . . . and he had glimpsed Greyface in a savage tussle with a wounded, lone wolf, while Greenface stabbed down on the creature, eventually driving it away, a scene of attack that had lasted only seconds, a brief disorientation during a class on Economics.

And the traces of woodland and grassland were there in one swab of every three.

Garth visited him twice during the summer, but could not persuade the boy to come to the dig and help, although Angela gave a willing hand and regularly reported to Jack on the progress of the excavation.

By the early winter, the distracting sense of proximity of the bull-runners had faded considerably and Jack felt his life become his own again. Now he risked a second visit to the Hercules shrine, where the revealed masks of Greyface and Greenface were carefully protected behind a frame of toughened glass. As he looked at them this time he felt only plaster and stone, no life at all, no resonance.

'They're dead,' he said, and when the glass was opened and he touched the blind eyes he just shrugged. 'I was frightened before. But there's nothing to be frightened of now.'

Garth seemed to have been expecting this. 'Then come with me,' he said. 'Come and see the new find.'

In late October, telephone engineers laying cable in the area behind Spittlefield, close to Castle Hill, had breached the roof of a deep chamber, ten feet square, eight feet in height, and with a small access portal from the west that had been sealed in antiquity. The room was filled with the bones of animals, mostly skulls. The way to the next chamber was downwards, through a stone trap-door.

Garth could stand upright in the skull room, standing on a wooden platform that had been carefully placed so as to avoid disturbing the bones. With Jack at his side he pointed to the earth below.

'It goes four chambers down, maybe more. That's all we've been able to reach. The whole sanctuary area spreads out to the west and slightly to the north, chamber after chamber, each embedded more deeply within the complex, accessible by a single door, or shaft. This one is free of rubble, but beyond and below it the chambers are impacted with the earth itself, and a lot of them are probably obliterated.'

'This isn't Roman . . .'

'Damn right. Nor Greek. And it certainly isn't Celtic. Older than all those times.'

Jack stepped down to the floor without thinking. Garth crouched beside him, watching as the youth bent down to touch the crumbling skulls, with their wide horns. 'Bulls. The skulls of bulls. What is this place?'

'It could be pre-Minoan Crete; it could be pre-dynastic Egypt. It could be Turkey, the Levant, as far east as Persia . . . anywhere where the bull was sacrificed to worship. The walls are mud-brick. I'm inclined to think Turkey, Levant, maybe Egypt. But older by centuries than the Hercules shrine, than Minerva of the Shoe Shop, than the Lord of Animals under Market Square. It's what Glanum is all about, the concentration of temples.'

'But in Exburgh? They came all this way from the Middle East to *Exburgh*?'

Without thinking, Jack had picked up a bull skull, one horn shattered, one stretching two feet, curving up from the bone, still polished white. If he felt the shrine shake, it might have been imagination, traffic, or the contact with the runners. There was a hard breathing somewhere around him, and the sense of something vast moving furtively through tall grass.

But the mood passed quickly and he placed the dead bone down on the dry earth floor, by the well into the dark below, the chamber underneath.

There were no paintings, no frescoes, no carvings, no symbols anywhere in the room.

Just bones.

Just wrongness.

He said, 'Is this the heart of Glanum?'

'No. Where we are now is on the edge of the heart. As I said to you, the sanctuaries get older the closer you get to the centre of the city. Wherever you find Glanum, it's always the way: the heart in the corpse is always inaccessible. But we've come damned close in Exburgh. And since the corpse is still warm . . .'

Jack watched the man in the half light from the street, aware that John Garth was talking more to himself than to the student in the pit.

'How many Glanums are there?' he asked.

'As many as you can find,' Garth answered darkly. 'Glanum has left its shadow across the world, and it has been doing so for longer than you can imagine. Are they close? The bull-runners?'

Suddenly chilled, Jack said, 'No.'

He hauled himself onto the wooden ramp and climbed the ladder from the cold room into a street that hummed with traffic; he stared up the slope of Castle Hill to the sheer walls of the Castle itself. He thought: Solid sandstone. The hill is solid sandstone. There's nothing underneath but rock and mantle. There could never have been a city there!

The town of Exburgh bustled, seeming to widen with every passing month as a new ring road was built, and rows of terraces bulldozed down to make way for a supermarket, and a wide, well-appointed parking area.

The excavations were prettied up and made presentable, and the tourists came in the spring and summer months, fascinated by the frescoes and the given story that Glanum was a city of shrines, a city whose heart was hidden below the Castle Rock, beyond the abilities of contemporary excavation.

Jack worked at weekends in the small museum, collecting tickets, selling pamphlets about Glanum, postcards, and other Heritage Industry publications. On occasion he acted as a guide, but Angela was far more effective, being less inclined to exaggerate the truth and thus avoid awkward, probing questions. In any case, Jack could not abide the skull chamber. When he descended into the room he heard echoes of the running bull and his hackles rose and his concentration drifted. But the skull-room was the gem in the excavation tour, since it belonged to a culture that could not possibly have been present in the country unless brought in under exceptional circumstances.

Towards the end of the summer vacation following Jack's final school exams, Garth arranged for a trip to the country, supplying a minibus and driver, hampers of food, cold-boxes of wine, beer and mineral water, and such an air of mystery that his invitation was hard to refuse. Jack and his parents, Angela and hers, and three of the students who had been regulars on the Glanum dig crowded into the small van and sang and laughed their way into the hills, into the high hills, and then down to a wooded river site where a tarpaulin was stretched on the ground, and a series of canvas sun-breaks were stretched between branches to create patches of shade in the intensely hot height of the day.

Garth prowled the shallows of the river, black jeans rolled up, feet bare, his heavy arms bronzed, almost as dark as the leather vest he wore. What he was looking for he never said, but continued to hunt the water's edge while the food and drink he'd provided was consumed with all the enthusiasm and inelegance of a typical picnic. Perhaps he stayed apart from the rest because he was smoking, one cigar after another, the pungency of the fumes hanging heavy over the glade.

Because it was hot, and because they were now very close,

and because it was dangerous and they were game for any-thing, Jack and Angela slipped away from their families and made frantic if furtive love for half an hour, screened by rocks and dense bushes of wild, yellow rose. Hot and sticky, glow-ing with achievement and an adolescent sense of triumph in the deception, they dressed and emerged from their hiding place, to find Garth leaning against a tree, smoking, his gaze on the ridge above them, the top of Mallon Hill.

'We were just, er . . . we went for a walk,' Jack said, aware that Angela's gaze was furious, a clear statement: what the hell are you doing? We don't have to explain ourselves.

Garth nodded. 'There's nothing like it. Nothing like it at all.' His smile was enigmatic.

Still staring at the ridge, he ground his cigar between thumb and forefinger. 'Feel like another? Walk, I mean . . . I'm sure you do. Come on.' He was wearing patterned, brown leather boots with pointed toes, but covered the uneven ground with as much facility as if he'd been wearing proper hiking boots, Jack, in loose trainers, found the going easy but Angela, in sandals, lagged behind, swearing loudly, and struggling on the hill, whose slope was murderous.

At the top, Garth stripped to the waist. His lean body running with sweat, he stood with his hands on his hips, breathing slowly and deeply. When Angela arrived at the summit she tossed her useless sandals at Jack, sat down and picked at her feet, which were bleeding from several small cuts.

The air was very clear here, without the constricting humidity of the woods by the river. As quickly as she had become angry she became at peace, flopping back to stare at the clouds. Jack, sitting by the tall man, knees drawn up, watched her for a moment, stared at the sweat saturated T-shirt which was clinging to her body as she drew breath to relax, but he was finished with sex for the moment and waited for Garth.

This was not just a walk for walking's sake.

After a while the man said, 'Can you see movement out there? I don't mean the cloud shadow . . .'

Jack scanned the hills, the woods, the expanse of flowing, open green, sun-saturated, shadow-flecked.

'Just a flock of birds in the distance. Otherwise, no.'

'What can you hear? Put your head to the ground . . .'

Angela was sitting up, now, watching curiously.

Jack leaned down and listened through the grass. At once, the struggling of the bull-runners came into sharp, auditory focus, and he smelled forest. Greyface was carrying a bleeding carcase, an animal of some kind, Jack couldn't be sure – they were too distant. He just knew that they'd been hunting.

Apart from the bull-runners all he could hear was the faint sound of voices from the river and the thump of his heart, magnified, it seemed, through the earth itself.

When he told this to Garth, the man glanced down and smiled. 'Listen *through* all that. Can't you hear the movement?'

Jack concentrated. He tried to hear beyond the rustle, struggle and murmuring of the two people who were running, close by.

And at once he heard the slow creaking of great stones!

'It's like movement . . . deep in the earth . . .'

He felt the ground vibrate. Angela watched him closely, eyes narrowed against the sun's glare.

'Can you hear something?'

The sound that was rising from below him was like a deep thunder, coming in waves, the sound of an earthquake, he imagined, or mine workings, but far away, far away . . .

'There's something down there, something moving around.'

But Garth said, 'There's nothing there. Just echoes. Pre-echoes. There's nothing there yet, but it won't be long. I had a good feeling that it would stay around . . .'

'I can't hear anything at all,' Angela said. 'Echoes of what?'

'The white whale,' Garth said with a smile, pulling his

biker's vest over his broad shoulders. 'This is where I leave you, Jack. I need time to think, time to prepare. Veronica will drive the bus home.'

And before Jack could say a word, he walked out across the hill, tugging his broad hat over his damp hair, descending the rolls and folds of ground until he could only be seen occasionally, a diminishing figure walking to the west.

For a while, Jack thought the man had taken off for the afternoon, requiring solitude, and he went back with Angela to the river and the picnic.

In fact, that was the last he saw of Garth for more than a year, the man having clearly decided to abandon the exploration of the hidden city.

He left without a word, without a note, and when the rains of October began to wash against the earth of the scattered shrines, the pits that dotted Exburgh, they were covered over and preserved for later excavation.

8

Jack eventually saw Garth again on two occasions. The first was shortly before Christmas, three days before the end of the long winter term. With two other boys, Jack had left the school grounds for the latter part of the afternoon, quickly changed from school uniform into jeans and leather jacket and walked down to the city centre in search of last minute suggestions for Christmas gifts.

As they strolled through the neon-lit darkness of the main street, aware that a fine, icy drizzle was starting to fall, Jack glimpsed the tall man emerging from the shoe shop above the Minerva shrine.

'That's Garth . . . *Garth*!' he shouted.

'Who's Garth?'

'An old friend. The guy digging up the old city. Christ, don't you know *anything*?'

Jack ran through the crowds until he came to the ring road. Garth was already across on the grass verge, walking towards the high wall of the church on the opposite side. Again Jack called to the man, and this time Garth looked round, squinting through the traffic. In the early evening darkness it was hard to read the man's expression, but Jack was in no doubt that he had been waved away.

Garth had turned, then, and disappeared around the building.

Jack went back to the shop and asked for the manager.

'I came here a year ago with the archaeologist, John Garth? He took me downstairs to see the temple.'

'Yes, I remember. You got claustrophobic. Very frightening. I suffer myself, which is why you won't *get me*—'

'He was just here, wasn't he? I saw him.'

Ignoring Jack's youthful impatience, the manager agreed. 'Went downstairs to listen, he said. Up against the rock statue at the end of the passage. I don't know what he was listening for. Do you?'

Jack shook his head. 'Has he been here before? I mean recently?'

'No. Not for months.'

'If you see him again, could you ask him to call me? It's really important.'

Jack wrote his name and telephone number and left it with the man, then on impulse asked, 'Could I see downstairs again?'

'I don't see why not. I'll have Shirley come with you, just in case . . . if you like . . .'

But Jack wanted to be on his own. 'I'll be OK. I just want two minutes.'

He went straight round the covered sanctuary to the small door that led to the claustrophobic tunnel. He'd forgotten that the narrow entrance would be locked against the public. But behind him, soft steps on the metal stairs announced that Shirley had been sent down anyway; she peered across the model below its glass case. 'You all right?'

'I feel fine. I wanted to see the rock statue. Do you have the key?'

The woman came over. She was very small, slightly built, probably only a few years older than Jack himself. Her small hands were heavy with rings, an engagement ring gleaming with blue-tinged diamond light. She opened the small locker by the door and gave Jack access to the passage, switching on the fluorescent light, which flickered several times, then glared. When he reached the far end, against the rough rock, the odd shape, the muscle shape in the stone, Jack pressed his ear to the cold surface, closed his eyes and listened.

Breathing!

He pulled back, alarmed by the deep and sonorous breath that he had felt being drawn. Then he slapped the stone shoulder of what Garth claimed was a buried statue and listened again.

A swirling pool, breath heaving and sucking from its centre . . .

Again he was startled by the image that touched his senses. For a second he had felt sucked down, face blasted by an icy wind from the subterranean deep.

He went back for a third time, fingers spread on the rock, ignoring Shirley's tentative call checking that he was safe and not frightened.

And for a moment he was in the sea, rising dizzyingly to the surface, twisting as the water flowed over him, reaching for the light above. Except that it wasn't water; the light was coming closer, but he was struggling against drowning, and the world around him was heavy, black and stifling!

He threw himself away from the rock, choking and gasping for breath. He could hear the woman calling to the manager.

'I'm all right! I'm coming back.'

He crawled along the narrow tunnel, banging his head, aware of the pink, anxious oval of the assistant's face. She helped him brush the dust and dirt from his clothes, straightened the collar of his black leather jacket and locked the passage.

'You've seen a ghost?' she asked with a smile, and Jack laughed, remembering earlier words in a similar situation.

'I don't know. There's something under the hill, though.'

'Yes. A billion tons of sandstone! The shop's closing, I'm afraid.'

'I'm on my way.'

Christmas came and went, the traditional orgy of television, attempts at games, visits from and to relatives, near-death by turkey, chocolate and cocktails, secretly consumed wherever his friends' parents were less strict on such under-age abuse than his own.

He was a reluctant passenger in the back of the car on New Year's Eve, as his parents drove southwest to the moors for four days of bracing, damp, treacherous walking. Angela had been invited to join them, but she had cousins visiting from Australia, two boys of her own age. And besides: she was working on a *paper*, an actual, formal piece of work which she intended to submit to *Nature* magazine.

Jack slumped and sulked. He was aware of his bad mood, aware that it wasn't really like him, but damned if he'd do anything about it. He watched the saturated landscape, hardly sharing the enthusiasm of his parents as they began to reach the deep country, with its signs and signals of a long forgotten past, the monoliths and grave mounds, the bleak castles slipping from the high hills where they had been built to stand forever. *Why does she always have to be working?*

Angela, he had to acknowledge, annoyed him as much as she thrilled him.

His small radio screeched to the strident, wonderful sounds of the punk rock band PIL. On each occasion that he was instructed to 'turn the racket down'—

'And stop singing that you're the "Antichrist". We've got the message. Jesus! have we got the message . . .'

'It's the song. The words of the song.'

'You don't say . . .'

—he obeyed (*they were laughing at him*) then inched the music up by degrees. The tape played endlessly – he'd only brought the one – his only comfort as the moors approached.

By the end of the journey, he felt seriously like falling head-first into Grimpen Mire – the muddy bog of Sherlock Holmes fame – to be dragged down until the black dogs swam for him, to be eaten in celebration on the rocks, the *Antichrist*, a victim of the old earth and its old powers.

His imagination shifted into overdrive.

What a story he would tell when the new term started!

But instead, he walked and complained, and almost sobbed with relief when he was left in the hotel's television lounge for most of the evening while his parents tucked into the *a la carte* menu, and shared hiking stories with an older couple who were walking the whole way from one end of the country to the other. (They hadn't got very far then, Jack thought, until he realized they were almost at the *end* of the journey, eleven hundred miles down, sixty to go.)

Angela called during the evening, but all she wanted to talk about was whether or not he'd had an encounter with the bull-runners, and to enthuse to him about something she'd read in her research.

'Primal, primitive words and images might sometimes slip into a sort of sump, like a pit. They're discarded, not needed by the main memory systems in the brain. But they form archaeo-stories which occasionally become sufficiently complex to filter back to the conscious level.'

'Archaeo-stories.'

'Yes. I read about them in a French Canadian journal of psychology. They're events or images, or whole stories that have sort of created themselves out of our own reading, our own imagination – our experiences. They surface because they become energized from—'

'You've been reading French Canadian journals of psychology?'

'Yes. Yes, I have. I've begun to understand what's happening to you, Jack. Do you want to hear about this?'

'What language are they written in?'

'The journals? French, of course.'

'I'm stuck here, up to my neck in mud, bog and black dogs, missing you, thinking of you all the time, and you're reading *French*.'

There was a moment of stunned silence. 'The work is fascinating. Jack, I think Jandrok's *archaeo-story* might explain—'

'I want to be in bed with you,' he whispered. 'I want to be making love.'

'Jack! Keep a grip! My parents often listen in.'

'Are they listening in now?'

'I haven't heard the *bips* on the line. I don't think so.'

'Do you miss me?'

'Of course. Of course I miss you. Jack, you're only away for four days. I'll see you next week.'

'How're the cousins?'

'Big, loud, rude . . . very self-centred! But rather nice.'

'Have they tried to seduce you?'

He heard her gasp of irritation, could imagine her annoyance. 'What do you mean *try*? Didn't have to *try*, Jack. It's three in a bed every night. You're *pathetic*. Grow up!'

The line went dead on her angry voice. Jack mimicked her fury into the mouthpiece then slammed the receiver down.

Why did I *do* that?

After a fitful night's sleep, he got up and showered at six in the morning, dressed in walking clothes and stared out at the sweeping rain, the waving trees, the tumbling, tormented clouds rolling in from the Atlantic.

'Great day for a walk!' he sneered at the world outside. Then thought, *so let's go walking!*

When his parents came down to breakfast, he had already finished eating and was standing, fully clothed and ready for the elements, grim-faced and twitchy.

'Hurry up,' he said, to the amusement of other guests in the breakfast room. 'Let's not waste a moment of the day. Let's get *walking*.'

His father smiled at him half-heartedly. 'It's too wet for the moors. They'll be too dangerous. We thought we'd take a coast drive, look at some castles.'

'Not to cast any aspersion on the joys of a coastal ride, I'm for the moors. The black dogs are waiting for us. I feel a family like ours can take them on and triumph.'

His father stared at him, frowning. 'Shut up, Jack. It's too risky to walk in weather like this. The mud softens up . . .'

'Then I'll see you later.'

'Where the hell are you going?'

By the time his father had gathered his wits and come out of the small hotel into the rain, Jack was standing in the bushes, concealed and grim. When the man on the steps disappeared inside again, he ran quickly through the grounds, across the main road, and began to pick his way across the fields to the rise of land that marked the bleak moors.

In two hours, he was high above the town and could look back at the grey stones and slates of the hotel itself, nestling among black winter trees in the curve of the river. The rain had eased, but was still strong; importantly, the wind had dropped and the wind-chill was no longer as discomforting and dangerous as it had been earlier.

There were a few other people striding up the slopes, some of them with dogs which ran in a bedraggled, miserable way rather than leaping and barking for exercise. Jack followed them, pacing along the muddy path, stopping only when he saw a distant shape, a solitary figure moving along the ridge, dark against the grim sky, ascending a path towards the main Tor.

Something about the stride . . .

He pressed on. Sheep moved away from him, almost silent in the downpour. A vixen moved around them, a huge creature, rust-red and lithe as she trotted cautiously downwind of the flock, looking for anything lame or small. After a while she vanished into the mist and the sheep relaxed.

He was suddenly alone on the moors, no sign of life, animal or human, just the dull if verdant bog grass, the grey, mist-shrouded rocks of the tors, the swirl and drum of rain. He struck out for Wolf Tor, the highest point, and after crossing a ruined stone wall, an old boundary marker, he found a crude path that wound towards the summit.

Between one glance at the Tor and the next, the tall man

had appeared there, watching him, rain pouring from his leather hat, glistening on the long raincoat.

This was Jack's second encounter with Garth before the Spring, and he sensed at once that something was wrong. He trudged along the path, wiping the water from his eyes, aware that the man was standing in the lee of the craggy rocks, smoking and staring back.

Face to face, Garth looked pale and haunted, his gaze watery, unfocused, cast more to the wide and bleak land below this summit than to the breathless boy in his anorak, jeans and muddy boots.

'How did you know I'd be here?'

Garth ground the cigarette against the massive grey monolith beside him. 'Angela told me. I paid a visit to her father two days ago. I thought it might be an idea to see you. Especially out here.'

'On the moors?'

With a cryptic smile, Garth said, 'Wide, wild open spaces – easier to dowse. Easier to hear. If there's anything below the earth, moorland like this reveals it quickly.'

'I saw you in Exburgh – before Christmas. You ran away . . .'

'I had things on my mind. I couldn't talk to you just then. But I've been keeping an eye on you, Jack.'

Jack stared at the man, cold in the rain, tugging his weatherproof tighter around his neck to stop the icy trickle of water down his neck.

Garth asked, 'Dream of Greenface lately?'

'A little. It comes and goes; it always has. There's a strong feeling of a bull in the tunnel, below the shoe shop. I got scared again.'

'You went back?'

'I went back. There's a real *life* in that place. Just like you said. The hidden city is alive.'

Garth stood for a few moments in silence, hands in pockets, watching the boy. Then he said, 'You might be in trouble,

Jack. I can't be sure; but I thought I ought to warn you. To take care.'

'In trouble?' Jack shivered at the words.

'They won't let you alone. The bull-runners. You're their channel to freedom. They're coming closer. Can you feel that?'

'Not for a while, now. I hear them, but they're not close. Can you? Do you see them too?'

Garth shook his head. He lit another cigarette, huddled against the rain, his face momentarily wreathed in coils of an almost blue smoke.

'Glanum *is* alive. You're right. But not the ruins below Exburgh. That's just an echo in stone. It's important to make the distinction, Jack. What's alive is in *you* and in *me*. We're part of the same haunting, but it's coming at us in different ways. The bull-runners have you in their sights; I have Glanum in mine.'

'What do the bull-runners mean to the city?'

'To the city? I don't know. To the *heart* of the city? They belong together. Jack, I've been hunting Glanum for longer than you'd believe. Since before the Sixties!' he added with a grin. 'I've been hunting it so long I've forgotten when it started. I've even forgotten *how* it started . . . except that . . .'

He had drifted for a moment, eyes narrowed, thinking hard, remembering. Then he shook his head.

'When *you* surfaced, Jack . . . when I found you – with your link with the bull-runners, I knew I was close to the end of the search. But I forgot the danger – to you, I mean. And since I can't tell exactly what's going to happen to me from one Godforsaken moment to the next, I thought I should find you. To tell you – warn you – that you might be in a lot of trouble.

'But wherever I am, I promise you one thing—'

He squeezed the life from the cigarette and flicked it into the rain, then tightened his coat and tugged his wide-brimmed hat lower across his face as he smiled at the boy.

'—I'll keep an eye on you!'

And he turned and strode down the hill, a blurring figure in the misting rain walking deeper into the moors, heading towards the quaking ground, the low tors and fifteen miles of dangerous desolation. Jack wanted to call after him, but no words came. He watched silently until the city dowser was obscured by rain and distance, then turned back to the hotel.

Garth was on his mind all the time, now; in dreams, at school, even when with Angela in the privacy of his house, his parents at work. When he articulated the 'presence' of the strange man, it was always in words that suggested a final reckoning was coming close.

'Something's going to happen . . .'

'But with Garth, not the bull-runners.'

He hadn't experienced any dramatic closeness of the bull-runners for a long time, now, and yet, especially when he was out on the hills, he could hear the woman's breathing, her torn, ragged breath; his limbs sometimes ached with running when he had been standing still. There were shadows that alarmed him, of beasts rising from the marshes, or emerging from the swollen, roaring river down which he *sensed* he was swimming.

But they were not close. Only Garth was close. He was abroad in Exburgh, hugging the shadows of the old city, walking at dusk across the neon-lit streets, smoking, always smoking, glancing round, following the signs of the hidden town, kneeling at the ghosts of the shrines.

'He's keeping an eye on me.'

'How do you know?' Angela turned in bed, her fingers walking across Jack's chest, marking out each rib until he squirmed. She was pungent with a perfume called *Opium*, and with sweat, her long hair tousled, damp and matted across her forehead.

'I just feel it. He's here . . . he's close.'

'Why hide?'

'I don't know.'

'If I hadn't met him, I'd think he was another of your *archeo-stories*.'

She had meant the reference to be a moment of humour, but Jack repeated the word in exasperation and Angela turned irritably away, propping her head on her hand, picking up the book by Jack's bedside and snorting with derision as she saw that it was a 'Help to Pass Advanced History' book, a time-saver for slow students.

Jack was hopeless at history. He should never have agreed to take the subject in his final year.

Angela's paper had been rejected by *Nature*, and then by two psychology journals, and then by *New Scientist*, *Science*, and finally by the local paper. Most disappointing of all, when she had sent a copy of her essay to the Canadian scientist whose work had so inspired her, Jandrok had sent back a kind but short note through his secretary to the effect he was fascinated by her theories but regretted he had no time to deal with individual correspondence on the nature of his ideas.

She had taped all the letters of rejection to the inside of her school locker and could occasionally be found staring at them, and willing harm and despondency upon the authors.

The paper had impressed her teacher, however, and under his tutelage she was preparing for a University course in Psychology, attending an evening class and reading more widely in the subject. The school curriculum was insufficient to address the level of her understanding, and she was clearly being marked out for a top college of further education, probably at Cambridge.

The unexpected sound of a car pulling into the drive interrupted both tension and passion in the mad scramble for clothes. By the time Jack's mother had opened the front door, both pupils were staring at open books on the dining table, their overt dishevelment put down to natural, youthful scruffiness.

9

He was laughing, chin up, and shaking his head . . .
Greenface was exploding in his face, sunlight making her glorious as she leapt from the stained glass of the church window . . .

Garth followed, reaching down to him, shaking him . . .

'Quiet! Jack, be quiet! Sssh!'

Jack came out of the dream and sat up. The bedroom window was open, the air in the room crisp and fresh. Garth settled back on his haunches, a crouched shape by the bed, his body rank with sweat, his breath heavy with the smell of tobacco.

'Who's Jocelyn?' he asked quietly.

'Jocelyn?'

'You were moaning the name Jocelyn when I came in through the window. So who is she? Your new girlfriend?'

Jocelyn?

Jack's head cleared suddenly. 'Jocelin! He's a priest. In the book I'm studying. *The Spire.*'

'Never heard of it. Who wrote it?'

'William Golding.'

'Him I've heard of.'

Jack was still disorientated. What was Garth doing in his room at – he checked his bedside clock – four twenty five in the morning.

'What are you doing here?'

'I've come to fetch you. I'm expecting to leave today. It's taken longer than I thought. I need some help.'

'You're leaving?'

'I'm leaving. What's it about? *The Spire.*'

'A priest.'

'Jocelin. We already got that far. But what about him? Why does he make you dream?'

'He wants to build a spire on his Cathedral. But it's going to be too high, too heavy. The foundations won't hold it. But it's his dream and he won't listen to common sense.'

Garth seemed taken with the idea, looking away, thinking hard before he said quietly. 'Like the Tower of Babel, then. Building for personal glory rather than the glory of God.'

'I don't know. I'm not sure . . .'

'The Spire isn't ready to be built. The human mind that wants to build it is too far ahead. Dreaming. But the building won't accept it. The earth won't accept it. Am I right?'

Jack didn't know. He'd prepared several set-answers to do with the book, and with William Golding in general. But mediaeval priests and the construction of churches in the Middle Ages held as much interest for him as . . . well, mediaeval priests and the construction of churches in the Middle Ages! If the *Antichrist* had featured, Beelzebub, Satanism, maybe some exorcism, even a minor demon or two, the story might have taken on a different dimension.

'It's a bit dry. It's about more than the story itself. Subtext, metaphor, all that stuff.'

'I know. I know,' Garth said wearily. 'All that stuff.'

'Lots of vertigo, though. That's cool.'

'But a dry book. Like stone? Like earth?'

'Yeah. I suppose so.'

Garth smiled. 'Or maybe you just don't get it. Yet.'

'I suppose so.'

'And the earth itself may have some surprises for you. Get up, Jack. Get dressed.'

'Why are you here?'

'I told you. I'm expecting to leave today.'

'Leave for where?'

'Good question.'

'What's happening to you?' Jack asked gently, suddenly sad.

'The White Whale,' Garth said, winking at the boy. 'Come on. Get dressed. And make a substantial packed lunch. We have some walking to do. *Vertical* walking,' he added with a leathery grin. 'As opposed to horizontal.'

Jack left a note on the breakfast table, pretending that he had left early for a swim before school, a less frequent occurrence now than a few years ago, but a suitable enough explanation for his absence.

Garth had hired a car, a sleek, peacock-green Renault whose back seats were now pushed down to make sufficient space for two heavy coils of rope, each with a gleaming grappling hook at its end.

'You *can* drive, can't you?'

'No. Not officially.'

Garth spun the wheel too hard for its power-assisted steering and the car skidded and screamed on the road as it sped away towards the hills. 'Well, that's too bad. You'll just have to take a chance. It's easy enough to handle.'

As he spoke, he crashed the gears, which complained with ear-splitting stridency. He frowned as he stared down at the gear lever. 'I'm used to automatics; this was all I could get at short notice. Where's the overdrive?'

'You're about to hit the kerb!'

'Shit!'

By the time they parked, in the thin woodland that ran along the bottom of the Mallon Hills, the day had developed into strong sunshine and warm breezes and Jack felt he had aged ten years, the result of the dowser's appalling driving. From the car park they could see the traffic heading to Exburgh for the start of the working day. But away from all that, the hills rose in silent, solitary splendour, cloud-shadowed and brilliant with dew. Everything here was fresh, unspoiled, the new season bringing a scintillating green to the land.

They struck off through the beechwood, found the path, the kissing gate and then the rough track that wound up the first of the hills, towards the Mallon valley. Garth led the way, his long oilskin coat and heavy leather pack slung over one shoulder, a coil of rope over the other. Jack carried the second grappling hook, and his own knapsack with roast beef sandwiches, two apples and a chunk of game pie.

At the first summit they gazed over farmland, the river valley itself, and the wooded slopes of Windover Hill, a good hour's stride away. Garth crouched down and listened to the wind. His face almost shone in the bright sun.

'I know this place so well, now,' he said. 'I know the springs, the windbreaks, the snow-shelters, the pipes and caves that riddle the rock.'

Jack watched the man carefully. Aware of the attention, Garth turned on him, still crouching, then pointed to a clump of trees and a dry-stone wall, half-way down the slope to the winding brook below.

'I've lived there for more than a year. There's a deep crevice, runs a hundred yards into the hill, quite dry. I've had some dreams there, some wonderful dreams.' He laughed. 'I'm a sort of bear, Jack. I hibernated over the winter to make sure I was in the right place.'

'The right place?'

Garth stood, stretched, then picked up the rope and his pack.

'It's been a long hunt, but I'm at the end of the trail, now. I'm sure of it. And it's partly thanks to you. When I found Glanum, I found my quarry. But it was a long search . . .' he added, almost sighing. He stooped quickly and tugged up a small tuft of grass, rubbing the moist earth and roots between his fingers as he again stared down at the boy. 'I'm going home, Jack. Or I'll die in the attempt. That's why I asked you to come with me.' He put the crushed grass to his nose, closed his eyes as he inhaled briefly, then let it fall.

'But don't be concerned,' he added. 'You're in no danger yourself. I promise you that.'

'Up on Muldon Moor, you said that I *was* in trouble.'

'In trouble, yes. But not in danger. If I die, you'll remember what you've seen. If I don't, I'll be keeping an eye on you. You'll always have a friend in me, Jack. Over the years I've made that promise many times, and always kept it. Now let's walk. I'm getting hungry and I can smell that game pie . . .'

The game pie?

'That's *my* lunch,' Jack murmured as he followed the man down the hill.

'All supplies to be shared,' Garth said with a quick, amused glance back.

She was crouching, watching him, the green patterns on her face writhing like living creatures. Her dark eyes were wide, her expression one of curiosity; and behind her, the man in the cloak of scalps and feathers stood impatiently, his attention on the world around them, his energy concentrated on survival. 'We have to go . . .'

'We're so close . . .'

She reached towards him, her fingers brushing his cheek. The earth was shaking; Greyface hunched up slightly, alarmed by what was happening; rocks shuddered and shifted, trees shook, leaves shedding, boughs cracking, the ground itself seemed about to open . . .

Jack opened his eyes. Clouds scudded above him, and the tremor in the earth passed away. It was warm, with a light breeze, and he was stretched out on the ground, still sleepy. The shadow of a man passed over him and he sat up, to see Garth pacing restlessly about the hilltop, staring into the distance.

'I fell asleep.'

The man seemed impatient, silencing him with a gesture, a hiss. 'It's close, now. If I say get the hell away, you do just that. Do you understand? You just run. Get out of the hill.'

'I saw Greenface. She said she was close . . .'

For a second Garth stared at him, face in shadow, body dark against the bright sky. 'I expect she is. Was the man with her?'

'Yes.'

'Threatening?'

'Worried.'

The hillside seemed to vibrate. Jack stood up and looked around. They were facing the deep valley. Cloud shadow ran across it. The wind gusted.

'What's happening?'

'It's nosing for me. See those trees?'

Jack looked towards the copse, two hundred yards away. Garth said, 'You go there, you stay there, among the trees; you simply wait; you hang on, you don't move. You certainly don't try to stop me.' And then he cried out, startling Jack. '*Look there*!'

'What? What is it?'

Long coat flapping, Garth had started to run along the hill. He was pointing into the distance. 'There! There it *is*!'

Something was moving through the valley. Not cloud shadow, Jack realized, but the land itself, folding, furling, a ripple in the green earth, like wind on water, a pattern, turning to flow towards them.

'Bring the ropes!'

Jack dragged the heavy coils with their metal hooks and flung them at Garth's feet. The man stood silently, letting the wind blow at him, his gaze following the wave-motion in the valley.

'It knows I'm here. But I don't think it recognizes me. This could be dangerous. Back off from me, Jack. Get away from me.'

'I feel strange.'

Around him, the world was in bright shadow. The earth rumbled, the wind raged, the grass chattered. Looking round, Jack realized that nothing was right, not even the sight of the world. His senses were merging, melding almost, and Garth's breathing became sonorous, his voice booming as he turned and waved slowly, a hand waving slowly, *get away, now, get away.*

'What's happening?'

The hill seemed to swell below him, the whole world shaking.

Get away, Jack. Get out of the path. Get to the trees or you'll be sucked into the wake . . .

'Garth! What is it?'

Across the valley, a vast shape moved through the trees, throwing woods and grassy slopes into flowing waves, cutting the land with stone towers and high walls, white features that passed like scythes as they rose above the green, then descended again, vanishing from sight. 'It's moving round – to the north. It's coming up the valley!'

Garth hauled the ropes as he ran over the ridge, disappearing for a moment, before returning, face wet with effort, brow furrowed. He listened hard, looked round, then seemed to sense something below him. He slowly lengthened the grappling end of one of the ropes, starting to swing it. Jack watched the man, felt the unreal breeze. Everything around him was unnaturally bright. The earth thrummed with movement, a rising and falling vibration that made his legs shake.

Garth said urgently, 'You're standing in two worlds, Jack. What you see is the hunters' world, unreal in its way, but dangerous. You should back away *now*. To the trees. And hold on tightly.'

Jack was about to say something, but he hesitated as the air around him became suddenly still – almost frozen.

That was when the world exploded behind Garth.

The walls of the city rose so swiftly and so steeply from the earth that Garth was thrown down. The stone behemoth moved rapidly across the hill, sliding past Jack as he watched open-mouthed. The air was filled with thunder. The walled beast stretched higher into the sky, then plunged again, among a stand of shivering beeches.

In the few seconds that the city had broken the surface he had seen the shattered walls, the grinning gates, the streaming trails of vine and creeper that swathed the ruins, the bristling roots of twisted trees growing through the stones to form writhing, human shapes upon the white-washed blocks.

The great tower had moaned as it passed, audible through the thunder, the sonorous echo of wind in a vast chamber, or a deep cave. A dark figure was clinging to its top, peering down at the small creatures below.

As suddenly as it had reared, the city had gone, and where the earth had been broken there remained no sign of the damage. But below Jack, the world shuddered, the hill threatened to shake itself apart.

'It's going round!' Garth shouted.

He stood up from where he had fallen, brushed at the smears of grass and mud on his clothes and again began to swing the grappling iron.

'Here it comes!'

He was swinging the iron in a wide loop, his back to the boy. 'Goodbye, Jack!'

This time, Glanum came straight at him, breaking the surface of the land, rising steadily towards the man who waited; a great gate gaped, an arched maw with bull's horns and wide, animal eyes carved deeply in the stone. The tower that guarded the gate shed stones and earth and broken branches. Jack saw statues, dark buildings, pillars and towers within the walls, a ragbag of structures, some dark, like mud, some bright, some white, some swathed in the lush green of a forest.

At the last minute, as it seemed the city would crush the tiny figure of Garth, it seemed to twist away, diving again at speed, throwing up a billow of rich and stinking earth, scattering trees in the hunters' land, leaving their shades just visible in the world beyond the dream.

Garth ran forward and threw the grappling hook, tossing it high on the wall behind the tower, jerked from his feet as the iron grasped the raw stone, swinging wildly against the massive battlement wall. His body was dragged, and he hauled himself along the rope, trying to walk the wall, his raincoat flapping about his bony frame. The city dived, and Garth went down with the descending beast. As he vanished below the hill, he managed to turn and glance at Jack, and he seemed to be shouting something, but he was hanging on for his life and he was soon swallowed.

For a moment there was silence. Then back along the valley the tower broke the ground, the arch of a gate, the heads of the beasts who guarded it, the red-tiled roofs of several buildings.

The hill shook one last time.

Then the air cleared, the strange light dissipated leaving just the blue of the spring sky. Around Jack the earth was as normal, the second rope, Garth's leather pack, lying exactly where he had flung them.

After a while, Jack shouldered the pack, but left the rope. He walked to the north along the valley, imagining the wake of the city. By late afternoon he was back at the car, bemused, still stunned by what had happened.

He sat in the car till dusk, then realizing that his parents would be frantic about his whereabouts, he found a telephone and called them.

But before he drove carefully back to Exburgh in the rented car, he cried for several minutes, though whether with fear, or confusion, or simply the loss of a friend, he couldn't tell.

PART TWO

Through the Bull Gate

10

In the years since Garth had made his spectacular departure from the world, hauling himself up the wall of the ghost city of Glanum, Jack had more or less come to terms with the experience and had largely ceased to miss the man, although each time he returned home from university he prowled the excavation, or walked the Mallon Hills, hoping to see the grey hair, the flapping coat, the curl of silver smoke.

No trace of the White Whale remained on the hills where Glanum had manifested itself that day. That Garth had disappeared without trace wasn't in question – attempts to find him, to piece together a life for the man, proved pointless. He was known for his archaeology, his talent for dowsing, and he had spent time working in Europe. But he was as trackless, as alone in his life, as any mirage.

What Jack had seen, he had seen, though. The experience was real to him. And although Ruth, the professional, was disinclined to accept the monstrous unlikelihood of a city emerging from the earth to swallow a man, Angela recorded every word, began at once to fit the moving city into a broader Scheme of Things.

'External and internal phenomena,' she said to him. 'You can't equate the two because you assume that *you're* the source. But if you are only the *channel* – if the source is nothing to do with you *yourself* . . . then the source may manifest in many sorts of ways.'

At the end of his final term he had failed to get a place at Cambridge, where he could have worked alongside Angela, and settled instead for Norwich, which at least gave him easy access to his friend. He was reading mathematics – he'd been excellent in the subject at school – but in his second year was bogged down, bored rigid by the reams of theoretical equations, even complaining that he was now confused about long division.

Time fascinated him, though, and he was a tireless fan of a young, disabled research fellow at Cambridge, Stephen Hawking, and of the wild, wonderful American, Richard Feynman, whom he met twice. Their publications acted as his touchstone to intellectual comfort, his response to them, the worlds of imagination they opened, helping to massage his confidence. A confidence that had recently taken many knocks.

In their first year apart from each other, Angela had become heavily involved with a robustly athletic New Zealander, a mature student in the Department of Psychology, specializing in Lucid Dreaming. The relationship distressed Jack to the point of distraction and he broke off all contact with Angela. Her new friend introduced her to the delights and disasters of canoeing, a sport which they undertook along the lakes and rivers of central Finland, and the gorges of the Carpathian mountains. Their affair lasted a full twelve months before collapsing, the glamour vanishing as suddenly and startlingly as the cold words – delivered without emotion – froze her heart.

'It's been fun. But I never commit for more than a year. I'd hoped you'd realized that. I tried to be clear without being . . . crude?'

Incensed, she was speechless for an embarrassingly long moment. 'No. No, I hadn't. Realized it! You *weren't* clear. And it's exactly a year to the *day* since we first went out! Did you keep a diary or something?'

'Certainly I kept a diary. I keep a diary of *everything* I do. How am I to study my own Lucid Dreaming if I don't have full life reference? Come on, Ang—'

'Oh my God . . . You shit!'

'Angie— come on. We're both adults . . .'

'*Shit!*'

Terrified of contacting Jack again, but desperate to do so, she finally found the courage to telephone him, was unsurprised by his coldness and caution, but delighted when he suggested meeting in the woods near Hockley Mere, a place of primordial beauty, timeless, little disturbed by human endeavour. Here, they moved away from the forestry research station that had been their rendezvous, walked for two hours in the stillness of the lakes and woodlands, then drank a warm bottle of Chablis, which Jack had forgotten to enclose in ice packs. It was a hot April day, the whole place in new bud, new life, and Angela cried for a long time.

'I *have* missed you. I'd just felt there was something *missing* from us. And he's going so deeply into the mind – his work's so challenging . . . But he was such a bastard . . .'

Jack didn't know what to say. He didn't want to think of the other man, this bright New Zealander. He didn't even know his name; his heart was still crushed with envy. So he just put his arms around Angela and held her very limply until she moved closer and began to look at him through moist, then more appealing eyes.

He'd expected her to proposition him, and was already aroused and ready, the last twelve months having been a time of sublime and frustrating failure when it came to making new relationships.

'Shall we meet again?' she said, then laughed. 'When shall we two meet again . . . in Hockley, Exburgh . . . or in . . . Spain?'

This was a modest attempt at humour and Jack responded to it, but he was disappointed since it clearly signalled her intention of returning, imminently, to Cambridge. Jack summoned up the courage to say, 'Do you want to start seeing me again?'

'Of course,' Angela said, but she was remote, frowning as she presumably thought of the implications of the idea. 'Jack,

I'm not sure. Not yet. I couldn't wait to see you, to talk to you, when my life just fell apart. Well, fell apart it *seemed*. He wasn't worth it, of course.' She looked at him fondly. 'I *did* want to see you. I never wanted to lose touch.'

'Kiss me.'

She hesitated, then acceded, and he held her for a long time, even though she'd broken the kiss after a few seconds.

Chancing his luck he said, 'If you come back to me, I'll not let you go again.'

'That sounds like a threat.'

'It isn't. Just don't come back to me unless you're sure. I need you very much. I love you, I'm sorry I never told you before.'

'It must have been hell for you. Steve was . . .'

'I don't *want* to know the bastard's name. I just want you. Come back to me – but please! Only if you're sure.'

She was slightly startled. She agreed silently, then added, 'I know I'm going to be sure. Give me a few weeks, that's all. Just a few weeks. But Jack . . . you *have* to come to Cambridge. Steve's been doing – sorry . . . The Department of Psychology are doing some really interesting stuff with dreaming and a new thing, computer generated *Virtual Reality*. It's going to be big. It's going to change lives! And it might be a way of getting a *visual* record of the bull-runners.'

'I don't want to talk about this now . . .'

'No, of course not. I understand. But *have* you seen them recently?'

'They're around. They've not presented any primary visions, not for a long while. I really *don't* want to talk about that. OK?'

'I have to go.'

'I know. That's why I don't want to talk about anything but us.'

She grinned over her shoulder. 'As I said to you once before, you're my life's work. I'll be keeping my eye on you!'

'You and John Garth both, it seems.'

I I

Years had passed, years of inner silence, years of change. In the early summer, to celebrate his birthday, Jack took Angela and their five year old daughter, Natalie, to a 'surprise' location in France, an old farmhouse in the mountainous Perigord region, ramshackle but fully equipped, and with turkeys (noisy and disgustingly messy), hens (noisy but egg-laying) and small black-spotted pigs (clean, quiet, but unwelcomingly curious) as their garden companions. The farm belonged to a work colleague of his, a man in his fifties with no family commitments who had bought the small house years before, visited the place for two weeks every year, and otherwise took pleasure in 'lending' it to friends for their own holidays.

The girl loved the animals; Angela loved the walking, through deep gorges, along the wide, slow rivers that flowed out of the central highlands; Jack enjoyed the canoeing, slipping away from his cares and duties to drift lazily below the steep cliffs, perforated with caves, covered with gnarled and stumpy oaks and proud pines, precariously growing from the rock, a literally vertical forest above the winding waterways.

Like all good things, this time away from the pressures of work came to an end, and after ten days Angela took her leave of the farmhouse. She was scheduled to attend the *Konference Nove Psychologie* in Prague, and was giving a paper on 'The Source and Meaning of Limbic System Echoes'. The paper had been written well in advance and she had spent her two days' 'preparation' simply memorizing Wendy Cope's splendid parody of W S Gilbert (*A Policeman's Lot*) on the subject of

'Patrolling the Unconscious of Ted Hughes', the darkly myth-
ical British Poet Laureate at that time.

In order to make one of her points during the presentation
she wanted to be able to look up from her notes and sing the
lines.

It was typical Angela: anything for effect.

So with sadness, but anticipation, she made her farewells to
the farm ('But I shan't miss you damned turkeys!') and Jack
drove her to the airport, before returning for the last few days
of the holiday.

Distracted without her, and now unable to take a kayak on
the river – Natalie was too young – he took his daughter to the
nearest gorge and descended the steep path to the wide, grassy
bank with its thin pebble beach in the shallows. It was here
that they'd had most of their picnics. The girl paddled and
Jack swam, though the water was icy. They lay back on the
grass and basked in the sun as it moved high overhead. Everything in the valley became steamy and drowsy. Canoes and
kayaks drifted past, the paddlers' young voices hollow and
echoing, fading into the distance . . .

After a while, Jack got up and stretched his arms and legs.

He continued on along the river, wary of the steep slopes
with their concealed paths, and the bushy hawthorn that
could easily have concealed danger. The sun was still bright
and the sides of the gorge were dropping to more open land.
He cut inland for a while, struggling through undergrowth,
wading across muddy streams, aware that there was a smell of
smoke in the air, woodsmoke, a settlement close by.

At some point the river turned and the land opened out into
dense forest, with the mountains now behind him. He was
approaching the bank again, and could hear the laughter and
chattering of several young women. He moved towards the
treeline and peered from the shadows, his heart beating hard
with the humidity and effort of his long journey.

There were five of them, all dressed in patchwork skirts and simple shawls. They had black hair tied in tight ringlets, all except the tallest and eldest who had fashioned her own luxurious locks into an elaborate pony-tail, high on the crown, flowing down around her shoulders. They were playing on the rocks that dropped to the river itself, which here was wide and sluggish, bordered by woodland on the other side.

The girls were making linked loops of flowers into a single, draping necklace. When the flower ring was finished each of them in turn put it around her shoulders and ran twice around the group, laughing, sometimes almost hysterically, though the joke was lost on Jack.

The tall girl was the last to wear the necklace, and when she had completed the ritual of running, to the rhythmic applause of the others, she flung the ring of bright blooms into the water.

The five girls crowded together, watching how the flowers moved on the turbulent surface, one of them jumping up and down and clapping loudly in her excitement.

It was she who turned suddenly to the far woods, looking nervous. There was movement there, dark shadow.

At once the excitement stopped. The girls murmured with apprehension, huddling down and peering across the river. From his watching place, Jack could sense the movement too. There was a strong, strange smell on the air.

A moment later, a loud series of bellows pierced the tranquility with shocking effect. Huge curved tusks rose above the trees and five elephantine creatures charged through the edge wood, massive, shaggy bodies crushing the undergrowth. Their trunks were held high above the tangle of the forest. They thundered down the bank to plunge into the river, lowering tusks and shaking the long, amber hair that swathed their heaving flanks.

The girls had screamed and fled as the five mastodons waded into the shallow river, heads swaying so that the curling ivory from their jaws raked the water.

Suddenly they stopped, lowering trunks in unison to drink. After a few minutes these winter beasts turned into single file and began to walk up the river, belly deep, in the direction of the village.

A figure moved past him, a shadow in the bright, cold sun, head low, body low, darting to the edge of the water and disappearing beyond the rocks where the flower girls had played. Jack rose quickly to follow, alert to possible danger, and as he came closer to the river he was aware that—

Someone was calling from the flowing water. And he walked with less caution, more concern, to the bank . . .

Disorientated: he was in the shadow of high, gloomy cliffs.

Natalie was floating away from him, calling hysterically . . .

He sat up! And blinked, staring in confusion at the struggling form in the river, now more than a hundred yards away. The shock hit him like a hammer blow, and he screamed as he jumped to his feet, running to the water's edge.

Floating away from him!

'Nattie, Splash your arms! Oh Christ . . . !'

He ran along the bank, but trees intervened and he struggled to find a way through. The river was slow, but Jack himself was a slow swimmer and he was afraid that if he entered the water it would take too long to catch the drowning girl. Natalie went below the surface and Jack screamed again, screamed for help, looking desperately back along the river, but they seemed quite alone.

He flung himself into the water, crawling with all the strength his panic could muster, blinded by water, choking on water, unaware of the cold, unable to see the fair-haired girl he loved so much.

Then he heard Natalie's cry, and tried to shout, 'Keep splashing your arms! Keep kicking the water! I'm coming. Daddy's coming!'

He was aware of something sleek and yellow sliding past him, the cold splash of water on his face as a paddle nearly struck his nose. Exhausted, he trod water, saw the slim kayak swerve around the struggling child, then suddenly turn over.

When he had swum further he saw a girl dragging both Natalie and a kayak to the shore, Natalie's arms around her neck. When Jack struggled to the narrow, muddy 'beach', she was rubbing the shivering girl's arms and laughing with her.

'Thank you . . .' Jack said, and the canoeist stood up, glancing at him. She was tall and German, probably a student, wearing a black bikini bottom and a life-jacket over a saturated T-shirt.

'She's OK, I think,' she said. Jack hugged his daughter, crying with relief and the after-shock of his day-dream.

The girl had squeezed down into the kayak and was pushing herself back into the river. She seemed very confident. She had kept hold of boat, paddle and child, despite being knocked over by the abruptness of her turn.

'Thank you again!' Jack said. She looked at him sharply.

'She's a nice girl.'

'Yes.'

'You are lucky to have her.'

'Yes. I know. Thank you again . . .'

She drifted into the middle of the water, then began to paddle vigorously. As she rapidly vanished round the bend in the river, the ambiguity of her words struck home and Jack felt sick.

If Natalie had been terrified in the water, she showed no signs of upset now, as if the German canoeist's brief words with her had exorcized all terror. She played happily as they walked back to the farm, unaware that her father was shaking and himself in sudden apprehension.

He had been dreaming, but the dream was the same as in those days when the bull-runners had infrequently but powerfully invaded his mind's eye. And yet they hadn't been there – or had they? The female figure had been in silhouette – could it have been Greenface? He'd seen no sign of Greyface – unless he'd been watching from the Scalpcloak's eyes! And the lucidity, the immediacy of the vision had been exactly as he remembered it.

Mastodons, tundra-creatures, charging through a forest into water, scattering girls from a primitive village, interrupting their flower ritual . . .

He could still smell the monsters; he could still hear the screams of the girls, fleeing for the thin security of their tents, their stockade, their parents.

Was it part of the same sequence of visions that had haunted his childhood and his adolescence? Ten years without the bull-runners; ten years without any sense of Glanum as more than a stone shadow; ten years in which he had thought himself free of the Otherworld. But ten years of disappointment for Angela, who was eager to turn her training and understanding on the phenomenon: 'I promised to keep my eye on you, and now there's nothing to keep my eye on!'

He realized at once, as he led Natalie up the winding track to the road and their holiday home, that he had to return to England. Without Angela, he was now a risk to his daughter, no more, no less than if he were subject to fits of epilepsy. He couldn't afford these lapses with so precious a life at stake.

What clawed at him was the thought of the two-day drive to their home in England. There was no way he felt able to risk the journey, so he called Angela at the conference hotel in Prague and waited for her to return. She arrived by taxi a day later, triumphant – she had already presented her paper when the urgent call from her husband had been put through to her – and with mixed feelings of horror, at her child's near death, and excitement that encounters with the bull-runners might be returning.

When they went to bed that night, Angela was passionate and close, her libido fed by the kudos of success, and perhaps by the more primal need that surfaces when a family has been threatened, the need for survival, for replacement. Throughout the mating, Jack cried silently against her shoulder.

Once at home again, he dictated a detailed account of the *shimmer*, which Angela noted carefully.

'Was there any sense of the runners?

'No . . . except that . . .'

It was so hard to define, like trying to explain Angela's presence in his dream, his certainty that a middle-aged man was her own partial presence . . .

'I was watching from the tree line, behind the girls. I have a sense of my own face looking out, a striped, grey face, concealed in the light and shade of the underbrush, watching curiously. Perhaps I was Greyface . . .'

'No sense of the woman at all?'

'None at all. Maybe it was just a dream, a daydream. Maybe it doesn't connect.'

Angela was scrawling furiously, pushing her auburn hair back over her head, absorbed by her thoughts; after a minute or so she wound back the tape and started to transcribe it.

Jack went outside where Natalie and her cousin, Ben, were splashing in the paddling pool, supervised by Ben's minder, a cheery Australian girl who made sudden gasping sounds and begged a beer. Jack popped back into the house to fetch a cold lager, then went down to the bottom of the garden, staring out across the downs to the distant line of hills.

A patch of woodland, a copse known as Battle Clumps, marked the part of those hills where the city of Glanum had flowed from the Deep, surfacing to entice, to capture John Garth, ten years ago.

It was this view of the Mallon Hills that had finally convinced them to purchase the house, a ramshackle property on two floors overlooking Exburgh from the south, needing so much modernization and decoration that family life had operated constantly in the dust and debris of builders, the chaos of refurbishment. The large garden was mostly given over to an orchard, with paddocks beyond where a few sheep and three retired horses grazed. Its sense of boundary with wild country made it popular with Natalie's friends, and they always seemed to have visitors.

He looked, now, at the trees on the horizon that marked the drop down to the valley where Garth had hidden and lived for more than a year, and he felt, for the first time in ages, a need, almost a compulsion, to go back to the shrines of the hidden city, to the masks of the travellers, carved in antiquity, according to conventional wisdom; faces that had seemed alive when first exposed.

Angela wanted to come with him, to watch him as he returned to the Hercules shrine, curious to know what was happening to her husband; but Rachel would be leaving at three in the afternoon, so Natalie would have to be supervised. 'Why don't we all go tomorrow?'

He stood in the low-ceilinged room, looking at the bespectacled and beautiful woman, at the flow of her precise handwriting, the tumble of hair, and he heard:

running

And Greenface was close to him, her breath sweet, the sweat on her body oily, staining her tunic, making the green tattoos on her face seem to writhe like snakes as she came towards him

running

Close now, and desperate. She was alone. Greyface was not around. She was behind him, around him, before him

inside him.

'They're coming back,' he said to Angela, who at once rose from the table and came to him, feeling his skin, smelling his skin, looking closely for any sign of the *shimmering.*

'Are you sure?'

'No. Not sure. It feels like it, though.'

'Then you shouldn't go out now. Stay home. If they're close, we can record it.'

'Not that close . . . Not yet . . . I need to go . . .'

He was gasping for breath. Why?

'Got to go,' he stammered.

Hooks pulled him. Memories of Garth were strong. He could feel the city shifting below the town, imagine the ochre crumbling from the walls, the masks, the frescoes . . .

'It's something I want to do alone.'

'You're not to drive. Jack, I absolutely insist on that! Your driving days are over. I'll phone for a taxi.'

'I agree. Quickly, though, quickly . . .'

She'll follow me, he thought as the taxi turned in the road to take him the two miles to Exburgh. She'll find a way to took after Natalie and she'll follow me.

Greenface was calling to him. He started to whine, holding his eyes as the woman's pain surfaced. She was calling to him, she was terrified. Greyface was close behind her, angry, his voice a low thunderous rumble as he challenged the woman, demanded the impossible, some impossible thing, some deed, some duty, something that terrified her, so that

came close, looked through his eyes

The taxi dropped down the steep road to the old town. Church spires and office blocks gleamed in the late afternoon sun; the river curled, silver and still, around the town centre, flowing towards the setting sun.

'Here! Here's fine!'

He was almost above the hidden heart of the city, on the narrow road by the steep slopes of Castle Hill, where a handful of people wound their way to the ruined walls and Norman Keep at the summit. Below him, Glanum pulsed like a waking beast.

He walked further into the town, towards St John's in the distance, following a course that had less to do with modern thoroughfares than with a feeling of communication with forgotten alleys, hidden walls. And after a few minutes he came to the Hercules pit.

He paid his money and went down the ramp, a remote figure among the few tourists who passed the plaster masks with a brief look, attracted more by the colourful frescoes on the north wall.

Jack faced the masks, looking between them, challenging the blind eyes to open, trying to see beyond them.

'You were dead. I thought you were dead.'

Cold plaster remained sightless across the centuries.

'Leave me alone. Leave me alone, for God's sake. I have a child now, and I nearly killed her . . .'

For ten years their world had drifted away from his, taking them into silence, into the distance of space and time. Ten years of peace . . .

The woman's breath was suddenly hot on his neck. His sense of smell was excited by the oils that streaked her body. His head echoed to the thunder of her heart. She was frightened. She was being hunted. She was charged with energy, alert to every sound, every movement in a world of shattered light and shadows.

Jack left the sanctuary and walked across the park. Shadow trees shifted in and out of his vision. He made his way steadily towards St John the Divine's, where the suicide gate lay buried. Turning a corner, Greyface suddenly leered at him, ice-eyes flashing, teeth bright through the clay mask. When Jack stepped back with shock, he collided with a man carrying shopping, nearly knocking him over onto the cobbled stone road.

Since they were the only two people in the street, the action must have seemed deliberate, and the older man struck out at his confused aggressor. Mumbling his apologies, Jack fled through Market Square.

At last he came to the river and crossed a bridge, walking away from the city's heart. But he turned back, thinking 'Urban area', and stared across the water at the spire of

St John's and the bulk of Castle Hill. A canal boat, gaudily painted in red and green Victorian designs, was chugging slowly against the flow. A laughing couple were struggling with a rowing boat, oars splashing uselessly as they circled helplessly. They were drifting slowly towards the dark maw of a cave, a vertical gash in the immense cliff that Jack could see shadowed, straddling the water.

The cliff seemed to be rising from the earth, a ghostly movement that disorientated him. When a boulder, carved with crude faces and symbols, its wet surface catching a heavy, alien sun, slid suddenly, translucently into view right before his eyes, he again staggered back, turning among the trees, the dark rising columns, aware of a glimmering light – *shimmering* – somewhere to his left. He seemed to be sinking, but . . .

It's coming up from below!

Greyface was calling to him, taunting him. The hunter was circling, out of sight, sending shadow birds scurrying from the bushes. Piercing whistles, mocking laughter, mingled with the dull roar of traffic.

Jack panicked and started to run. A hand grabbed him, slapped his face.

The shadows faded, a less alien sun caught his eyes, made him squint as Angela held him, shaking him, her words slowly coming clear.

'I knew you'd watch over me,' he gasped with relief.

'Come on. Jack. Come on. We're going home. You're a danger, and not just to others.' She scanned him, searched his face, amazed. 'You're glowing – like fire. We have to get this recorded. Come on, Jack. Come home . . .'

But the hold of *Glanum* was too strong.

He let Angela take him back through the streets, to the municipal car park, but he insisted she drive him to his parents, to their house above the city. Here, with the sound of running loud in his ears, with the stifling presence of a forest he could not see, with the scent of blood and sweat from two people who were so close he could almost touch them, he stood at the bottom of the front drive and looked down the hill.

As if it were yesterday, he could remember Garth strolling towards him, coat flapping, smoke coiling from the stub of his cigar. He could see the man's shape against the setting sun on the glimmering roofs of the town, and like the ghosts that haunted him, he felt he could reach out and take Garth's hand.

You're the boy who sees other worlds . . .

You're the man who dowses for lost cities . . .

'What happened to you?' he whispered, and a gentle touch on his shoulder made him turn. Angela put her arm around his shoulders, followed his gaze to the sprawl of Exburgh. 'What happened to who? Who are you talking about?'

'Garth.'

'Oh yes. Of course. You miss him.'

'I hardly knew him, but yes. I miss him. What's happening to me? It's come back, but it's different. It's like they're . . .' he reached out, running a hand through the warm air, rubbing the air against his palm with his fingers. 'It's like they're right beside me.'

'You said the city was rising. Are you still seeing the city?'

'Yes . . . but more distantly. Like a photograph projected on a wall – the real and the ghostly mixed together.'

It was like a dark shadow above the churches, the town hall, the multi-storey car parks, the clutter of structure that makes a modern town. If he blinked he saw reality, but if he looked hard enough he could see a hill, groves of trees, the clutter of red-tiled buildings, a shadowy, shimmering illusion of something that might once have been, but which might also be his imagination.

Is this how it was for John Garth? Is the world he inhabited an overlapping vision of the alien and the real?

He said, 'But Greenface is behind me, watching over my

shoulder. She keeps talking to me, murmuring things, touching me . . .'

Sensual. . . that touch . . . he couldn't tell Angela, but the touch of the alien aroused him, as if she had always been intimate with him, and now looked to him for strength, for companionship.

'Can you understand what she says?' Angela was examining him closely, disappointed, perhaps because the film of 'otherness' was not now present on his skin.

He thought of the woman, let her breathing grow loud, let his mind slip away from Angela.

'Time to come through . . . found gate . . . at last . . . searched so hard . . . look after me . . .'

'Oh Christ!'

Angela grabbed him, turned him sharply to face her, watching his eyes.

'What is it? What? Come on, Jack. What's happening?'

'They're coming through . . .'

She practically dragged him to the car, while his parents stood concerned and unhappy. He sat in the passenger seat, strapped by the seat belt, watching as Angela talked briefly with the older couple then returned to the car, reversing out of the drive with a speed approaching the dangerous. She stopped just once, at neighbours, to pick up Natalie, and within an hour Jack was washed, naked, monitored, videoed . . . and crying . . .

'Damn!'

Angela turned off the camera, came over once more to inspect her husband. Jack let her turn his face this way and that, enjoyed her hands on his body, tolerated the gradual detachment of the chemical pads and electrodes, listened to her sighs of frustration.

He wanted her. Naked, his skin cool, he suddenly wanted sex, and tried to tug her back to him, his head clearing fast.

'Let me clear away the equipment, first. For God's sake, Jack, you nearly killed yourself today. Again!'

'Take your clothes off.'

'Let me get cleared up, let me get Nattie to bed, let me scan the data and *then* we can play.'

He lunged at her. Greyface laughed, watching from behind him. The hunter easily blocked the blow from the woman, tripped her and tugged at her skirt and blouse.

'This is nice,' Greyface said. 'The hair colour. Like amber. I like it. Long hair like amber. Wind it round your hand.'

Greyface showed him how to pin the wrists with a single, powerful grip. The girl was in the doorway, screaming, but the sound was swallowed by the forest, disturbing nothing more than animals.

'Gently. Gently!' Greyface mocked him. 'This woman *loves* you . . . Give it to her *gently*!'

Far from gently, Jack stretched down to suck the woman's breast.

And suddenly Greyface reached out and jerked him by the hair, pulling him away, laughing. 'Get up. Get *up*, you fool. I just want you to know that we're close.'

He was standing, naked and shaking, powerfully aroused and bleeding from the scratches Angela had been able to inflict upon him before he had disabled her. In the doorway, Natalie was a huddled, silently sobbing figure, watching everything.

Angela stood, tugging down her skirt and closing her blouse. She ran to her daughter and hugged her. 'It's all right, darling. Daddy's dreaming. He didn't mean it. It's all right.'

'He was hurting you!'

'No he wasn't. He was just dreaming. Come downstairs, everything is all right. Daddy was having a nightmare.' She glanced furiously over her shoulder. 'Put your pants on, chief! Get downstairs!'

And then, with a quick frown, 'Greyface?'

Close to tears, still numbed by what he had done, all Jack could murmur was, 'I'm so sorry . . .'

'*Greyface?* she insisted.

'Yes . . . Oh Christ . . .'

'I thought so. I could smell him. Jesus, he's old . . . he's from somewhere *old*! Dress and come down.' And to the child, 'It's okay, Nattie. Everything's okay.'

With the girl settled, they huddled by the cold fire, curled up on the broad sofa, sipping vodka and tonic.

'I hope we did the right thing,' Angela murmured, swirling the ice in her glass. 'What *do* you say to a child who sees an attempted rape by her father on her mother? Christ, I need some advice. I think.'

'You seem to have done fine. She's quite settled.'

'Maybe trauma can do that to you.'

'I don't know.'

'Nor do I. With the near drowning, and this . . . I really do think it's take-advice time. Any problems with that?'

Jack drained his glass, trying to block the sounds of the forest, the breathing behind his head, the tantalizing and painful feeling of his body about to split, like the silken pupa of a moth, splitting open to release the traveller within.

'No,' he said awkwardly. 'I don't have a problem with that. My problem is the sound in my head.'

There was nothing showing on his skin, no *shimmering*.

They had already talked through the events of the day, the glimpses of a shadow city, overgrown and ruined, rising from below Exburgh. Angela's wrist ached with taking notes. She had filled three hours of tape, getting Jack to analyse what he had experienced almost down to the prickling response of each individual hair on his neck.

But once home, there had been nothing, and although the chemical analyses of the various pads that had absorbed his sweat would be some days in the analysing, from the encephalographical point of view he had shown no more neurological disturbance than a man daydreaming.

Angela was frustrated. 'It's like trying to photograph a fabulous beast. Every time it's seen, there's no camera. Every time there's a camera, no beast.'

'There's a beast. Make no mistake,' Jack said, and reached for the bottle to refill their glasses.

They were running him down, hunting him like an animal, and he fled across the broken land, between the rocks, the bushes, over dried streams and along the dry mud gulleys of the other world. They were running him down . . .

He sat up in bed, his head throbbing with pain. Angela slept beside him, exhausted by thinking, writing and alcohol. The video blinked at him, the three hour loop catching his every breath, the shimmer on his skin.

He held out his hands, aware of the haze of light in the darkness.

'Angela . . .' he breathed.

They were close behind him, screaming at him and he covered the wild land with long strides, his chest bursting with the effort.

They were running him down . . . an animal . . .

He staggered from the room, hitting the door, wrenching it open and walking unsteadily out onto the moonlit landing. The sound of the pursuit made him wail with fear. His legs wanted to move in rhythm, in sympathy with the shadow-creature that fled the hunters. Every muscle in his body was aflame, every sense heightened so that the world outside this darkened house drummed upon him like a persistent, shocking rain.

And something made him think: *record this.*

He found his way back to the bedroom, but he couldn't call out, couldn't raise the sleeping woman. The red light on the camera flickered and he stared at it.

Watch me. Keep an eye on me . . .

Then he went to the wardrobe and crouched before the mirror, aware of the glowing face, the gleaming, sweaty flesh of his body, his belly heaving, his hands spread on his thighs, light seeping from his hair, from his eyes.

They were coming through!

He tried to scream, but all the sound of his voice was sucked into the vacuum that accompanied the passage of the man. Greyface leapt from him and Jack felt his body torn from the inside out. He shuddered, shedding the gleaming shadow of the hunter, who turned and cried out as if with pain and a fury of triumph.

'Catch me *now* if you can!'

In the mirror, Greenface ended her fusion with the kneeling man, and again Jack's body was wrenched. Like a woman struggling out of tight-fitting clothes, the glowing green body detached from him, then saw Greyface, who lunged.

'We made it through!'

'No!'

Watching from isolation, helpless, immobile, Jack saw the woman turn and run to him. She came out of the glass, out of his own pale reflection, and

burst into him

He swallowed her. He heard her running, fleeing deeply down, while in the glass Greyface scowled and drew away, drew back into shadow, his voice growing distant.

They had come from inside him. Not from a world in parallel, but from inside him. As he knelt, watching Greyface fade as a grinning eel draws down into the murk of the bottom of a pool, so he felt the woman in his mind, retracing her steps, crying out with fear, with exasperation, lost in a land that hunted her.

And that land was Jack Chatwin himself. And she was running home, oblivious of danger, a frightened spirit, returning to her source.

Greyface loomed above the kneeling man, his face twisted with fury.

'Fetch her back!'

Jack couldn't speak. He was paralysed, all but his eyes. His tongue was heavy, his face locked. The woman ran into him, a shadow in his dreams. Finally, Greyface crossed the darkened room to the window. He looked at the distant glow above Exburgh, above Glanum, then passed into the hall. Watching in the mirror, Jack tried to scream. Angela turned in her sleep, disturbed by the sudden sound of their daughter, crying out. There was noise downstairs, the back door slamming. Distantly, Natalie wailed. Frozen inside his body, Jack realized that Greyface was running to the hidden city, Natalie taken in response to the loss of the woman.

As Angela woke, so the spell broke and Jack staggered to his feet, screaming, 'Call the police. He's got Nattie!'

From the window he saw the glimmering shape of the man, moving fast across the field at the bottom of the garden. A brief glance into the girl's room established that she had gone. He tugged on gardening shoes and an old raincoat from inside the utility room and began to run, covering the garden in seconds, leaping the wire fence and striking out into the darkness.

Behind him, Angela was shouting. Lights in neighbouring houses were beginning to glow.

For a few minutes he thought he would die. He was terrified of Greyface. He could not begin to understand the process by which this monster had appeared in the bedroom, at night, from his own day-dreaming mind, all he knew was that the monster had his daughter, and that she was in terrible danger . . .

Suddenly, she was there, a pale figure in white nightie, hands clasped in front of her, a frightened face on a motionless body.

Jack dropped to his knees in front of her, grasped the girl's shoulders.

'Nattie?'

'I'm cold.' He looked around, but there was no sign of the

man, or the glow that had briefly been associated with him. The girl was beginning to shake, but she wasn't crying.

'Nattie, are you all right? Did he hurt you?'

She shook her head. 'He told me a funny story. He's nice. He said to tell you something.'

'Tell me then.'

'You've taken something of his. You can't keep her for ever. Fetch her back. If you don't, he'll take something of yours.'

'Will he, indeed! What else did he say?'

'Nothing.'

'What about the funny story?'

Natalie frowned, thinking hard, then shook her head. 'I've forgotten it. But it made me laugh.'

You can't keep her for ever. Fetch her back . . .

12

Five days later the woman came back, a shadowy, frightened presence at the edge of the forest, close to a wide river that surged and bubbled over dark rocks.

It was a maddening haunting. She inhabited the edge of his vision. However hard he tried he could not quite see her, but he dreamed of her, watched her as she hunted small game, smelled the fires she lit, in a clearing among stone ruins, sometimes caught snatches of her song.

Eventually she came to a church, at the side of a wide square, where a crimson sun cast a perpetual twilight. Here, she hid in the dark spaces, ate when she could, slept and cried below the corrupt statues of strange gods.

He imagined, too, that he could feel her uncertainty. She would not leave her own world again, but she was if not helpless without her male partner, at least less adequate than before. She called to him, pleadingly, then angrily. At night she huddled, taking sleep in short naps, always wary of danger.

She was thinking that she should return, back to the source, the scene of their crime.

This is how she thought of it: their crime. Jack knew that she was frightened of the city, the stone towers, the hunters from that ancient place who followed the bull, seeking revenge for a deed whose nature eluded the watching man.

Jack felt like a voyeur; at the worst of times, which were the most lucid, Greenface crept so far to the river's edge, crouching there, that he could smell her scent and see the way her eyes glittered behind the mask of paint. But the sun was bright and she was part of the green, an inhabitant of two worlds, an inhabitant of the shadow.

During this time, the video recording of the 'auto-exorcism', as Angela called it, was computer enhanced, analysed electronically, scanned at various wavelengths, even played to a professed psychic. None of the techniques were able to enhance the flash of shadow that had been caught visually, the shape that Jack had quite literally *shed*. It was amorphous, lasted one fiftieth of a second, but obscured the thin gleam of moonlight on one of the polished wooden bed posts.

For the first time in their life together, Angela's questions, and her notes, were half-hearted. The shadow was physical evidence of the phenomenon to be added to the observable *shimmering* that had been part of Jack's boyhood. The realization that one ghost was abroad in the city, and one holding back through fear, begged careful thought, not just in regard to what was happening, but of the consequences, and it was the obvious consequence that was now terrifying the woman, since she lived every day with her husband's almost palpable fear.

Greyface had physically taken their daughter. He had threatened them. He was not far away, and perhaps, like the woman within, he was watching them constantly.

'Let's move away. For a while, at least.' Angela spoke quietly, cradling Natalie, who was drowsy. It was mid-evening and they were sitting in half-light listening to music.

'How would that help?'

'The male is embroiled with the city. You seem to feel that, so to move away . . .'

'I don't think distance is a factor. I think he'll come wherever we are. I don't know what to do . . .'

They put the girl in her room, locked the windows, then locked every door and window of the house. Before he went to bed, Jack watched the old town for a while, but the only light was from cars, and the late-night disco in the Grand hotel.

He was woken at three in the morning, opening his eyes as

a gentle pressure on his shoulder roused him. Natalie was standing by the bed, her fingers on his bare skin, squeezing rhythmically. He sat up and the girl's hand dropped away.

'Nattie?'

She stared at him, half-smiling.

'He wants to talk to you.'

For a moment her words made no sense. 'He wants to talk?' Then he understood, the knowledge like a shot to the head. 'Christ!'

And he realized with a further moment's shock that he could smell grass. He reached down to his daughter's bare feet and felt the smooth, dew-moist blades from his freshly-mown front lawn. 'You've been out! How did you get out?'

'Followed him out.'

'Followed *who* out?'

'The feathery man. He danced in the garden with me. He told me a funny story.'

Angela had woken with the loud sound of voices and now grabbed for her housecoat. She was alarmed and angry.

'What's going on?'

'Natalie's been to a disco.'

'What?'

'She's been dancing outside. With a hairy, feathery man.'

'She can't have been!'

Angela went quickly downstairs, her natural concern manifesting as exasperation.

The front door was open. It hadn't been forced, it had been unlocked. The key was still in place, but it was the spare key, which was usually kept hidden in a tin on the freezer. Natalie had known it was there, a fact that Angela had forgotten.

Arms folded, she walked down the path. The street lamp illuminated the lawn, and she pointed to where the girl had run around the single gleaming silver birch that graced the garden.

Jack was watching from the bedroom window, Natalie in

his arms. He could see, clearly enough, that there were two sets of tracks on the wet grass around the moon-silvered tree.

'Tell me the funny story,' he whispered to the girl, but again Natalie shrugged.

'Can't remember it.'

'But it made you laugh.'

'Yes.'

'What was he dressed in, this man who danced with you?'

'A bird cloak, lots of feathers. But with hair on it. Different coloured hair.'

'Does he have a name?'

'Yes. I've got to guess it.'

'Like in *Rumpelstiltskin*? Like in the story?'

Natalie repeated the name from the fairy tale, but she could never get it right, this time managing Rumplit Skinny, which made Jack laugh, and his daughter giggled too.

Guess my name, little girl.

Guess my name like in the story.

Guess my name and I'll . . .

And you'll what? Guess your name and *what* would happen? He kissed his daughter on the cheek, then whispered, 'I want you to promise me something. Will you promise me something?'

Natalie squirmed in his arms. She was getting tall, and she was heavy, but she clung around his neck, blinking as she stared into the night. She hesitated, then nodded silently.

'I don't want you to guess his name. I don't want you to dance with him again. I don't want you to go outside at night. I don't want you to listen to his funny stories.'

'They make me laugh . . .'

'He's not a nice man, Nattie. Promise me that if he tries to talk to you, you'll come and tell me first.'

The girl nodded again, huddling into her father's bosom. Then she said suddenly, 'He wants to talk to you!'

'I know. You've already told me. And when I talk to him I'm going to tell him to stay away from us.'

But where to go? Where to talk to this creature?

And as if his thought was transparent, the girl said, 'He's by the cave in the cliff.'

'What cave? What cliff?'

'The big cave, silly. By the funny building. There!'

And she pointed out across Exburgh. 'There!' she said again, her expression of irritation older than her years. She was pointing towards the church, whose tower could just be seen against the sky. Jack turned as he held her so that her pointing finger drifted, but when he asked her to show him again, unerringly she found the spire of St John's.

'There! Silly . . .'

'The church?'

'The cave in the wall,' she said.

The entrance to the labyrinthine passage, Glanum's suicide gate to the city of shrines!

With Angela's words of divided loyalty fresh in his mind ('Tell him to leave us alone; but find out what you can about where they came from . . .') Jack walked through the quiet streets towards the church, encountering little night activity until the main shopping centre, where the bright mall was filled with teenagers, fresh from a 'rave' in the Exburgh Hotel.

Beyond the precinct the church rose darkly against the drifting cloud. The sounds of music and revelling faded behind him and he crossed the cemetery, coming round to the front steps, circling the building twice, before suddenly detecting the scent of water, and old, cold stone. He was standing, facing Castle Hill, looking inwards to the heart . . .

Almost at once, the hidden city rose to confront him, night-shadow in the darkness, surging from the earth. A wall faced him, but a thin entrance began to glow, faint blue light defining a crack as if in rock. He was aware that he stood in a crowded grove of trees, where dangling wooden shapes clattered in a light breeze.

Greyface stepped forward, leaning against the rock wall,

squeezing his body through the narrow gap; waiting, watching. His eyes sparkled. He seemed to be draped in rags, but Jack could see the broken splay of feather, the lank fall of scalp hair. And there was the sheen of polished stone, a wide-bladed knife, resting on his hip.

'Have you brought her back?' the Scalpcloak asked.

'Who are you? Why are you doing this to my family?'

'You have someone I need. Give her up.'

'I can't. I have no idea—'

'Give her *up*! She can't have gone far, the land was too difficult. Bring her back and your life is your life, and your darling daughter can sleep in peace.'

'Who are you?' Jack whispered, and the ragged figure stepped out of the crevice in the cliff. He reached out and gripped Jack's face in a hand that was broad, heavy-fingered and callused, twisting the man's head this way, then that, the fingers bruising skin.

The clay mask was cracked and the eyes ferocious.

'I'll take your Natalie,' Greyface murmured. His breath smelled of blood. 'I'll take her bit by bit. I'll steal her spirit, shade by shade . . . I'll build my partner from the life of one you love . . . *unless* . . .'

He smiled, released Jack and pushed him away. He stepped back into the darkness, and a girl giggled. A moment later Greyface reappeared, pulling the shivering, naked figure of Natalie into view.

'My God!' was all Jack could shout before stumbling forward, only to be repelled violently by the dark-feathered and hair-cloaked hunter. Natalie's eyes were black and wide, her mouth open, her hands clutched tightly against her chest. She watched her father without comprehension.

'I left her safely . . . in the house . . .'

Greyface pushed the girl behind him.

'Only a shade, Jack. The first of many. I shall pare her down, layer by layer, ghost by ghost. You can keep the flesh, much good that will do you. Unless you *fetch her back!*'

A moment later he had gone and Jack ran after him, squeezing into the rock crevice and feeling his way blindly along the cramped passage beyond.

The tunnel twisted. It echoed with sound, which might have been the retreating hunter, or just a subterranean wind, booming and surging somewhere ahead. The walls were carved: he could feel the lines and curves, but it was pitch-black, and the ceiling was getting lower.

When he cracked his skull against rock for the third time, and felt blood oozing from the graze, he backed away from the further darkness, aware that he had begun to experience a primal fear that was quite irrational, that he had begun to imagine the rock passage as a crawlspace, that he was a child, crawling through a longing, loving mother, hard-wombed but enticing. He was dizzy with the feeling of sex, and fright, and he felt his way back to the grove of trees, staring at the crescent moon above, listening to the dull clatter of the grotesque wooden masks that were slung from boughs and stone arches.

He took a tentative step forward, and

suddenly tumbled down the steps of the church, twisting his wrist and ankle painfully, ending up on his side, the dark tower of St John's above him, a scatter of summer stars behind a spreading, gentle cloud.

He stood, holding his wrist, turning slowly on the spot as he looked for any sign of the sanctuary, but Greyface had withdrawn. All Jack could think of was his daughter's *shade*, an echo of the girl, which the bull-runner had implied had been drawn from her, leaving her less than whole.

And he remembered meeting John Garth on these steps, years ago, and being asked what lay below. He had answered 'the crypt', but Garth had said, 'the suicide gate . . . the labyrinth . . . to the hidden city.'

The suicide gate, then – if this illusion, this vision of magic was correct – the gate was a crack in the cliff, and the city lay beyond, concealed from the world by the earth itself.

As he started for home, Jack turned to the church.

'I'll be back,' he said aloud, aware of the melodrama. But unable to rid his mind of the gaping, giggling monstrosity that had been the shadow of his daughter, he picked up a stone from the flower border and slung it at the church. And again shouted, 'I'll be back!'

13

He paced around the kitchen, pretending to do things, watching the girl as she sat quietly at the pine table, making a clown puppet out of cardboard pieces. Her tongue was wedged firmly between her lips as she concentrated, her only sounds were little grunts of irritation and effort.

'How do you feel, Nattie?'

She looked up, frowning, eyes bright, hair a little stringy with cow-gum. She didn't speak and Jack went over to her, leaning down to meet her gaze. 'Do you feel funny in any way?'

'No,' she said. 'Just thirsty.'

'Ginger beer?'

'Yes please.'

He fetched the drink. The girl slurped noisily, then had difficulty removing her sticky fingers from the glass. Tongue between lips she leaned forward to press the next part of the red clown from the card.

Jack walked the length of the kitchen again, staring out at the orchard, across the fields to the distant hills. He strode back to the hall, patting the girl's shoulder as he passed her, picking up the newspaper from the telephone table. But in seconds he had again paced to the back door, his heart beginning to race.

I'm going mad. I'm cracking up. I've got to stop this . . . Where the hell is Angela?

The phone went and he ran to it quickly.

'What's going on, Jack?' came a man's voice at the other end. 'Are you ill?'

'Oh. Hi, Bob. No . . . I mean yes. But not seriously. I think my blood pressure's up. A really bad headache this morning.'

His section manager was clearly irritated. 'Crap. You're too young to have blood pressure. And you were scheduled to be in the marketing meeting at eleven. Without you we could only complete half the agenda.'

Oh Christ!

'I'm sorry, Bob. I should have called in.'

'Yes. You should have. Are you on medication?'

'No. Just resting. I'll be in tomorrow. Can we reschedule the discussion?'

'Already done. Tomorrow at nine. And that's a.m. You *will* be there? With the ExoNel file?'

'I won't let you down. Again, I'm sorry. It was a hell of a weekend; a family problem, two sleepless nights.'

'Okay, Jack. No harm done. Just make the meeting at nine. If you need to spend the rest of the day in a darkened room, we'll sort something out.'

'Thanks, Bob.'

Damn!

It had been a very foolish oversight. He'd been awake all night, sitting either in or outside the girl's room. The ExoNel meeting had completely slipped his mind. Angela must have got up and gone to work as usual . . . and now he suddenly remembered breakfast, her conversation, her assumption that he was going to work late. Events cleared in his head, a dream breaking. He'd missed an important discussion; thank God it was only a preliminary brainstorming and not the presentation to clients. He bit his nail angrily, standing by the cool glass of the back door, letting the cold surface soothe his forehead. Natalie held up the first clown and he admired it, then felt her brow.

No temperature. No signs of illness. No signs of change. No signs of anything wrong.

He made her add up to fifty again, listening for the slightest hesitation. He made her do the alphabet. He made her sing two songs, though she soon tired of his persistence.

Nothing was out of place, out of speed, out of rhythm.

What had that creature been, then? What had that ghost been? It had looked so like his daughter.

Again the phone jarred, this time Natalie's school. She'd been missed, and again he went through the routine apologies, this time saying that the car had let him down, and he'd been forgetful.

Yes, Natalie was fine; she was doing creative work, and yes, he'd practice the song with her that she'd be singing in the school play on Parents' Day.

He sat down across the pine table from the studious child, sipping strong coffee. Natalie asked him if she could go to school, now. She seemed quite keen, but when he said, 'Not today, darling. I want you to do some paintings for me,' she accepted the answer with only the slightest sigh.

At midday, Angela called.

'What's going on? Why aren't you at work?'

'I'm not leaving her,' he said. 'I just feel frightened. I can't explain it.'

'Natalie? She's there?'

'Painting.'

'Didn't the Robinsons take her to school? I saw them driving up when I left this morning.'

'I sent them away. I'm not letting her out of my sight.'

'I thought we'd agreed at the weekend: to behave normally, not to disrupt her.'

'You didn't see what I saw,' he said, and felt tearful panic quickly surfacing.

'I'm coming home . . .'

As the line went dead, the back door was shaken loudly, rattled on its hinges. Natalie was staring at it, solemn and quiet, quite motionless. *What had she seen?*

'Was that the wind?'

'I think so,' the girl said. The garden was empty. The day

was still, bright, no breeze that he could discern at all. He checked the lock; it was still firm. He strained to see left and right in the garden, but could perceive no movement, no shadow, no shape of human or beast.

Christ, I'm cracking. Maybe it had just been a delusion, the whole thing at the church, the grinning ghoulish child . . .

But it wasn't a delusion, he knew it. He had spent his life being haunted; he had witnessed a city sailing majestically through the earth, and he had absorbed the image, and consoled his affronted psyche; he had accepted the phenomenon, made it a part of his life, with the echoing and screaming of the running couple. He had probably always known that there would be a moment when it would go too far, when something would have to give.

He had seen too much, now; he had passed the point of acceptance. But instead of going crazy, – he was protected against insanity, a lifetime of living with ghosts had done that for him – instead, he was frightened so deeply in his heart that each time he drew breath he felt sick. It was a panic that was welling up, a wave of terror that he was just, *just*, keeping at bay, but it was coming closer, and it was focused through his daughter, because his mind had spewed out a scalp-cloaked animal man, who had his claws in Natalie.

Jack could feel that touch, almost scent the blood. The door had rattled, the air had shifted, and it hadn't been the wind. He was being watched, closely watched.

There were other eyes upon him too and he almost howled his despair as he felt the woman shift towards him, to take over his mind's eye.

Where is he? How do I call him back?

There was no language, just a certainty of meaning expressed through her green-faced gaze, the emanation of fear and loss that came from her body as she crouched in the twilight, in the shadow of ruins. She watched his world through his own eyes, but seemed not to hear his words as he shouted loudly, then tried to talk *inwards*, to find some way of communicating with the huntress.

The green on her face flowed across her skin, an optical effect, an illusion, distracting him from the dark deeps of her eyes, from where she surveyed the world of her own nightmares.

Where is he? How do I call him back?

'You can't. You can't! Come out of me! Leave me alone! Go back to him, follow him, run with him, leave me alone!'

Natalie was shrieking in terror.

He's got her again . . .

'NO!'

Natalie was sobbing hysterically, slamming the kitchen door closed against him as he stumbled to save her from . . .

'Leave her alone!'

He pushed at the door, but the key had turned, the security lock. He kicked frantically at the wooden panelling, splintering the wood.

Natalie was screeching, fumbling at the door to the garden as he kicked his way into the kitchen to save her.

'Natalie!'

'Go away! Go away!'

He watched her as she slammed the kitchen door behind her, running hysterically through the apple trees, towards the high fence that separated their garden from the paddocks. He felt his knees give way, slumped down on the vinyl flooring, aware of dry fragments of cat food, a pencil, the top of the tube of gum.

'Oh my God . . .'

He's got her. I'm helpless.

Greenface whispered in his ear: *Where is he?*

'Who are you? What are you? Why can't you leave me alone?'

Bring him back.

'He wants *you* to go to *him*! Leave me alone!'

We were wrong to leave . . . we shouldn't have run . . . bring him back . . .

The pain in his face was like a fist as he smashed into the pine table, staggering to his feet. Then there was shattering glass and he was cut and the sudden stumble down the concrete step. He bludgeoned the trees with his body, aware of the slow fall of unripe apples. The red twilight confused him. The deep shadow frightened him. He turned and turned again in the place of temples, searching for his daughter among the rose-tinted stone, while Greenface, running at a crouch, followed his every step, keeping her distance, curious and watching.

I can't help you. I'm going back . . . tell him to follow . . . back . . . And as she slipped away again, as the blue sky struck his senses and he smelled the summer earth, heard Natalie singing; and Natalie laughing; Natalie giggling and running . . . out in the paddock, among the spreading chestnut trees, where the sad, grey horses spent their days.

The girl was imitating a fairy, arms spread, twirling and twisting below the cover of leaves. He walked towards her. She saw him suddenly, screamed and ran, racing in a wide arc, easily avoiding him as he staggered towards her, calling for her. She reached the house again, leapt across the spray of glass from the shattered window of the door.

My God, she's running from me. Running from her own father. What have I done? How have I frightened her?

She had locked herself into the bathroom. He knelt outside the door calling for her. Part of his mind, a rational part, kept saying to him: don't make things worse. You're not in control. Don't make things worse.

The loving part was desperate to hold her, to make sure she wasn't hurt.

Natalie yelled for help.

Greyface twisted his hair, jerked back his head, tugged and jerked in emphasis to the words. *She should have followed me. You stopped her. Bring her back.*

'I can't.'

In a sudden moment of fury he turned where he was slumped, struck at Greyface, tried to grab his arms and twist them into submission, but he found himself staring at Angela, his grip bruising her. She eased his fingers from her arm, kissed him quickly, reassuringly on the mouth.

He melted into her body, hugged her as he cried. 'I'm cracking up. I'm so fucking frightened. It's just . . . suddenly. Come on. I know it's sudden, I know it makes no sense . . . oh shit . . . it makes no sense . . . I'm so frightened . . .'

Inside the bathroom, Natalie kept yelling; but for a while, Angela held him, whispered in his ear and stroked his hair.

. . . also, he says, she just appears, like someone stepping in front of him. Although he describes the sensation as 'echoing', as if she's moving around outside a rock chamber and keeps appearing at a cave mouth, peering into the darkness. And he peers out, and glimpses the strange lands, the ruins, whatever landscape she happens to be in.

I think this might be evidence for the portal-access theory; the windows will be our way of glimpsing the Deep beyond the Hinterland; I'll try and suggest that he thinks 'oracle'. Such a contact site, if I can persuade him to participate, will fit comfortably with whatever fiction is evolving in his own particular Deep. There are definitely elements of pre-history there, but again, are these *natural* RIR's superimposed on an *unnatural* Greenface and Greyface 'source'?

Everything he describes suggests these creatures are human, and we grow towards the idea that they are *old*; elements *themselves* of pre-history. But without Midax I don't think we can establish whether or not they are brain-specific, or external intrusions into Jack's *psychome*.

He's frightened, at the moment, and not receptive. Natalie is involved, he thinks, although I've seen no sign of anything wrong myself. One of the runners has 'everted', inhabiting outside space. This angle is complex and will need some defining, but probably not yet. In a week or so, though, I'd really suggest you take him in and test him. If you can use him, this is an opportunity, as they say, not to be missed.

I'll make a formal proposal later, but thought I'd E-mail this for you to start thinking about the idea.

Angela, 5.30 am, Tuesday.

Greenface had left the twilight and passed quickly through woodland, emerging by a deep, icy pool fed by a wide fall of water from the towering cliff above. Here, she bathed for a long time before stalking the shallows, half-crouching, watching for fish. This naked hunt was unsuccessful, and half-way through she seemed aware of being watched, tugging on her white-shell tunic and running again.

Soon she came to a place where the land fell away and a vast plain opened before her, wooded and mountainous in the distance, gleaming bluely where a vast lake sprawled across the earth.

For a long time she stood there, and Jack felt drawn to that great distance, drawn to home; but as always with these moments of shared vision, he felt her hesitation, her fear before she started to run again, and the glimpse of Greenface faded into darkness, the darkness of his room, a darkness broken by a thin crack of light where the curtains were not quite closed.

The door to the room was open and a white-gowned figure stood there, watching him. The girl was holding a mug of coffee and she walked cautiously to the bed.

'Is that for me?'

'Mummy says you're not very well.'

'I'm not. I'm sorry I frightened you yesterday. I didn't mean to.'

The mug was hot and he drew a quick breath as he tried to

find somewhere to put it down. Natalie was solemn as she stared at him, then came to a decision and jumped under the covers with him. They sat, propped up on the pillows, and watched the light grow.

'Have you been out dancing?' Jack asked.

'Nope. Mummy's been sending E-mail and I've been reading.'

'Early risers.'

'Couldn't sleep.'

Angela came in carrying her own mug of coffee. 'How's the head?'

'Sore. Spinning. I've seen her again, this time in a waterfall. She's heading deeper, heading home. I don't know what to do.'

'Who's heading home?' Natalie asked.

'A strange woman with a green face, and two spears, and a blowpipe which she uses with great accuracy.'

'Oh, her,' Natalie said matter-of-factly.

'Yes. Her,' Jack said, with a sidelong glance at the girl. 'Have you seen her?'

'No. My bird-friend talks about her though. I think he's married to her. He misses her.' She looked round sharply. 'Are you going to get her back? When are you going to get her back?'

The sudden change in voice startled Jack. For a second he felt sick, staring at his daughter, looking for a sign of the grey mask among her own pale features. But Natalie just said, 'Will you paint her for me? Then I can show him.'

I'll take your Natalie. I'll take her bit by bit. . .

'You're not to show him anything. Do you understand? *Nothing*. You're not to *see* him, Nattie. Do you understand me? Can you understand what I'm saying to you . . . ?'

His voice was rising. The girl huddled below the covers, eyes wide as the angry face of her father loomed over her.

Angela tugged his arm. 'Easy, Jack. Take it easy. Jack . . . !'

'She's not to dance with him,' he said desperately. Angela's face swam in his vision. 'He's going to take her,' he mouthed silently. 'Bit by bit. I don't know how, but I don't dare think he's bluffing. Bit by bit, Angie. How will we know?'

She took his hand in hers, stroked his fingers. 'Jack . . . you've always resisted working with Steve Brightmore. And I know you're reluctant to let him try to document your . . . visions. But I think it's time you tried something. Something that won't harm you, can only help you.'

'This Midax stuff?'

'It works, Jack. It's going to be a fabulous tool in therapy; not to mention psychometry. If Greenface is accessible, you'll be able to confront her. If she's there, in here . . .' she tapped a finger on his forehead, 'I'm confident you'll be able to interact with her, to persuade her to . . . whatever . . . come out, join her partner, leave you, leave you in peace. She doesn't belong there, Jack. The chance to cut her out and discard her is in your hands, and in Brightmore's research.'

She looked at him long and hard. The name Brightmore rankled him; her continued familiarity with the New Zealander offended him. They talked a language he didn't understand, shared enthusiasm and humour based on work and observations that excluded him from understanding.

Bloody Brightmore!

'Please?' she asked. 'We can't risk too many yesterdays. Even if it's all psychosis, you're doing yourself some serious harm. Please?'

He thought hard for a few seconds, then whispered, 'I suppose it makes sense. But won't I be vulnerable? And won't that mean Natalie is vulnerable?'

Angela didn't answer. After a while she sighed and slightly shrugged.

'Yes. I'm afraid it does. But if there's a chance of it working . . .'

He lay back, his hand gently touching his daughter's hair as she listened to her parents. 'Okay. Let's give it a try. When do I start?'

PART THREE

M.I.D.A.C.S.

14

'I dream in my dream all the dreams of the other dreamers, and I become the other dreamers . . .'

'At last!' a male voice said. 'I'm here, right behind you, Jack. Where the hell are we? In a plane? It's all very hollow. Very angular.'

Angela's presence in his dream induced a moment's dream-shock, since she was in the form of a man, and out of sight. And yet though she spoke with the man's voice, it was unquestionably Angela.

She said, 'This is beautiful. I'm getting startling colours – some shape as well. Are we flying up a hill?'

'Yes. Very slowly.'

He was in the front of a small, single winged plane, peering through the blur of the propeller. The pilot was behind him – Angela's presence was located behind the pilot, at the back of the craft.

The plane was indeed flying up a hill, rising in almost absurd slow motion. Below, the hill was a sequence of tiled and marbled baths, coloured in luxurious blues and greens and blacks, the water gushing from the mouths of lions, giants, grinning gods and ghoulish gargoyles. Azure blues and scarlets gave way to mottled mosaics, and silver moonbursts, each bath occupied by a few naked humans, of both sexes, drenched and diving in the spouts of liquid.

'Water?' Angela guessed. 'It is. Water. I can just make it out. And people . . . You know what water means . . .' she teased. Jack watched the ruins of the buildings on either side, thinking about the detail, the columns, the statues, the intricacy of the arches. The plane ascended slowly and he sensed the summit of the hill approaching.

'What does water mean?' he asked, manipulating the dream, confronting the Outsider in the dream (this was, after all, the purpose of the test).

'In most people's case: sex. But there are so many Roman baths – I'm beginning to get a good VR focus. Maybe you need a shower? Oh God, look at him!'

Through her masculine voice, she laughed. Below, a Herculean male was being scrubbed with huge brushes by four lithe young women, his hands above his head, as if hiding from the pain.

'You're *weird*,' Angela said.

'It's a dream!'

'Not mine, though, I'm relieved to say. God, Freud would have adored this.'

'I can't control what surfaces.'

'Obviously.'

'It's an archetypal image – symbolic.'

'Rubbish. You hanker for a good *scrubbing!*'

'Behave yourself.'

'Why? I don't *mind* if you put a few nubile girls into the baths. I shan't be *jealous*. Just as long as you put *me* in.'

'Can you see the baths? The faces on the waterspouts?'

'Vaguely. Try staring at one spot. See if the focus sharpens.'

But Jack ignored the dream suggestion and turned in his seat. The pilot was a blank-faced man, face white as a ghost, skull-like, dressed in ancient flying gear and flexing a 'joystick' easily from side to side. For some reason his hands were bandaged. Behind the pilot sat his old geography teacher, Mr Simmons, a fat faced-man with greasy black hair, who was looking earnestly at the passing ruins, the bathers, the brilliantly coloured marble baths.

'Christ, I hated you at school!'

Jack struggled for a moment for full presence in the dream, then managed to say, 'Smile at me?'

'I can't,' Angela/Mr Simmons said. 'I'm caught up in the visual side. I don't have control. I'm just a passenger in this intersect.'

Jack himself lost control, then, finding the dream shifting, like a jump in a broken film, to the high part of the hill. They were still flying slowly over the white coral of weathered ruins, but a great bull's head was towering from the ground, horns curved elaborately, almost meeting above the broad, red features, the empty eyes.

'It's the shadow-horning,' Angela said, beginning to drift into dream incoherency. Jack was aware that she was saying, 'It's the bull.'

'I don't want to fly too close.'

'Dream, dream, dreamers into the surfacing.' (She was actually saying: 'Maybe they'll surface now . . .' meaning the bull-runners.)

Angela's voice, blurring, was also different in tone again. She was an actor from the 1950s, whom he knew but couldn't name, grey-haired and very smooth. More importantly, she was referring to Greyface and Greenface, but in this dream, lucid though it was, he could not hear them, he could not even remember how he called them. When he tried to control the lucid state to focus on the bull-runners, they twisted out of *sense* into *incoherence*, and he saw two characters from Star Trek, one of them speaking as Captain Kirk, but with the face of his grandfather, recently dead.

Greyface and Greenface belonged in another region of this *pre-conscious* as Brightmore called it.

'I don't like the look of this,' Angela said. But already the dream was decomposing, the elements of TV science-fiction blurring the crystal image of the Roman baths, the ruins, the monstrous bull's head.

As quickly as he had felt threatened by the looming creature, the lucid state dissolved, and though Jack kept control of his own ego-presence, searching briefly for Angela, he had drifted into a picnic scene, some soft reflection of his school days, tinged with anxiety and a sense of wandering away from the security of the group. He managed the escape line, 'Coming up for air!', but drifted on, slipping into normal sleep, normal dreams.

CatREM18
Term: 05:16:Day3

He woke suddenly, fully alert, yet surfacing into a world of madness, where the conversation he could hear was surreal and the movement of people random. As he focused his mind on the chaos, he realized that Angela, Steve Brightmore, and other members of the MIDAX team were animatedly, excitedly and jokingly discussing the 'Hill of Baths'.

'Jack's *back!*' he called out as he sat up on the couch. The huddle of researchers dispersed and Angela came over to him, her face ruddy, glowing.

'You're a natural! Jack, you're a natural. You throw such a strongly defined Optical Resonance Image . . .'

'Do *what?*'

'*Optical Resonance!* We can *read* you! I could *see* those ruins – the water! I was there, flying *with* you. You're a natural.'

The New Zealander, Brightmore, came over to shake Jack's hand. He had long black hair tied back in a single plait, and dark stubble on his lean face. He watched Jack distantly, but with curiosity, attempting a smile.

'That was a good test, Jack. You really pump out the O.R.I's.'

'I do my best.'

'How often did you dream lucidly as a child? Angela's right – you're really strong.'

'I didn't. Much. Maybe a few times, the usual thing – flying over tree-tops, being swung high in the air on the end of a huge rope, hanging on for dear life.'

Brightmore glanced at Angela with a quick smirk, then said, '*Those* weren't lucid. Lucid is different. Your lucid dreaming is so much a part of you, you probably think it's part of reality. Such a *powerful* O.R.I. I'm really impressed, Jack.'

'Thank you, Steven.'

'The VR scanner was picking up the neurone-firing pattern and interpreting it in *seconds*. Did you sense the interaction delay? With Angela?'

'Interaction delay?'

'Like on the phone, long distance. A hesitancy in response.'

He hadn't. He said so.

'Good. T-lag compensation. That's quite common. But I say again, you're a natural, Jack. Your Midax is almost begging to be released and let loose.'

'My Central Self. My ego.'

Brightmore laughed, this time making Jack's adrenalin surge with irritation. 'Central self! Ego is different. *Id* is different. Old-fashioned words, back in favour. You have ego and id personalities, hundreds of them.'

'And this is good?'

'It's not *bad*. Your Central Self is a rational fusion of *some* of these. The rest are scattered, *eyes* watching from the *unconscious*. But your Central Self is *rational* – it's strongly shaped, strongly formed, and when it goes *Mostly Isolated*, *Defined* and *Autonomous*, it will have direction and purpose! Angela and I should be able to interact with you at the higher level of the pre-conscious. The Hinterland. The region before the Deep. We'll be there to take your reports . . .'

'The Hinterland,' Jack echoed. 'Pre-conscious . . .'

'A kingdom all your own, Jack. A part of the mind shaped by you, unique to you, your own world, filled with the familiar, but utterly original. Think of a chess game. Recognizable pieces; unique game-play. No two alike.'

'Kings, castles, knights and pawns.'

'Pieces in the game, but *no* game the same. Let's go again. Do you mind? One more dream, just for practice.'

'And then?'

'And then we'll start *isolating*. We'll start breaking the rules!'

15

'I dream in my dream all the dreams of the other dreamers . . .

'But all I see is a church, growing out of a cliff . . .

'Is anybody there croaked the raven, raven, dream dream, jeannie, dream . . .'

Get a grip, Jack. You're almost there. Give us a visual source for the voice . . .

'. . . like the Cathedral at Notre Dame . . . hundreds of human statues round the big door at the front of the church – all faceless – great doors, hanging open. Feeling of desertion. The red cliffs . . . all around, encompassing, high above . . . hundreds of caves and . . . movement. Reminds me of Petra, hot rocks, the desert, the buildings cut into the desert cliffs, like Rose-red Petra . . .'

Go into the church, Jack.

'Oh God! Huge, absolutely huge arched dome, light everywhere from windows, dust and rocks and broken pews, and chickens everywhere, running everywhere, enormous statues everywhere . . . gleaming white.'

Take control. Find a visual source and take control.

'Woman in armour, holding spear and sword . . . Joan of Arc . . . de Triumph . . . white stone armour . . .'

Bring me in.

'Come on in, Angela . . .' *Find a source for Steve. You need to hear him.*

'Lovely Jesus. On the Cross. All pained and twisted. That's

my Steve, you bastard . . . Come on down from that bloody tree, Mr Brightman . . .'

Jack. Get a grip.

'Get a grip on Angela, you got a grip on her . . . caused me pain . . . no pain to you . . . never commit for more than a year . . . pain in the head, the thorns, the hands . . . come on down, you bastard, come and join the dream dream jeannie . . .'

I kept hearing rock songs, like *Jean Jeannie*, that old David Bowie number . . . no, I know it wasn't called that, but you know the one I mean . . . and echoes of Heavy Metal. The church was just like that Cathedral in Reims, in France – acid-rain scoured statues of the apostles, the saints etcetera in columns beside the big, oak doors. But the Cathedral was embedded in an immense cliff of red sandstone, as if it were *growing* from the cliff. When you told me to go into the place, the church itself seemed to squeeze towards me, like something growing, something organic. The steps were wide and white marble, and I think I recognize the influence of that George Pal film, *The Time Machine*: a sense of running into desertion and decay. The inside of the church was straight out of Turner, but I can't remember the painting. We saw it at the Royal Academy once, wrecked pews, broken statues, all those chickens and the fabulous shafts of light catching dust which was almost motionless in the air . . . *Ewenny Priory*! That's the one. Ewenny Priory, all ruins and light and dust. Perhaps this symbolizes the decay of my religious belief? Am I supposed to speculate about these things in the Hinterland?

I approached the altar space, aware of a big crucifix, with the figure of Christ, loin cloth, crown of thorns, dark beard, eyes closed; but in a side chapel there was a brilliant white statue of Joan of Arc. Her hair was long and curled. She had armoured greaves on her legs, and an impressive breastplate, shaped for what I can only assume was a fairly impressive bosom below. Lots of chain mail, and a spear and sword, and her armoured foot stamping on the snarling head of a dragon.

When you said to put Angela in the statue it was quite incredible: Joan creaked, twisted and looked around, then came down off the plinth, walking in jerky motion at first, then more smoothly. How very silly! But it seemed real at the time. I've watched so many films, so I suppose I could describe the movement as Ray Harryhausen segueing effortlessly into Terminator 2, you know, that effect, what do they call it? Morphic something? Not Resonance, that's different. *Morphing*, that's it. The smooth special effects you get.

Joan became splashed with colour, especially round the face, and walked over to me, crouching down, a stone woman with Angela's features but huge, hugely built, a marble, marvellous giantess.

Then the Christ detached itself from the Cross. I'm sorry Steve . . . I wasn't in control, and still resent you. Obvious statement. Funny that I can articulate it here and now, but I didn't mean to subject you to so much blood. The unconscious works in mysterious ways. Funny, though, you were hitching up your loin cloth at the front like you do with your jeans, always checking everything's in place, and it was held together with studs and turned faded denim blue as I thought of it.

So I had Christ and Joan of Arc, crouching in front of me, really earnestly, talking to me – your voices – and that's when I started to laugh.

(Sorry about that.)

Are you getting all this? It feels strange; I'm writing furiously, sitting just outside the church, on the steps in fact, and the sun is low, and red, and everything here is very still and deserted, like the end of the world. I seem to be writing on a heavy parchment, and the pen is a fountain pen, something I never used at school, but it feels good, so maybe this is the fulfilment of an unrealized dream.

So many unrealized dreams, so much to fulfil if Natalie's to be safe.

Odd: as I wrote that last I was feeling concern for Natalie. Is that important? My external world feelings are still strong in this Midax state. Which makes me remember that I'm to look for the aperture, and Greensleeves, but everything is so silent, glowing like red dusk, red twilight, yes! I think the way through is close, don't know why I say this, why it feels like it feels, but behind me, the way through is close.

Am I in a Midax state? It's hot, I could do with a drink, and I'm sitting on hard steps below a ruined church, looking at other temples, like Roman temples, basking in end-of-the-world red sunlight.

Back to what happened: the two statues quite quickly became 'certainties' of each of you; they still looked like Christ and Joan, but your own characters started to belong to them.

You asked me to define Midax again – *Mostly-Isolated/Defined-Autonomous-Central-Self* – and Christ in his blue loin cloth said, 'That's good. That's very good. You have a fifty percent split; that's the best yet. When we can isolate your Central Self at 80 you'll get the instruction to locate one of the access channels between the Hinterland and the Midax Deep. You'll go in after Greenface, then, but you'll be on your own. So keep writing, keep practising control.'

And I said, 'I want to come out. I want to make love. I want to see what's behind the armour.'

The statue started laughing. It said, 'Randy bastard. About time too!' and I said, 'But I'm going inside . . . and I may be gone some time . . .'

So then you asked me to imprint the church, and the carved cliff, with its windows and entrances, and try to mark a route back when the Midax state dissolved. I'd like to come out, now. The statue is walking up the steps. Christ is still crouching, watching me, wiping the blood from his eyes. It's getting brighter, like a car's headlight, a glare, a glare, blinding . . . glare . . .

DISPATCH ENDS

'Excellent! Jack. Excellent! You went well beyond normal LD control.'

LD? Oh, right. Lucid Dream . . .

Jack sat up, realizing that his right wrist was aching. Someone was massaging the muscles, flexing the fingers. Angela's face, smiling, came into focus. His arm was still strapped to the 'scribble-pad'; he looked at the ferocious scrawl from the pen attachment and realized it made no sense at all. 'Can you read that?'

'Of course. It's no worse than a doctor's prescription.'

'It's just straight lines.'

Brightmore was fussing with the headpiece and laughed. 'If you look closely you'll see little bumps and twitches. We use Direct Computer Interpretation—'

'DCI?'

'DCI. Yeah. It prints out the text almost as it comes from the pen. It makes assessments where it's unsure, that's why we get you to repeat so much of what we say. Gives us a direct comparison.'

'ADC?'

Angela laughed as she worked the blood supply back into fingers that were now tingling. 'Not *everything* comes down to acronyms.'

He thought, RSI for sure, if I keep this up. He flexed the fingers. 'How fast was I writing?'

'Faster than you'd believe possible.'

'FBP?'

'Shut up. Idiot.' Amused, she leaned over and kissed him. 'Bet you feel like an LSP, though . . .'

It took a second: 'A long slow pint? Yes. I was thinking of

beer for most of the transmission. The church was hot, the sun was hot, it made me feel very thirsty.'

Brightmore was fascinated by that statement and made a long note, nodding as he typed at the console.

'So what's *that* in capital letters?' Jack asked after a moment.

'Rats!' The New Zealander said. He was frantically backspacing to correct an error.

'Rats?'

Brightmore glanced over his shoulder, grinning. 'Real Appetite Triggered. *Somehow.*'

He had tried to understand the neurology and psychometry of Midax, but found that he could not mentally articulate the central concept: that his Central Self, the apparent existence of his own point of view, could be partly condensed and given identity and direction. And that once this was done, he would effectively be able to treat his dreams as a virtual reality experience, not just manipulating them, but existing in them, able to interact as if in real space and time.

Like the unfortunate policeman in Wendy Cope's parody of *The Pirates of Penzance*, he would be able to patrol his own unconscious, to confront his own nightmares.

As far as the Midax research group was concerned, under the patronizing and bullying Steven Brightmore, he was a gift from the gods. The whole project had been centred on dreaming, and in particular on a way to locate and explore the channels that connected the conscious and the unconscious mind, which passed through the region currently referred to as the *pre-conscious*.

The pre-conscious was a focus of argument and counter-argument, a region, or a pattern in the brain of primates, whose nature and complexity were hotly contested.

The Midax group, by working on isolating and making autonomous a fragment of the dreamer's own consciousness, hoped to go – indeed already had gone – deeper into the wild world that fed nightmares.

Jack was a natural, and perhaps had been so all his life; there was some debate about whether his easy ability to isolate his CS existed by nature, or had been induced by the haunting influence of the bull-runners. This, and other questions, might become clearer after the first journey inwards.

That said, several of the Midax team, aware of his claimed experiences with emerging ghosts, both human and stone-walled, were dubious, despite Angela's persuasive discussion and description. It made no difference, however, since Jack was the perfect test subject.

Bizarre though his quest would be, if he could locate Green-face – whoever, whatever the entity was – and persuade her back to a world she feared, he would be triumphant. If not, the experience would still have been useful to the Midax team, and only his time would have been wasted.

This had been the sixth test transmission from the more superficial LD state and Brightmore wanted to run two more such experiments, to satisfy himself that he could produce a sufficiently autonomous 'Ident' of Jack Chatwin that it would survive the deep-coma state that would accompany the Midax voyage itself.

Jack couldn't sleep that night following his encounter with Jesus and Joan; the images were so real, the experience had been disorientating and wonderful. The more he thought of the cliffs, the temples, the distorted façade of the cathedral, the more he was drawn back there.

He prowled the house and the garden aware always of the glow of light from Exburgh, sometimes aware of a shadow on the town, the shadow of a city.

He wanted to go to the gate, to the cave, to call Greyface and challenge him to be patient. But a part of him felt that Greyface already knew he was going inwards, and that the encounter would be no more than humiliating, unless it were to be frightening. He was constantly aware of the shade of Natalie, lost in the labyrinth of the suicide gate, hidden below and within the town.

At four in the morning he heard her laugh out loud. She was still in her room and he ran up the stairs from the kitchen, opening the door and watching as the girl jumped up and down on the bed.

'What's going on?'

The girl laughed hysterically and flopped over onto her back, bouncing on the covers and then lying still. She was hugely amused, squirming away from her father as he went over and tried to put his arm around her. 'Have you heard any funny stories this evening?'

She nodded. She was backed against the wall, her hands in front of her mouth, restraining infantile and incomprehensible amusement. From the bed, Jack asked, 'Is he here? Is he nearby?'

A shake of her head, but then the words, 'He'll be watching you.'

'Will he? That's nice. How will he be doing that?'

'Don't know. He'll be watching you. And me. Flesh and shadow. He said: flesh and shadow. We're all in the same dance.'

Giggling.

'Dancing, dancing,' she said, and ran to the window, banging on the glass, banging at the night, at the light of the stars, banging on the window and shouting, 'Dancing! Dancing! All in the same dance!'

Jack eased her away just as Angela appeared in the doorway ('What's going on?') and came over to sit on the girl's bed, stroking the young brow, the soft hair, murmuring, soothing, calming.

Natalie started to drift into sleep, but as her eyes seemed almost closed for the night they suddenly opened, engaging Jack.

'All in the same dance, Daddy,' she whispered. 'Don't

forget. All in the same dance. Fetch her back to him. That's what he always says: fetch her back to him.'

Jack kissed her on the brow and she curled up, comfortable.

'Tell him . . .' he whispered. 'Tell him, if you see him again . . . Tell him I'm doing my best. I'm doing my best. Tell him to leave us alone.'

Natalie giggled again, then yawned and stuck a thumb firmly in her mouth, curling up below the duvet, feigning sleep as she sought happy dreams.

16

On the wall above Brightmore's wide-screen AppleMac were lines from T. S. Eliot:

> Between the idea
> And the reality
> Between the motion
> And the act
> Falls the Shadow
>> *For Thine is the Kingdom*

'And that's where you're going, Jack. Into the Shadow. Although we call it by different names. The Hinterland . . . the French prefer *Interland*. In the US they still call it the pre-conscious, but that's too broad for the Kingdom.' He glanced round. 'And thine is the Kingdom! It's a place of your own making, exclusive to you in many ways, but inclusive of much that we all have in common. Look . . .'

On the screen he had drawn concentric arcs to create three bands, like a rainbow, labelling the outer zone *Conscious*, the inner *Unconscious* and the central *Pre-conscious*.

'This is only a schematic, you understand. The layers don't really exist . . .'

'Thank you.' *Infuriating man!* 'I'd got the idea . . .'

'Nothing gets between conscious and unconscious without passing the pre-conscious. Easy? The pre-conscious is riddled with wormholes, but they're very selective. So when you dream: images and fears, moods, emotions – and the energetic psychic manifestation Carl Gustav Jung labelled *archetypes*, all of them flow *up* to the pre-conscious, and partly penetrate to awareness, the more so in lucid dreaming. The important thing to understand – and this is only the beginning of our understanding – is that *as* they transit the pre-conscious, so they create Form! Shape! And Story!'

'F.S.S., in fact.'

'Precisely. Form. Shape. Story. But all of a transient nature, quickly decaying. What gets through gets used. What stays in the pre-conscious is fragile and *normally* fades in nano-seconds.'

'So would this be where writers get their inspiration from? The Deep Well?'

'The innovative ones, certainly. Yes. Of course!' Brightmore was at the keyboard, tapping out a detailed note to himself, intrigued by the thought. 'Writers, *any* artist prepared to let deep images surface over time rather than forcing ideas to a deadline; writers prepared to touch a little deeper, rather than just scouring conscious memory . . . Yes. This *is* the well of inspiration.'

He moved the pointer on the screen to the outer band denoting 'conscious'. 'The reverse is true of memory passing – for the sake of understanding I'll say *down* – *into* the unconscious. As *this* passes the pre-conscious – you've already accessed the Hinterland, one skin of the beast, if you like – so it creates Form, Shape, Image, Creature, Story . . . that persists! And persists for the rest of your life.'

'So it's permanent,' Jack said irritably.

'Exactly!'

'Undying.'

'Undying,' Brightmore agreed.

'A land full of unfit heroes.'

'A kingdom all thine own. How's your quantum theory?'

'Always bad,' Jack said. 'Sufficient to get a degree, but I'm long out of touch.'

Brightmore wrote the words 'Fields of potential' along the narrow band that depicted the Hinterland.

'Fields of potential?'

'Fields of potential. Are you familiar with this thinking?'

'Remind me.'

'Like the Universe we inhabit – before it took on shape, at the Big Bang – the pre-conscious is unstructured, unformed but packed with *potential*; it only hardens into the illusion of Memory! Event! and Story! when it's observed by the conscious mind. That observation sets up a persistent structure, a fixed image, a fixed world, if you like.

'Now: where it meets these *fixed* structures on the way *up*, the normally fast-decaying seepage from the Unconscious can then inhabit the Hinterland on a more permanent basis.'

'Worlds in collision . . .'

'Worlds in collision. Exactly. And that, Jack, is precisely what you are going to encounter when you journey to the Shadow: a world substantially drawn from your conscious experience, which we call Received Image Representation, mixed and made muddlesome by ancient echoes from the Unconscious, the limbic system in particular. The Saurian mind, as some of our American colleagues delight in calling it.'

'You mean I'll see *dinosaurs*?'

After an uneasy moment, Brightmore smiled. 'It's a sort of joke, you see.'

'Really? I didn't get it.' Jack cast a despairing glance at Angela, who shrugged, amused. *Stop being sarcastic.*

'The reptilian brain . . .' Brightmore went on. 'It's an old expression for the primitive brain, the primal urges.'

'Thank you, Steven.'

'But will you see dinosaurs?' Brightmore shrugged. 'Who knows? Depends on your childhood reading. If you do, they'll be RIRs. From the conscious filtering *down*. Do you see? From your imaginative experience in films, in books, in museums. What was that boy's name, Angela?'

Angela frowned, shaking her head. Brightmore added:

'The one who encountered marine monsters from the Jurassic – in a landscape straight out of the End of the World!'

'Oh . . . right . . . Whitlock, I think. Michael Whitlock?'

'Michael Whitlock!'

Jack was irritated by the feeling of being excluded from this discussion. 'And he was . . . what? What was he?'

'He was a boy who accessed his own Hinterland – in a chalk pit, wasn't it? – and could make imaginary objects real. Or so it was claimed. He had other things wrong with him, but his own private Hinterland was rich with Received Image Representation. RIRs. He was a lad of twelve. You've lived and seen more, of course, Jack, but as an adult your imagination is probably far less effective, so it's likely to be a more narrowly-focused landscape than that particular boy's. You probably won't even recognize your "real" life when you see it; that's one of the purposes of this trip. Bring back an account of the Deep beyond the Hinterland! The only other thing to warn you about: we have no way of knowing how dangerous your experience will be.'

'Dangerous? Dreaming, dangerous?'

Brightmore controlled a moment's exasperation. 'You won't be dreaming. This is not dreaming, Jack. You *must* be clear about that before you go. And besides, a shock strong enough to kill doesn't only have to happen in the waking world. One of the population groups of the Hinterland, we think, are Early-Trauma-Induced Protecting Entities – multiple personalities, as they are commonly known. *E-tipes*, if you want the acronym! They are permanent because they come from the neo-cortical experience of trauma. Others, such as past lives, visions, *myth-imagoes* – or *mythagos*, depending on what source you read – are more diffuse, coming from the primal Unconscious. But don't forget – if they've latched onto a landscape in the Hinterland, then they'll be *functioning* – and you can interact with them.'

'And Greenface? Greyface? The bull-runners?'

'They don't fit at all with what we understand. The whole

of your *shimmering* experience is an externalizing of the Memory, Event and Story activity inside your skull, but we can't know from which zone they have surfaced. Always assuming, of course, that they haven't lodged in you from outside—'

'Like parasites . . .'

'Like parasites. Assuming that isn't the case, then the only way to locate their origin is by questioning them. You have one of those entities outside and one inside. Since I can't comprehend on any level how an escapee from your pre-conscious mind can be living in a ghost city, I'd prefer to concentrate on the science and send you inwards. The supernatural I'll leave to Angela and Ghostbusters.'

Angela made a derisory sound from across the room. 'They're connected, Steve. The potential field *inside* has *everted* and inhabits external space. What's so hard to conceive in that?'

He said nothing, and Angela added, 'You're so uncomfortable with anything that isn't encased in bone. I'm criticizing you, Steve.'

'I'm aware of it.'

'Inside skull: This good! Outside skull: This not good. Am I right?'

Ignoring her, Brightmore swung round from the screen, thoughtfully watching Jack. 'The *shimmering* on your body . . . it did actually stink, didn't it?'

'It did. Of marshes on one occasion, desert on another, woodlands, forest a lot of the time.'

'And a glow, a real glow, real light—'

'And sound,' Angela reminded him. 'I could hear distant sound.'

'But nothing recorded, nothing on the video.'

'Not the sound,' she said. 'The light, yes. The organic chemicals, yes. But the voices . . . only perceptible by one or two of us.'

'Only you, actually,' Jack said with a quick glance at her.

'Only me, of course,' she responded with a frown.

Brightmore said: 'Conclusion: that the presence in the conscious mind of the entities and their baggage of landscape and emotion affects the body's metabolism. This produces a reflection of the complex carbon chain chemicals in their environment, includes a more obvious visual aura than those many people can already detect, and all this is biologically possible. But the *sounds* Angela heard – voices, panic, whatever – those were illusory. Either that, or you're part of the *shimmering* game as well.'

'He *does* treat it like a game. I can't deny it,' Angela said as they lay close together in bed, turning the pages of Jack's notebook. 'Christ, your handwriting's awful. I'd never realized how awful. I can hardly read it.'

'A sign of brilliance, according to my mother.'

'But not of illumination. What does *that* say, for example?'

'Swamp, Interland, Savima.'

'Oh, right. Steve's been laying that on you, has he? It's part of Jandrok's work. You remember Jandrok?'

'I don't remember Jandrok. No.'

'He's the French psychologist who gave me a hard time when I was writing my paper on archeo-stories. Ten, eleven years ago? You were away on the moors, feeling horny. We'd only just started to *do it*. You were *missing it*.' She nipped his ear and squeezed him affectionately, stroking him gently. 'Remember now?'

'*Please!* I'm trying to concentrate.' He turned pages deliberately. 'I'm looking for the bit about Dinosaurs. If I'm going to meet T. Rawhead Rex in this Shadowland, I want to be prepared.'

He had meant it light-heartedly, anticipating a smile, but Angela turned sharply away and picked up her own book.

'I've done something wrong?' he asked carefully, staring at her naked shoulders.

'A little less of the Rex,' she said angrily. 'A little more of the . . .'

'A little more of the . . . ?'

'Shit! Forget it!'

'A little more of the "shit, forget it"?'

She let her book drop to the floor, exasperated, but stayed turned away from her husband. 'I'm sorry, Jack. I'm concerned about you, that's all. I don't know how dangerous the trip's going to be. And I don't like being left alone with Natalie. I don't like this *Glanum* place. You see it, you seem to take it for granted. But I can feel it too. It's like being in an icy, stone alleyway, a cold wind blowing, just stone walls and a feeling of desertion. Steve is probably right. I *am* a part of it.'

'Then don't pull away from me. Angie? Please don't pull away from me.'

After a moment she turned over, meeting his gaze briefly. Her smile was very thin. 'Let's have a look,' she said tiredly. She tugged the notebook from his hands and turned the pages. For a minute or so she scanned the content.

'You can read it? Despite my coded scrawl?'

'Just about. This is more or less a summary of Jandrok's structure for the pre-conscious. Swamp, Savima, Windom, Maelstrom and the Deep.'

The full horror of Brightmore's seminar came back to him, but he liked Angela's closeness. She was – of all things – very reassuring, and he needed reassuring. 'You're so sexy when you use strange words. Those strange, incomprehensible words. Those strange, *dirty*, incomprehensible words.'

'Shut up and read.'

'Talk dirty some more,' he teased.

'Not funny.'

'Go on. Say "Savima".'

'It's a fusion of Savannah and Anima, and relates to archetypal landscape. Shut up and read.'

'I don't want to read. I want to *Rawhead.*'

'I haven't the energy.'

'Your body is a field of potential. Weren't you aware of that Angela? A field of potential. A veritable *meadow* of potential.'

She was amused at last. 'Oh God. And now you and your dog, and a bottle of pop, and Old Mother Riley, *and* her cow, all want to *mow* that meadow?'

'I love that song. God knows why. As English folksongs go, it's a bit obvious.'

'It's the adolescent in you. Weren't you aware of that Jack?' She tossed the notebook to the floor.

'I love you,' he said. 'Let's Rawhead.'

She looked up at him, and for a second he thought she seemed confused. But she whispered, 'No. I don't want to *Rawhead*. I want to make love. Let's keep Jandrok and all the other *rawheads* for the cerebral side of things.'

'I obey.'

'I'm glad you obey.'

'I'm glad you're glad I obey . . .'

17

'From the earlier tests, you'll have seen how the level we call the Hinterland is confused, malleable, certainly dreamlike. Although you have some control, there are other factors at work in the shaping of the zone. Mainly, though, the Hinterland will be constructed out of your own idea of crossing-over places, thresholds, if you like: gateways, forest edges, churches, walls and so on. However you visualize the abstract notion of the barrier between conscious and unconscious.

'We'll send clothing, supplies and survival equipment through with you, but check it carefully; it may not hold its integrity during the transmission. Once at this first level, you'll have to look for the ways deeper, if that's where the woman – Greenface – has gone. But it's likely she'll have left signs, traces of her presence. Again, from your earlier description, she was watching you from there, from the main Hinterland . . . or at least, from somewhere similar.'

There were so many questions to be asked, so much to be explained, so much reassurance needed . . .

'Will I always arrive in the same Hinterland?'

'Short answer: Yes. Qualification? Hope so. So far, our research suggests that once you've hardened the passage inwards, paved the way, if you like, then that will be your base camp whenever you enter the Hinterland. At any time in your life. But remember: it's confused. It's malleable. It's dreamlike.

'From this surface skin of the pre-conscious, there will be hundreds of portals to the deeper zones—'

'And I'll recognize them . . . how?'

'I was coming to that. Probably simple paths, or caves, the space between trees; arches of carved stone, doorways, small pools of water, beckoning figures. Think *fantasy*. There's nothing new; everything in your head is programmed by the familiarity of mythology, and has been for more than a million years. You might even look for the edge of an overhang or cliff. Abrupt breaks in physical space are often linked with the tunnels. Also, keep watching for shifts in time; and for any broken integrity in the space around you, or the event that's occurring. One thing we're beginning to find is that some of the leakage from the conscious mind surfaces in the pre-conscious in discreet form: it might be someone you know, a grove or glade, a cave, maybe an oracle! We might be able to talk to you if you find such an inlet into the Deep.'

Brightmore was almost on a high as he talked, his fingers flying across the keyboard as he typed notes, thoughts, speaking aloud to Jack, who sat nervously on the couch inside the Midax frame, which would soon be his home for a day or more.

His lightweight rucksack was open before him, half packed, the clothing in, the pistol and knives wrapped carefully. He looked almost forlornly at the camping supplies, dried high protein foods, sugars, packet soups. He had always enjoyed camping and trekking through Europe's mountains, but somehow . . . it didn't feel right to be eating packet soups in a dream.

He watched Brightmore at work. He'd had this briefing before, but he was encouraged and reassured by the psychologist's repeated description of the realm to which his subject would soon be dispatched.

'Won't I be able to catch fish? Eat the fruit of the Hinterland's lush orchards?'

'Of course. If they're there. If you're successful. I meant to ask you . . . Have you ever hunted game?'

'No. I don't like the idea of it.'

Brightmore laughed. 'Then pray for a foodstore!'

'How do I get back?'

'We bring you back, or you return on your own. From the Hinterland you can call us easily enough, so just make your way back to the white-stone plaza – the church. I want to suggest to you that you don't stay in the Midax Deep more than a week as you perceive it. OK?'

'OK.'

Brightmore swivelled round from the AppleMac then came over to the Midax frame, checking the glucose drip, the leads, the contacts. 'You'd better finish packing. You need to memorize everything that's in the bag. Then say your goodbyes.'

He was matter of fact, almost curt, more interested in the project than in the subject, or at least, that's how it appeared to Jack as he slowly filled the Gore-tex rucksack, pressing spare boots and rainproof trousers onto the top, then drawing the strings tight.

He went to the children's room and sat with Angela for a few minutes, watching Natalie as she played with Owein, Brightmore's slightly younger son. The girl was totally in charge as they fitted together the parts of a model magic castle.

'I think I'd have been happier being told I would simply be dreaming. I'm so full of the idea of a long journey it feels like I'm leaving for ever. And for the rest of you it's only a day.'

'It might be longer for us. We'll be with you all the time, and let you explore as long as it seems to us that you're safe. Maybe as much as four, five days.'

'I don't want to get stuck there for years.'

'You won't. Nobody yet has entered the Midax state for more than a day; and they all said their subjective experience had lasted less than a week. So it's goodbye for a month maximum.'

'A month . . . I've only got packet soup for a week!'

'You've got survival rations for a month. Assuming they come through. All you need to find is water.'

'Water? Water on the brain! Plenty of that! Ah well, time to go, I suppose.'

'I'll try and be with you,' Angela said. 'This is a first for me too.'

He hugged Natalie, and kissed her. He tried to look into her eyes, but she was earnestly trying to return to the magic castle, an ordinary child, with an ordinary child's self-centredness.

Angela took him back to the Midax frame, then kissed him.

'Bon voyage. Behave yourself!'

PART FOUR

Beyond the Hinterland

Chapter 8

Beyond the Equation

18

I have emerged safely in the Hinterland again, the evening
world of red sun and broad shadows, and I have found clear
evidence that someone has been here recently, living in the
cathedral. It is not exactly the same church: the statues
around the great doors are no longer saints and bishops, but
hunched human figures with grotesque faces. The doors are
the same, but there is now a second entrance to the left, a
vast, vertical wooden gateway between the upright forms of
animals: lions, chimaeras, horses, and two great bulls, all on
their hindlegs, all curiously distorted, with their inner limbs
and the bulls' horns forming the arch above the doors. Across
the piazza, other buildings crowd together, white-façaded,
marble-pillared.

Shortly after surfacing, I ran down the steps, away from the
church and the Bull Temple, and looked back, my eyes finding difficulty in focusing against the crimson glare of the sun.
The red cliffs still rise behind the cathedral, a great curved
wall enclosing the ruins and the piazza in a tight embrace.
This massive curtain wall of rust-red rock opens towards tall
woods, formed of broad-trunked, twisted trees.

Everywhere I look there are gaps and tunnels, passages and
even a valley stretching away from this place of my imagination. This is a more complex Hinterland than before,
more enclosed yet more defined. The cliffs above me are not
hard-edged rocks but flowing, organic curves, as if the limbs
of human giants and the trunks of massive trees have all been
petrified and pressed together, slowly rusting.

Sharp lights glint and gleam among the folds of the cliffs,

and in places I can detect traces of carving around the narrow fissures and crevices that suggest portals into the deeper world. But the façade of the rose-red city of Petra has gone, eroded, perhaps, made older, or perhaps obscured by new growth.

Although I have spoken the contact code aloud, there is no response, no sense of the presence of the outside world, of Angela, keeping her eye on me! For a few minutes in this strange land I've felt very lonely, more than a little afraid. But I know there is a routine to be followed. It just doesn't seem to be—

Nothing is quite as I—

It's so *twilight* – end of the world. Cold wind from the woods, though. I guess that's my way out, my way deeper . . .

There was a routine to be followed, and despite my confusion, I held on to that mental list as if it were a talisman. Or do I mean touchstone? The routine included entering the church and trying to re-engage with the talking statues, but the sight of those monstrous creatures guarding a second sanctuary – the Bull Temple – has made me apprehensive. It took a while to understand why – the connection with the bull-runners – and I suspect that this is because of some slight 'jet-lag' in my memory.

Despite the ranks of fabled, fabulous and monstrous beasts that guard the gates, the main figures are the bulls, their heads extending out across the steps, curved horns casting long shadows across the piazza. They frighten the spirit in me, and I am avoiding wandering too close to them.

I began the routine by inspecting what had been brought into existence with me.

The clothes I'm wearing are intact, corduroys and leather jacket, and the compass and my watch are through as well. But the pistol is now a flare gun and the knives have mutated to vegetable knives, short-bladed and ideal for paring but not, I suspect, for defence. The rainproof pack has mutated from a carefully prepared bag, designed to support a long hunting trip, to the sort of back-pack I might take on holiday to the Mediterranean, full of summer clothes and sandals; there are three pairs of bright blue paisley swimming briefs in place of my rain-proof over-trousers! The packet soups have changed to packs of toffees, and I feel a certain comfort in that. I'm not unduly concerned about most of the items that have changed, since the only items of any true worth are the photographs of Angela and Natalie, taken on that holiday in the Perigord. I've brought two, just to be on the safe side. Earlier, I sat for a long time on the stone steps staring at the pictures, trying to imagine Natalie standing by me, holding my hand, touching my face, so physically close to me while here I'm preparing for a journey beyond the cliffs, to a territory that has never been mapped, and only ever glimpsed a few times, images that suggest great danger, great hardship.

It didn't take long to establish that this is no lucid dream. Try as I might I cannot manipulate or control the illusion around me. I'm beginning to think of myself as Mr Eighty Percent. Too much of my central self has been condensed, re-defined and set loose for it to have the full control of dream imagery and the seepage from the unconscious that exists in the lucid dreamstate.

Whatever was within me has formed, defined, hardened and is waiting, and I will be no Merlin, able to summon change at will.

There is the very real experience of being in very real space, and time itself runs quite normally, according to my watch and to my own innate *sense* of time. The sun stays low, and the shadows defy the passage of the seconds on my wrist, but I can report that this is no timeless dream, but a defined reality in which it takes me nearly five minutes to walk to the edge of the woodland, and the same nearly five minutes back again.

The tunnels through the trees bring a fresh smell and the sound of a waterfall. For a moment, earlier, standing in the breeze from beyond the forest, peering into the sylvan gloom,

I thought I heard human voices, but it may have been nothing more than animals, birds perhaps. From that position I could see back to where the red cliffs curved into the distance, obscuring the land beyond, and I am certain that I saw furtive movement against the red sky, a small shape ducking down, then moving quickly to its right before crouching again and peering into the valley.

Was it Greenface? I still don't know. At this time I can see no signs that it is she who has been living in this particular borderland.

Time to explore, now.

Later . . .

Having walked the area of the piazza, peering into some of the buildings with their scatter of fallen statues and floors littered with broken pottery, I returned to the cathedral, to the 'Christian' gate, avoiding the Bull-Gate with its two grotesque, ebony bulls' heads. Inside the church was a clear echo of my previous visit: the dust, the light, the signs of this place having been long abandoned, the running, noisy chickens, pecking at the crumbling plaster, the stone floor and the weedy plants that were springing up through the cracked flagstones.

On the altar, Christ was agonizing on his tree, but with his face upturned, his mouth and eyes opened as if calling out, his body a slim, extended post-modernist representation of the crucified carpenter, the thorns from his crown curling out like the horns of a bull, but that feature, I'm sure, is my own fearful addition to the scenario.

Where Joan of Arc had stood previously, so proud, so robust, so ice cold in marble, now there was a different female figure, no less statuesque, no less magnificent in her form of white marble, but armoured differently – metal-scales and armoured greaves, spiked gauntlets and a belt of throwing knives slung across her shoulder. A tumble of long, full hair had been carved so intricately in the stone that even a stray, wind-blown strand curved delicately from her brow, snapped off at my clumsy touch. A raven's wing was the pin that fastened a short cloak above her left breast.

It was as I started to leave the church that I caught the faintest scent of wood ash, a moment only, but sufficient to tell me that a fire had been made here, and sure enough, after a few minutes of searching by the stone walls of the church I found the traces of a small hearth, almost completely concealed. The footprints in the dust were small; and by the fire itself I found a single cockle shell, bored to take a thread.

I breathed her name aloud, wondering if she was still close.

I might not have found the remains of her food but for the sound of snarling and crunching from a deep recess below a stained glass window. The creature that was wolfing down the scraps of the chicken meal at first struck me as a fox, but when it turned on me, baring its teeth, I realized that this was no fox that had ever hunted the nightland of my own world.

It was the size of a hound, and its red fur was streaked with black. The bush of its tail flexed left and right, rather like an angry cat's. From its muzzle, four horny knobs stuck out like cancerous growths. A tall ridge of black, stiffened hair ran from between its eyes to its tail.

I backed away, but the creature was as afraid of me as was I of it, and it suddenly loped away to the piazza, uttering shrill, piercing sounds, a high pitched bark, perhaps signalling to others of its kind.

Within the recess were the feathers, bones and charred remains of the meal, along with the entrails of the chicken, which had been carefully wrapped in leaves and smothered with mud, an obliteration to the senses that had worked so far as the ur-fox was concerned.

Her footprints were in the dust everywhere, and I could see, now, how she had pursued her prey as it had flapped and clucked in panic about the church, catching it with her spear

– I found traces of blood – and taking it to the small chapel for its preparation.

That I assumed the traces were the work of Greenface was a simple instinct, not a reasoned conclusion. I had, after all, seen her near this place in my visions. But if such creatures as that grotesque and ancient fox inhabited my world, then other humans too might be around, and the source of those voices beyond the trees might account, equally, for the surreptitious feast within the sanctuary.

I had been in the Hinterland for several hours and began to feel hungry and tired. There had been no change in the light outside, but my watch marked the real-time passage of from ten am to six pm. Nothing had changed, and nothing changed when I again attempted to influence the lucidity of my vision, to create movement, presence, to bring the voices of Angela and Steve (You! The both of you! I'm beginning to forget that this is a communication to people who are reading my report!) to bring *your* voices, your presence into the piazza.

I am on my own, to an extent that induces a feeling of claustrophobia. The twenty percent of me that is watching the main self at large is now panicking, wants out, wants reality, is perhaps lying upon that plush couch, in its web of wires, twitching or thrashing, perhaps murmuring from its fragmentary dreamworld. It has been abandoned, but it is still aware, and perhaps it is that residual awareness that feeds back into the Hinterland as furtive movement, frightening shadow, a brooding wood, an enclosing mood that seems directed to one end only: to get me away from here . . .

Ah! I think, then, that perhaps there is another explanation for this anxiety. Yes of course, the Hinterland is only the thin, conscious border that protects me from the raw unconscious. Here, I have constructed images and icons that combine both mystery and hope, sanctuary and afterlife. The cathedral, the shrine, the opening passages, the voids, the womby channels calling me back, the tunnels of light, the breezy glades, the never-neverlands in which I fantasized as a child, all . . .

Calling to me? But they can't *all* be the way through . . . Can they?

And surely I would never have constructed the Bull-Gate!

It exists there, reaching from the red cliff, a parasite on the rest of the ruined sanctuary. I do not believe it to be the gate I seek, rather, it is a gate to avoid. I notice, in contradiction of my statements a few hours ago, that the creatures that surround the heavy gates themselves have grown bigger, fatter, almost older; they are reaching further out across the steps, casting long shadows as their necks crane forward; their animal faces turn away from the sun, stretching round to watch the woods that hide the distant waterfall.

So there *is* change here, but it is not of my doing. I suspect, therefore, that I am certainly not alone, or at least, that I am not the only influence on the world that confines and contains me.

I slept for a while at the back of the cathedral, emerged briefly to establish that there had been no change of any devastating or inherently threatening nature, and then climbed the spiral stairs to the bell tower. From here, by squeezing through a narrow window, I could walk along the sharp angle of the roof above the main body of the building and reach that point at which church and cliff were joined, a seamless junction as if the rock had simply been carved at this point into the precise, angular dimensions of the place of worship.

I climbed the cliff for a long time. The rock was hard, the smoothness of its surface consistent with petrified flesh, but still amply pitted and cracked by weather to make the ascent no more than a difficult scramble.

High above the church and the Bull Temple, looking out across the wide piazza, I could see the swathe of the forest and the sudden drop of a steep-sided gorge, distantly, where a thundering waterfall sparkled and misted in the ruby twilight.

I could see no signs of life, not even the flight of birds above the canopy nor the stealthy movement of deer at the edge of the woods themselves.

Intrigued by what lay at the top of the cliffs, I climbed on for what seemed like hours. The slope curved away and soon the cathedral was lost below me, and I was surrounded only by rock and the red sky. And yet the climb remained as difficult as before, a steady ascent at a high angle past the fissures and carved entranceways that I had seen from the piazza.

I ventured into one such passage, a horizontal, oblong opening framed with galloping and tumbling horses, manes flying, bodies curiously bloated. I realized, after several minutes, that this was probably the entrance to a tomb. The tunnel became narrow and tall after the initial scramble through the hole, and began to wind into the mountain towards a source of stale air. The walls were hung with clay figurines and shapes made out of grass and flax, some simply of dyed cloth tied to shank bones or long wooden poles. It meant little to me, and the journey inwards was unrewarding, so I returned to the hot cliff face.

I had hoped to find one of the sources of the gleaming, silvery light, but they were elusive, catching my eye on occasion, but refusing to be at the end of the rainbow when I arrived to inspect them, breathless and sticky with perspiration.

At last I gave up, abandoned the climb and descended again cautiously to the ruins below to rethink my strategy.

I was still out of sight of the church when I heard the creaking trundle of a cart and human voices.

Eight ragged looking figures, five men and three women, hauled two heavy carts across the piazza. The carts were piled high, though whether with booty or supplies was impossible to tell since the bulk was concealed beneath skins. They were moving towards the base of the red cliff, between the Bull Temple and the obsidian mausoleum, shouting at each other, struggling with the weight. As I watched, two men and a third woman came running down the steps, carrying the statue of the crucified Christ between them.

The carts stopped. The ragged band argued noisily. From inside the church came the sound of stone being smashed and various calls went out to the two sanctuaries. I had the feeling that the words meant: 'Enough, now. We can't carry any more.'

Two more figures appeared, running lightly down the steps, children, I thought. One was carrying a fragment of a stone limb, weaving beneath its weight across his shoulder, the other some icons. Behind them, two more came, struggling with part of a woman's head – the head of the Raven Warrior – and they were cuffed and shouted at, but ran ahead of the carts to the overhang of cliff, where a temporary camp was made.

I remained on the roof of the cathedral, or in the bell tower, for a long time, aware that two of the older men were prowling round the piazza, shading their eyes and scrutinizing the twilight slopes above them. One of them seemed to watch me for so long that I felt sure he must have seen me, but at last he moved away, and of course I was so dusted with red – as was the cathedral – that I would have been just one more shape against the landscape.

Now a third cart emerged from the forest, pulled by an ungulate of grotesque appearance, all sagging grey skin, heavy horns, and dripping muzzle. Four men pushed from behind, two women, young and long-haired slapping the beast's flanks. A fifth man strode behind them, weighed down by a massive leather pack, his face hidden below the flop of a cowl. As the cart continued, he stopped for a while and looked back towards the woods, as if searching, then strode towards me, passing by, heading to the Bull-Gate and disappearing below the jutting heads and horns of the guardian beasts.

I finished the descent to the church below, where I expected to find the chickens slaughtered for the fire and my pack rifled, or stolen, leaving me without the precious pictures, *icons* of my external life. In fact, the chickens were quietly brooding in the far corner, caught in the dusty light from the Lady Chapel, and my pack was still secure in its niche. The only damage was to the statues and holy pictures, for these had all been either broken or taken, and it was oddly sad to see this destruction. I was especially grieved at the broken body of the Raven Warrior, whose discarded corpse lay across the wooden seats of her chapel, her arms broken, her spear snapped in two, her head taken as I had observed from the cliff.

Christ was missing completely, of course, and his cross was upturned against the marble altar.

As I kicked through the dust and the shattered stone, partly angry, very puzzled, I realized that a figure had arrived in the open doors to the church and was standing there, watching me. As quickly as I had seen him, he had gone. I was about to follow when a scuffle and raised voices alerted me to the squabble between two adolescent males. They were arguing over a triptych, and as they tugged at the painting so it split into its component panels. Angrily, and with a suspicious glance in my direction, these wisp-bearded youths gathered up the pieces and scurried from the hall, still bickering.

A little later, a wind blew up from the direction of the forest. The icon hunters had formed the three carts into a windbreak, erected animal-skin walls, and lit a fire that burned brightly against the face of the cliff. I watched them again from the bell tower, saw how they formed into four distinct family groups around the blazing wood and began to prepare their meals. And it was at that moment, as they prepared for their food, that I realized that I was still inhabiting a dream, to an extent at least . . .

I had assumed that these were icon stealers, accumulating their trade-goods by pillaging and looting. But as the Christ was dismembered and the carcase laid across the fire, so I saw that this was a form of cannibalism. The statues were regarded as a source of food, and the limbs and broken stone were heated until they cracked, then distributed among the family groups, who proceeded to consume them with all the fervour and happy conversation of a group of friends at a Sunday barbecue.

It was visual madness. It was a reflection of the absurdity of dream.

How I longed, as I watched them from my vantage point, for some interchange, some conversation with the outside world, with the thinking, rational minds of those of you who watch.

Perhaps these icon-eaters were the last of the lucid but ridiculous aspects of dream, inhabiting this twilight Hinterland, as real and hard as the stone-stuff they consumed, but still a function of expressed desire, or fear, rather than memory and imagination.

I listened to them for several hours, sitting in the church, watching the dust swirl in the rising wind, the chickens run, the light from the high windows shift and darken as clouds swept over the blood-red sun.

Eventually the newcomers slept, and though it was still twilight, I slept too, grateful for an escape from the exhaustion that had accompanied my long and arduous climb.

I woke to the sound of drumming and the smell of fire. The chickens were flapping around in panic as one of the youths from yesterday chased them, laughing, prodding at them with an iron-tipped lance. Swirls of smoke came into the cathedral through the higher windows, but there was no fire that I could see.

The drumming, meanwhile, kept up its rapid, rhythmic beat outside.

Seeing me awake, the young man walked over to me, shouldering his spear as if it were a rifle. He had long fair hair, a broad smile and a thin, downy beard. His clothes were primitive, leather-stitched together, but I saw a bone cuirass below his loose jacket.

He reached a hand to me and I thought he was about to help me up, but he passed me a small piece of wood, then laughed and left the church. The wood was a fragment of one of the triptychs, and I could see the edge of a face, a piece of building, a distant hill. I tossed the fragment into my pack, then followed the strange young man to the source of the drumming.

They had set fire to the Bull-Gate. With their carts lined up, the vandals stood in a wide arc around the marble steps, staring up as flames raged upon the heavy wood, and smoke billowed and obscured the jutting bulls, the stone creatures. Two men crouched behind the drums, striking them with thick wood batons and much energy. Across the piazza, the cowled man was walking in and out of the ruins, striking at columns with his staff, kicking through the rubble.

There was a sudden cheer and the vandals raced to the burning gates, picked up the blunt, cut trunk of a tree, laced with ropes, and charged the doors. Their first attack was successful, the Bull-Gate shattering inwards, flaming wood falling from the broken bars. Now the carts were hauled up the steps and each in turn dragged through, the animal being pulled and bullied as it struggled to escape the fire, but eventually disappearing into the sanctuary, following the drums.

In all the confusion I had failed to notice the cowled man cross the wide space and ascend the steps. He passed through the fiery gates, now, and the youth with the fair hair and fine beard, and two others, used their own staffs to push the doors back into place, blinking against the smoke, wary of the swirling flames.

As the gap into the Bull Temple closed, so the cowled man glanced back, and though I couldn't at that time be certain, I thought I recognized a face from my youth, a face I had missed for years, the face of the man who dowsed for the hidden cities of the world.

Finebeard was watching me, I realized, staring out from the midst of the flames.

Fire suddenly exploded as bitumen or tar ignited and he pulled quickly back as heavy black smoke roiled down the steps, acrid and choking.

The fire raged for an hour and the great gates were

consumed. When the flames had finally died down, the whole piazza was covered with a dark ash, the air heavy with burning. Around the open gate, the two bulls were now leaning heavily towards the forest, their heads turned, the shadows from their horns making pointers on the ground, indicating a direction I should take.

Intrigued, less fearful now, I entered the Bull Temple and walked along the vast hall, aware that an encompassing darkness lay ahead. The walls were intricately inscribed with figures, painted with murals, covered with design, none of it at all meaningful. The hall seemed to swallow me and when I shouted, the voice echoed and echoed, each sound becoming fainter, but never actually dying.

I went outside again to the piazza, looked up at the gaping muzzles of the aurochs, and decided to follow their advice.

I returned quickly to the cathedral, thought of my meagre supplies, and swiftly caught two chickens, trussing them wing and beak and tying them, alive, to my pack, where they hung silent and in peril until their later, swift dispatch.

As I made to leave the Hinterland, I looked again at the fragment of wooden painting given to me by the fairbearded youth, and this time turned it over in my fingers.

A crude green face had been scratched on the other side. Open eyes watched me.

I was still studying this enigmatic fragment when a shadow fell across the entrance to the church and the youth himself appeared there. He carried his own leather pack, the sturdy lance and a cluster of knives, dangling from his belt. He was smiling at me, then beckoned, pointing towards the forest and the waterfall.

'Yes. I'd already decided to go.'

He left the church and I followed him. He was singing loudly as he strode towards the evening woods, then glanced back and laughed, again beckoning to me.

Catch up! Come on! A long way to go . . .

19

I have no idea how many deep channels led away from the Hinterland, but that Greenface's return route to her own country would have been through the waterfall should have been obvious. When she and her Greyfaced companion had passed *through* me, that night, I had glimpsed the fall and the gorge in the background and been aware that they had come from that same direction. Now, I found traces of her in a rocky overhang, close to the raging water but in a place sheltered from its spray. I know they were the remains of her camp – she had cut her hair as I had seen her doing on two previous occasions. The dry black locks were scattered in the ashes of a small fire.

A path of sorts led down the side of the gorge, levelling out to a narrow ledge that passed behind the falling water. I could hardly believe that the carts of the icon hunters had come this way, but the marks of the inner wheels were clear on the slope and where the ledge was narrowest and most precipitous there remained the droppings of the nervous animal that had been urged along the path.

Behind the fall a cave system opened into the rock, a honeycomb of passages, some open to the sky with water pouring through them, others leading downwards into an echoing abyss, others winding through the mountain, wide tunnels along which the icon hunters had dragged and pushed their carts with enormous difficulty, as my companion described it.

I had never known that dreams had such a hard time of it, away in the sleeping mind! We emerged into the eerie silence and heavy resinous air of a pine forest which smothered the hills and the sides of a deep gorge, opening out ahead of us. I could see the gleam of lakes in the far distance. We had left the twilight behind; this was a bright, summer world. Behind us, the waterfall was a dull murmur in the rock, a shadow sound as if it belonged to another place, another dream.

Finebeard was pointing to one of the more distant lakes. I could, I thought, just make out small boats spreading out in a fan from a shoreline settlement, where smoke drifted in the air. He reached into my pack and removed the crude image of Greenface, holding it away from him, indicating the route he was sure she had taken.

There was a confidence about him, a youthful certainty, and although he could scarcely have been out of his teenage years he conveyed an air of direction; he was my guide, I realized, and had been released to the task, perhaps by Garth – or the man who had resembled Garth – or perhaps by my own *need*, made manifest in the Hinterland, the true starting point for the long search ahead.

Curiouser and curiouser, as Angela would have said.

Taking back the shard, I introduced myself, and Finebeard laughed as he repeated the name 'Jack'. In his own language, perhaps, the word was scatalogical. His own name was unpronounceable, a gibberish of several syllables that sounded, when I mumbled it, like William. And William was what I named my guide, and again he chuckled.

It took most of the day to descend the mountain and traverse the pinewoods to the broad blue lake, and the village. There were trails of sorts, spreading out into the land around like the veins of a leaf: passages to other worlds, to other regions, some of them marked with poles or stones, some clearly to be avoided – from William Finebeard's caution – some familiar to him. Had the icon hunters really hauled their wagons all this way? He indicated that they had. Where they had come from, the mountains on the far side of this community, the terrain was far harder, the valleys deeper. He had joined them a few months ago, when the snow was thick and extra hands were useful for hauling the carts. The icon hunters never rested, never stayed in one place for more than two or three days. Their life was one of constant movement, following the clues and stories that they heard, looking for the religious shrines and sanctuaries which they could loot and use as trade along the way.

My life, even in my dreams, it seemed, was full of sanctuaries. They haunted me.

A deep ditch, filled with a tangle of vicious-looking thorn, was the only barricade around the fishing village. Smoke rose from each of the low houses, and there was a great deal of shouting out on the lake. Several fishing coracles were being paddled to the shore, dragging a wide line-net behind them. The surface of the lake thrashed and sparkled with fish.

A series of weird cries went up suddenly and the lake activity paused for a moment. Two of the bigger boats began to haul for the shore while from the largest of the huts a group of women appeared – the source of the warning – holding bone-tipped harpoons. William called out and waved and the atmosphere of caution changed. A different ululation sounded and the lake activity reverted to the normal task of dragging in the nets.

Two boys carried a wooden plank to the ditch and laid it over the thorn, and we walked carefully across into the community.

I had no idea who these people were. The women wore brightly coloured dresses and shirts, mostly scarlet and yellow. Their hair was tied up on the crown below odd, round hats that were pinned in place. Their skin was creamy white, their eyes very pale. The men wore long buckskin shirts over leather leggings and the same round hats perched on hair that was shaved to the scalp in a wide band from forehead to nape. The left sides of their faces were variously scarred, the older the man the more the cuts. They were almost completely free of familiar jewellery or trinkets – semi-precious stones or painted shells – but rather clattered with fragments of religious painting, metal crosses, sun-circles, stars and gleaming moons, shards of grails, plates, incensories and tabernacles, drilled for the leather strings that slung them from elegant necks. One woman wore the parts of a painted slate diptych slung front and back and tied across her shoulders, a bizarre and heavy garment that showed images of a boy carrying fishes, dancing women with elaborately coiffed hair, and long-necked geese, their bodies broken off where the slate was smashed.

We were led to the largest of the houses, to an accompaniment of shrill cries and calls from the men out in the boats. Inside, the floor dropped down, five feet or more below the natural level of the ground. Light streamed from the roof. A fire burned in a recess in the stone wall. We sat on coarsely woven mats and drank a disgusting, syrupy drink, warm and sweet, certainly alcoholic, and I dread to think what else.

Wherever I looked around this lodge, images of gods, goddesses, animals and symbols stared back at me, from simple madonnas on faded canvas to coiled snakes on bark, from elaborate labyrinthine patterns in several colours scratched on polished stone to the stark imagery of Axe or Cross, or severed heads in clay. Candles of all shapes and sizes burned dimly. Like china and pictures in a suburban house, this lodge was decorated with a striking but chaotic jumble of bad and meaningless taste, each item interesting in itself, but without any context save their prettiness and tradeable value.

William asked me for the image of Greenface and showed it to the headwoman, who sat chewing by her husband, staring hard at me from eyes set deep in her hard, lined face. She nodded at the image and passed it back, then proffered a wooden bowl full of dried strips of fish. These again were disgusting, but some acid in the leathery flesh made the mouth water. I started to chew and realized that I could never swallow this foul offering; I would be chewing for ever, or so it seemed at the time.

Greenface *had* been in the area. William already knew this

since he and the icon hunters had seen her on their own travels. He learned from the headman, whose name was strange but meant Five Cuts to the Face, that the woman had haunted the rocks and trees above the village for several days. She had frightened the children, but done them no harm. She had stolen fish on two occasions, but on a third had left four crudely carved harpoon hooks, so the theft was adjudged as trade.

The woman had been incomprehensible to them, from the far-away, but a frightened woman nonetheless, and someone in search of a way across the lake.

One evening they had left a small boat outside the thorn hedge that extended into the lake. She had taken it gladly, at dawn the next day, and Five Cuts had watched as she had paddled into the lake glare, soon to be lost from sight.

The headwoman, leaning forward on her knees, the odour of fish rancid on her breath, pointed at my pack, indicated that I should turn it round. As I did so she smiled and held out her hands for the trussed chickens. She was nodding vigorously and I passed them across to her. She snapped their necks with a movement so quick that I missed it, took off the twine and passed it back to me, then called to one of her daughters, three of whom were sitting in the gloom, close to the door and the ramp to the floor. The youngest girl ran over and took the carcases to the fire-side, where she started to pluck them with astonishing speed.

William was still communicating in sign and expression, some words too that perhaps he had picked up on his travels. I gathered that he was asking for a boat to follow Greenface, and after a while he fell silent, hunched forward, waiting for Five Cuts to think.

The old man stared at me then spread his hands. They wanted to trade, of course, and his gaze was on the pack. But I had nothing to trade that I could spare. The chickens were earning us a meal, and probably hospitality over night. William had nothing but essentials either, and he looked at me rather despairingly, or perhaps hopefully that my own pack would reveal some worthwhile item.

I couldn't give away the flare gun, or my knives; the sleeping gear was essential, as were the medications, changes of clothes, the photograph of Angela and Natalie. There was nothing of value that I could spare. Unless . . .

I reached in and drew out one of the pairs of paisley swimming trunks. The bright colours impressed the headwoman. Five Cuts frowned and reached for the garment, studying it before – predictably, I suppose – he put them over his head and looked at me solemnly. I nodded enthusiastically, trying to say, 'Suits you very well. The headgear of Kings in my world.'

His wife was laughing hysterically. He removed the bathing costume and passed it back, then said something to the woman that again set her off in peals of laughter. She studied each of us in turn, then nodded at William, who shuffled uneasily as Five Cuts rose and indicated that he should follow.

In the corner, by the fire recess, the young girl was chopping the chickens crudely, watching me almost wistfully as the heavy stone knife rose and fell, cutting uncomfortably close to her fingers.

In turn, I was led from the main house to a second, brighter and airier place which was nevertheless overwhelmingly heady with the smell of fat, flesh and furs. The pelts of various animals were pinned out on wooden frames. Two women and a thin-armed youth were at work with bone scrapers, stripping the fatty tissue from the skins prior to curing them. The headwoman gave me a scraper of my own, a block of pumice, showed me briefly what to do and knelt me down at a piece of hide a full six feet by four. As I knelt to the task, she patted my head. As I hesitated – the smell was overpowering – she kicked my backside.

The other three laughed. They were all chewing vigorously – disgusting lumps of a fishy gum – and one of the women reached up and touched the side of her nose, causing her companions to exchange glances and chuckle.

No thanks.

I bent to the task of curing with a vigour that surprised me.

William Finebeard, in the meantime, had been taken over the ditch and up into the woods. His hands were quite raw when he came down for the stew of fish and chicken that was served up about two hours later, as darkness was covering the land. I had by then processed two hides only. He had logged and stripped the bark from two trees. He had then dragged the trees into the village and been shown how to cut the trunks lengthwise, insert stone pegs at hand-width intervals, ready to split the resinous wood into crude planks.

Shortly before we ate, a muscular man with fierce eyes but a ready smile and two cuts on his cheek came into the lodge, kneeling down before the older couple, then joked with them. He was clutching a great bundle of broken bone harpoons and was exhilarated and loud, high on the catch of a fish that looked like a sturgeon, but was five times the size, and ten times as hideous. It was dangling from a gallows in the centre of the village, a focus of much excitement; I'd seen it as I left the curing house.

Two Cuts tossed the broken hooks towards a mat in a corner of the lodge, for later repair, then crouched by the cooking fire for a moment, stirring the stew and talking to the eldest of the three girls.

After a while he came and sat with William and me, taking my companion's hands in his own and examining the blisters. Whatever he said, it was approving and concerned. He called to the eldest daughter, exercising an authority that suggested he was married to her, then went to his corner, bending to the task of removing the bone blades from the broken hafts of the harpoons.

The older girl came and sat opposite William, rubbing oil and ash of some sort into the blisters. She was called Ethne and her eyes sparkled as she worked on the wounds, speaking quietly and I felt wryly, since William smiled and laughed with her.

Her young sister – Thimuth – came over to me and took my hands, her own eyes shining with energy and excitement. She could have been no more than twelve or thirteen, precocious and lively, the touch of her hands on mine signalling more than soothing. But Five Cuts spoke to her sharply and she drew away, scowling and disappointed, spitting into her hat before placing it back on her head and sulking back to the cooking fire and the stone pot with its simmering, smelly soup.

We sat in a circle to eat, and William and I were encouraged to fill our bellies. In truth, the mix of fish and chicken was tasty and I was soon full and feeling tired.

By firelight, later, I watched Two Cuts back at work in his corner, the headwoman sitting and talking with her middle daughter, who was stitching cloth, and Thimuth curled into a tight ball below a blanket, watching me. Ethne was still working on William's sore hands, and talking quietly. Five Cuts himself sat staring at me curiously. When I met his gaze he frowned, glanced at my companion, then back again.

Slowly he shook his head, a clear warning.

Now something became clear to me which should have been obvious all along. There was more than soothing going on between William and the eldest daughter. With everything except language – they were contriving to sound innocent – they were loving each other, sharing their souls! No wonder William had been so willing to come back. These two were not strangers to each other by any stretch of the imagination. My friend's attention was half on the harpoon mender, sitting in the gloom, and half on the beauty who sat before him, and affection and desire flowed between them as tangible as a scented summer breeze.

You young rogue, you . . .

The clutch of harpoons was repaired and Two Cuts ceremonially presented them to the Headman and his wife. He went outside with Ethne, then – they were clearly betrothed – and William spent a long time scratching at the ground with a stick. Ethne didn't return; she lived in the lodge during the day, but slept elsewhere.

We were both exhausted and I was glad when blankets of animal skins were brought to us and I could entertain sleep, disturbed only by the sound of constant chewing, and by my friend, in the very small hours, who rose beside me, indicated graphically that he needed to urinate before slipping from the house. He didn't come back, and at first light I saw him at the lake edge, staring across the water.

I had certainly hoped that our efforts of the day before would have been sufficient to earn the transport across the lake, but the headwoman worked us a further full day, mercifully releasing me from curing duties after a few hours and setting me to splitting logs. William was raw-handed but exuberant in the evening, and we were presented with three long harpoons, a warbling whistle, and a pound of fish-gum, which I held to my bosom with exaggerated pleasure as I thanked them profusely.

Our boat was shown to us, our boatman was an older man – Four Cuts – who would take us to the far shore, returning the vessel when we were safely landed. Such boats were at a premium, it seemed, and we were given instructions on how to signal in the future should we need to be returned.

We would stay the night and depart first thing in the morning.

William's need to urinate came upon him astonishingly quickly, as we dozed by a smouldering fire-glow and listened to the mastication of fish-gum. The young girl's eyes sparkled as she watched me, but she had been warned away from me and did no more than occasionally spit into her round hat and sigh. When William slipped from the lodge she half sat up, but seemed more concerned that her parents shouldn't see him go.

In fact, Five Cuts was awake also, watching me from a position on his side. I could not fathom that gaze, but I was glad we were leaving the next day.

The girl was shaking me awake. She had kindled the fire and was holding out a shallow dish of very meaty fish and vegetables. There was no one else in the hut, and I noticed that my pack had gone, as had William's. What was happening?

I was still bleary in the head, probably from the combination of unexpected manual labour and my intake of a thinner, more palatable version of the syrup that had accompanied the chicken and fish meal of the previous evening.

I wasn't hungry, tried to be polite, then saw that the girl had tears in her eyes. At first I thought they were for me, but sudden angry voices outside, and her quick, nervous glance, told me otherwise.

Where was my friend? Where was the young rogue?

I splashed cold water on my face and with the trembling girl following, stepped out into the bleak dawn. My host and hostess were by the lake, and the boatman was waiting for me. I could see the packs stowed at the front of the blunt-nosed vessel, and a small breeze was catching in the half-sail.

I walked down to the shore, aware that this was an angry community, now, that we had outstayed our welcome. There was no sign of Ethne or William, no warmth among the people who had gathered on the beach.

'Where is he?' I asked. Five Cuts indicated the boat. I was to get aboard. Everything was stowed, I could see . . . packs, harpoons, two dull-scaled, smoked fish, a bag of fleshy fish gum . . .

'I'm not going without him . . .'

'Get aboard!'

I refused, turning back to the village, determined to find my friend, but William was there before me, two hundred paces distant, walking across the bridge over the ditch, walking straight to the boat, walking stiffly . . .

As I made an attempt to go and meet him, the old woman, the headwoman, dragged me back.

'Get in the boat!'

Her words, incomprehensible in themselves, were charged with meaning.

'Are you all right?' I called to my friend. He smiled at me, but it was a thin gesture, and he seemed in pain. He was wearing his leather shirt, but was naked and fully revealed below, holding his heavy trousers over his arm, holding them to his side as he kept in a straight line towards the boat.

What have you been up to, you dog – as if I need to ask . . .

There was something wrong. Behind him, Two Cuts appeared, striding over the bridge, pacing down towards the beach and the boat; in his hands, five harpoons. On his face: anger, terrible anger.

I don't know how or why the thought occurred to me, but I realized suddenly that this was a walking race between two men, the wrong-doer and the wronged. It was something about the deliberateness of the pace; either could have run, but each walked, and each walked with increasing desperation, the furious man behind struggling, it seemed to me, to get into harpoon range.

'Come on! Make a run for it, we'll get off-shore and row until we drop!'

As if he understood me, William Finebeard shook his head. He was close, now, and he *was* in pain, I could see that so clearly now. There was blood on the backs and insides of his slim legs. He made eyes at me, a look that said, 'Get aboard,' and a look that said, 'Don't interfere . . .' Behind him, Two Cuts had raised a harpoon above his shoulder, still walking. I started to run, determined to interfere if I could, but a powerful slap to my face stunned me. The old woman danced around before me, slapped me again, turned me round and kicked me so hard that I stumbled towards the bobbing boat.

I resisted still, and looked back in time to see Two Cuts fling the harpoon. William screamed out and staggered, but stayed upright, his face contorting in pain. He reached behind him and snapped the shaft – God, that must have been agony! – and kept on coming.

The point had struck him in the middle of the back. He ought to have been dead.

'I'm going to help him!' I said, but Five Cuts took my arm in a vice-like grip and practically threw me into the boat, where the boatman held me down by the shoulder. A few seconds later, with Two Cuts close enough to whisper in his ear, William walked a path through the red skirts and black cloaks of the villagers, splashed heavily into the lake water and fell forwards into my waiting arms. I hauled him into the wooden hull, and felt the tug of movement as wind took the sail and the boatman used his long paddle to push away from the shallows.

If I was aware of this, it was from the edge of my vision. I was still recoiling in shock at the sight of the forest of broken harpoon shafts that grew like spines from my young friend's back. There were seventeen in all, all cut through so they would break easily, all firmly embedded.

What I didn't understand, as we pulled away, was why the angry partner of the eldest daughter had not finished the job. He had had a clear chance to do so.

Already, Two Cuts was walking back to his hut, the remaining harpoons cast aside, his body as stiff and lithe as a wildcat's. Behind him, young Thimuth followed, head bowed, though she glanced back quickly towards the lake, and I raised a hand to her.

The boatman was silent, guiding the small vessel out across the deeps, his attention fixed on catching the shifting, impulsive breeze.

William was breathing hard, face down on the floor of the boat, head slightly turned towards me. I tried to comfort him and he smiled, then met my gaze and winked – I think it was a wink – but there was something about him that said, 'It was worth it.'

We were well off-shore now and I started to remove his heavy shirt, thinking that the sooner I cut the harpoon heads out of him the better his chances; although the boatman was silent and remote from us, he was from a culture where such wounds must surely have been frequent, and might have practical suggestions.

William stopped me, eased himself onto his side, grimacing with pain as he did so, then relaxing, taking his weight on his shoulder. His eyes were watery, his mouth slack, but by sign and suggestion he told me what had happened. And why, in fact, he was still alive.

William and Ethne loved each other, having met on the young man's previous visit to the icon hunters. They shared a magic that must have existed from the earliest of times: the magic of recognition, the chemistry of passion.

Two Cuts was not bonded to her yet, but it was a match that had been agreed within the small community. When the fisherman had found the lovers in the forest – he had heard her cry in the night, her cry of pleasure – both lives were forfeit, or only William's, provided he undertook the Walk to the Shore. If he agreed to the Walk to the Shore, then the girl would be spared, free to live her life, free of all shunning, all punishment, all scorn. It was the way of these people, and a cruel one for the man involved.

Two hours before dawn, William Finebeard and Two Cuts had begun the walk to the shore, Two Cuts following at a distance of two harpoon throws behind the man he was challenging, free to launch up to twenty, of the thin fish-stickers, free to kill if he could get close enough, required to lose honourably if the man he pursued outpaced him.

They had walked from the ridge, down through the pines, and along the shore. If at any time William had broken into a run, the girl's life was lost. If he had fallen, his own life was lost. It was as simple, as brutal as that, and for four hours he had walked the walk of his life, despite the fact that Two Cuts' aim was impeccable, and each time he'd thrown a spear, the blade, a long, thin piece of bone, the teeth recurved, had found its mark.

Finebeard grinned and pulled me close. He murmured my name, then repeated it. And what he indicated to me then was the thought that had puzzled me as well. He said, 'He could have killed me. But he didn't. He thinks he's driven me away. But he hasn't. I love her, Jack. This is something that perhaps you can't understand . . .'

I wanted to say to him, oh yes I do. There are some things that never change. He had been prepared to lose his life to save the girl's. He had run that risk so that he could go back again.

We were in deep waters, and the boat tossed, although a brisker wind was carrying us forward nicely. As I held William's hand, I thought he started to laugh. I smiled and leaned towards him, only to realize that he was weeping, though whether he cried with the pain of his wounded body, or that from his broken heart, I couldn't tell.

I stroked his face and he looked at me with glistening eyes, then held his hand to me, thrusting the fingers to me, and the odour was familiar, an aroma that in different times would have been erotic and arousing, but which now seemed a fading memory of a hopeless love.

He brought the hand to his mouth and kissed it, smiling, hugging his fingers as he hugged a memory of the elder sister. Then he closed his eyes and sighed, and the sigh was like a song, fading on the wind. And shortly after this, the breath went from him.

20

The boatman was guiding the craft to a muddy shore among the trees, but as I looked into the distance I saw, about a mile away, a white stone tower, half obscured by green. It was an image all too familiar to me, and I urged the man to tack slightly, to sail along the shore to a place where I felt certain Greenface had once ventured, though whether she would have returned to the place – she and Greyface had seemed afraid of the tower – was an argument I suppressed for the moment.

The solemn man agreed, but pushed me back, as if to say, *Sit down! Now!*

I clutched my stomach and held onto the rough wood and blackened leather of the hull. The lake was so wide that in its middle the waves had rocked us like the sea, and I was feeling sick. But I soon recovered when I noticed the beached boat, the same boat, as I understood it from our captain's gestures, that days before had been given to Greenface.

We came onto the mudflats and reedbeds below the ruins, crumbling walls spreading out along the shore and up the wooded hill, the white tower most prominent of all. The boatman helped me with the corpse of William Finebeard, dragging it through the reeds to higher, drier ground, where five small horses were grazing, though they scattered at our approach. Before I could express any thanks, the man had passed me a small leather bag, which from its feel contained a liquid. He indicated that I should rub this unguent into the wounds on William's body, and I said, 'He's dead. It'll do no good. The man is dead.'

The boatman raised his eyebrows, kicked the body, then turned and waded back to the tethered craft, pushing off from the mud and catching the wind.

A moment later a hand with a vice-like grip grasped my ankle.

Too stunned to feel pleasure for a moment, I looked down at the anguished face of my friend, twisting up from the earth. He was making exaggerated licking motions with his lips, trying to smile.

'Christ! I thought you'd died. I wept tears for you!'

I found water and moistened his mouth. He was in severe pain, now, and befuddled as he surfaced from the coma. But he was alive! And I was overjoyed – and if I'm honest, relieved – I no longer felt so alone again. My guide was back.

All thought of Greenface had fled for the moment. And if I was aware that the woman had been afraid of these white towers, then I had either forgotten, or suppressed the concern, because it was to the base of the tower that I dragged the revivified and groaning carcase. I fetched the packs, the harpoons, the fish gum and dried fish and then began to ease the man's jacket off, aware that his back and legs were caked with drying blood and that he was in a terrible state.

As the heavy cloth of his shirt came away, so I saw the reason that he had survived. Before the Walk to the Shore, he had turned the bone cuirass around to cover his back – I discovered later that he'd had an inkling of what would lie in store for him if he'd been caught with Ethne and had prepared accordingly – and though fifteen of the bone harpoons had penetrated his flesh to the depth of half an inch, their full power frustrated by this crude defence, only two had struck deeply. I was moderately certain that no vital organ had been hit, although clearly one of the strikes had severed a major vein, accounting for the massive blood loss.

Most of the bone blades dropped out when tugged; four had gone deep enough for the teeth to need to be cut free. I poured the boatman's unguent onto the cuts and rubbed it in, while my fair-bearded friend howled again. There must have been iodine in the dressing liquid, since his back turned yellow, but any characteristic smell was overwhelmed by the pungent aroma of the preparation's main ingredient.

Fish, of course.

Even the deepest of the wounds had clotted by now, and I was certain it could not have inflicted internal injuries, since it was high up on his shoulder. I washed the rest of his body with cold water, then dressed him as best I could before fetching the mountain-survival bag from my pack and tugging it around his shivering form. I made him as comfortable as possible, placing him face down, and put two of our own harpoons next to his right hand.

As William slept, I looked at the bag of medicine. The boatman had been prepared for this moment, I realized, prepared to help a wounded man, not a dead one. And it occurred to me, now, that the young and athletic Two Cuts should have clearly been able to overtake the struggling man with ease, on that long walk to freedom.

He had chosen not to.

So perhaps there had been no intention to kill the young man, an intriguing element of the duel, a puzzling aspect of the brutal walk.

I constructed a windbreak and built a fire. Then, clutching the third harpoon and a vegetable knife from my pack, I walked into the treeline and approached the base of the tower itself.

Now that I examined it closely, the ivory tower was revealed as exactly that – a towering column of shards and lengths of polished bone, broken towards its top to give the illusion, from a distance, of crenellations. It was cold to the touch, almost unnaturally so. It must have had a diameter of fifty yards or more. There were round openings in its walls, high above my head, and I was reminded of pores. I could see vegetation and the dark masses of large nests, tangling and nestling in the spikes and cracks of its shattered rim.

Why had Greenface seemed so frightened of this silent, shining pillar? Or had I misconstrued the scene? I had been a child, they had been glimpses, I had had a vivid imagination and my stories turned on fear, on chase, on quest, indeed, on the childish yet primal and ever-potent trappings of fairy-tale.

She had certainly passed *back* this way, however, and I climbed the wooded hill, away from the tower, looking for signs of the woman but finding none as I explored the fragments of stone and ivory wall that had once reached from high ground to the shore and the tower itself.

At the top of the hill, leaning against one of the massive pines that crowned the ridge, I looked back to the lake, reassuring myself that all was peaceful and safe down at the shore, where William lay healing. Then I picked my way over the summit of the hill, to see if I could discern a way ahead for us, and my life seemed to stop for a moment, my senses stunned by the vision that was laid out before me.

From just below the ridge to the high cliffs in the far distance, the whole land was slowly turning, a vast whirlpool of thick forest and white ruins, steadily draining down to a centre that was obscured by mist and shadow. Everywhere, the cliffs were crumbling, sheets and pillars of rock crashing into the dense canopy to be swirled downwards. And yet, the towers and turrets, the gleaming white walls of castles or shaped outcrops of white rock that were being carried by the turn of the land, seemed from the pattern of the flow to be spreading *out* from the sinkhole itself, to pass, increasingly battered and broken, to the outer edge of the turning land!

The earth before me shuddered, shook and groaned as it was both swallowed and recreated – two swirling streams of forest, land and ruin, moving against each other, an entwining spiral.

I followed the winding path towards the deep cut that separated me from the edge of this whirlpool of forest, aware of the vibration of the hill below me, the increasing sense of instability, the proximity of change, of sudden destruction.

Creatures, too, were moving away from the shifting wood. Whether they had come from the centre of the maelstrom or not I couldn't tell. I heard their movement through the trees, listened to their growls, chatters and cries. Three creatures of enormous size, their skin almost black, and thick like an elephant's, moved across my path, each towering above the trees, walking on massive legs. The tallest turned to look at me and bellowed. Its head was wide, tapering to a short trunk which flexed like a cat's tail. Tiny eyes challenged me. It stamped a huge foot against the ground and I felt the tremor.

It moved away, a creature from the long-gone time of the world, some precursor of the elephant, but almost bronto-saurian in its shape and movement. And as it cleared the path, crashing through trees, I glimpsed a slim and furtive human shape.

Greenface!

She was watching me. She seemed startled to see me, glanced round nervously, then ran into the cover of the under-growth. I ran towards her, shouting out. Something struck a tree close by, then I felt a glancing blow on my shoulder and was aware of a shaped stone crashing into the bushes behind me.

I stopped and pulled into cover, watching through the trees, scanning the light, and soon she moved into the open again.

'Please don't run from me!' I called. Could she understand? Christ, she was an inhabitant of *my* world.

She shouted something at me, which I took as a good sign, but which communicated nothing intelligible. 'Don't be frightened,' I called again. I realized I was holding the harpoon and quickly stuck it in my belt. A second later I felt a stinging pain in my leg and saw a short, thin dart hanging from my trousers, the point having grazed my flesh. I pulled it out of my clothing and kept it.

She uttered the high, bird-like trill that I had so often heard in my early visions, and immediately was gone, vanishing silently, certainly heading towards the edge of the arboreal drowning-pool.

I was about to follow when a creature that looked like a cross between a warthog and a jackal darted into my path, snarled, salivated, backed away and erected horny spines around its neck, a dangerous looking frill, signalling clearly that it was about to charge.

I fled. The creature bounded after me, but stopped when I turned suddenly and threatened with the harpoon. Its stink was overpowering. Canine teeth jutted from pugnacious jowls and its tiny eyes narrowed, gleaming yellow.

The land shifted, the trees around me bowed slightly, seemed to stretch from their roots. The hog, whatever it was, took steps backward, then slunk away.

I returned to the summit of the ridge from where I watched the steady spiral flow around the sump for more than an hour, hoping that I would see the woman again, wondering how, if at all, I was to traverse this moving land.

A different trill, on the whistle that Five Cuts had given me, reminded me that I had a friend, someone whose life was in my immediate care, and that there might be danger back along the shore of the lake.

Again the whistle, and again I returned to the camp. A day or so had passed since we had first landed here.

William Finebeard was up, fully clothed and agitated, in pain still but substantially recovered from the exhaustion of the walk and the wounds. He beckoned to me urgently as I slipped and ran down the last slope, then quietened my questions, leading the way along the edge of the lake, away from the tower. I could see already that the dry mud shore was marked with the hoof-like prints of several animals. After half a mile, William held me back and pointed to the tree-line.

Five small, horse-like creatures were grazing at the lower branches. They were probably the same animals I had seen previously. Their colour was a deep brown, with black stripes over their rumps and manes of brilliant gold. As they reached up on their hindlegs to browse they revealed stubby toes at the sides of the central hoof. Small-eared, smaller faced, as high as a tall child at the shoulder when on all fours, their relationship to horses was obvious enough, and I felt sure they were an extinct precursor of that animal.

William's idea was to catch them – or two of them – and use them as transport.

'And how do you propose to do that, exactly?'

'I don't propose to do *anything*,' he indicated. 'You build a trap. I'll drive them into it, then you close the trap on two of them . . .'

'That simple, eh? And then?'

'You smack each on its face in turn. That stuns it. Get on its back, tie yourself with rope to the creature's neck, and ride with it until it's exhausted.'

'You've done this before?'

'No. But I've heard about it.'

'So have I. A lifetime of westerns.'

He didn't understand, of course, but clearly he had encountered the *experience* of taming what I believed to be a species of *hipparion*, and knew it could be done. Indeed, he established that the icon-hunters sometimes traded for these creatures, though hunger usually fated the beasts for the pot – stewed with sacred statues? – and away from the duties of carriage.

Despite his confidence that the proto-horses could be tamed, William's injuries and my nervousness combined to cause failure and bruising.

The hippari were moving slowly through the trees, paying little attention to anything but their meal, and we set up a leg-snare below a thick bunch of cut leaves, dangling juicily from a branch. As the small herd came by the smallest of the horses began to nibble and stepped into the snare, but when I yanked it tight the animal charged us, turned and kicked out with its hindlegs, its haunches flaying wildly left to right, the sharp horn on its vestigial toes suddenly scything the air like sharpened kitchen knives.

It landed a glancing blow to my arm and I withdrew. The creature reached down and worried at the rope, leaving it where it lay. It snorted, then turned to the shore. Suddenly all five hippari raced along the lake's edge, kicking in that wild way, turning inland a half mile distant and disappearing from view.

I helped my young friend to his feet, aware that he was in pain through his smiles.

'Perhaps not the *best* idea you've had, William.'

'I'm sure it worked for the icon-hunters,' he seemed to be saying, as together we limped back to our camp.

I made William rest and recover for a full day, against his stronger instincts, his more reckless wishes. He wanted to go back across the lake, back to the eldest sister. As I sat with him, among the bulrushes where the shore was drier, listening to the sounds of the prehistoric forest behind us, I could feel his love, his loss, like a strangling grip. He smiled, he frowned, he laughed out loud as he muttered words, he wept and smashed his fist into the dry mud.

Time and again he said her name, shaking his head, so angry with fate.

And so I was in a quandary. By the swirling wood, Greenface might still be prowling, gathering courage as I would have to gather courage to pass into the maelstrom of that sucking land. I could get to her, I could try to establish contact with her, I could embark upon the persuasion, the attempt to bring her back to the violent entity that was her male shadow.

But here was a man who was shuffling between the deeper world and the Hinterland, held in an endless cycle of hope and despair by the simple fact that on the far shore of the lake, in a community of prehistoric fisherfolk, was the woman he loved. So simple, so agonizing, and if William was a representation of that basic drive, the basic conundrum that has haunted lovers from Australopithecine times at least, my own response was probably of a similar great antiquity to those ancient and forgotten forebears:

I simply couldn't abandon him in his time of need. For the moment, his desperation for the companionship of the woman he loved powerfully outweighed my own need for the resolution of a problem, for the seeking out of Greenface; for the saving of Natalie. I can't explain it, but for a while, at least, I abandoned my daughter instead.

We sat long into the night, by a fire which I kept stoked high with wood, and slowly and carefully ate the fish that the boatman had given us. We laughed as I consigned the fish-gum to the deeper waters – speculating that it might creep back during the night and sneak into the pack again – and lay back and talked, he in his language, I in mine, and somehow despite the strangeness of the words, we understood each other.

I had made the mistake of trying to 'identify' William's base-culture from his clothes, which were distinctly medieval. In fact, he had traded for the garments with the icon-hunters, whom he had joined a year or so before, shortly after what he called the Great Cold.

'What did you trade?'

'Part of what I was carrying, the least part, though the icon-hunters aren't aware of it.'

'And what exactly were you carrying?'

His pack was very small; he had crude weapons, winter furs, odds and ends of wood and bone, nothing that could be called tradeable.

'Ten steps from the winter dance,' he said. 'And the knowledge of how to mark them.'

'How many steps altogether? In the winter dance.'

'I don't know. As many as exist when all the steps come back together. There are summer dances, and spring dances . . .'

'Autumn dances?'

'Yes. Of course.'

'And the knowledge of how to mark them. How's that kept?'

'Marks on wood, marks on stone. All together, they make a great dance.'

'But you only know ten steps, and only from one season. Why is that valuable?'

'It's valuable if you've lost it. It's valuable if you don't understand its meaning. It's especially valuable when all the steps have returned from exile, in whatever sons and daughters have now become the dancers.'

'What was the winter dance for?'

'To encourage the spring.'

'Fertility stuff,' I said with a smile at the earnest man. 'I'm sorry I asked. I'm disappointed. What happens if you don't dance the winter dance?'

'No spring comes. There are no fish in the rivers. No meat for the spear. No life on the land.'

'But has that ever happened? I mean . . . that the dance wasn't danced and the spring never came?'

He seemed amused. 'Of course. That's why the Great Cold came. It was too late to save the land, so the dance was sent into exile. A song played through bone pipes by children will bring us together again. However many, from wherever we are, and when we share our knowledge, and the dance is danced, the spring will return.'

'The Ice Age. I understand, now. You're a creature of the Ice Age. Well I'm damned. I had you far later than that. But who sent you into exile?'

'My last winter father. My own father sang his song to me, but my last winter father was a long gone man, and a wise one. He shared the dances among his children and they went away from the tundra, away from the cold, waiting to come back when – (and here he spoke a name which was almost unpronounceable) – has died from the poison of (another name, another confusing image).'

I felt like saying to him that in the libraries of my own land his story was listed in a thousand different ways – The Wasteland, most notably – his fears were now demons, his hopes now gods, his own part in the dance an element of myth that would have been pieced together like an ancient skull, fixed and fiddled to make it conform to the current way of thought and culture.

The moon rose over the far shore, a moon as I have always fancied it existed in legend, quite huge, almost full, a silver jewel that made the lake gleam, the land filled with night shadow.

We moved back into the crude shelter, and soon William was asleep. I dozed for a while and woke to the gentle sound of splashing water.

The five hippari had returned and were spread out along the lake's edge, drinking and grazing the reeds. They moved almost silently, constantly alert, the leader in particular watching the wooded hill, the gleaming tower, the paths through the forest to the dangerous world beyond.

And then, as I watched these ancient creatures, I saw a swifter shadow, a human figure darting across the muddy shore, stooping and drinking, then gathering a handful of the taller rushes.

I rose and walked towards her. She saw me, hesitated, eyes bright in the moonglow. A moment later she ran again to the trees, head low, body lithe.

'Greenface . . .' I whispered, then called her name more strongly. 'Please come back.'

I was apprehensive, aware that my skin still itched where her dart had struck me, but went anyway to the spot where she'd vanished.

'Greenface!' I called again, not too loudly. There was only silence. After a few minutes I returned to the ivory tower, but when I was a hundred yards from where the woman had slipped into darkness I heard furtive movement behind me, someone going deeper.

She had been there. She had watched me. She had heard my voice.

I don't know why, but I felt she was curious, or linked to me in some other way. And it was a feeling, an instinct, that carried with it the tenuous thread of hope.

21

I was being shaken awake, violently, urgently. William was struggling out of the foil and felt survival bag, shouting at me to 'Get up! Quickly! Up!'

I quickly grasped the crisis. The woods behind were being trampled and crushed with a nightmare noise as dawn signalled new arrivals at the shore.

We had time to grab our packs and supplies and fling ourselves into the lee of the white, bone tower. Seconds later, elephantine legs, mottled grey and black, pounded the scrub where we had been lying, shattered the crude windbreak, carrying the first of four of the huge, short-trunked creatures down to the lake's edge.

They bellowed and roared, waded into the water and used the short snouts to drink and spray each other. They defecated, they wallowed, they enjoyed themselves. Then one mounted a second and the water churned, the air reverberated with trumpeted irritation as she tried to escape the attention.

All along the shore of the lake, creatures had come to drink, frolic and annoy each other. Dense, dark flocks of birds circled and squabbled, while solitary winged giants, feathers gleaming with metallic golds and purples, swooped and snapped at their smaller kin in an aerial dance that flowed and swirled, then suddenly exploded like some avian display of fireworks.

A snarling in the bushes preceded the slavering jaws of one of the fox-jackals I had seen in the Hinterland. Other, similar sounds, and the flashing of green, quizzical animal eyes, suggested more than one of these beasts was investigating the possibility of a human breakfast.

Most sinister of all, the sleek, red-furred body of a big cat slunk around the tower, dawn-light catching the curved fangs that curled below its lower jaw. *Smilodon*, the sabre-tooth. It watched us for a few seconds, breath rasping in its lungs, then slipped into the forest, scattering birds from the canopy.

The lake-side restaurant was open, and my Ice-Age friend and I had no safe table among its customers.

Nevertheless, I practically had to haul William away from the waterside. He complained bitterly, trying to shrug me off, almost pleading with me. There were no tears in his eyes, but a frown on his face that aged him with its forlorn despair.

I tried to tell him that there was no way back across the lake, not without risking the eldest sister's life, indeed, without forfeiting his own, but of course he knew this and indicated that if I would help him for a day, he would stay with me three days. That was all. Just three days in my quest for Greenface, and then – and this was the deal – the two of us (three, if the woman was amenable to the return to the Hinterland) would build a raft and return, by night, to the village, where he in turn could find his loved one and aid her to freedom.

In the meantime, he would start to build a stronghold here, where the ivory ruins of another people would be the shell from which he would construct his fort. Even as he spoke, he was pacing out the distance – here the stables for the hippari that he would capture and tame, there the harbour, out across the reedbeds; the watchtower was obvious, and up on the hill, among the fallen walls, the main body of the city – to which he would bring Ethne; and in which he would spend his life with her. Of all the nightmares I had expected to encounter in the hidden land of my unconscious, frustrated love was not one of them. But then, neither had these encounters with the ancient world of mammals, although I should have anticipated such a presence in the Midax Deep after witnessing the fights between Greyface, Greenface and some of the more rampaging of the grotesque creatures.

For a day, then, I helped him mark out the borders of his hold, using lengths of creeper and broken branches to define the limits of his fort. We assessed the woodland for its use in making fences against the behemoths which constantly emerged from the maelstrom, stumbling and thundering towards the lake. We avoided all talk of strategy, of the way he would 'invade' the fishing village to bring Ethne to his new-found land.

The following dawn, we began the steady climb through the pinewoods, away from the tower, towards the dull sky above the shifting earth. I had expected William to be astonished by the sight beyond the highest of the ridges, but he simply scanned the distant cliffs, then looked to the right (I had no idea of compass directions) and pointed.

Had he been here before?

'Not here, but somewhere similar. There are many of these moving lands. Some suck forest and the white towers into the darkness, some, like this one, bring them out to the light. The trick is to navigate around the outer circles. Don't penetrate too far towards the centre. Otherwise you become lost in the Eye.'

'Not a good thing to do?'

'Not if you want to go home.'

'You seem to know a lot. What's within the Eye?'

'I've heard no songs that tell the answer to that.'

'Then how do you know it's dangerous?'

He grinned at me. '*Because* I've heard no songs that tell the answer to that!'

For all his good humour, William was weary, now, and the deeper of his wounds had begun to bleed again. I could smell it, and in this primeval landscape, such a scent should be avoided. I quickly washed him, patched him again, aware suddenly and with some concern that he needed two or three stitches, surgery beyond my capability or resources; but I got him moving. I was looking for a sign of Greenface, half suspecting that she was not far ahead of us, perhaps torn between full escape back into the Deep of her world and an attachment to the ghost in the machine of the land which she inhabited.

'You should return to the lake,' I said to him, but he wouldn't hear of it.

'She's close, Jack. I'll stay with you until she comes to you. A promise is a promise. She's *close*.'

And indeed, after a few hours following the natural ledges and ridges of the country towards the high cliffs that might mark the beginning of new territory, we found her first direct communication with me, two crossed branches in a forest glade that opened from the dry path of a winding stream. She had tied one of her bone darts so that its point indicated the lake. Two locks of her hair were tied to the crossed boughs, each matted with fresh blood.

Leave me alone. Go back.

William intuited the meaning as quickly as did I, and was exasperated when I simply took the dart and dismantled the cross.

'She can't be more than a mile ahead of us. Don't you see? She's running, but she can't hide. The moment I entered her realm there was a link between us and she has to sever that link to be free of me.' William smiled sympathetically and shook his head, then indicated that when he had been a boy a close friend of his had been trampled by a juvenile 'tusker' (a mammoth) and had talked a similar sort of nonsense ever after.

For the better part of two days, Greenface led us on a labyrinthine chase through the hills and valleys that circled round the swirling Eye. She was a fast runner, but not skilled at hiding her tracks or traces. Our limited talents in noticing the signs of our quarry were compensated for more than adequately by that laxity.

Twice I saw her, surprised at how far ahead of us she had run. On the first occasion I glimpsed her as a distant shape moving over a bare hill, crouching as she searched for danger; on the second, she was standing between two towering cedars, her arms stretched out like Christ on the Cross, staring back across the valley to where William and I picked our way carefully down the steep slope. She was against the setting sun and remained there motionless for the twenty minutes that I stood and stared at her. Was she again saying: *leave me alone*? Or was her behaviour an echo of the rituals that had imbued her life when once she had lived upon the earth, a prayer at dusk amongst the dark wood of the great trees?

'She'll set traps for us,' William had warned, two days ago, and his words had made us cautious, and therefore slowed our progress, and Greenface was escaping.

Now I threw caution to the wind – a metaphor that I mimed with a slash across my throat and a puff of air across my palm, tossed away carelessly, gestures that again exasperated the Ice Age hunter-dancer – and ran on ahead, slipping and sliding down the defile to a thin sparkle of water, and the cedar-covered slope beyond.

The figure of the woman stayed still for several minutes more, then abruptly disappeared.

I stood among the cedars, dwarfed by their massive size, made calm and clear-headed by their heavy scent and the semi-tropical heat that bathed this new border. Everything was very still; the tremor in the earth had gone. I was not at all sure which way the Eye lay, whether behind me, or ahead. I had become disorientated and I could easily have been going deeper into this unconscious land, or back towards the place of churches, bulls and channels, the Hinterland where Angela could send me signals.

I was lost, and I felt the vast distance between my isolated eye and the full return to consciousness as a form of panic. Suddenly, I wanted to go home. Suddenly I had had enough.

Behind me, William gasped up the slope, flexing his neck with discomfort, probably from the unhealed wound, dripping with a sweat he had rarely known. A man of the cold, a carrier of the winter dance, he was more alien in this hot forest, this tranquil place of giants, than I was, and it was clear now that he had come as far as he could manage in his determination to assist me.

'There'll be traps,' he said again, shaking his head. 'You mustn't do this. You mustn't pursue so carelessly. She's warned you enough. She doesn't want you, my friend. Give up the ghost . . .'

'I can't.'

'Jack! Give up the ghost!'

'I *can't*.'

And yet . . . I could. I was frightened. William saw my hesitation and breathed a sigh of relief, fitted neatly in between his striving gasps for breath.

'Let's go back to the lake. It's getting hot.' A breeze stirred the giant cedars. A voice whispered 'Fetch her back' and a shadow ran around me, a small girl.

I turned to follow the dream, or memory, an illusion, anyway, reminding me that even now, as I voyaged in my own machine, Natalie was playing with the grey-faced phantom, listening to his funny stories, shedding ghosts of her own, perhaps, peeled away by the entity that had escaped me, as it waited for me to fulfil a bargain: a life for a life.

I had to go on – *and yet I felt called back!* – I had to make a last try to catch up with the woman . . .

Was I being called?

Disturbed by the sense of anxiety that pervaded both this forest of towering cedars and my own perceptions, I sent William back to the camp.

'You don't need to come any further. Why don't you wait for me by the lake? We'll cross together, to rescue Ethne.'

His eyes brightened suddenly. 'You *will* help me then?'

'If I can. And with all my heart. A promise is a promise.' I looked through the forest. 'I need one more try for Greenface, though. If I can't catch her now, I'll have to think again. But I'll come back to you first.'

'Thank you. I feel very weak, just now.' He was glad to be released, I realized. 'I need you, Jack. If I see her, I'll want to kiss her. I need you to remind me of the danger!'

'I'll do that, all right.'

William gathered his things and walked away from me, already thinking again about Ethne. As he departed he stumbled slightly, glancing back apprehensively. I could see smears of crimson on his waist and left arm. He was bleeding again, he had exerted himself too much. But he was a strong young man and now, with the pressure of running off him, he would have time to recoup fully before attempting to cross the lake.

'I won't be long,' I called. He turned and stared at me, raising his arms in question.

I called again, 'I'll come back to you within a day or so. But *wait* for me. I'll not be long!'

He smiled and nodded, raising a hand in parting. He was soon gone, dropping down the slope as he retraced our earlier passage from the lake. I felt very sad to see him go.

This forest, though, was a wonderful place, its majesty and tranquillity reached to my heart. A rich, golden light filled the spaces between the monumental trunks of the cedars. The ground was soft and yielding as I walked. The wind was musical as it flowed in the clearings, a murmur of comfort.

Like an animal, all senses pricked, I moved between the pools of light, and I was at peace here; but there was something else, something I knew with all my heart.

Greenface was close by!

She had waited for me. She was watching me from among the trees, a shadow against the buttressed columns, moving around me, behind me, always keeping out of sight.

I walked for an hour without looking back, then stopped in

a cedar grove and talked out loud, reasoning that since Grey-face had been able to communicate with me in his various, violent, persuasive ways, the woman too might understand the language of the man in whom she moved.

'Your partner has a hold over my daughter. I think he means to kill her unless you return to him. I don't understand why. He wants you back. I know you're afraid, but I don't understand your fear, and I don't understand your partner's anger. Please come back with me. Please complete your journey . . .'

She was so close.

And yet she stayed in hiding.

A few minutes after my loud talk to the forest I heard movement ahead of me and continued to jog and walk along the rough track. I hoped to see the woman, to glimpse her again, but she was circumspect, now, in the way she observed me, and besides, William's advice about traps had begun to haunt me. I was alert for snares and trip-wires to such an extent that my attention was not focused.

I tried a merry dance-and-dart around the sprawling roots of the silent giants, hoping to surprise her, to encounter her, even to entice her with the simple humour of my capering.

Birdless, this forest, no creature stirred in the canopy to suggest her movement, her alarm at my antics. I was a lone man going mad with the scent of cedar, tripping on the ground-briar that grew in profusion.

But she *was* there, waiting for me, and she caught me at dusk, with the sun reddening and deepening, a light reminiscent of that in the Hinterland . . .

For some time the land had been descending towards a narrow valley, a steep sided gorge, blocked in the distance by the sheer wooden wall of some as yet inidentifiable structure. Whatever had been lodged, askew and broken at the bottom of the valley, was huge, and as the darkness grew deeper I could make out lights and movement in its region, but no further sense of anything other than that.

I was so curious about this vast construction, which

seemed almost to grow from the valley walls, that I had stumbled into the trap before I realized it.

Whether by charms, magic or otherwise, or by a skilful manipulation of the thorny undergrowth, a cage of yellow briar-rose curled suddenly around me, snaking from the earth, flexing from the bushes, winding into a prison that nipped, snagged and tugged at me. The scent of the rose was sweet, the prick of the curved thorns unbearable as I tried to move. I stood quite still, therefore, embraced by the tangling bush, listening to the stealthy approach of the woman who had snared me.

She circled me twice at a distance like a prowling animal, studying me. She seemed almost naked, having rid herself of the heavy cloak, the belt of clattering knives, the small roll of fur, the blowpipe and spears. By the last glow of twilight I could see the complex design of green lines on her face, the patterns on her tight, hard chest, above the loose tunic with its glitter of shells, the scars in neat rows down the front of each thigh. She wore tight sandals on her feet, strapped firmly to her calves.

'I'm hurting,' I said quietly. Even breathing drew thorns into my skin. It felt as if the briar-cage was tightening slowly.

'Who are you?' she asked suddenly. 'Why are you following me?'

Her voice was very soft, the accent lilting, the words, at least as I perceived them, English, which surprised me but didn't startle me. *I know you!*

'You travelled in me,' I said. 'There was a man with you. I saw you often in my dreams. Don't you recognize me?'

She stood. Without the cloak she seemed willowy. She was as tall as me. She came over, dark eyes shining, and peered through the briar. The sudden curiosity in her face served to melt the hardness. She was lovely to look at, full-lipped, high-cheeked, dark-eyed. I can't find better words to describe the subtlety of her beauty which was not in any way marred by the intricate patterns of green lines and small designs that were pricked out on her skin.

'Yes,' she whispered. 'Now that I look at you . . . I've seen you in my dreams too. And you are the face that guarded the horn gate. I was frightened of you. I couldn't pass through.'

'Do you have a name?'

'My name is Ahk'Nemet.' (This is a phonetic attempt at the word she used to indicate her name.)

'And your friend? The man you were running with?'

'Not my friend. My brother. His given name is Baalgor. It's a common name.'

Not her friend? I had seen them making love; years ago, I had described the passion with relish to the eager children of my class at school.

'Baalgor has sent me to bring you back to him.'

She spat on the ground, suddenly angry. 'I wondered why you were following me. Go back to him. I intend to return to the wounded land.'

Those were her words. *The wounded land.*

'I've run long enough. I can't run any more.'

'Where is the wounded land?'

She smiled. 'Where a land lies bleeding and abandoned. Where else? It's my home. I belong there. I should never have followed Baalgor. I should never have done what I did.'

Intrigued, I asked, 'What is the name of your land?'

'Gl'Thaan Em,' she said, and I repeated the phonemes, aware at once of their familiarity. *Glanum?* Could the two places be the same?

'I know that land,' I told her from my thorn cage. 'Only I know it as a city. Called Glanum. A city of shrines.'

'There are many shrines in Gl'Thaan Em,' she said, imitating my own expression. 'They are the Bull places, the sanctuary woods, the revengers, the snorting pursuers of the destroyers – like me, Gl'Thaan Em is the wall that holds the beasts; but now it is the wounded land. Baalgor and I did the wounding. He has escaped through the horn gate. But for me, there is only one thing to do: go back and die. I must do it. The Bull place that follows me is too close, and to die beneath its stones is to die for ever, and that frightens me.'

'What did you do to – Gl'Thaan Em – to be so afraid?'

'What does it matter? I couldn't cross the horn gate, so my only life, now, is to go back and hide among the shadows. I'm tired of running. I'm tired of being followed. You're no bull-revenger, but you threaten me, and I can't live with your shadow over mine.'

The rose thorn tightened slightly, cutting into my face and arms so painfully that I cried out.

'I have a daughter. Baalgor will kill her unless I bring you back.'

Ahk'Nemet was already walking away, scratching at her backside beneath the tunic, shaking her head. She fetched her furs, cloak and weapons from behind a cedar, stepped back into the gloom, a slim shape against the fires burning along the top of the wooden city beyond, where the valley narrowed. She was staring at me again.

'I have a life too.'

'Then come with me. Come back through the horn gate and persuade Baalgor home to the wounded land—'

She laughed. 'Can a camel graze on the mother moon?'

I assumed her metaphor was intended to express impossibility.

'All my life I've dreamed of you. I saw you running. I saw the bull. I saw the white towers, the rivers, the cliffs, the fights with nightmare creatures, the vigorous sex you seemed to enjoy with Baalgor, the way you hunted. I watched you open your bowels each morning and bleed with each moon. I've felt your fear, your hope, your pleasures and your distress. You're a part of my life, Nemet. Baalgor too. You live inside me. *I* am the gate through which he passed. And I'm the gate *you* refused to open. I am a dream within my own dream, and you are a dream within the same dreamer. I *am* that dreamer. And my daughter's life is being scoured out, cored from the inside like a ripe fruit. I have one life, one daughter, one chance to save her. Please come back with me. Please come back to Greyface.'

'Greyface?' She laughed out loud. 'Baalgor?'

'Yes.'

'It's true. There's the grey of death in him, and the grey of his beard, and that white clay he uses to blind the eyes that cover his body soon goes grey. Greyface. A good name for the eye in a corpse.' She hesitated. 'But I can't help you. I have to go home.'

'What about my daughter?'

'Teach her to fight. Or have another child.'

Her callous words inflamed me. I felt a call home as urgent as any need I could imagine, and I tore at the briar, ripping my flesh, but broke it down, careful of my eyes, shedding the cage and howling with rage and pain as I stumbled down the valley, looking for the running woman, listening for her.

'Come back! Oh Christ, come back!'

I glimpsed her. She was in the night shadow of the towering wooden wall, below the carved and fire-illuminated totems that leaned out from the ramparts. I could hear animals, a cacophany of sound inside this fortress; and drums beating a fast tattoo, and the screech and whine of ancient instruments. She had gone towards a low gate, a simple hole in the wall with, as ever, the skull of a horned animal leaning out across it. For a second I saw her figure, crouching, then darkness took her. By the time I reached this gate she had vanished. I peered into the tunnel, aware of the redness of the light at the far end. Ducking down, I went in, feeling my way below the thunder of drums and dancing, and the vibration of the creatures that were being paraded within this structure.

Suddenly I was on the side of a hill, blinking against the deep red of a familiar sun. There was a swift movement behind me, but I was too late to turn and defend myself, and a foot kicked me between the shoulders, sending me tumbling into the unknown.

'Leave me alone!' she called after me, but I was lost already, slipping down the slope of land, falling endlessly it seemed, the sun moving above me, the glitter of silver catching my eye, until—

I came down in dust and bruises to rest against the angled roof of the church.

This was the Hinterland again.

Somewhere below me, my name was being called, and I began to move as if in a dream, surfacing from a sea of unconscious towards a brighter light, the steady chanting of my name.

I thought briefly of William, waiting for me by the lake shore. How long would he wait before recklessly crossing the water to Ethne, to a place where his death was assured?

'Sorry, William . . . she tricked me . . . but I'll be back . . . a promise is a promise . . . I'll be back to help you . . .'

PART FIVE
Flesh and Shadow

22

He had imagined the return from the Hinterland would be like coming out of a dream, but the sensation was quite different. Instead of experiencing confusion, the dissolution of reality, in fact the journey, his close encounters, remained as real, as painful, as they had seemed at the time. The trap and the trick by Greenface were minutes only in his past. He could still smell the odour of the thundering beasts inside the wooden-walled town, still hear the dancing and music and he was in pain from the rose thorns. Nothing fragmented into ghostly disconnection. He might simply have stepped through a garden gate from one house to another.

'I was so close,' Jack said as he sat on the couch and was shoulder-massaged by strong fingers, while a wan-faced Angela pulled and stretched his tired fingers. 'She tricked me – she's afraid to come back, but I have a hold on her. I've got to try again . . .'

'For the moment, just relax,' Steve said, passing him a glass of water.

'I'd rather have a beer.'

'I'm sure you would. But no alcohol until we've debriefed your Midax shadow.'

'Hurry, then. Hurry. I've got to get rid of this taste of fish gum!'

But there was something wrong, he could sense it in the atmosphere of the room, he had known it from the moment the Midax state had terminated – and it was transparent in

Angela's demeanour. They had called him back from the Deep because there was difficulty at home.

'Natalie? Is it Natalie?'

Angela encouraged him back to the couch, calming him. 'Natalie's fine. The ghost of Greyface has been back, more funny stories, but she seems fine.'

'*Seems* fine?'

'She's *fine*. There's nothing to worry about!'

'Then why was I called back? I'd almost reached the woman. We even spoke for a few minutes. If you hadn't interrupted, I might have made a better contact.'

Steve was watching him solemnly, arms crossed. 'You have a slight problem. Something we hadn't expected.'

Angela helped Jack to stand and led him to a mirror. At once he realized he was in *real* pain, not remembered pain, the sting of thorn, an itching on his right leg where a small arrow had grazed his flesh. In the mirror he could see the marks of briar-rose on his cheeks, forehead and chin, all of them iodined and treated. Every wound he had inflicted on himself in his escape from the cage was open and had been bleeding in his *real*-world body.

'Like stigmata . . .' he breathed.

'*Exactly* like stigmata,' Steve said from across the room. 'As I said, we hadn't expected this. We could almost follow your disasters by the bruises and wounds that erupted or appeared on your body.'

It was a shocking thought and Jack stared across the room, trying to understand the full implications of the phenomenon. 'Then I'm in actual physical danger in the dream?'

'So it would seem. And it's *not* a dream, Jack.'

'I know. I know. But . . . if I get killed, I don't come back . . . Is that a fair assumption?' He rubbed the more painful of the cuts, which was still seeping.

'That's hard to say. A difficult experiment to set up, as I'm sure you appreciate.'

'But if I *did* die in the Deep – it now looks like I'll die on the couch! *Shit!*'

'We don't *know* that, Jack. Everything on your body is superficial – deeper trauma may be prevented by your mind's own will to live, its own defences. Not *everything* that's happened to you is detectable. No food in your gut, or changed blood sugar, for example, just a certain "fishy" taste in your mouth . . .'

'Fish gum! God, it *didn't* go away.'

'So relax. But next time, treat rose bushes with more respect. Please?'

Jack agreed, too tired to argue further, too weary to confront Steve's apparent complacence. But he was thinking of *stigmata*, those marks that could spontaneously appear on the bodies of devout, deeply religious, entranced or hypnotized subjects.

What journey into the unconscious, what events beyond their own Hinterlands, might be the reason for the appearance of such wounds? He had a sudden, appalling vision of journeys towards crucifixion, the pursuit of self sacrifice in the deeper mind, where a dream-time torture could result in a spiritual suffering in the ordinary world.

But what if they died there, hanging on the tree? Or drowned in the crystal waters of a lake? Or crushed by the feet of creatures from Prehistory?

The 'reports' he had made whilst in the Midax Deep were fragmentary. His account of the Hinterland was very clear, his experience transmitting to the sleeping body, with its wired-up pen and paper, and producing an eighty-percent coherent description of the events there. But almost from the moment he had passed the waterfall the periods of automatic writing had become sporadic.

Watching the pattern of the writing, the frequency of the fragments, Steve had begun to form the intriguing idea that within the pre-conscious realm there were 'echo channels' (for want of an as yet better description), echo channels to the conscious mind, like small, breezy passages through which echoing and enhanced glimpses of the pre-conscious could be achieved. He likened them to the seepage of water down a mountain-side which drained the hill despite the full, raging tumble of a river. The river carried the potent symbolic and representational sensory experience from the pre-conscious; the drainage pores simply relieved the pressure.

Jack's real-time experience beyond the Hinterland had occasionally 'echoed' through these pores in the mind/ under-mind barrier, and because of the Midax conditioning, the sleeping body of the journeyman had scrawled an account of what was happening for those few minutes, before relapsing into a motionless, coma state.

To get the full story, Jack would have to re-live the whole several days, and he did this now, in as much detail as he could remember.

Later, he watched Natalie as she and six other children, two of them boys, danced a circular dance to music from *The Jungle Book* played on a tape recorder. It was an hilarious experience. Natalie always took one extra pace to the left when the rest of the group had swung to the right. And one extra step to the right when the rest of the group . . .

The confusion, the expressions of concentration and anxiety on the children's faces, reminded Jack of his own attempts at dancing as a teenager, at school and at Exburgh's two discotheques. A flamingo in failed flight, Angela had described it. 'But you're so cute – it doesn't matter'.

He'd never understood 'cute' – it was an imported expression that for a while found popularity with the girls in his school. He just knew it was a good thing to be.

He was called away from the play-group and back to the brainstorming session in the conference room, where a book of prehistoric animals now lay open among the scattered sheets of the transcript of his journey.

Earlier, there had been a great deal of amusement at the

transformation of his clothing into bathing trunks. There was a 'wild card' factor in the process by which the central self rose independently in the Hinterland, but it seemed that whatever reality had been bent going in, it remained immutable for the duration.

More intriguing was the apparent circularity of the deeper world. Jack had certainly imagined that he had been travelling *away* from the cathedral and the Bull-temple, only to turn up on its far side. This phenomenon may have been linked to the Eye.

The world within had been shaped by his own imagination, his experience, and the experience of his life and his race. There were more puzzles than there were likely to be answers: why did the Fisherfolk and the Ice Age adventurer not speak his language, yet communicate with surprising facility in sign and gesture, whereas Greenface and Greyface spoke an *accented* English. Their origins must have been different to the other human forms populating the Midax Deep.

One by one he identified the extinct mammals he had witnessed. Some of them had held a special fascination for him as a child, when he had visited natural history museums in Washington and Arizona, travelling with his family.

'The small horses you saw,' Angela turned the book towards him, 'two small toes beside the hoof, were probably *hipparion*, early grazers, extinct about two million years ago.'

'I'd remembered. William wants to tame them.'

'The huge creature might have been an elephant of some sort, but more likely *indricotherium*: a hornless rhinoceros, foliage browser, found in Asia, biggest land mammal that ever lived, which is why it's probably being generated in the Deep.'

The picture of this giant was indeed a reasonable reflection of the crushing monsters that had come down to the lake to drink at dawn.

The question, now, was the extent to which these reconstructions were behaving according to evolution, or to imagination. If the latter, then he might, for future journeys, 'evolve' a tame horse, and easily-hunted sources of fresh meat. He might de-construct the *smilodonts*, the sabre-tooths, and the beady-eyed hyenas.

The love affair between William and the elder sister was curious, because it was a story, romantic, vengeful, noble, passionate, but still a story. What did it reflect? Aspects of Jack's own sexuality, and experience? His fears, frustrations, buried concerns, secret hopes? Or was it an element of early myth, part of the core of legends that had arisen with awareness in the early human populations?

The one thing that seemed quite clear was that the woman, Ahk'Nemet, was a free agent in this landscape; she and her companion had travelled here, but by all the signs were as alien to the world within as was Real-Time Jack himself.

It had been a long, long day, and Jack was exhausted. He went to the play-group and Natalie came running from the room, face glowing with effort and enjoyment. She was startled by her father's cuts and grazes but let herself be picked up, prodding painfully at the wounds.

'Where've you been?'

'Fishing,' he said, carrying her towards the exit. 'And hunting tiny horses with black stripes and three toes. And running away from giant elephants with short trunks and no tusks and legs like huge trees. And shouting at hungry hyenas and sabre-toothed tigers. And watching forests swallowed into a whirlpool in a valley. And dodging darts blown at me by a woman with a blow-pipe and green tattoos all over her body—'

She closed his tips with two, tight fingers, curious: 'What were the tiny horses called?'

I might have known. Horse-obsession!

'What were they called? *Hipparion*, family *equidae*.'

Natalie thought that was a silly name for a horse. 'Can I ride one?'

'Got to tame one first. They run very fast. And they kick very hard,' he added ruefully. 'Also, you'll need a time machine to about two million years ago.'

The girl suddenly wrinkled her nose. 'You've been eating fish.'

'Unfortunately.'

It was astonishing how his 'dream' had changed his breath.

'You need to brush your teeth.'

'I intend to do a damn sight more than that to them.'

Sand-blasting the inside of his mouth came to mind. But he felt it would be inappropriate to mention this to his daughter.

Natalie's arms were around his neck and she was getting heavy, but seemed to need this comfort. He had been 'away' from his family for four days. As he carried her from the research building to the car park, Angela walking behind with Steve and still in intense discussion, the child placed her hands on her father's face and stared at him with a look that was neither childlike nor adult – a simple stare that froze his blood, accompanied by the words, 'You shouldn't have given up.'

'Natalie?'

But he knew that this wasn't his daughter.

'This is going to cost the girl,' she said coldly. 'How much time do you think I have? You fool! I'll kill everything you love unless you open the gate!'

And before he could speak, she *slapped* him, a hard blow that brought Angela running.

'What's happening? Oh Christ . . . Jack?'

Suddenly the girl giggled and squirmed in her father's arms. Jack's face was stinging and Angela could see the reddening mark. 'He's here?' she whispered, but Jack shook his head. *I don't know.*

Natalie said, 'There *aren't* any elephants with short trunks and no tusks. That's just one of your stories.'

'And quite a story it is too.'

'I want to ride a hippa. A tiny horse.'

'I'll see what I can do.'

Feeling sick with exhaustion and uncertainty, he let Angela drive him home.

23

The day after his return from the Midax Deep was difficult for several reasons. Primarily, his sleep had been disturbed by lucid, crazy dreams, echoes of his experience during the controlled journey, but maddeningly accurate on many of the points that he had either missed, or chosen to ignore. And in particular: that William had been a fair-haired, fair-bearded reflection of Steven Brightmore, and the affronted fisherman, the sturgeon-catcher who had harpooned him to the lake shore, then shunned him from the village, was . . . himself.

He had woken in a state of damp, cold anxiety, and was made more irritable to find Angela in her small study, poring over the day's transcripts, scribbling marginal notes and talking to herself.

'Come back to bed.'

'I can't sleep, Jack. This is too wild. My head's buzzing.'

'I need to hold you. I'm wild too, my dreams, they're crazy. I feel very stressed.'

'I know. You're sweating like a man with a guilty conscience! Make some tea. Oh, and check on Nattie, would you?'

Too confused to demonstrate the sudden anger he felt at his wife's apparent complacency, he stalked the house in the deep dark, and finally made tea when he saw the first, faint glimmer of light along the ridge of hills behind the house.

And as if awakened by that same first light, the girl came into the kitchen clutching her favourite stuffed toy, a grinning fox, and declaimed that she wanted to find a tiny horse to ride. She was wide awake, raring to go, urgent to find a black-striped, three-toed *hipparion*, and her activity was so noisy, so determined that the rest of the world awoke, and the birds stirred, and the light increased nervously outside, brought into being by this small focus of energy.

Having been unable to sleep, now Jack felt tired. It was four-thirty in the morning.

He spent the first part of the day ringing round to riding schools and stables. 'A small horse, preferably black or grey, three toed if possible . . .'

Natalie was racing around the house, already convinced that she was going to ride a 'hippa'. She became frustrated towards midday when no arrangement had been made and Jack began to think that he was being manipulated, just slightly, just ever so slightly . . .

At last he found a stable that might supply the required beast, but the riding hours were at weekends only. 'It's really important. I'll pay your price. My daughter is five, she's ridden twice before, she's quite competent. It's a very special treat.'

And at two in the afternoon he was standing by a paddock gate, watching his helmeted daughter bouncing on the back of a scraggy-looking Shetland pony, an animal in its declining years, its back so sagging in the middle that it might have spent a lifetime carrying gold bullion, a look in its eye that could kill: but black and grey, temporarily dignified by being identified as the last representative of an extinct species of the *equidae*, and not at all inconvenienced by the humane amputation of its second and third toes which, Jack had explained to the girl (guilty at the continuing fabrication) had been essential if the horse was to be ridden by a human being.

She'd believed him, of course. Storytelling was his trade!

He had expected to return home at five o'clock, but Natalie had tired of the ride, refused the chance of an ice cream, and the traffic had been easy through Exburgh. He pulled into the drive an hour earlier than arranged and was incensed to see Brightmore's blood-red Lotus sprawled, rather than parked, across the gravel, its front wheels embedded in the flower borders.

'Steve's here! Steve's here!' the girl said, surprising him with the unexpected intimacy of her relationship with Bright-more. And as she ran to the front door, Jack banged his palms against the steering wheel, bitter, angry, confused, willing himself not to look at the bedroom window to see if the curtains were closed, but he did, they were, and for a moment he sank into himself, feeling cold and very clear in the head.

Then he laughed quietly. 'Harpoons at dusk, you bastard. You walk ahead of me.'

The front door was open and his daughter was waving him into the house. 'Daddy! Come on, Daddy.'

He slammed the car door, used his key to quickly scratch the paintwork of the Lotus, just above the brake-light (felt good!) and then smiled.

Angela was in the kitchen, making coffee with one hand and pouring lemonade with the other. She looked kempt and relaxed.

'Was it a good ride?' she asked as Jack entered the room, flinging his jacket onto the table.

'I don't know. Was it?'

Angela frowned. 'Did she have a good ride? On the pre-historic horse?' She emphasized the last words, playing the game with him for the child.

'Half an hour's mad gallop.'

'It was fun,' Natalie said, draining her glass of lemonade noisily and with great finality. Angela watched Jack carefully.

'You all right?'

'Where's Steve?'

'Outside. Smoking. He'll be in in a moment. You seem strange. Has something happened?'

'I don't know. You tell me. What the hell's he doing here?'

Angela got his drift and turned away from him, unplugging the percolator then folding her arms. 'We've been working out a strategy for your next journey . . .'

'And it was necessary to do that in the bedroom, of course.'

'No. Of course not. Jesus! Jack . . .'

'The fucking *curtains* are pulled.'

'That's because someone is *resting* there. Laura! Steve's assistant. Remember? She's got a migraine. She's been sick. I didn't think you'd mind her using our room.'

The glare held, and Jack felt sick himself, turning away from his wife.

'I'm sorry. Christ, I'm sorry.'

'So am I,' she said. But there was an odd tension in her voice. He fought to ignore it.

'No. You have nothing to be sorry about. It's me. I'm still a bit crazy about Steve, I suppose. He was in my dreams last night. He was part of the Midax journey. It's something deep-rooted. I know you had a bad time with him a few years ago, and I know that everything's professional now . . . but I can't . . . I can't shake it off.'

She didn't speak for a moment, wouldn't look at him, and his mouth went dry again.

I don't want to know. 'I'm sorry,' Angela repeated, her face tense, her eyes half-closed. She looked as if she was about to cry. Everything in the kitchen was in high focus, sharp edged, very clear, and he started to understand.

I don't want to know. Not now. Not yet . . .

'You don't have to be sorry, love. It's me. It's my mad imagination. I need to stop being so bloody paranoid.'

'Jack . . . We need to talk . . .'

No!

And Brightmore was suddenly in the doorway, brushing his fingers together, first looking quizzically at Angela, then at Jack himself. 'Everything OK? Not intruding, am I?'

'Your front wheel has gouged into my flower border. What sort of parking is that?'

'Hello Jack. How're the wounds?'

'Healing. Though some wounds heal slower than others.'

'I'm sure that's true. Laura drove, by the way. At my

request. Always pass the buck, if possible.' He grinned. 'I was writing my report on your Midax transfer. I didn't know she was ill, and I didn't notice the damage. You want me to move the car?'

'Forget it. And if it's of any interest to your report, coming out of a Midax journey is far more of a re-adjustment than just coming out of a deep, lucid dream. I'm very shaky. In the last hours in the other land I felt called back here. Now I feel very strongly called back to the world . . . wherever it is. It's like I've abandoned people, and a place, and the mission isn't finished.'

Brightmore was instantly professional. 'This is important. Can I get a record of what's happening to you? How you feel?'

'Of course. Walk ahead of me. I'll bring the harpoons.'

'I'm sorry?'

'Nothing.'

Angela still stood by the cooling coffee percolator, her head low, her arms folded. Brightmore glanced at her then walked into the small study.

Upstairs, the toilet flushed and there was slow, unsteady movement back to the front bedroom.

An hour later, Brightmore drove Laura back to Cambridge, and Jack started to regret his transparency, his moment of uncontrolled irritation. He had given himself away, of course; the New Zealander had instantly made the connection between the reference to harpoons and the earlier account of the Walk to the Shore. And that look between him and Angela, that quick glance, the question expressed in the merest narrowing of eyes. *Does he know! How the hell could he know!*

I don't want to know! Not yet . . .

Natalie had made a drawing of the wild, tiny horses. There were ten of them, running among tall trees, and although the girl was only five, the effect of her imagination, combining what her father had told her and what she had experienced on the decrepit, grey Shetland pony, was astonishingly vigorous.

'This is as good as a cave painting!' Jack informed her. 'It's got a real feel about it. I can hear those little devils snorting as they stampede.'

'What's a cave painting?'

He sat down heavily. He'd forgotten the extent to which Natalie questioned everything.

'It's a painting in a cave: usually of hairy elephants called mastodons and horses with huge fat bellies.'

There aren't any hairy elephants, silly . . .

'Is there a hairy elephant in the zoo?' she asked.

'No. Only in the permafrost.'

What's the permafrost, Daddy?

She was frowning. 'Why do the horses have big fat bellies?'

Damn! Why do you have to be so unpredictable?

'They ate too many hairy elephants.'

'Horses don't eat elephants. That's one of your stories!'

'I suppose it must be. Anyway, what's wrong with stories?'

'*Steve* doesn't tell stories.'

'No. I don't suppose he has the time.'

She was fussing with the green canopy of the giant trees. 'He makes Mummy laugh. He tells jokes.'

'*Isn't* that nice.'

'When I'm playing outside with Baalka, he tells funny jokes to Mummy. I can hear them.'

Baalka? Playing with Baalka? What the hell do you play?

Torn between two concerns, Jack said, 'I always thought you liked my stories.'

'I *do* like your stories.'

'And I like your horses. Though don't forget they had *three* toes on each foot.'

Extra toes, eighty in total, were duly crayoned in, a tedious process which Jack watched with patience, his mouth dry, his mind an insistent chant: *I don't want to know. Not yet. Not yet.*

Angela came in and praised the crayon drawing. 'Time for bed, young lady.'

There was no protest. The girl packed up her crayons, slid from the chair and ran to the tall window, looking out over the garden towards the city.

'He's not here yet,' she announced, and ran back across the room, grabbing her drawings and scampering up the stairs. In her own room, she undressed, ready for a bath. As Jack stood in the doorway, Angela sat the girl down and said, 'What have we said to you? Haven't we asked you not to play with . . . Baalka?'

'I won't get dirty,' Natalie said earnestly. She looked at her father, her pale, pretty face suddenly sad. 'I like dancing with him. He doesn't hurt me. If I say he's dancing too fast, he always stops. He always brings me home. All he takes is a dream, and I've got lots of dreams. Baalka said so. Oh please . . . don't stop him coming.'

She was looking at her father, ignoring Angela's stern words, her affectionate hug, her reassurance that it *was* alright to tell Baalka to go away.

Jack whispered, 'If she wants to dance with Baalka, maybe she should.'

Without looking up, kissing the girl's fair hair, Angela said, 'Why?'

He wanted to say: because he's peeling her life away, strip by strip. Because she's incomplete, though she seems fine. Because there's a shade of her in the *shimmering* and I don't know how important it is to get that ghostly echo back. Because! Because! Because maybe we should keep the bastard happy. Maybe if he thinks I'm trying, he'll bide his time.

And most of all . . . maybe he could be reasoned with . . .

'Will he come tonight?'

Natalie grinned and nodded. 'Every night. But he doesn't hurt me.'

'When you're tired of dancing, tell him you want to come home and go to sleep. Promise me?'

'I promise.'

'Goodnight, then.'

'Night . . .'

'Sweet dreams . . .'

Angela followed him downstairs to the kitchen. 'What are you going to do? Why are you suddenly encouraging her? I thought you said Greyface was dangerous. I only have your word for this, Jack. You realize that, don't you? If you tell me something, I have to believe it. It's only you that can see it! Why the change of heart?'

'It's not a change of heart,' he said, levering the top from a bottle of beer. 'It's a change of strategy.'

'Meaning what, exactly?'

'I'm going in. I'm following him in. Tonight, when he comes out to play, I'm going into the *shimmering* to play a game of my own. Any objections?'

'Yes. It sounds dangerous. And I need you. Are you sure you know what you're doing?'

He drank beer, watching her angrily. 'Of course I don't. I feel like I'm in some crazy film. Cities slip out of the earth, whirlpools suck forests, prehistoric animals crush my breakfast, my daughter dances with ghosts, my wife screws a man she once told me she thinks is a shit. Of *course* I don't know what I'm doing.'

Her arms, already folded, tightened more as she watched Jack through narrowed, pain-filled eyes. 'I don't love him, Jack. It's just good chemistry. It's over now. I promise it's over now.'

'Good chemistry,' Jack said, and held the bottle before him. 'Like this beer. When the soothing alcohol gets inside me, it makes good chemistry with the *gastric juices*, then good chemistry with the *blood plasma*, then with the *pleasure* receptors in the *brain*. Good chemistry! Yes, I think I can understand that. I don't *love* this beer . . .' he masturbated the neck of the bottle . . . 'I just want it inside me, *doing* things to me—'

215

'Shut up Jack. I told you. I don't love him. It's finished.'

'Until the next time I go inside after Greenface. Four days, Angela! Four fucking days I was helpless. You could have waited four *days*.'

Gently, she said, 'I've waited five years. You've not exactly been *attentive* since Natalie was born. Christmas and birthdays, the night before you went into the Deep. I gave in for two days, two days only, two days when the chemistry was right, because when you're on the edge, like, *you* know . . .' (she struggled for words, head shaking) '. . . like on the edge of something really big in your field, and you were there, our first *real* Midax voyager, well . . . it gets intense. So yes, we made love . . .'

'Made *love*?'

'OK! We *screwed*. For old times' sake! I'm sorry. It was chemistry. I don't intend to take a degree in the subject. Because I love *you*.'

'Do you? I wonder.'

'Don't wonder. Just believe.'

'Let me have another of those chemical *beers*. *Then* I'll see if I believe. But I'm still going in after Greyface. I have Nattie to think of. I have to be *attentive* to her. I have to *keep my eye on her*. Remember that expression?'

'Of course I do. You're drunk . . .'

'Your words, years ago. I was your Life Project, Angela! You were going to keep your eye on me. Funny, isn't it? I thought you were being romantic, I thought "keeping your eye on someone" meant looking after them. But you just meant studying me like a man looking down a microscope at a chicken embryo.'

'I did *not* mean that. That's a cruel thing to say. Please stop drinking. Christ, how much have you had?'

He opened the bottle and raised it in a toast. 'Not a lot. And yes. Cruelty! Here's to *cruelty*. It's in our lives whether we like it or not. In the shape of Greyface.'

He drained the bottle and smiled falsely, an angry and

pained expression, childish, confused, but very determined . . .

'That's why I'm going in.'

'Going in?'

'To the *shimmering*. I'm going in. *After* him. Beard the bastard in his den. Bury him in the ghost of Glanum, then kick Brightmore in after, seal the entrance, pick up our lives.'

24

At three in the morning Natalie slipped quickly from her bed and went silently downstairs. Jack emerged from the shadows in her room and followed her to the small utility room. The girl was standing on the step-ladder, effortlessly opening the hinged window which was kept permanently locked.

So that's how she gets out.

In seconds, the child had slipped through the narrow gap. Jack checked the lock and saw that it had been tampered with, then followed his daughter into the back garden by a more orthodox exit.

She was already on the wooden fence that separated garden from field, her white nightgown bright in the moon. By the time Jack had eased his heavier body over the fence, the girl was dancing and laughing, skipping in a wide circle around the huge horse-chestnut that dominated the scattered trees in the paddock.

He walked across to her, but kept his distance, circling the child as Natalie circled the tree, talking to someone, her hands reaching out to an invisible grasp.

She was oblivious of her father, but her dancing companion was not, for she stopped suddenly and looked puzzled, looking towards the man who stood in the moonlight but calling for 'Baalka'. Jack felt the ghost very close to him, but it was pure imagination that suggested eyes and the soft touch of breath on his lips.

'What have you done to my daughter?' he said to the night

air. 'Leave her alone. I'll go after Ahk'Nemet again, but please leave my daughter alone.'

The reply to this request was the sound of Natalie's laughter, the sight of her running across the field, round the houses to the road into Exburgh. Jack followed. The girl stopped suddenly, then turned and ran back to the house, but for a fleeting instant he saw a flash of her shape continuing towards the road, like an after-image.

Natalie crawled back into the house and pulled the window shut. A few seconds later he saw her at the window, then she'd gone, presumably back to bed. Angela had woken and was standing anxiously at the back door, a coat over her sleeping-shirt.

'Where is she?'

'Back in the house. She uses the utility room window.'

'I thought it was locked! We always keep it locked!'

'The lock's been opened, forced, I think. Anyway, she's safe for the moment.'

'Did you see Baalgor? Baalka? Whatever . . . ?'

Whatever!

He shook his head. 'He was there, but he's gone back to the hidden city. I'm going to the church.'

'What church?'

'St John's! That's where the gate to the inner city lies. I'm sure it's the way in.'

'Be careful, Jack.'

'As careful as I can.'

The doors into the church were locked and Jack trotted back down the steps, casting a double shadow from the lights above the porch, illuminating the façade of the building. Suddenly, Natalie cooed at him from the shadows in Mourning Passage. The ethereal child, in her ghostly nightgown, had a hand in front of her mouth, as if suppressing a sound that had been uttered mischievously. As her father approached, so she backed away, crouching slightly, feigning apprehension.

The moment Jack faced the shadows of the alley, the *shimmering* opened before him, the cleft in the rock, the stone pillars, the standing stones among the heavy trees. The suicide gate. Cool breezes blew at him. This was a different night in a different world, and the ghost of his child was running away, running into Glanum.

For a long while the passage continued as he'd remembered it from a few weeks ago, a narrow tunnel, a natural fissure in the mountainside that was dank and slick with water seepage, dangerously unpredictable as it suddenly dropped away, deeper into the ground.

The sound of someone running preceded his cautious entrance, but though he called to the girl – or whatever the girl was, this *shade* of his daughter – there was no reply.

That time before, Jack had panicked as the passage opened into a rock-hewn chamber, an immense vault illuminated by grey light. The stink of fear in this place, the buzz of wailing voices in an otherwise empty, echoing rock cavern, had been too much. But he crossed the chamber now, and it occurred to him that he had passed the Hinterland of this particular world, an altogether bleaker and more sombre experience than that in the world of Ahk'Nemet.

A second tunnel led deeper, but . . . He emerged, eventually, through a stone gate into the sombre city beyond, facing high grey walls, curved alleys, towering buildings. Everything here seemed warped and grotesque, perspectives changing as he moved slowly through the streets.

He began to run, his legs powered at times by panic, at other moments by hope. There were small squares with drab fountains, and areas where the doors of the houses swung lazily, protecting only shells. Elsewhere, the gruesome shades of people, cowled, like lepers, he thought, moved about the alleys, aware of him but unafraid of him.

He became exhausted, his body seizing up, his breathing laboured. And as he realized that he needed to rest, so he became aware of the passage of time: he had been exploring this urban shadow for more than eighteen hours, although the light had not changed, such light as there was.

He found a gate into a small courtyard, where the stone floor was broken by stunted bushes and trees. The broken windows of the house opened into empty rooms, crumbling plaster walls and cracked floors on which traces of mosaic could be seen, but colourless.

He was hungry, but sleep called more urgently, and he crept into the deepest of the shadows and closed his eyes.

On waking, he checked his watch. He had slept for three hours only, but he felt revived. He was thirsty and soon found a fountain, drinking messily from its sluggish flow, aware that he was watched – it was the girl, he was sure – but sensing that he was not threatened.

For several hours, then, he wandered through the labyrinth of streets, calling out, answered by echoes, sometimes by silence. In one place, in a small square surrounded by marbled buildings, wild horses grazed the rough grass that grew between the cracked flagstones. They bolted at his approach and ran the streets, twenty animals surging through the maze, lost for a while, then reappearing. They eventually came trotting back into the square, nickering and cautious, eyeing the stranger constantly as they began to graze again.

He passed through five gates, some plain, some decorated with the motifs of animals, grotesque human faces, one of them with a frieze of migrating human beings, animals, carts and children, a thousand small, intricately depicted characters, the story of some long forgotten journey between historical lands.

The walls grew higher, thicker, the light darkened, and eventually he came among monolithic tombs and shrines. The sky overhead was developing into a storm, a great spiral of swirling clouds, slowly turning above the centre of the city.

He watched that sky for a long while before familiarity pricked at his senses: here, in clouds, was a similar storm to that which had been engulfing the trees and ruins in the Midax Deep.

Am I below that other world?

It was a strange thought in a strange place; there was no sign of any of the structures and ruins that surrounded him being sucked into the sky, nor of the crumbling cliffs of the Deep plunging through the Eye, onto the grey city below.

But I'm close . . . I feel I'm close . . .

And as that insight captured his imagination, so he heard the sudden, sonorous call of a horn, ahead of him, where a river glimmered among the tombs, and drawn to it by curiosity he made his cautious way down the hill.

As he crossed from the street to the wide steps leading down to the mooring-wall of the river, he was pleased to find the greyness turning steadily, as he approached, into brilliant sunshine, and the sound of festivities and revels became an ear-shattering delight. Far from being a sombre call, the blast of the horn was part of a great celebration on the river, where full-sailed barges drifted and collided, people swam naked, streamers coiled from decks and music screeched, squealed and whined, encouraging dancing and the beating of drums, and the swinging of blazing torches in dangerous fashion.

The steps were covered with sprawling, brightly-dressed couples. Glass shattered, metal flagons were tossed across the stones, aromatic scents and the odours of cooking filled the air as smoke wreathed and coiled from incense braziers and stone-lined pits, where meat charred and sizzled.

It had the feeling of a wedding, but the noise of shouting and laughter were sucked into the sky, leaving Jack oddly remote, a man surrounded by hollow sounds, a ghost who moved among the revellers without impinging upon their awareness, although he was solidly a part of them.

He picked his way to the river's edge, stepping over mooring ropes and landing planks, crossing the river from decorative barge to decorative barge. He was aware of the idols and statues that grinned and grimaced from their deck-side shrines. He stopped cheekily to pick at a golden plate filled with fruit and pale meat, then tasted a scented wine from a clay jar, while pausing briefly to watch the strange, swaying dance between a naked couple. Their full-fleshed bodies gleamed almost incandescently with oil as they circled each other, mirror images in motion, if not in form, their eyes locked, their lips coming closer to the final, initiating kiss which, erotic though it was, heralded a sudden, all-embracing intimacy that Jack blushed to witness.

As he stepped onto the far bank, the light dimmed again, and the sound of the party faded to a distant echo.

Ahead of him, temples loomed in the half-light and a massive, shadowy form moved among them, glimpsed in the alleys as it prowled restlessly, watching. It was taller than the buildings and Jack glimpsed heavy legs, quizzical eyes, a bulky shape, man-like, keeping its distance in the sanctuary gloom. A moment later a second giant walked behind it and the two behemoths slipped away into the shadows.

'Titans. They won't hurt you.'

He turned at the sound of the voice. Natalie – the shade of his daughter – stood behind him, smiling nervously as she stared up at him.

'Did you see the horses?' she asked.

'Yes.'

She looked round quickly, ruefully. 'I'd like to ride one. But I can never get near them . . .'

'Natalie? Are you . . . is your name Natalie?'

'I dream with her sometimes. By the big trees.'

There was movement distantly and a wolf or large dog bayed. Shade glanced around, her face a picture of childish apprehension. 'This way,' she gestured, but suddenly changed her direction as the flag-stoned street itself started to shift and rise, becoming an arching back, the shoulders swelling as giant arms pushed the creature up from its subterranean waiting place.

'Another Titan?' Jack shouted as he fled behind her.

'K'Thone!' she seemed to call. 'Always breaking up the city. Come *on.*'

Shadows, always shadows.

The white-robed girl ran barefoot through the labyrinth and Jack followed, one moment stifling in the heavy air, the next welcoming a gusting, freezing wind that poured between colonnades and arches.

Where are you taking me?

He could suddenly smell water. Shade was scampering towards a low arch beyond which steps led down to a wide pool. This was fed by a natural well that rose somewhere in the carved rock surround, to pour slowly through a series of brickwork pipes. As Jack crouched by the fresh pool he was aware of movement above him, cutting off the light from the windows that opened into this water sanctuary. Shade was washing her hands, splashing her face, wetting her feet, rubbing vigorously at the soles and heels and muttering to herself.

'Sore. The streets are hard and I get lots of cuts. Do you want to drink? It's fresh. I often come here to drink.'

Jack took her advice, aware that the rock around the spouts on the other side of the pool was carved into female faces. They stared at him through wide or slanted eyes, and seemed to be kissing him with parted, half-smiling lips. There were five mask-spouts in all.

'Whose place is this?

'The women's place,' the girl said with a nervous giggle. 'But it's OK, they're not here at the moment.'

'How do you know?

'The water swirls when they're here. Like a whirlpool. And it smells like blood. And you can see silver light everywhere. Strips of skin from the Moon. They're hunting with their dogs, deeper in the city. Hurry up, though. If the hunt's been good they'll be back with their kill before you hear their horns calling.'

There was an odd quality to her words, something in part exciting, since it was frightening, and in part familiar. Natalie herself didn't talk quite like this; the language seemed too advanced for a five year old, or at least, for the five year old he knew and loved.

He had to remind himself that this was just an echo of his daughter, a part of Greyface that was simply playing with him, drawing him willingly deeper into a web, deeper into the heart of the ghostly city.

Shade had finished her freshening and led the way out of the pool, racing up the steps, leaving wet footmarks on the cold stone.

'Come on. Come on,' she barked childishly. 'Quickly.'

Outside, she ran towards two massive stone statues representing fabulous beasts, mythic perhaps, but beyond his experience: bird-headed and bird-winged, their cold eyes gazed into the city from squat reptilian bodies, long tails curled, scaled bellies scraping the ground as the wide, lizard legs seemed poised for sudden movement. They guarded the passage into a drab, monolithic building, a face of dressed stone without decoration, open double doors that were narrow but high, an impression of total darkness within.

Jack called her back. She seemed impatient, doing an odd little hopping dance, anxious to draw him deeper. 'You *must* come.'

'I'm tired. I need to rest. I'm frightened, Shade. I need to go home. There's something wrong; I came in good faith, I came with promises, to seek guarantees . . .'

'Stop it. Stop it,' she snapped. 'Silly words. Silly words.'

'I came to see Baalgor. But he's just playing games with me. I made a mistake coming here. Now I want you to come back with me. Come home with me . . .'

He reached out a hand to the suddenly furious child.

'Come on, Shade. You don't belong here. You're part of a different world. You belong with someone else. Come home with me.'

And do what? Stitch you back into Nattie?

'I belong *here*!' she screamed, but she was backing away, her face breaking into a tearful mask of fear and uncertainty.

He went towards her, not knowing what he could achieve, and took her by the shoulder, fighting her as she struggled, subduing the flailing of her hands with his stronger grip.

'I'm taking you back, Shade. You'll have to show me the way.'

She snarled at him, shockingly feral. 'And if I do? You fool! He'll just come again. Skin by skin, he'll take me. The inside skins, not the outside skin. Pretty, pretty child, that's all you'll have, never loving, never living. But she'll be *here*. All of her, all the inside *Nattie*. All of me. I love this place, Daddy. If you take me away, I'll just come back. I'm protected by a stronger man than you.'

He drew her small body towards him, furious with these weasel words, these 'not-her' words, this ghostly programme that Greyface had instilled within this echo of his daughter.

'There is no-one stronger than me when it comes to you, Natalie. *Natalie*!'

As he emphasized her name he discovered that, strong though he was, her teeth were stronger, and as they chewed through his flesh he screeched with pain. She slipped away, running to the bird-headed monsters, whose stone wings rose quickly as she approached, their beaked faces turning, lowering, to form a guard against the deeper temple.

Hesitating as these monsters threatened him, he could only watch helplessly as Shade squirmed between the marble jaws, slapping one of the creatures which opened and closed its mouth with a crack of stone.

The splayed legs shuffled, the guardians approached him for a moment, moving rapidly, then settled. From behind them, the tall figure of Baalgor – *Baalka* – approached, his face mottled where the pale clay mask had broken and fallen away from burnished skin. His eyes were like jewels.

The girl now clambered on to his cloaked shoulders,

giggling helplessly as she struggled to find a purchase on the man's back. Greyface both helped and hindered her, a typical fatherly tease, tugging here, pushing there, half-smiling as the girl struggled to sit on his shoulders, finally allowing her into position, her legs dangling down in front of him, her grip safely in his long hair.

He came within striking distance of Jack, who began to smell the scalps and the bloody clumps of feathers on the long, foul cloak. The clay that caked the body below was finely cracked, crazy patterns, and daubed and striped with colour, as if Greyface had wiped the juices of meats and berries on his belly.

'Who are you?' Jack whispered.

Man and girl watched him, the same gleam of confidence and arrogance in their eyes. Baalgor ignored the question.

'I've seen you play with Natalie like this. It's tiresome, tiring. But all shades come with echoes of their past, and these things have to be accommodated.'

'You've stolen other souls, then.'

Greyface shook his head, glanced down as the girl squirmed, slapped at her leg. 'Easy, now!' And Jack felt a surge of heat to his face.

Don't you hit my daughter . . .!

But he kept quiet. The bull-runner watched him.

'Are you calling to her?' he asked after a moment.

'Who?'

'Who do you think? You've named her *Greenface*. Natalie tells me you've found her name is Ahk'Nemet. That means she's spoken to you. Are you trying to persuade her? I need her with me, Jack. I intend to have her . . . your daughter's life is my price. I've made that clear enough, I think.'

'I've come to ask you to let her go. Give me back the . . .' he remembered Shade's words. 'Give me back the *inside skins* you've stolen. Give me back my daughter – all of her: I'll seek Green – Ahk'Nemet for you. I came very close—'

'I know.'

'I can get close again. I'm prepared to help, but I can't make promises. The journey to find her is very damaging, very wounding. And she didn't want to come when I encountered her.'

Greyface seemed irritated. 'I know.'

'Well if you know, then you must know how difficult it is.'

'She doesn't want to come! If she'd wanted to come with me, she'd have done so. *Of course* it's difficult.'

'But I'm trying, dammit! Look at these cuts. That's wild rose and harpoon, and a blowpipe dart that still hurts! Your companion is a vicious hunter.'

'I know. You'll have your work *cut out*.' He laughed. 'Why are you here, talking to me? You should be pursuing her. Shouldn't he, my sweetheart?'

This last was addressed to the smiling girl, who leaned down across Greyface's head and let the man nibble her fingers. All the while he did this, Natalie watched her father. Greyface's touch was on the girl's legs, his fingers on her thighs, an innocent intimacy which Jack would ordinarily not have noticed or been concerned with, but which he found, now, to be an incensing, infuriating, deliberate gesture. He was being taunted; he held his temper in check.

'Tell me something,' he said hoarsely. 'Why do you need her so much? Greenface. She doesn't want to be with you; she doesn't seem to *need* to be with you. Why do you need *her*?'

'She has something that belongs to me,' was the grim answer from the clay-cracked face.

'Tell me . . .'

Shade giggled, tugged at Baalgor's ear, then whispered to him. The man said, 'The talisman of Estradel. A sword, its blade polished from obsidian, inscribed over the generations with the charms and sorcery of the Estradoth. Its grip is fashioned from . . .'

Breaking off, he turned slightly to the girl, who again whispered in his ear.

'From the green-veined ivory of the One-Horn, the pommel

surmounted with the crystal egg of the Forgotten Bird of Orax.'

Shade was still whispering.

'When the sword kills, it passes magic into the corpse; such corpses, when resurrected—'

'Enough!' Jack said wearily.

Greyface grinned. 'What fun. What fancy. Obsidian is a good stone, I remember hearing of it. I've never touched it.'

'Nor, I imagine, have you resurrected a corpse containing that small fragment of magic. The living dead, walking the deserts among the forgotten tombs, doing your bidding.'

'You remember the tale, then?'

'I made my childhood fortune describing what I saw of you and the woman. You ran through places that to me were pure fantasy! I created stories to go with the visions.'

'I know. Some of the powers you described were astonishing to dream. They gave me hope. I was born with the talent to scour, to skin, to shape shadows. It was what they *put* in me. It was magic, but it was – is – mine.'

It occurred to Jack, now, why Shade's words had sounded so familiar. She was speaking in terms, and in the style, with which he had always told his stories.

He said, 'What I saw never made much sense to me, but the visions were vivid, colourful, adventurous . . .'

'I liked the stories you told,' Greyface said. 'More than your daughter does, although she remembers every detail of them. Don't you?'

He teased the girl for a moment and Natalie laughed, clinging on to the broad shoulders, watching her estranged father with cruel disdain from the restraining grip of the man she adored.

Greyface went on, 'When you told them as a child yourself, I imagine I heard them, but in dreams, or in visions of my own. We were running very hard. The bull was always very close. The hunter was always closer to us than we realized, moving through a land to which we had no gate. It was always behind us, and we had to run faster than a star falls. We were constantly in terror, constantly on the alert. I became aware of someone, or some place, drawing us close. Odd dreams, strange music, lands I had never seen nor could imagine, names that were very foreign, cold winters I had never experienced, lush, stinking, shadowy forests that were unlike the great, scented cedar forests of my own country . . .'

Forests of Cedar? The Middle East!

'My sister experienced them too. *Stop it!*'

This admonition was to Natalie, who was squirming and trying to get into the big man's arms, hanging onto the long hair, causing pain. Greyface cradled the child, swaying slightly, rocking as if trying to get her to sleep. Shade curled into the foul cloak against his breast, completely content.

The Bull-runner never took his gaze away from Jack.

'It was you, of course. God to our mortal lives. The dream to our sleeping hours. The hope beyond our waking nightmare. We followed your call blindly, not knowing who or what it was that beckoned to us. But when we passed the gate I saw you clearly, and knew you for the mortal man you are. You are nothing special!'

'I know. I never claimed to be.'

'You are nothing but a carrier of the old dream, the place to which we escaped. And having run the dream, I escaped from it easily, and Nemet could have too, but she was frightened to find that her great hope was nothing but a lie, a land so remote from her own land that it had no meaning. She had courage, but not enough. And she had too much remorse, which is why she is running home. But she can never undo the wrong. Not without me.'

'Then why don't you return as well? And *leave* my dream. Let me live my life in peace.'

'Catch!' the man said, and Shade was flung towards him, screaming. Jack caught the girl who at once raked his face with her nails, struggling out of his arms and running back to the stone guardians. She vanished into the gloom of the mausoleum and Greyface folded his arms.

'If you spill water on the ground, can you bring it back to the cup? Of course not. If you put fire into a woman, can you stop the rising of new wings? Of course not. I was put into my mother's belly by fire and stone, marked to be born, to be raised, to be sent to the sanctuary wall. Likewise my sister . . .'

'I don't understand. The sanctuary wall? Which sanctuary? Where? When? Where were the Cedar Forests?'

'. . . But we grew too fast, we grew too close. We were too aware. We learnt what was happening to us, and we planned to escape. We learnt how to destroy. And what we destroyed can never be undestroyed. To go back is to die. To go forward is to live, even though we are a lifetime's walk or more from our beginning place.'

'Then why don't you go ahead alone? Or do you love her?' The question seemed to stun Baalgor, or perhaps to confuse him. But after a moment he shook his head, as if pityingly, and his voice was soft. 'Of course I love her. Nemet is my sisterwife. We were born to each other; we are a *part* of each other. I need her. She has the skill of the trail. Without her, I have no proper direction. Without me, she has no courage. No determination! We were *born* to each other. Which is why she is so hesitant, and why you can persuade her. Otherwise – the art of direction can still be raised in the young. Those skills, too, were *born* to me. And bit by bit I shall create a new sisterwife from your daughter. She led you through the city without difficulty. Without her, you would have been hopelessly lost. She's begun to learn, to understand the trail. It's a beginning, but there is still a long way to go. A great deal of *peeling!*'

He came up to Jack, reeking of flesh and blood from the cloak. He reached out, grabbing Jack's hair and twisting his head to left and right. Jack stood still, allowing the pain, the anger. He felt physically helpless, though he could have struggled against the violence. But a deeper confusion made him wait, made him take the brutal touch.

Who are you? Where do you come from? How could I have been your gate?

How do you control my daughter?

He would have to go back into the Deep. He couldn't bear to think of Natalie running wild with this scalp-cloaked monster.

'I'll try again,' he whispered. 'Please don't touch my daughter until I've tried again.'

'Hurry, then,' said the grey-faced man, releasing Jack and turning to enter the darkness of the temple. 'Hurry!'

PART SIX

At the Maelstrom's Edge

25

Winter had come to the Hinterland, but I surfaced from the Midax dream, sheltered and dry in the overleaning bulk of one of the great bulls that guarded the Bull Temple. The landscape was silent and soft with a deep covering of snow. This was a dawn world, now, and the light was harsh and brilliant.

A set of tracks, clearly human, led towards me, then away again towards the winter forest and the gorge. This same person had rifled my pack as I slept, but from the compression of the snow around me it seemed they had stayed for a while, hauling me into shelter, waiting for my emergence from the transition.

Perhaps impatient, or simply cold, they had eventually departed. I tried to see signals in the snow-spoor of my love-lorn and vigorous friend William Finebeard, but the fact is I was more inclined to see Greenface in the trail, and whether by some lingering smell, or subtle sign, I was convinced she had been here, searched me, and was now close by, perhaps in some place where the winter was abating.

The great bulls, the thrusting, leering statues that guarded the entrance to one of the temples, now were looming skeletons, their bones carved from black marble, though with horns of gleaming ivory. The hollow skulls stared down at me, the cavities and sockets in the carved faces giving an illusion of curiosity.

This dreamlike state hardened slightly, becoming lucid, yet still unreal. I was half in the Hinterland, half in the process of arriving, but I could hear and smell the winter, and was aware of the approach of horses from the gully.

I stood in my shelter and watched the riders wade carefully through the silent wood, entering the hushed piazza, fanning out to form an arc between the church and the temples opposite. I counted fifteen, heavily cloaked, their mounts bigger than the prehistoric horses that had browsed along the lake-edge in that time, days or years past, when I had first been here. The animals were swathed in coarse blankets, muzzles gleaming with guards of copperish metal.

A horn-blast startled me. One of the riders was standing in his rope stirrups, the metal horn held against chafed lips. The sound was a sustained low note rapidly ascending, like a ship's siren, repeated three times, then three times more.

The horsemen shuffled, mounts restless in the cold, all swathed in the frost from their lungs. They were clearly uncomfortable in this place, and those four or five riders who quickly dismounted and waded into the ruins, searching, were disgruntled and irritable at the task.

The leader eventually called my name, a cry taken up by the others, a summoning muffled by the winter but loud enough to carry to the higher cliffs.

William? Was that William Finebeard who shouted and called for me? I walked towards him, aware that I was a ghost in this ghostly place, and as I approached I was convinced that this man, bearded and advanced in years, was not my lost friend.

Nevertheless, I moved before him, calling out, and two of his companions were aware of me, trying to restrain their restless, skinny equines, prodding spears at my shape as they turned in the deep snow, shouting in alarm.

Half the troop scattered at once, beating their screaming horses back to the gully and the waterfall. The others stared at me, not responding when I spoke to them. They could see but they couldn't hear. Eventually, they, as well, *gave up the ghost*, turning and riding away, although the leader – who had seemed unable to engage with my incorporeal presence – pointed vaguely to the church, bellowed my name several times more, coupled with that of 'William', before following his men.

In the church I found a crudely painted wooden plaque, slung from one of the columns. It was marked with the icon that I associated with my friend, the simple, snaking corner of a maze, a quadrant of the Winter Dance, and included the representation of the *paisley* pattern, with which William had associated me after the fiasco of the swimming shorts. A vertical list of symbols, ten in all, could mean nothing else but the number of times he had revisited the Hinterland, or sent his colleagues here, to search me out.

Ten visits . . . ten years? And perhaps visits from a William whom I would not recognize, for this Hinterland was different, now, familiar in many ways, but changed, from flesh to bone, an empty place, soulless, a *version* of the Temple City in which I had first arrived.

I re-packed the canvas bag, then slung it across my back, alarmed by its weight. After wading through the snow, away from the Hinterland, I slipped and slid across the icy ledges of the frozen waterfall before finding the treacherous track down through the wooded slopes. From here I could see the distant lake, still visible despite the haze of winter mist, where I hoped to find the village again, and perhaps some way of crossing the water to join forces with the fair-bearded youth whom I had abandoned in another time.

It was a freezing and difficult journey to the lake, and I spent three days travelling, sheltering where I could, conserving my supplies. Eventually, I hauled myself from the treeline and smiled at the sheen of ice before me. The white surface was broken in places, exposing the blue gleam of water, and I knew I had found the lake.

Half a day later, close to dusk, my hopes of a warm fire,

warm food, the comfort of people who might have forgiven me for my friendship with William, were dashed.

How much time had passed was hard to tell, but at some point, years ago, the fishing village had been fortified, a massive line of defences against the land on one side, the take on the other. And at some time after that, the city had been besieged and sacked. The great walls were broken; the charring of fire was in evidence everywhere. If the grisly remains of humans lay scattered about the fallen stones, the snow had mercifully covered them.

A harbour had been built as well, crude stone piled between thick uprights of cut trees. In the wide, deep haven, the hulks of burned ships lay, broken and ice-endowed, prows high, sterns in the mud. Like fallen marquees, the once-colourful sails lay caught in the frost. These ships had been lean and sleek, longboats, I imagined, but they had been destroyed as they lay quiet in their berths. They were useless.

Inside the walls of the fortified town there was sufficient shelter to make a camp, and I chose the ruins of a house whose tree timbers had survived the destruction. It was only after I had lit the fire, and was busy tying hides and the remains of blankets to the frame, that I noticed the icons and carvings on the poles, and realized where I was. This was the chieftain's house, that same house where William had silently courted the eldest daughter, and the young Thimuth's lust for me had been sternly rebuked by the watching parents.

Dire-wolves prowled the ruins during the night, and I kept the fire blazing and my back firmly to a tall wall, a sharpened pole between my knees as I sat, watching the hungry creatures. There were three, perhaps four, one of them a huge 'alpha' male with fur so stiff with its own preening that its ruff took on the appearance of quills. This monster kept a watchful eye on the fire whilst its mates scratched and tore at the hard earth, resurrecting the stinking limbs of the dead where they had been summarily buried.

And so of course I couldn't sleep, even though my instinct told me that these creatures would not attack.

At dawn I was simply too exhausted to stay awake, and several hours later opened my eyes to find snow drifting across the scene of last night's grave-digging, and the lake as silent and beautiful as any lake in Finland. Freezing, I soon started the fire again, and changed from damp clothes to fresh ones.

For the rest of the day I hunted the winter forest without success, sought for any means at all to follow William's raiders across the lake to the ice-tower shore, and finally, at dusk, came back to raise fire again, to further weatherproof my shelter, to prowl among the ashes of the dead, trying to imagine what might have happened here. With the light going I went to the lake's edge and skipped shards of stone across the frozen surface, the sound ringing hollow in the bitter frost.

And it was at that moment, unguarded and lost in thought, that the sensation of a city appeared to me, a brief moment in which, with the ice shaking, ghostly towers rose above the lake, a broken wall, an open gate surmounted by the familiar horns of a bull. It was intangible, insubstantial, and I experienced it more by a dream awareness than by sight, but the city moved around me, hovering in the winter air, for all the world as if it were watching me, or listening. I saw at once that this was the same ghost city that had burst from the earth on the Mallon Hills, many years ago. It was Glanum!

I turned around, called for John Garth, felt uncannily as if someone had touched my cheek; but then the sensation was gone, the ghost towers slipping back into the ice. I was left with my focus on the far ridge, where earlier I had hunted small game and proved myself adept only at striking bark.

There was a small fire burning there, a ruddy glow in the forest's gloom. As I watched and listened, I heard the sound of the small horses, and of men laughing.

There were three of them, and in the morning they rode

slowly along the shore, peering up at the ruins, almost cursorily kicking through the traces. Of course, when they found my shelter they searched it and dismantled it, but since by then I was securely hidden back along their trail, they failed to find me.

I don't believe, however, that it was me they were searching for. There was an anger and a frustration in their actions which did not concur with their search for me in the Hinterland.

I found a good place to hide, close to a mound of snow, by some dense brushwood. I was alarmed when the three riders came back towards me, dismounted, stripped their equines of blankets and trappings and blew a shrill horn blast. And immediately I was glad that I hadn't burrowed, for extra shelter, into the mound of snow, for it erupted with a great blast of stinking warmth and a huge man, heavily furred, luxuriously bearded, sprang up, throwing back the crude wicker frame in which he had been lurking. He stretched and farted, tossed out a sword, a throwing axe and a spear, then kicked away the rest of the snow, roaring good-humoured abuse at his companions.

There were a few minutes of drinking from a leather gourd, then the horses were driven away, back into the frozen forest. Being tamed, they soon stopped, bewildered and alone, caught between the cry of the wild and the certainty of feed from their erstwhile masters.

As soon as the guardian had relieved his painful joints and satisfied his waiting appetites, the brushwood, which I had seen but not considered, was cleared from around the black-tarred hull of a small boat. After throwing their equipment and the harnessing into the hollow shell, they dragged and hauled this vessel to the ice, where it slid and slithered towards the water, the four men trying to keep control, laughing as it twisted in their grasp, possessed of a life of its own.

At the edge of the ice, they flung themselves aboard. The

boat plunged into the icy waters and they struck around them with poles, then used simple oars to paddle away from this alien land.

I watched them enviously, but suddenly they started to cry out, and I felt a certain horror too as I saw the vessel list, then start to sink. They had thrown themselves overboard at once, but this winter was too strong and the water like the bony grip of death. They could not get further than the edge of the ice, against which they clawed and grasped, but across which they could not crawl. Like that ice in the heart of the betrayed, this simple edge, this slender gate, was a barrier that could not be passed.

It was not possible to listen to their shrieks without feeling impelled to help. I slipped across the frozen lake carrying a coil of rope and flung it to the nearest man. It failed to reach him, though he grabbed for it, stretched for it with a determination that made his wan face suddenly flush. Below my feet, the ice moved and a crack appeared. I backed away to safety, releasing the rope, which glided, snakelike, into the wretched man's grasp at last.

As he vanished below the grey surface, silent and resigned to death, so he tied the rope around his neck. His impassive gaze was on me to the last.

The four equines were huddled miserably in the lee of one of the broken walls, their breath frosting thickly, two of them pawing at the hard ground. I found more rope in the ruined town and gently persuaded the creatures to let me tether them loosely and lead them to a more sheltered place. But I had nothing with which to feed them, and I would have to release them to their own devices before too long.

I spent the day hunting again, and collecting what pathetic and inadequate fodder I could – no more than some straw from what had once been a bed, and the pale emerald leaves of an evergreen, whose bark was a series of jagged points, a primitive tree which might easily have poisoned the horses, but which in fact seemed to perk the creatures up as they chewed the slender vegetation.

As the light began to go at the end of my second day here I decided to abandon this visit to the Deep and return to the Hinterland, and by calling, to surface again in my own world. But as I huddled by the fire, behind the palisade of sharpened branches, I saw a figure move steadily across the lake, walking carefully on the ice. It was a bulky shape, dark and broad, and whoever it was carried a long spear in each hand with which it steadied its movements. The moon was behind clouds, but the lake-water glittered. The figure crouched as close to the edge of the shoreline ice as it dared, peering to the far coast. It must surely have seen me earlier; the fire was bright, the noise of burning wood loud.

I prepared for the worst, and when at last the human shape came slowly back to the land, picking up a leather bag and walking cautiously into the ruins, certainly aware of me, I rose defensively to confront the stranger.

By the faint light of the fire, dark eyes in a green face watched me from within the heavy cowl of fur.

She came to the defences and shrugged off the heavy winter skin, shivering as the cold air hit her, but quickly coming to the fire, unafraid of me, her weapons left beyond the fence.

'You were in my dreams again,' she whispered. 'So I've been expecting you. But I'm not following him. I'm not coming with you. You've found me, we can talk, but I'm not following him. I need to go back.'

'You've been in my dreams too,' I said. 'I didn't expect to find you in this sort of winter, though.'

'I've been here for years. When the winter changes, it's like cloud shadow running through the valleys. The spring comes faster than a man can run. Everything melts, everything is mud, drowning mud where the valleys are deep and the hills shift or the rivers rise and spread. Then the trees blossom and bloom, and the heat comes and the earth bakes. It will happen at any time. Then you can have your boat and cross the lake again, if that's what you want. The bitumen caulking can be replaced easily enough, the gaps in the hull patched.'

She cast me a look, a half smile, and I realized that she was telling me she had sabotaged the horsemen's vessel. I whispered, 'So that's why it sank so fast.'

'I didn't expect it to sink so close to the shore. If they'd come onto the ice, I'd have killed them. They've been hunting me for sport while they've been looking for you. They've run me almost to ground too many times. I simply shortened the odds against it happening again.' She smiled, her dark eyes shining. 'But at least you have a boat.'

And Greenface had food! Earthy flavoured mushrooms, which she had gathered in autumn and carefully dried; highly spiced strips of fowl; dry, hard cakes of unleavened bread; and fat, sharp-tasting olives.

'You have to know where to look. There are traders everywhere. Gather what you can, where you can – if you have something to trade, this edge of the world is not an unpleasant place to exist.'

This *edge of the world*?

'This is the edge of the world,' she repeated, when I asked her what she meant. 'What more can I tell you?'

'Tell me about your life. Tell me where you come from.'

'I was born in a valley, below forested hills, in a camp that moved with the seasons between those hills and rivers, between fresh springs and the walls of great sanctuaries. The land was hot and lush; the creatures of the forests were terrifying; the creatures of the river were huge and menacing. As a child, with my brothers and sisters, I swam in dangerous waters. My father took me in his boat, up the river, past many of the wooden and stone figures that protected the land from those who sailed the water. He traded and talked, using words that were meaningless to me, but which he had learned through his life by courage and with dedication. I often dream of him. He was such a tall man, his beard in ringlets, his hair tied around the crown with a circlet of polished blue stones, his hands so strong and dark, each finger with a leather ring, his belly hard and scarred, his legs tattooed to show his knowledge of the lands to north and south.

'I helped him sail the boat, sitting on the cargo, tugging at the deep sail while he leaned against the tiller, shouting at me, always angry, always making me work a little harder. But when the voyage was finished, the trade completed, he would dress in his loose tunic, black and yellow, and let his hair free, and open the leather gourd of fragrant wine. We would let the current take us, slipping down the river below the stars, drinking and laughing, eating figs and olives, invoking moon and river to give us safe, sweet passage. I would curl on his belly in the night, wrapped around him, safe in his broad arms, fulfilled by his love, satisfied by his food and kisses. How could I have known what he planned for me? I listened to the strange tongues he spoke, and saw the hungry glances of the men he spoke to, but I never dreamed that he would send me to the sanctuary of beasts. I never dreamed it. He betrayed me. He betrayed us all.'

She caught herself in melancholy reminiscence and straightened up, spitting on the fire, which hissed spectacularly. Her speech had been slow and soft, her gaze all the time upon the flames. Now she reached for an olive and chewed it quickly, silent again.

'Is that why you're running? Is that why you're pursued? Because you disobeyed your father?'

She was quiet for a moment, then said, 'No. By that time, I was already marked. Only I didn't know it. And not just me . . .'

'Baalgor too?'

'Baalgor . . . and others. Seven in all. After the terrible deed we all scattered to the stars, some to the north, some to the south. Baalgor and I stayed close – he was my brother – the others I think running alone. I imagine they perished quickly.

The lands we entered were those of demons, put up to snare us. A man alone would have had no chance. The two of us managed to keep the hunters at a distance until we came to the edge of the world, and realized we could run no further. Then we started to look for the Gate, but by the time we had found it . . .'

She hesitated, and recognizing that I had been that gate, I spoke impatiently. 'By the time you had found it?'

'By that time, something had changed. To reach the edge of the world reminded me how far I had come, and I felt called back, called back to make retribution. Baalgor was furious, and we became great enemies. Eventually he went through the Gate, but I refused to follow. Enough now. I'm weary and cold. No more talking until the spring.'

She put two pieces of wood on the fire and watched the new sparks fly into the winter night. Then she fetched the heavy fur and came close to me, and now for the first time I saw the skins she wore as masks.

She was nervous at first, making me sit away from her in the fireglow. But one by one she peeled three layers of skin from her face, each coloured in different ways, each containing, tattooed, part of the complex pattern of marks that had made her face so fascinating.

I was astonished at the careful revelation. Each layer she handled as if it was a spider's web, gently folding it, then rolling it, touching the mask to her body as she proceeded, speaking quiet words, and at times lowering her head and kissing the back of each of her hands.

With the removal of the third skin-mask, only half a face, came the sight of Nemet as she truly was, a skin of light hue, full-lipped, wide-eyed, high-boned, a beauty that took my breath away. She quickly applied dabs of an oil to her skin, which was lustrous in the fire, the green lines of her own tattoos glowing. Her hands were shaking slightly. She dragged a thick-toothed comb through her black hair, pulling it to the side and working at the knots and tangles, watching me all the time.

'You look so different,' I said helplessly.

'Different?'

'Without the skins. There was always something hauntingly beautiful about you, very primitive . . . but now . . .'

'I'm ugly?'

'Hardly that. Just different. A different person . . .'

'But not different at all. Just naked.'

'And beautiful. Very beautiful.'

'You sound like my father.'

I felt embarrassed, watching her as she first combed her hair, then peeled the clinging clothes from her body, massaging her shoulders, breasts and belly with the same sweet-smelling oil. She shuffled closer to the fire, shivering slightly. I wondered if she would invite me to anoint her back – the thought thrilled me, an excitement combined with guilt – but she simply dressed again, then closed her eyes and swayed as she sat, whispering words that had no meaning for me.

At the end of her prayers she became still, staring at the flames, perhaps remembering the past. She seemed melancholy again.

'Were you praying?'

Nemet glanced up at me, then smiled slightly. 'Saying goodbye.'

I wanted to know so much about this woman. The last time we had met she had trapped me and tricked me; now she was here, more intimate than I could ever have imagined, confident with me, trusting, sharing a winter's night and a warming fire. 'Saying goodbye to . . . Baalgor?'

'To my sisters.'

'Your sisters? How many sisters?' I felt a chill as she picked up the small pouch of skins and kissed it. 'Three, of course. Two of them dead, one skinned but quick enough to run! I wonder where she is? I've been wearing their faces since I fled the sanctuary. But it's time I let them go. They've helped me enough . . .

'Bless them,' she added as an afterthought.

'They've been eyes for me to look into the shadows, and a sweet tongue with which to talk to strangers, and a sharp-scented warning of the dangers of strange wild beasts in the demon land. But I don't need them, now, not now that I'm going back. If I'm careful, I can find their broken bones and give them proper burning, a proper earthing before the sanctuary takes me. I owe them that, since my father is dead and my mother buried with him.'

'What was your sanctuary called? Where in the world can I find it?' I asked, but Nemet threw cold ashes at me, angrily.

'Enough of this! I'm tired, I want to sleep. I want to wait for spring. We can talk then. In the meantime, just sleep against me, and hunt ahead of me. It's too cold to do anything else, and I'm too tired.'

26

Exactly as Greenface had predicted, spring came in the form of a sudden, warm wind, a passing of brightness on the land. The snows melted, the ice turned to slush, and the forested hill behind the ruined settlement began to colour with a fresh, bright green. I stood among the trees, watched the rapid bursting of the bud, marvelling at a sight which owed no allegiance to nature, only to imagination: my own imagination, my deepest dreams.

Soon the forest was in full leaf and the heat was splendid. Steam rose from my heavy clothes, and the world smelled damp and rank. Wild creatures returned to the land, their movements noisy in the new growth, their shapes bulky, their cries occasionally articulated as they found the old trails, and the paths to the lake.

Two of the four small horses came nosing up to me as I returned to the camp on the shore, a third staying to graze the lush foliage. I tethered the animals and they seemed content. Their companion arrived later, stamping at the ground and backing away from me as I approached with the halter. When I threw aside the rope it became calm and came and grazed about the walls. A strong minded animal, then, and being slightly larger than its mates I marked it as my own steed for the future.

The boat was in deep water, but not yet silted. With Greenface I swam down to its hulk and we pushed it upright, freeing it from the rocks so that it might be dragged more easily. Greenface swam like an eel, a wriggling, slender shape, all legs and arms as she struck for the bright surface then doubled up to dive again, her black hair streaming about her face, her limbs smooth and silky as they gently kicked to keep her in her place.

She caught me looking at her, seconds before the strictures in my lungs sent me spiralling to the air again, where I gasped for breath then plunged to the wreck, uncomfortably aware that the touch of the water on my naked body, the sense of freedom, the sight of the woman, was giving away my arousal. Greenface teased me with a kiss the fifth time I dived and I almost choked. She was ascending above me in a stream of bubbles and I floated up after her, rising to the surface with my hands gently running up the length of her body, touching her sex, the swell of her buttocks, her belly, the taut flesh of her breasts, and finally the lean, beautiful angles of her face.

She was looking at me with hunger, her hands on my shoulders, treading water slowly. Then again she kissed me on the mouth, a brief contact, her tongue a sensuous touch upon my lips. With a sudden laugh she kicked away, swimming strongly for the shore. 'We need ropes and horses,' she shouted, and I followed the lithe, naked woman to the tethered animals.

We had already made lengths of rope from the nets and cables left after the destruction of the fishing village. We swam down with them, securing the small craft on the lake bed, then used the equines to drag the vessel to the shore, diving to the slowly moving hulk, pushing and struggling to help it through the sediment. After several hours its prow was above the water. Later, we dragged it to the shore and hauled and heaved it over to inspect the damage.

'We can cut new wood to fill the holes,' she said. 'And melt old pitch from the broken fishing boats to make it waterproof. The sail is in good condition, but the mast is snapped half way down. So you'll have to cut a tree to make it good. First, though, go and find the saddles and the harnesses.'

'Why?' I asked, interrupting her flow of thought. She seemed expert at everything she suggested, running her hands over the savaged hull, testing the depth of the bitumen waterproofing, examining the rigging-rings and cords on the waterlogged canvas sail. She seemed the very antithesis of Greyface's description of her: a woman without determination.

She glanced up and smiled. 'Horses can swim. We'll make wooden frames to help them. It's only half a day's sail across this lake, and we'll be dragging them with us. They couldn't do it in the winter, but in the summer they'll survive.'

And so I returned to the lake and swam in search of the leather saddles, the primitive trappings. I found two sets only and returned them to the camp, wondering how I might attach stirrups to them, but decided the effort was too much trouble. The horses would be good pack animals if not good mounts.

Two days later we crossed the wide water, beaching several miles away from the earthen and tree-palisaded walls of the stronghold that William had constructed around the tower of ivory and its white stone walls.

We lost the most robust and most independent of the horses on the way, perhaps because of its extra size, perhaps because of its age. I was sad to cut the creature free, but it was exhausted and in distress and a quick death was assured as it sank below the choppy surface of the lake.

With the small boat hidden in the forest's edge, Nemet set about making a shelter for herself, a corral for the three remaining animals. I left her, assured by her that she would remain until I returned, and walked the shore to the fort.

In two years, William had worked hard. Where before we had huddled in the shelter of ruins, now a vibrant city straddled the shore line and hills. Its harbour reached out from the bulrushes, a high wall, the wooden poles topped with carved heads, animal and human, and flapping flags. Five ships were tethered, bright pennants blowing from single masts, smooth, narrow-bladed oars gleaming in the pale sun. Animals struggled in corrals, smoke filled the sky from hearths, everywhere was activity and noise.

And yet I walked through the open gate in the imposing

earthwork wall that had been raised across the shore, stepping between the burning torches, without being challenged. The white tower was cordoned off, but I could walk round it into the main body of the stronghold, where much woodland remained, though the hill in places had been levelled into platforms to take small houses. Everywhere were tents, some square frames, some in the conical shape more familiar from the Americas. Two longhouses stretched in parallel in the centre of the space, torches burning in the sunlight in front of each. There were carts and wagons everywhere, and dogs and pigs squabbling over the scraps that littered the ground.

Almost as soon as I was inside this part of the enclosure I was noticed; a young man leading five horses came over to me curiously, followed by others, men and women both, all bedecked with icons and variously clothed. There were no older children running around, although some of the women carried infants. Distantly, inside a circular corral, two of the hippari were being galloped on the tether, responding to the gruff, sharp instructions of a fair-haired youth.

There was also a forge – I could hear the ringing sounds of metal being shaped – but it was out of sight, behind a cluster of tents.

The response, as I say, was mostly of curiosity, and I tried to indicate that I was a friend of William's, and had come to see him. It was a grizzle-bearded elder who finally caught on, and seemed to understand my connection with a man who was, I soon gathered, their tribal leader. I was led to one of the longhouses, pausing only to watch as five bedraggled riders came in through the gate, spears hanging heavy in their arms, steam rising from the exhausted hippari. They were angry and they smelled of blood, walking brusquely to one of the larger tents, ignoring everything around them as their horses were led away.

For a while it was very confusing; I was given food and water and offered several small objects of a religious nature, which I took with a smile, waved, stroked, kissed, hugged and generally played with, watching for some sign of approval from the small group who sat around me in the longhouse. There was a gathering of softly spoken people at the far end, and smoke from a fire was billowing about the centre of the lodge. Two small dogs yapped and fussed in the gloom, continually chased away by the people around me, who seemed to be waiting for me to address them.

After a while, one of the five riders entered the lodge and came over to me. He was very young, but already his face was crisscrossed with what looked not so much like cuts as scratches, and the scratchmarks of wild animals, rather than a lover. His name was Perendour. His hair was long and lank and he had shed the draping uniform of leather and dull metal for a filthy grey and voluminous djellaba. Watching me through dark, lively eyes, he extended his hand and I shook it. The act, a simple one, seemed to please him, indeed, seemed to tell him, or confirm in him, everything he wished to know. Now the alcohol was delivered, an earthy, stale brew in which all manner of detritus swirled. It would be good for the bowels, I thought, and shared the toast. It was a strong drink and I consumed it with circumspection, picking at the dry meats and fruit in the bowl between us and listening to the knight's conversation as best I could.

William and his entourage were several days' ride away, in the high mountains, searching for an oracle. He was with his new bride, who was a lively and 'kicking' mare. She had two scars on each cheek, and I realized that this was the fishergirl, Ethne, from the sacked fortress across the lake.

William – who Perendour referred to with a slight deference, confirming my belief that William was either Chief or Prince in this stronghold – had never given up hope of my return. Far from being angry at being abandoned, he had believed I had been taken by demons, but was aware that I had courage and would return if I could find a way. Every season he led his growing band of hunter-warriors to the Bull Ruins beyond the lake. This time for the first time he had sent his men alone, but already a rider was on his way to find him.

He would want to return immediately, to see me. He had missed me with all his heart, and was often to be found wandering in a melancholy state along the lake shore. Only the raid and the liberation of Ethne from her oppressive father and husband had cheered him.

I soon worked out that his followers were the icon hunters I had seen on my previous incarnation in the Hinterland. The ragged band who prowled my own unconscious had all too readily fallen in behind a man who promised them the booty of many cities, and whilst their first attack had been to satisfy the needful love of their leader, even now they were planning to enter the Eye itself, to the source of cities.

I listened and tried to understand the various fabulous legends that were told about the Eye.

Already, several knights were lost, sucked down into the earth in their valiant but vain attempts to unlock the gate. The oracle might help in William's understanding of the quest ahead of him. His determination, his pure charisma, held together this growing and increasingly organized band of traders.

As for why they had hunted Greenface, the answer lay in the simple fact of the factionalism of the group; the men who had stayed behind to hunt the woman for sport were late recruits to the stronghold. I debated whether to mention their deaths, and decided not to, but I felt that had I done so the news would not have been greeted with any real concern.

A second thought, then, was whether to suggest to the woman that she came into the shelter and greater warmth of the fortress, but I detected a callous unconcern among my hosts that suggested it might have been unwise.

They did not particularly like strangers here; only my identification as William's great friend made me welcome. And besides, there *were* questions about the hunters, a puzzlement at the length of time they were taking to follow back across the lake.

*

At some time in the evening, weakened and warmed by drink, I thought of Greenface, waiting for me a few miles away. I became angry, outraged at the way she had been hunted, and began to articulate an incoherent protest, which was greeted with laughter and understanding of my state of inebriation. No-one could comprehend my actions, my assertions, but it was clear that I was drunk, and as quickly as I had begun my rant, I ceased it.

I was led to a berth at the far end of the longhouse, a small chamber separated from the rest of the communal space by a loose curtain of hides, overlain with strings of clattering bones. I had no doubt that these were holy relics, stitched together from the hands and feet of a thousand saints.

As I lay down on the soft mattress, helped into position by an overly physical matron, her body redolent with the scent of incense, I saw above the bed, pinned to a cross beam, the picture of Angela that had been such a comfort to me in my previous incarnation in the Hinterland.

The photograph of the smiling woman, taken with the newly born Natalie in her arms, was set between the sweet-faced, pale-skinned innocence of the Virgin Mary and the open-mouthed, enticing allure of the goddess Kali – the three faces of mythological woman: innocence, experience, destruction.

And I stared at my wife, and loved her, and began to entertain feelings of guilt for the fact that I was drawn so intimately to Greenface.

When I slept, I slept deeply, but was woken before dawn and encouraged to come and help fish the lake. As grey light illuminated the three beached ships, their rigging slapping against the masts in the crisp breeze, I waded into the water with a length of net, part of a ten man group which fished the shallows quite effectively before disbanding to other duties.

After a sumptuous breakfast of honey-glazed fish, aromatic and nutty bread, freshly baked, and succulent olives stuffed with fragrantly spiced meat – a meal that was a rare treat, judging by the delight and surprise that the mini-banquet evoked – I begged time to myself and took a pouch of purloined bread and fish along the shore to the camp where Greenface should have been waiting for me.

At first alarmed to find the site deserted, I soon found her heavy clothes furled up and hidden carefully; her travelling things were scattered about. From the sounds in the forest, high on the hills behind the lake, I guessed she was hunting and would return later.

I left the provisions and returned to the earthworks.

I waited here for two days, and in that time I didn't find Greenface, although the food I took to her was consumed, and the hidden shelter showed signs of having been used.

Then at dusk of the third day among the icon hunters, riders came into the stronghold, exhausted and dishevelled, their primitive horses steaming and screaming in an odd evocation of the more familiar 'whinny'.

I soon gathered that William was lost. He had ridden too close to the Eye, and though the band sent to fetch him back could see him, he was beyond their reach, and seemingly unaware of the danger he was now facing.

For a while the fort reacted with a sort of mindless shock, an aimless sequence of gatherings, discussions, silences and shaking of heads. I gained the impression that to go where William had inadvertently journeyed was the same as being dead, and the only thing stopping the mourning process was the fact that his soul could still be seen. And indeed, when the wild riders came to me, crouching before me in the Mongol fashion, elbows on knees, hands together between them, the discussion became more earnest than any yet.

They were looking to me, now, to understand how to guide William from the great distance that separated him, and Ethne and the others, from the enchanted world of the lake, the herds of hippari, and the prospect of adventure in wild realms.

'I can't do it without a guide,' I said. 'I need a guide myself. As soon as I've found her, I'll return.'

I went to the sheltered hide, frustrated to find it still empty. 'For Christ's sake!' I bellowed to the hills. 'Don't abandon me now!'

I passed the night by the water, listening to the movement of creatures beyond imagining, wary always of the giant beasts that came so swiftly to the lake's edge to drink.

And at dawn, just as I was drifting between sleep and wakefulness, the lobe of my ear was tugged, startling me.

'I've missed you,' Nemet said, her eyes sparkling, her breath moist on my face as she stared at me, searching my expression, perhaps for signs of betrayal. 'That fish!'

For a moment I was puzzled. 'That *fish*? What fish?'

'With honey. You left it for me. Wonderful!'

'Oh, *that* fish! I know. It's been red carpet treatment since I told them who I was.'

'Red carpet?'

'They've honoured me. I'm their chieftain's lost friend.'

'Honour *you*. Hunt *me* like a beast of prey.'

'Not all of them. I think you can trust them. I need you, now. I have to go to the Eye. William is trapped there, and his hunters think I can help. Will you come with me? You seem to know your way around this *edge of the world*.'

Nemet grimaced, then shrugged. 'I don't. Not really. I know the way back to the city. You mustn't put too much faith in me . . . Jack.'

It was the first time she had called me by name, and whilst I was pleased to hear the sound of my name on her tongue, she clearly was adjusting to a great change in her relationship with me. She repeated, 'Jack. *Jack.* Strange name for a strange dream-man.'

'It's a nickname for John. It's one of the oldest names known. It's probably no more than an early sound, one of several designed to distinguish between individuals. It's simple . . . like me . . . It needs direction . . . like me. Help me? Nemet?'

'I don't know.'

'*Please!*'

'I don't trust the people in the sanctuary . . .' she meant the stronghold. She was staring along the shore, frowning.

'They won't hurt you if you're with me. They need me, now. I just don't know what to do. It's not that I'm afraid of the Eye . . . I just don't understand it.'

'And you think I do?'

'More so than me. Your own sanctuary lies there. You led me a merry chase last time I was in this edge of the world. Nothing seems to surprise you.'

'Everything surprises me. I was born to expect that. Surprise keeps me moving. Perhaps that's the difference between us. Surprise takes you . . .' she suddenly laughed. 'By surprise. It stops you dead.'

'Yes.'

'Yes,' she repeated softly, thinking hard. And then she smiled, placed her hands on my face and leaned forward to kiss me. 'If I come with you – keep your friend's hired assassins away from me.'

'I promise.'

'Good. But I make *no* promises. I want to go home, Jack. I want to finish with the torment. I'll come with you as far as I can, but please don't try and keep me.'

'Of course I'll try and keep you!'

Again, she smiled; again she kissed me. 'I know. So I'll say goodbye to you now. That way . . . when I leave you I can do so without guilt. Goodbye Jack.'

'I'll follow you to the heart of the world.'

She laughed out loud, standing and gathering her belongings together. Then she said something that astonished me with its insight. 'You *are* the heart of the world. There's nowhere else for you to go.'

27

I should have foreseen the outcome of the perilous journey to the Eye of the land.

I had been seduced by Ahk'Nemet's closeness and intimacy, and I had not truly believed her warning words. It seemed unlikely, as we ascended the wooded mountain slopes, rise upon rise, deep into the mist, that she would try and escape before we had accomplished our mission. And perhaps I was right to think that, though I had forgotten one simple precept of human life: we don't always act in the way we mean. Deeper drives are often at work.

Burdened by charms, the horses heavy with religious icons, we followed Perendour and his band of four along the mountain trails. These mercenaries had a lazy way of riding, slouched in the crude saddles, rein-free arm dangling, heads drooping as if asleep. They were resting as they rode, but were nevertheless alert to every movement in the forest, erupting into a sudden gallop as a small creature unwarily gave itself away, surrounding the beast and using spears to dispatch it with brutal, gleeful finality. Fresh pig and colourful, surprised-looking birds were soon added to the loads on the two packhorses.

This was not the same route to the whirlpool of woods and ruins that I had glimpsed before, but soon the earth began to shake at times, deep tremors that startled the animals and discomforted their riders. The mountains were dangerous here, with slippages of grey rock, crashing trees, and the fragile, crumbling ruins of ancient buildings. Everything seemed to be on the move, but there was not, as yet, any of that sense of the world slipping-by that I had encountered in my previous pursuit of Greenface.

That changed as soon as we crested the last and most difficult of the ridges, winding our way through a gloomy wood of pines and birch, and finally emerging onto the lip of the Eye. Here, stretching away from us into the vast distance and descending into the depths, the rotating spiral of the earth could be seen.

'Now we *ride*,' said Perendour irritably, and kicked his steaming equine to make it trot along the precarious path.

I soon discovered that we had come along the wrong trail, and that we had a great deal of distance to make up. We rode, therefore, almost non-stop for the rest of the day as it was experienced here, resting only for the sake of the horses, when they threatened to drop with exhaustion. Away went the unnecessary supplies, the fresh meat included; the pack animals were now swapped around among us, extra backs for the burden of human weight.

Without tents, it was a miserable night; without sleep, kept awake by fear, it was a nightmare. The world creaked, rumbled and shifted as we huddled around a blazing fire, watching shadows in the dark. The hippari screamed, gnawing and struggling at their tethers, struggling for freedom. They would only be calmed by constant attention. By moonlight, we watched a castle wall ascend the slope. Regurgitated from the Eye, it rose above us over the hours, dark towers silent and leaning precariously as the land spewed it out. We crouched below the crumbling battlements helpless, like creatures fixed by light, unmoving, trusting to fate. It passed safely by us and later crashed into the forest, the sound of its falling sending birds screeching into the grey dawn skies.

Weary, but glad of the new day, we packed up and continued round the maelstrom, following broken roads and crude tracks where possible, searching in the fragments of habitation where we found them, looking for the oracle where William had last been seen.

At last Perendour called out, and we mounted up and followed him away from the ridge, towards the marble façade that had been built against a cliff. Bright in the sun, the carved stone was blinding. The forest had grown through the building, branches drooping from the angled windows, ivy entwining with the dancing figures of humans and grotesque animals that wreathed the arch across the entrance.

Nemet was affected by the ruin, cautious and anxious. 'I know this place. I've played here so many times as a child.'

'Here? Exactly here?'

'Somewhere *like* this . . .' she murmured, but was unsure. She added in a whisper, 'It's followed me too. This `is the place.'

I looked more closely at the carvings. The human figures of both sexes were dressed in either short kilts or shapeless robes; the women were shown with their hair in tight, waist-length ringlets, the men with beards and 'fans' of hair across their crowns. There were no weapons in sight, but the beasts were more fabulous than realistic, and small chariots abounded. There were ships, high prowed, high keeled, and stacks of what looked like amphorae and the skins of animals.

Over all of this, dominating the empty entrance, was a pair of watching eyes, a stone carving that communicated great authority, with just a hint of humour where the lids narrowed above the unshaped nose. It was a knowing look by all our judgements, and the stare seemed to follow us about.

What had at first seemed Grecian, at closer inspection was far, far older.

Perendour was prodding at the undergrowth blocking the entrance, looking for a way inside. I suddenly realized that Ahk'Nemet had become agitated.

'Don't go in!' she cried in genuine terror. She had begun to back away, wide-eyed and frightened, staring up at the façade of the temple.

'What is it?'

'Don't go in. Stop him going inside! It's the Watching Place. I remember, now – my father pursued me here . . .'

'You said you'd played here as a child . . .'

'I did. So did my brother. *Stop him*.'

Even as Nemet shouted this order, causing Perendour to hesitate in his movement through the undergrowth, the woman had run for her horse, flinging herself over its back before squirming round to grip the flanks with her legs. She kicked, smacked and bullied the poor creature into a jerking gallop that carried the two of them along the edge of the forest.

Unmoved by the strange woman's warning, Perendour had vanished into the overgrown temple. He called out; there was the sound of crashing about. He whistled, then laughed, and his companions turned to me and laughed also, raising their hands in that universal gesture that means simply: why all the fuss?

Their casual attitude was, not quite literally, the spur to my giving chase to Nemet. She was not a good rider, and though she seemed to race ahead of me when she heard my approach, at the edge of the cliff itself, she soon turned into the forest, ducking and weaving below the branches, finally flinging herself from the crude saddle and dangling from a bough. She hung there, stretched out and magnificent, her head slightly thrown back as she breathed softly.

I rode up to her and round her, then dismounted to stand below her, meeting her tearful gaze. I put my arms around her legs, my face against her belly, and she released the branch and came slowly into my embrace.

Her mouth was suddenly on my own, pressed hard, her tongue a deep and passionate presence, then a flickering, tasting tease across my lips. Her eyes remained closed all the time, her hands gripping my hair, pulling my face against her own, a wet, erotic, wonderful union of kisses.

She was still crying.

'Please don't run from me,' I whispered when the kiss broke. Her gaze was suddenly questioning.

'Then come back with me. Come back to the sanctuary.'

'I can't. I don't belong here. Besides . . .'

'I know. You have a wife, and a daughter, and Baalgor threatens your happiness. Are you thinking of her now?'

'Angela? Yes.'

'Do you think she's watching you?'

'She's a long way away.'

'But she knows. Don't you think she knows?'

Her words were not a tease, not a challenge; they might have come from my own mind, my own guilt at this encounter with flesh and face and the furious potential of a passionate union that was firing me and making me dizzy. The woman in my arms refused to unwind from me, her legs about me, her arms round my neck, her mouth touching me moistly, my eyes, my brow, my cheeks, my lips.

'Is this wrong?' she asked, and I answered quite truthfully that I didn't know. This woman was not real, although she was full, firm and fabulous in my intimate embrace. My fingers touched her and she arched her back, her warm breath sweet as she enjoyed the probing caress.

I didn't know if it was wrong. But the thought of Angela monitoring this overpowering foreplay made me shake. How could she see? Was a machine flickering? Was Steve sitting there, reeling off acronyms?

Subject entering phase of Pre-Sex Ecstasy; PSE growing! Limbic system activity increasing; physical arousal of Midax subject very obvious . . . reflection of VE (Virtual-Excitement) in the Deep Midax State.

This beautiful, tearful eastern woman had come from my past, from my dreams; I had entered the dream to find her; I had become that song of myself so celebrated by the poet. How could it be wrong to celebrate a love that was contained within my very soul?

The forest was quite still as I set Ahk'Nemet down on her

feet, then kissed her before kneeling before her and undressing her, running my mouth over the smooth skin of her belly, breathing her strong, moist scent as she held my head against her and gently stroked my hair. She lay below me, then, her eyes closed, her mouth half open, her breath shaped almost inaudibly into words of affirmation, her hands pressing me deeper, restraining me when I gave in to an urgency that was too animal for this strong yet seemingly slight and sensuous creature.

We moved together gently for what seemed like hours, and when she felt I was reaching my climax she took my hands and pressed them to her breasts, then again took my face in her slim fingers and drew me close for a hungry kiss as our bodies shuddered and sighed with pleasure.

'Beautiful,' she whispered.

'Yes. Beautiful.'

'Stay inside me. I can still feel the fire.'

'I had no plans to move at all . . .'

But shortly after, one of the hippari raced past, snorting and afraid, its trappings flailing as it panicked, panicking our own two horses, shattering the blissful intimacy.

'Something's happened,' Nemet said unnecessarily, tugging on her clothes. 'Let's get away from here. The Watching Place is too dangerous.'

'I can't just leave them.'

She almost spat at me, eyes bright with fury . . . or perhaps fear. 'Of course you can! Your friend isn't far. You don't need those *men!*'

Quite why I felt drawn back to the Watching Place I have no idea; a sense of duty? That would have been strange, since duty held no particular value for me; friendship, yes, but Nemet was quite right that it made more sense to ride away, to seek William alone. And yet I couldn't.

She was exasperated and angry, suddenly cold when minutes before she had been caressing me so warmly.

We rode quickly back to the shrine and found Perendour's

comrades in a state of agitation and indecision. Clearly, I imagined, something terrible had occurred to their man inside the temple walls; the horse had panicked because of the sudden shrieking of its master, hidden beyond the stone façade. None of the other knights had dared go into the ruins to discover the truth behind their fear that Perendour had been violently done to death.

In fact, the hipparion had bolted when a rock fall had frightened it. And the agitation was because of what Perendour had found, away from the Watching Place.

He was crouched on a rocky outcrop, staring across the valley at the circulating swirl of the maelstrom.

He glanced round as I rode up, then beckoned to me. Nemet hissed her irritation and kicked her horse towards the oracle. I dismounted and ran quickly to where the man was waiting. He pointed into the distance and after a moment taken to re-adjust to the strange landscape before me, I focused upon the small encampment.

'William!'

If at first I whispered his name, I soon shouted it, but Perendour tugged me down again, shaking his head. Indeed, my bellowed cry had failed to disturb the tableau of figures on the moving earth. So close, yet so far, my friend from the previous incarnation had not heard the sound of my voice.

And so I could do nothing but watch, and stare, and hunger.

From this distance, William looked no older than when I'd last seen him, a fresh-faced youthfulness, framed in the wispy blond of his beard. I could see he was laughing, kicking his horse into a gallop, cloak streaming as he was followed by the dark-haired girl from the farther shore.

She herself had transformed. There was something wild about her; I could imagine the sound of her shouting, of her laughter. She kicked at her steed, leaning forward across its neck, determined to win the race. Their companions, two cloaked men, trotted easily behind them.

The scamper across the land ended, the riders wheeled about, leaned towards each other and kissed.

Then William turned his eyes towards the pinnacle where I stood, and shaded his eyes, peering hard.

For a moment my blood raced. He'd seen us! But then I realized that his gaze had shifted. He was scanning the land as he saw it, but my own physical presence was not in evidence. The girl rode up beside him and leaned an arm on his shoulder. She was so pale of face, but perhaps that whiteness was simply a contrast with the extravagant colours of her tunic and trousers, gleaming peacock blues and greens. I couldn't see her scars, but her beauty was apparent, and her contentment with my friend was physically manifest.

Suddenly she had wrestled William from the back of his horse, and tumbled with him to the ground, laughing. Their companions discreetly turned and rode to a sheltered site. William and Ethne ran towards me, ducking down behind an outcrop, where the ground was grassy and fairly level. For a while it was hard to equate this carefree, playful young man with the ruthless attack on the fishing town, and the abduction – hardly against her will, it seemed – of the eldest of the chief's daughters.

I watched them for a minute only, for as long as they wrestled and rolled, energetically youthful, fighting with teases. When their mouths met, and they became quite still save for the slow unbuckling of belts and opening of shirts, I withdrew from my vantage point, sat quietly by myself and closed my eyes.

Later, Perendour came up to me, stabbing his spear towards the gorge, making spider movements with his other hand. 'They're moving off,' he seemed to be saying and I returned to the knoll.

They had packed their horses, adjusted their clothing, and were preparing to travel on. I wanted to ride down the slope, into the gorge that separated us, but Perendour was adamant that it would be of no avail. By whatever means William had crossed into the maelstrom, he would have to find his own way back, or be sucked down into the swirl of the earth.

After a while, my friend and his lake-girl rode on, then turned into a wood and were lost from sight. I was tearful for a few minutes, deeply affected by a strong sensation of loss and helplessness. I had wanted so much to meet William Finebeard again, a re-union he himself had hungered for, but he had eluded me, slipping through the time and the space of my own imagination, following a trail that was as much denied to me, the centre of my world, as it was to the scale-armoured mercenaries who even now were watching me with expressions that were solemn, uncertain, and distinctly shifty.

Where was Ahk'Nemet?

'What's happened to my companion?' I asked by word and sign.

Perendour rose from his crouched position and looked towards the white stone gate, the watching place.

'That woman is a witch. We should kill her and be done with it. Then maybe your great friend will find a way back to us.'

'Nemet is no witch.'

Were they saying 'witch'? And if so, what did they mean by it? An evil woman? A wise woman? Not the latter, certainly, since Perendour seemed quite exercised by the need to dispatch Greenface. She had, as I understood him, brought 'black charms and poisonous forgotten winds with her', to a world in which she 'did not belong'.

He went on, 'We occasionally see these people. They rise from the earth, or the lake, they come from the dark of the pit to beguile us, and shadow our vision with masks.'

'Nonsense.'

Perendour dropped to a crouch again, leaning forward between his knees and scratching patterns on the rock with his knife. He was thinking hard.

What had happened to Greenface?

On impulse I called out her name. Perendour glanced up, shouted something. The next thing I knew, one of his men, Gyldowen, had performed an odd, skipping dance, turning where he stood, doubling up . . .

And a spear-shaft, green-gleaming at its tip, was flying towards me, wobbling slightly in the air as it covered the distance in less than a second!

Acting by no more than reflex, I ducked. The ash shaft cracked against my head, blackening my vision for a moment. Perendour was on me in that instant, his flint knife above my left eye, held back by both my hands, but he was a strong man, far stronger than me, and his left hand clawed and scratched my flesh. I could hear his companions yelling with kill-fever, scrambling towards us.

The arrow that knocked Perendour from my body struck him in the temple, arriving with the hiss of a snake and the thudding crack of bone. He lay beside me, eyes staring and mouth open, one hand brushing feebly at the shaft. I scrabbled for the spear and succeeded in stabbing it into Gyldowen's thigh. He howled with pain and dragged himself away, then unleashed a jagged piece of slingshot that struck me above the nose. There was no real power in the shot, though the pain was excruciating, and I watched him blearily as he limped away, an arrow suddenly striking him in the shoulder, propelling him forward. He complained loudly as he staggered for safety.

I looked round for Nemet, but it was *Greenface* who approached, since she had tied her sisters' skins to her face again. The dyes and patterns of the tattoos made her wild once more, and somehow horrific. The skins weren't smooth; they sagged across her firm flesh and she looked ancient, as if that flesh were running from her skull, her mouth dragging down in a sinister leer. She glanced at me then ran quickly to the fallen man. The last of Perendour's companions was already far away in the forest, riding fast. Nemet danced around the head of the struggling man on the ground, her spear teasing and stabbing at Gyldowen's flailing, defending hands until, like a fisherman, she saw the opening to her prey and stabbed down quickly.

All frenzy left the knight.

As she approached me now, she held her short bow; an arrow was nocked. Just in case? Everything about her was tied, bound, fixed, ready for running. She bristled with feathers, gleamed with colours, flexed and twisted with muscular energy as she came to me, half stooping, very wary.

'I'm going home,' she said. 'Don't try to stop me.'

'We've had this conversation before.'

'I have to go. Unless I go, Baalgor will never release his hold on you . . .'

'I don't understand.'

'He needs me, Jack. He thinks he can entice me out again, out of this hell, into the enchanted garden, the place of dreams.'

She meant my own world.

'You might like it!'

'It might not like me. It's not my earth. Nor Baalgor's. We've been hunted as the Mudhawk hunts the snake, and the only way for peace is to go home, to find the city. If I go, Baalgor will follow, I'm sure of it. Without me he has no direction.'

'He says he doesn't need it. He can re-create you from my daughter.'

'He's a destructive man. He can burrow into your life, your lives, with the ease of a worm in a fig. But he can't get back what he needs from me. If you want to lose him from your life, then let me go. Or if you want an eternal life with me . . . follow me to the sanctuary. Take his place.'

There was something about the way she said 'eternal life' that suggested the life of the soul after a short and brutish murder. She was half smiling, aware of my hesitation, my distrust. 'It's all right, Jack. I shan't beg you to come.'

But I wanted to follow her! I wanted to stay with her, running this strange world, making our home in the lee of cliffs, or the bowers of the forest; I wanted to sleep with my face against her skin, my hands touching that smooth and supple flesh. Even through the skin masks of her dead sisters, her eyes sparkled with enchantment and longing.

She leaned forward to kiss me with a moist passion that stunned me.

'Goodbye, Jack.'

'Wait!' I called, moments later.

She turned where she stood, below the watching eyes of the gate. There was a smile of expectancy on her gruesome face, then a frown. At the same time I felt a different wind blow from the trees behind me; there was a faint aroma of perfume, and something like ether . . . like a hospital! Deep voices seemed to moan incoherently, and I thought I heard my name.

Ahk'Nemet suddenly cried out, shaking her head and throwing aside her weapons and pack. She ran to me, tearing away the masks.

'Not back!' she shouted. 'Don't go back!'

Angela called to me. '*You're hurting . . . Jack . . . come home . . . Jack . . .*'

Arms were around my neck, fingers in my hair, holding tightly to keep me. A mouth on mine, tears in half-opened eyes, a cry of grief muffled by the kiss. 'I'm not ready! I'm fine! Leave me alone!' I shouted as I broke the powerful grip of the Levantine-looking woman. Nemet thought, for a moment, that I was shouting at her, but I grasped her face, stared into the wintry skies, aware that the world was spinning, that I was dizzy.

I remember thinking, *You bastard, Steve! Leave me alone! You bastard! Angela! Let me go! I belong here, now. Let me go. Don't drag at me, don't keep watching me!*

Then Greenface was staring through me, looking round frantically, her face at first haunted, then distressed. I reached for her again, but she was as insubstantial to my fingers, now, as I was invisible to her eyes.

Weakened by the pull of another world, I sank to my knees, curled into a ball, tried to hold the last scents of the high forest, the older world, the woman from my heart.

Then hands were on my face, and a voice said, 'Got him. Thank God. I thought we'd never get him back. The bruising's not too bad. Why is he struggling . . . ?'

And Angela murmured, 'Why's he crying?'

PART SEVEN

The Moon Pool

28

Disorientated, damaged and furious, Jack came back from the Deep like a ghost, sharing his life, through his senses and thoughts, between the reality of the Midax room and the surreality of the forested hill and Watching Place that looked down across the maelstrom.

It was quite clear that he had been brought out too quickly, too abruptly; he had been too deeply immersed in the Midax state for a safe return, and only the concern for his bleeding, the fear that he might be in a skirmish against greater odds, had finally led Steve to agree with Angela to terminate the trip without first 'nudging' Jack back towards the Hinterland.

But Angela's expression, her demeanour, was transparent.

She had argued with Steve about the necessity of return not because of the scratches and cuts but because she, like the other technicians, was aware that Jack was in an intimate embrace. As with the wound-induced stigmata, so his body exuded the *smells* of his encounters, and when stale sweat from the quiescent, naked body on the padded couch had changed to pungent sex, Angela had become very angry. Despite Steve's carefully articulated explanation that Jack's *Midact* would not necessarily behave in the same moral way as Jack himself – that he was experiencing only the equivalent of a powerful erotic dream – her jealousy was entrenched and resolute, and she won the argument.

Jack was ripped *untimely* from the heart of his world.

Angela quickly regretted her brief loss of control. As soon, in fact, as her husband lurched screaming from the couch, tearing at his drip-lines and sensors.

It was clear that he was very ill, raging across the Midax room, his face dark, his muscles bunched, his wild gestures, his bull-like fury threatening to damage valuable and delicate equipment.

It took a paramedic to subdue him. Partially pacified, he was led to a recovery room. But though he was calm, now, in his eyes, as he stared at Angela, there was only a gleaming, boiling expression of hate.

An icy wind blew from the Watching Place, swirling from the maelstrom beyond. Storm clouds flowed across the forest and on the wind came the smell of fire.

Greenface came running, body held low, dark hair streaming. There was blood on her broad-belted tunic. She carried her bow and sheath of arrows, and wore her sisters' faces.

Behind her, four dog-like creatures chased towards her, leaping high in the air as they covered the ground, necks widened with frills of hair, backs stiffened with ridges of spines. They were higher than the woman, black-furred and streaked with amber. Narrow eyes were set close together above long, grinning muzzles.

Greenface turned and shot the leader. It stood up on its hind legs, the arrow embedded in its shoulder. All four of the wolverines straightened, heads lowering as they stared at their prey. They spread out, then, moving carefully on their hind-legs, forepaws hanging stiff, claws gleaming.

Again Greenface shot the leader, this time in the jaw, and the creature dropped from its upright gait, shaking its head and beginning to scream.

The taller of the females ran at the huntress. The creature, arrowstruck in the skull, kept coming. At the last moment it turned and swept out its hindquarters, legs extended, the claws raking Nemet's arm and stomach.

After this, the dire-wolves retreated, leaving the stench of the alpha male's secretion where it had marked the site of its defeat.

For several minutes they growled and called from the tree-line, close to the Watching Place, then were gone.

Greenface was shaken. She sat down on the rocky ground and lowered her head, her right hand clutching the claw-wounds on her arm . . .

As the encounter with her faded, Jack felt sun on his face and opened his eyes to the ceiling of the room; the window was open and the light was spilling in, making him squint. He swung his legs from the bed and looked around.

He could hear the sound of a woman crying; and his name was being called.

'She didn't go through,' he said aloud. 'She's waiting for me at the gate.'

Across the room, Angela shifted in her chair, then opened her eyes from the nap she'd been taking.

'Jack?'

She came over to him, hesitant at first, then more gladly as he stood and took her in his arms.

'Thank God,' she said, kissing him and tugging his hair. 'I thought we'd done you some serious harm.'

'She's waiting for me by the Watching Place,' he whispered. He felt fear and exhilaration, and the fear was for Ahk'Nemet, who was clearly in a dangerous place, alone, and with limited defence.

'Who is? Is it Greenface?'

'Greenface,' he repeated emptily. Then the circumstances of his departure from the arms of the woman came back to him. 'Why did you break the journey?'

Anger surfaced briefly and Angela stepped quickly back, but the shadow passed and he scratched his stubbly cheeks and chin. 'I wanted to go with her,' he said.

'I know. Or at least, I could guess. I'm sorry, Jack. I couldn't bear the thought of what you were doing. And besides, you looked like you were having all kinds of shit beaten out of you. You're very bruised again.'

'I was fine.'

'You'd also been in the Deep for fourteen days. We were getting concerned about letting you away for so long.'

'*Two weeks?*'

He tried to digest the fact. Previously, for what had seemed to be a longer visit beyond the Hinterland, he had been in the Midax state for only a quarter of that time. He stared at the floor for a while, then Angela almost sighed.

'Was she prepared to return with you?'

And of course he could only shake his head. 'No. No she wasn't. She wanted to go back to the city. She wanted me to go with her.'

Angela looked grim, her arms crossed as she stared at her dishevelled husband.

'And you wanted to go with her, I suppose. You wanted to follow her. You wanted to follow her?'

'Yes.'

'Of course. Of course you do . . .'

But he wasn't sure, now.

As he shifted back to reality, the passion in the dream was less intense, the urge that had been overwhelming him – to travel back to the beginning of things with Nemet, to help her atone for whatever she had done so long in the past – now seemed secondary to the sweet immediacy of his family.

'How's Natalie?'

'I don't know,' Angela said, and there was something almost tearful in her voice. 'But *I'm* not fine, Jack. Thank you for asking.'

'I'm sorry,' he said quickly, and reached for her, holding her very tightly. 'God, I'm sorry. I'm sorry, Angie. I'm still between two worlds. I haven't got my feet on hard ground yet.'

She was apologetic herself. 'Of course you haven't. I'm too impatient. Natalie is . . . strange. She's here, in the Institute. I don't like to leave her alone, but somehow . . . when we're home . . . somehow she always ends up dancing in the field.

Do you think she puts a spell on us?' She was smiling wearily. '*Someone* blinds us with charm when he wants to dance with our daughter . . .'

Angela's cold, tired words were like a blow to the heart, and Jack remembered the claustrophobic grimness of Glanum, and the crawling, mindless shade that was his daughter's reflection in that world. From love, he was suddenly back in the reality of fear, because he would have to go again into Glanum, to beg for more time, another chance.

Seeing the sudden anxiety on his face, Angela reached out to stroke a finger across his brow. 'Don't think about it, Jack. We should go home. Go home and spend some time together. Let's go up to the moors, go walking, find a remote pub with good beers and home-cooked food and stay until we feel like leaving.'

'I need a debriefing session, don't I?'

Though this time it'll be selective and discreet . . .

'Yes. Yes, of course. But after that . . . home for a while, then away into the moors. Without concern for the grey-green faces in your life.'

Jack stared at the woman, her own face bright, now, and not just with enthusiasm but with a need, almost a hunger, that he hadn't seen for several years.

And all he could think was:

but I WANT to be concerned for the Greenface in my life . . .

It was over two days since his return and Steve was anxious to hear the details of his experiences.

'How long would you say had passed since you were there before?'

'Hard to tell. Nemet suggested two years. Time enough for William and his mercenaries to have built boats, sailed the lake and sacked the fishing village. But to create the fortress? And for the survivors of the village to have built their own stronghold, and fleet? Two years doesn't seem long enough.'

'From what you could see of them, did William and the Fishergirl seem much the same age as before?'

'Very much so.'

'Then there may be a continuity of story on the level of your association with your friend William, but discontinuity of setting.'

'Each time I go back, I go back to a variant of the experience?'

'I think so. A third trip will help to get some hard and fast rules established. When you're ready, of course. And only if you agree.'

Greenface was singing; a love song; a song of longing; it was a warm night and she lay, covered in skins, below brilliant stars. Her words carried on the breathing wind from the earthpool, the maelstrom, beyond the place where she waited.

'Jack?'

'Sorry. She's very close. Still very close. She might be outside the room, that's how close she feels to me.'

Of course there'll be a third trip.

The other question that fascinated Steve was that of language. He made Jack go over and over again the sort of words and gestures that had been used by the knights of the fortress.

A linguist was brought in to listen and watch, and there was a great deal of debate about the fact that, even when communicating by sign, gesture and alien tongue, understanding was achieved remarkably quickly. Nemet, however, spoke English – or Jack spoke the apparently Levantine language of the woman – and so she clearly came from a different part of the unconscious world that was informing the Deep and the Hinterland.

Nemet and her aggressive partner – her brother/husband – were older, deeper, more a part of Jack than the others, who were most likely to have been constructs to cover the various personalities, shades of grey, that create the complex human individual.

Nemet was 'archetypal', though Steve was uncomfortable with the word. But she and Baalgor were part of an archetypal image, released, or revealed in Jack's case, but perhaps present in all the human population.

What they represented was hard to see, though their link with the City – or sanctuary, as Ahk'Nemet thought of it – their relationship with an event that had been City/Sanctuary based, suggested they came from a time when the human mind was growing aware of 'community'.

As with the chaos of their forms, their armour and their functions, so the language of the mercenaries was a mishmash of what Jack had *heard*, what he *knew*, and what was *innate*: a neurobabble that flowed like French, was heavily influenced by an early form of Welsh, and contained almost coherent passages of proto-Finnish, one of the earliest languages still in common usage, reflecting the common tongue of Central and Northern Europe in the period after the end of the Ice Age.

Although the words were meaningless to Jack himself, they were nevertheless part of the so-called Resurrection Imagery controlled by the brain's *limbic system*, those scattered memories that are resurrected in the human foetus during the third month of incubation . . . similar to – Steve showed him – but not quite the same as, the neo-Jungian notion of Experience-Programmed Common-Unconscious . . . or the post-Sheldrake concept of Transmissible Resonant Neuromorphs . . .

The hidden mind was a world of its own, a playground for any isolated ego that had decided to go a-roving!

Jack was weary; Jack was sad. He no longer felt at home. Home was beneath the stars, by the Watching Place, where the lithe woman, wearing her sisters' faces, waited for him. He became impatient with the Institute, irritable with Steve and Angela, and as soon as he had recounted what he remembered of the trip, saying nothing of his feelings or activities with Greenface, he called an end to the debriefing.

'Ok! Ok!' Steve said, as his persistent request for just 'one more session' began to arouse anger in the subject.

Jack calmed down.

'Let me out of here. For Christ's sake, let's end it. I'm stifling . . .'

'Yes. The session's over. Go home, Jack. Angela? Look after him.'

But Steve could never let go. He walked with the couple towards the playroom where Natalie was at work on a huge jigsaw with two other children.

'Nemet is an enigma. And Baalgor. We need to try and place them in time, and in the world. You need to try and understand what they did, where they did it, and who is pursuing them. Are you going into the *shimmering* again?'

'I don't know!'

'If you do . . .'

'I said, I don't know! Leave me alone, Steve. I've had enough!'

Brightmore tugged at his sleeve. 'I want to be with you if you do. I want to record the trip. There'll be a link with the Deep. There has to be. Let me come with you.'

Angela led her husband along the corridor, calling back to Steve, 'I'll be in touch. Your idea's a good one.'

But she added in an almost inaudible whisper, clearly not intended for Jack to hear: 'He'll take some persuading. Leave it to me.'

Natalie had a surprise for him. As they walked together to the car, the girl could hardly contain her excitement. She babbled about what she'd been doing while her father had been 'away', and she kept asking about the 'tiny horses'. Again and again, as they drove home, she asked whether he had seen any more of the tiny horses.

'Seen them, rode them, herded them!'

Natalie seemed concerned with the *colour* of the beasts. 'Weren't they striped with reds and greens?'

'Only the biggest and best. But yes. Striped with reds and greens.'

The girl giggled to herself. Her small hands clutched at her father's as they rode in the back seat of the car.

At home, Angela quickly opened windows to air the house. And after a meal of vegetable soup and garlic bread, Natalie made the presentation: her gift to her father.

Jack opened the box, aware that it rattled. Inadvertently, he spilled the contents on to the carpet. A jigsaw made of balsa wood painted with pastel. At first glance he thought there were a hundred pieces.

'Eighty pieces!' the girl announced proudly. 'I made it myself. In school.'

'Brilliant! Absolutely brilliant! Thank you, Nattie.' He kissed the girl, who squirmed away.

'Do it, then! Put it together.'

He picked out the obvious streaks of red and green (the horses), the straight edges, soon got the general idea, then joked and made odd connections, insisting that they were right despite the girl's protests that he was wrong.

'Horses don't have tails on their faces!' She looked shocked, realizing she had given the surprise away. 'I didn't say horses . . .' she said quietly.

'*Bears* don't have *tails* on their faces, did you say?'

'I didn't say bears . . .'

'I thought you did.'

'I didn't.'

'What *did* you say, then?'

'Nothing.'

'I thought you said "bears".'

'I didn't.'

'Lots of animals have tails on their faces, mind you.'

'No they don't.'

'They certainly do.'

'What animals?'

'The big-tailed Nose Bird, for a start. The tail-nosed Aardvark, for another . . . The short-tailed nostril fly . . .'

'No such animals,' Natalie announced uncertainly.

'There most certainly are!'

'No there aren't.'

'Are you insinuating that your loving father is a liar?'

She stared at him for a long moment.

'Yes,' she said with a sudden, mischievous smile. He looked shocked.

'Go and get your book of *Unusual Beasts*!'

'I haven't *got* a book of unusual beasts.'

Even more shocked: 'You haven't got a book of *Unusual Beasts?*'

'No.'

He shook his head.

'What a sad upbringing. All the wrong books. Well if you *did* have the right books, you'd see all *sorts* of huge and hairy animals with tails on their noses.'

'You're telling stories.'

'I am not!'

'Am!'

'Aha!'

He had fitted the final piece of the jigsaw into place and sat up straight to admire the painting of tiny horses, with tall trees in the background, and a human figure – he assumed the squat and dumpy man-thing was intended to be himself – riding the biggest of the beasts.

'This is wonderful! Just like the real horses.'

'I like making jigsaws. There's a special cutter that makes the shape. Are they like the horses you saw?'

'Identical. Thank you. I'll treasure this.'

'Did you see any other funny . . . *unusual* beasts this time? Did you?'

'Lots.'

'Not with tails on their noses, though.'

'Even stranger than the nose beasts. Have you ever seen wolves that stand up and run like human beings?'

'No. What colour were they?'

'Black, with golden streaks on their flanks and big, stiff ruffs, like spines, around their necks.'

Natalie ran for her paints. 'I'll paint them for you.'

'Their lair is by a big stone arch, covered with carved figures and animals.'

Let's see what you make of that . . .

For a while, then, as his daughter exercised her imagination over the subject of wolves, Jack pondered the jigsaw, amused by it, genuinely pleased with it. And as he stared at the crudely cut, naively painted image he realized that Natalie had drawn a second human figure: hidden in the trees, the green outline, clearly female, was blended in so well with the background foliage that only by staring hard could it be resolved.

He touched the green woman and wondered exactly who or what the girl had been meaning to portray.

Only later did the thought occur to him that perhaps Natalie had not been meaning to portray anything at all; that another hand may have been guiding the brush.

29

The Frouden moors rose behind the small town of Chagwick like brooding cliffs, always cloud covered and shadowy, the signs of time evident in the scars and runnels of the foothills that carried the rainwater from the vast expanse of craggy, marshy land that was the moor itself.

A long drive from Exburgh, and in a remote part of the country, Angela had arranged to stay with friends, artists and toymakers, at Stinhall – Stone Hall – in the tiny hamlet of Stiniel, a few miles from the Frouden hills.

Buried in a deep valley, almost completely hidden from the road by oak and aspen, Stiniel consisted of three houses, longhouses of old that had been converted inside to accommodate modern taste, but which from the outside might have been habitations out of history.

Natalie loved Stinhall. It fascinated her to think that below the flagstone floor of the house there were remains of even older buildings. She played on the turf maze in the garden with Toby, who was much the same age, while the adults indulged in the Stinhall hosts' wonderful hospitality.

The house was a treasure cave of puppets, paintings of folkloric figures, statues, green men, and creaky, eerie nooks and corners. It had a ghost, of course; and a wild man could sometimes be seen by moonlight, running along the edge of the woods across the fields from the kitchen.

While Brian and Angela supervised the spit-roasting in the garden of a haunch of local venison – the owners of Stinhall were nothing if not overwhelming in their largesse when it came to feasting – Jack helped Wendy create her Green-Man pie, a gooseberry tart in the shape of a face, decorated in pastry with leaves, branches, wild eyes and tongue, then painted green and red with edible dye. She had intricately carved waxy new potatoes into the shapes of beetles, to amuse the children, and created a 'fairy tower' out of pineapple chunks, apricots and slices of kiwi fruit.

'What's the point of cooking if you can't have fun?'

'Indeed. And what's the point of fun if you can't sink your teeth into a Green-Man pie?'

It was a warm, late autumn evening, perfect for a barbecue, perfect for sitting around by candle-light and talking, and exchanging news.

With Natalie under watchful eyes, Jack and Angela set out at six the following morning for the moors, and by nine were high above the surrounding land, buffeted by cold wind, striding out across the peat and heather, heading for infinity. They added grey stones to the cairns that dotted the wide land. They lunched below a craggy stump of rock called The King's Tor, then used map and compass to pick a route to the west, avoiding the danger areas of Old Gould's Pit and the Quaking Marsh, that would bring them to Windlash Edge, a cliff of more than two hundred feet, and a favourite ascent for climbers.

Here, with the wind in their faces and the sun now rosy behind thin clouds as it began to settle towards dusk, they sat, legs across the precipice letting the heady sense of 'old time' blow around and kiss them, drawing them almost out of time itself, so that they lay back and watched the sky, and smelled the scrub grass, the sharp earth, the crystal wind.

They held hands and closed their eyes. All concern, all confusion, was scoured from them. This was so peaceful, so remote, so private. They drifted together for what seemed like hours. It was almost like old times. Almost as good as when they'd first been together.

Almost. . .

'Let's stay here for ever,' Jack said.

'I need a pee.'

'Pee over the edge.'

'There might be a climber down there.'

'Pee over the edge – run like hell!'

'You would, too, wouldn't you? Time to get the hell down, anyway. Civilization beckons. It's two hours' walking from here to the bus station.'

Jack checked his watch. 'Oh Christ. Ninety minutes of light left. You're right. Let's move!'

The last part of the walk was along road, hard on sore feet and ankles, but safe in the darkness that had deepened in minutes. From the bus station they 'phoned Stinhall. Everything was fine. With an hour to wait, Jack suggested a steak; Angela argued for something spicier and they found a Thai restaurant in the town centre, asking for a table well away from the other customers.

'We've been walking for seven hours.'

No problem, the courteous waiter assured them from a safe distance.

It was after ten when the bus dropped them in the nearest town to the hamlet. In pitch darkness, below heavy cloud cover, they trudged along the country road, a mile and a half to the hot bath and strong tea that both, now, craved. Their torch cast feeble light on the trees and hedges, on the bright eyes of rabbits and two owls that were out, pursuing their own activities.

As they crossed the hill before the road dropped to Stiniel itself, flashing lights in the distance made them stop for a moment.

'Torches?' Angela said as she stared at the four criss-crossing beams of pale, white light.

'Torches,' Jack agreed. 'In the field behind Stinhall.'

'Natalie!'

'Oh Christ! He's followed her!'

They ran frantically, on feet that were stiff and sore. Angela slipped on the muddy hill, bruising her thigh, but irritably shook off Jack's helping hand.

They could hear Brian's voice in the darkness, and another man calling from across the field. By the time they'd run along the drive, through the turf maze garden and across the thin bridge that crossed the deep, scrub-filled ditch that divided house from farmland, the scatter of torches was spread widely.

Wendy was closest. She saw Jack and came running over.

'We think she's in the woods. Jack, I don't know what to say . . .'

'It's OK. We shouldn't have assumed she wouldn't do this here. She's done it before.'

'She played happily with Toby all evening, watched some TV, finished off the Green-Man pie; then went to bed, good as gold. Toby came down and said she'd started to laugh and dance in her room, so we went upstairs . . .'

'And she'd slipped out of the house.'

'I'm sorry.'

Jack reassured her. 'She's quite safe. We just have to get her home.'

A neighbouring couple had turned out to help in the search. If she'd run towards the woods, she was safe enough; but towards the bottom of the fields were pools and soft mud, a danger to animals, certainly to children. Felicity, the neighbour, had gone down to keep watch there.

Eventually they found her. Brian had gone into the deep wood and seen Natalie's white nightdress. She had climbed a tree and was sitting on a branch, twenty feet from the ground, swaying slightly and singing.

'Come on down, Natalie. That's where the trolls live.'

'Where's Daddy?'

'Coming up the field. Shall I get a ladder?'

'No, thank you. Just fetch Daddy.'

'You gave us quite a shock. We thought you were asleep.'

'My friend came and I wanted to come and dance with him.'

'What? Half way up a tree?'

'No, silly.'

Jack arrived in the woods, breathless, relieved to see his daughter. He could hear Angela calling behind him as she ran with Wendy. Jack had heard most of Natalie's exchange with Brian, who was shivering in the cold air. 'She must be perished,' he said urgently to Jack. 'I know I am. So I'm running home. Here . . .'

He took off his overcoat, then ran quickly in his pyjamas back through the dark.

From her branch, Natalie said, 'Send them away, Daddy. He wants to talk to you alone.'

Here we go again . . .

'Send them away!' Natalie said loudly, her child's voice teetering on hysteria. Angela and Wendy walked from the woodland edge, following Brian to the house.

Staring at his daughter, Jack said angrily, 'Come down right now. No arguments. Down! Now!'

'I don't think so.'

'Is he here? Greyface? Is he here?'

'*I'm* here,' the girl said with a smile, blinking against the beam of the torch. 'So of course he's here.'

He'd followed this far! Two hundred miles away from Exburgh, and he was still in control!

Frightened and cold, unsure as to whether or not this was Natalie – or Natalie plus Shade – who spoke to him from the high tree, Jack said simply, 'Shall I leave you here then? I'll leave this coat. Put it on. Keep warm; or do some dancing. Whatever, make sure you don't get a chill; and come down carefully from the tree when you come down. We don't want any broken bones.'

'Where are you going?'

'Back to Stinhall. To bath and bed. I'm tired from walking, so's your mother. We'll see you at breakfast.'

'Stay here!'

'I don't think so,' he said, imitating the gentle sarcasm of her own words. 'It's been a long day, and as long as you're happy out here in the woods, and as long as you climb down carefully, I'll trust you. Goodnight, Nattie.'

He walked away from her, picking out the path with the torch.

'Catch me, Daddy.'

'You just be careful!' he called back, but simple parental fear, uncertainty at his own strategy, made him glance back.

The girl was hanging from the branch by one hand, her body swinging, the white nightgown billowing about feet that twisted as if searching for a grip. She was watching him and smiling, face pale in the broad flood of the torch.

'Catch me, Daddy.'

And dropped.

Screaming her name, Jack launched himself back towards the tree, aware that she had twisted in the air, nightdress flapping, legs swinging up so that she would strike the ground backside first. But he had gone no more than four paces when the city rose before him, emerging from the earth at an angle across him, flowing about him, bringing with it the smell of old, cold stone and damp cellars.

It shimmered: he was there again, at the entrance to the cave, the *Shimmering* that would lead him to the heart of the ghost city. Natalie was not in sight. Wherever she had fallen, she was outside of his sphere of consciousness, and though he struck forward, beating hands against the rough-hewn stone at the entrance to the cave system, all he heard was the echo of his own despair . . . and the distant sound of water.

'Natalie . . .'

Somewhere here, right here, the child would have struck the ground. Was she broken? Had her spine snapped with the fall? A broken arm? He tried to feel through the new reality of Glanum, but the woods above Stinhall had gone, now, and ahead of him a voice called his name.

He emerged from the cave into the grey gloom of the shrine-city and faced the tall, white scaled woman who stood before him. The scales, he realized, were part of her tunic, slivers of white bone and shells made into armour, covering her from neck to mid thigh, hugging the narrow contours of her body. Long, fair hair flowed about a face as lean and elfin as any classical picture of the faery world, whose documentation in paint and puppet was the lifeblood of his friends in Stinhall. Eyes that glittered with amusement stared through the unruly fringe. A mouth, wide with anticipation, mocked a kiss, then a hand was raised, beckoning.

'Come on, Daddy. We have a long way to go . . .'

'Natalie?'

'Shade, you old fool. Don't you recognize me? Perhaps you don't. It's been a long time. Daddy's girl has grown.'

'Shade . . . ?'

'Come *on!*'

He was drawn to her.

'No!'

He turned and ran back through the cave system. Behind him, Shade followed, shrieking and laughing, he couldn't tell whether with amusement or fury; this ghost of his daughter was a harpy he couldn't and wouldn't fathom.

He was suddenly on the moonlit hillside, and he stumbled forwards towards the glow of light from Stinhall. Behind him, a woman shrilled her anger. He turned quickly, searching the illusory cave and the towering monoliths for a sign of his daughter, the tree-falling daughter (he was aware that he trusted to Natalie's natural, youthful litheness to have turned the fall into a perfect landing) but seeing nothing – *ran*.

Shade drifted after him, cooing and calling, white scales reflecting the moon.

Behind Shade, Glanum pursed its cavernous mouth, stretching for the sucking kiss, following him down the hill.

Angela was waiting for him at the bottom of the garden.

'Where is she? Where's Nattie?'

'Get into the house!'

'Where's my daughter?'

Jack turned. The *Shimmering* was flowing towards him, widening, will-o'-the-wisp shaping the entrance to the cave White Shade walking ahead of it, lean and beautiful, reaching for her father.

'Get into the house!'

'Is she still in the woods?'

'She's safe!'

He tugged at Angela's coat but she twisted away. 'Safe? You're mad! I didn't expect you to *leave her*.'

As Angela vanished across the bridge to the field beyond, Jack ran back across the turf maze, past the barbecue pit, towards the welcoming light of the kitchen.

Wendy stepped out to meet him, looking past him to the high woods. She was very calm, almost serene, her bright gaze fixed on something in the far distance.

'Who *is* that?'

For a moment Jack was too confused to think, but then he realized that Wendy could see the approaching shade.

'The ghost of my daughter.'

'She's beautiful.'

'She's just a ghost.'

'I know. She's still very beautiful.'

'I'm in trouble, Wendy . . .'

'Indeed, you are. Go inside the house. I'll try and talk to her . . .'

Wendy walked towards the glowing mouth of the cave, turning once to signal, 'Go in! Go in!' then crossed the maze and the lawn to face the spectral figure at the bottom of the field. Angela was lost in darkness, calling for Natalie up by the woods.

In the kitchen, Brian asked quite simply, 'Where's she going?'

'To talk to the woman. The ghost woman . . .'

'You shouldn't be doing this,' Brian said quietly, angrily. His eyes were fierce, covering the fact that he was terrified for his wife.

'I'm sorry. But she seems to know what she's doing.'

Of course! Neither Brian nor Angela could see the *Shimmering*. Only Wendy, always more highly attuned to the oddities and so-called *energies* of the natural landscape, could get a partial idea of what was pursuing her friend.

A moment later, the kitchen door was flung open and Wendy, dishevelled, her night clothes torn, burst into the kitchen, slamming the door behind her, leaning against it as she looked at Jack.

'What a bitch! Oh Jesus, what a bitch!'

The house shuddered. A puppet fell from the gallery on the open landing. The glasses by the sink rattled.

'I think we'd better get the hell out of here,' Wendy said. 'Sorry, Jack. Brian and I have charms . . .'

'We need the charms?' Brian looked even more alarmed.

'We need something! That's no ghost out there. You're on your own, Jack. You should have warned us.'

She fled through the house. Brian picked up the puppet, a four-foot high representation of a troll, then grabbed a knife from the table.

'We'll be under the bed at the back of the house,' he said with a wry laugh. 'What have you *brought* with you, Jack? Not termites, I think.'

'I didn't know it would follow.'

'You'd better take care of Natalie. Christ!'

The house trembled. Jars of dried beans and grains fell and smashed onto the flagstone floor.

The scaled woman was walking towards the light in the kitchen, shaking her head as she smiled, a parent approaching a misbehaving child. Behind her the night seemed to fold into the shimmering shape of the cave.

Jack withdrew into the sitting room, pressed himself against the stone wall by the small garden window. The wide fireplace glowed and crackled with the great log that burned there. The light of the flames cast shadows of statues and furniture about the walls. Toby's toys lay scattered where he and Natalie had played during the evening. The tall Regency clock by the door whirred and chimed.

Shade entered the room, drifting effortlessly through the stone. The cave mouth opened towards him, rank carved rock and gloomy entrance framed with eerie green light, flowing through the walls and open fire, bearing down upon the cowering man.

Glanum had come to fetch him again, and resigning himself, he stepped forward towards the log fire and the *Shimmering*, feeling cold and dampness wrap about him like the touch of hell.

30

White Shade was impatient with him. He was so slow, running and walking behind her as she led the way through the shadow city. Her frustration, her impetuosity, reminded him of Angela, as did her relentless drive forward, her constant reiteration of the need to get ahead, to get to the 'pool'.

'Where's the pool?'

'You remember! The well, the sanctuary where the women bathe and their dogs drink. The hunting spring. We hid there. Come *on*, Jack. You're not an old man. Run faster.'

Jack?

She was framed, slim and palely gleaming, between walls that crowded into him, a morbid place, its stones dripping anguish.

'I'm frightened. Everything's closing in—'

'Then run a little faster!'

'Where are we?'

'Don't you recognize it?'

'No I don't! Where *are* we . . . ?'

She looked quickly round and he thought she was shivering, uncomfortable for the moment. 'This is where they burned the bodies. They brought them here, some still alive, and burned them with pitch, and dry wood, and straw, and the blankets and clothes from their houses. They bundled them into the alley, because the stone walls stopped the fire spreading. And the fleas couldn't leap above them.'

'The plague?'

'Yes. The plague. And its victims. Hundreds, Jack. Exburgh has a very chequered history when it comes to human rights.'

'This is *Exburgh*?'

'This is Glanum, Jack. Glanum feeds on other cities, gorges on their shadows. You know that, don't you? Now come on!'

She was running again, emerging from the claustrophobia of the plague road to a plaza, where the rotting trunks of trees were formed into scaffolds and lean, black dogs rooted and fought as they prowled the square.

They came to the river again, where the hulks of the barges lay half-submerged in sludgy water, masts snapped and fallen, gaily-coloured trappings and sails now fire-blackened, or faded with time. Shade trod carefully, dancing over the crumbling decks among the ruins of the jubilee, crossing to the farther bank. Jack followed, stumbling, aware that the pile of yellowed wood that shattered as he fell was the rain-eroded remnant of a man.

Shade laughed. She seemed so at home here, a bright presence in the monstrous gloom.

He called to her.

'Last time I crossed this river, there was a party. It was so *alive*. It was a happy place. Debauched; delightful; an ancient wedding!'

'Digested, now,' she said with a chuckle. 'Digested and excreted. Glanum feeds on every sort of energy, every sort of mood. This is the rubbish dump! Come on, Jack. Keep to the road!'

He followed her between the bulging, grinning features of beasts, each shaped in smooth, black marble, each marking a monolithic tomb lining the wide road that led to a white building fronted by colonnades and topped with the stretching, winged forms of women.

Was that the Moon pool? If so, it had been substantially extended since he had last staggered into its cool, refreshing depths. But Shade skirted the place, hugging shadows, alleyways and the slippery banks of the streams which wound through the city.

At last she ducked into an entrance that was familiar to him. The steps were slick; he could see Shade below him, her image in the water broken and shining as she crouched above the pool, splashing the liquid on her face and neck. Carefully, Jack came down to join her. The whole place smelled dank; wet growth draped the stone faces of the women through whose mouths the spring water dripped.

But the pool itself was fresh and welcome. In the darkness, only the faint luminescence of the moon on Shade's dress of shells allowed his sight to adjust to the surroundings.

'What happens now?' he asked his daughter.

'We wait for my friends,' she said. 'Baalgor doesn't like them. He sent me to fetch you. I think he means to kill you. But that's not what I want. With my friends around you'll be safer than the last time.'

Confused, struggling to remember the previous experience of the *Shimmering*, Jack simply shook his head. 'I thought you were Baalgor's friend,' he said. 'I thought you'd do anything for him.'

'Jack, I've grown. Can't you see? Sometimes I go back to Nattie, I creep in beside her, we lie there together in the darkness and dream the same dreams. When she gets up to go to school I run along with her. It's funny to be there and here, to be young and old. I left Baalgor a long time ago, to hunt with the other women. But he catches me sometimes, and he's very strong. I know he can take the life from me, just as he's taking it from Natalie. I know he can take back from me what he's stripped from the girl. He can even give it back to her if he wants . . .'

'How?'

She ignored him. 'But Jack . . . I like being me. I like it here. I like the double dream, being with Nattie. She's part of my life.'

'She could be *all* of your life, the life you've not known. She's still growing up.'

'I grew up, Jack!' the woman said tersely. 'Baalgor saw to that.'

He didn't want to think about her words. 'It's not the same. Shade . . . Natalie . . . if you abandon him completely, we can start again. Get out of Glanum!'

'It's not the same,' the white shade echoed sadly. 'But I can't abandon him. What he's done to me, to your daughter, can't be undone.'

'You just said he could give back what he'd taken!'

What HAD he taken? Natalie still seemed so normal . . . except when she was 'possessed'. What had he taken? Why weren't the scars visible?

'Some of it. Maybe. I don't know, Jack. I just know I've moved away from him, safely away; but he's still close, so I take no chances. I'll do some of what he tells me, his carrying and fetching. But I won't let him hurt me any more. And I won't let him hurt you.'

He stared at her in the faint light, seeing Angela, seeing his daughter, seeing a young, courageous woman who belonged in two worlds. Like her father himself, in fact; torn between realms, increasingly at home in both.

'What do I do for the best?' he whispered, suddenly overwhelmed by fear.

'The best for what? For who?'

'For whom,' he corrected, and the shade laughed, echoing, exaggeratedly, 'for *whom*'.

'Got to get the language right,' he murmured.

'Got to get the language right,' she repeated affectionately, then went on, 'You want things the way they were. Too late. You want to keep things the way they are. You want this? You want the torment? Baalgor won't get any easier. He's a lost man, Jack. Without his Greenfaced sisterwife, he's slowly crumbling. You have to get them back together: her to him; or him to her.'

'And how do I do that?'

'How do I know? I'm your daughter's shadow, Jack. And I'm Shade. This is my world and all I know about it is what I see; Baalgor didn't talk to me about the centre of the city. Whatever's there, though, that's what he fears; that's where you have to take him. He lives in its shadow, but he's hiding from it. And that's where you have to drag him. *And* his green-faced partner. The centre of the city. It's what drives Glanum across the earth. It's what makes Glanum feed on the shadows of forgotten towns. It's what drives everything!'

The pool bubbled, water splashing suddenly onto the lower steps.

'Here they come,' Shade said. 'Don't be frightened.'

Even as she spoke the words, the surface of the water erupted. Four mastiffs, monstrous beasts, saturated and panting for air, came bounding from the well and onto the stone steps, shaking water from their stinking, matted fur. They turned to sniff and growl at the hunched man who crouched in their sanctuary.

One of them reared up, eight feet high, staring nervously at the intruder. A second lapped at his face, a deep rumble in its throat. Shade slapped at them. 'He's a friend. Easy . . . Easy!'

The dogs padded up the steps and three of them slipped away into a side passage. The fourth, its face speckled with white which caught the pale moon, crouched tensely at the top of the stairs, fixing Jack with its gaze.

White faces surfaced in the pool, staring through the water, almost dreamlike. The four women emerged in quick succession, throwing weapons to the hard floor, wringing out their hair, gasping for breath. One was very old, grey-haired, grey-tunicked. Another was no older than Shade, but her face was ridged with scars, or disease, it was hard to see in this faint illumination. The other two were mature and menacing, one wearing silver torques and belt over a leather tunic and sandalled feet, the other in shell armour, similar to Shade's, her hair cropped to the skull, a string of shell or bone fragments draped across her face, hanging from each ear, threaded through her nose.

This one hauled a rope from the pool. She, and the older woman, tugged for a few seconds and an animal, trussed and dead, was dragged into the sanctuary. Jack smelled the blood from its wounds.

Deeper in the place, the three dogs began to howl. The mastiff on the steps just growled in its throat, still watching the man it didn't know.

'This is my father,' Shade said, and the older and younger women laughed. Shade went on, 'He answers to the name of Jack. Jack? My friends have no particular names. They were eaten by Glanum much like everything else you'll find in the city. But the old woman scowls whenever you call her *Sefonnie*.'

'Sefonnie? Persephone?'

As he spoke the name, the old woman spat at him. She was gathering her arrows together where they'd scattered on her emergence from the pool.

'And this is Hekut,' Shade went on, waving towards decorated-with-shells, 'Nubissa,' the other woman, 'And Diana,' the girl.

'You certainly know how to pick your friends,' Jack said. 'Straight out of the wolf pack!'

'They're good hunters. In Glanum, you need to be. If you can't hunt, if you can't run, if you can't hide, you soon end up at the river-gate, grinning at ravens.'

'Does that mean "dead"?'

Shade laughed delightedly. 'It doesn't mean "making love".'

The women had moved away from the water, ducking into the passages, and now Shade led her father into a drier place within the Sanctuary, a small cell made warm with mats and candles. The dogs were eating, and from another place came the sounds of voices, laughter and butchery. After a while, Hekut ducked into the cell, glancing with a frown at Jack, and put down a clay bowl of cooked liver and tripes. Shade used her fingers to feed on the steaming offal, and when Jack satisfied his own hunger he found the simple meal surprisingly palatable.

After that he slept, his face to the cold stone, his back to his daughter. Shade rose in the middle of the night and went down to the pool; he heard her splashing as she bathed.

In what he imagined was the morning she shook him awake again and gave him water and a lump of honeyed cake. A pale, miserable light spilled into the cell as he ate with care and little relish.

'Hurry up. Hekut wants to go hunting with us. Do you need to shit?'

'I certainly do.'

She was so matter-of-fact about it.

'I'll show you where. Sefonnie thinks Baalgor is looking for you. He knows you're here. We'll try and surprise him. There's more cake if you want.'

'This is fine. Thank you.'

Hekut's mastiff bounded ahead of them, leaping like a giant puppy through the streets and shadows. The two women ran behind, Hekut carrying a clutch of thin javelins, Shade a sling and pouch of pebble shot. They rested frequently, finding water in a small, dilapidated temple to Apollo, sitting on fragments of the statue of the god as they sipped from the bubbling fountain.

Jack didn't recognize the route that Shade was taking him. Last time, the confrontation had been in front of the mausoleum, with its stone guardians.

'Baalgor withdrew deeper into the city when I left him, closer to its heart. It's dangerous for him, hiding so close to the enemy. He ran from them all his life; now he's using the tunnels in their own walls to wait for his sisterwife.'

What was at the heart of the ghostly city? A place where the Bull-runners had committed a terrible deed, causing them to run from an enemy that they only ever glimpsed as white towers and the snorting muzzle of the monstrous bull. When he again asked Shade what she knew, she simply shrugged.

'I only know that this city has grown on the ruins of other places. It scours the earth. It's settled for a while, as if it's waiting. Perhaps it's waiting for you, Jack. Perhaps the watcher is being watched.'

He listened to her words uncomprehending. There was something so knowing about this echo of his daughter; he couldn't tell whether she was lying to him, teasing him, or simply being truthful, sharing her lack of understanding, using language that would suggest she had known Jack-the-stranger all her life. How much *had* she taken from Natalie? And why had he been unable to see the change in his daughter? The thought of the small girl being cleverly scooped out, looking fresh and full on the surface, but increasingly hollow . . . the thought made him dizzy with panic. *He has to let me go*, he thought, with Baalgor's grinning face in his mind's eye. 'He has to let me go,' he said aloud, and Shade laughed as Hekut watched with solemn curiosity.

'He'll not do that. You'll have to get the two of them together again. One way or the other.'

'She doesn't want to come,' he murmured. 'She wants to go home, to face up to fate.'

Shade's touch on his hair was gentle and reassuring. 'From what I've heard – from Baalgor – you like Greenface rather too much. I think that's why he wants to kill you.'

Shocked by her words, Jack went quickly to the pool of water around the fountain and splashed his face. He felt hot and frightened. The memory of Nemet was strong in his mind and even as he remembered her he was aroused, and this confused him. He had been in a dream. It hadn't been real. And yet it *had* been real . . . and Angela had been upset by his actions in the Hinterland . . .

And Nemet was still waiting for him, whispering to him even now!

It was true. He could sense her, green-masked, hiding in

*the green of the wood, watching him, listening to his every
word, missing him as much as he missed her . . .*

How could Greyface have seen what was happening? How
could he have known?

He was still crouching over the dark water, drifting between two worlds again, when the dog began to growl, then
stretched to its full height, hackles rising, jaw gaping, teeth
exposed as it watched the entrance to the temple.

Greyface was framed there, his cloak of scalps and feathers
draped around his brooding form. He had assessed the danger
in an instant, stepping back into the street outside, calling for
Shade, challenging her to come to him, to trust him.

To Jack's surprise, she rose and went out, dropping her sling
and pouch of shot. Hekut hissed, tugged the mastiff and
followed into the street. Shade was in Baalgor's arms, Greyface grinning, his hand running over the woman's hair as she
stood in his embrace.

'Let her go,' Jack said. The dog growled and barked, Hekut
holding it back, one of her javelins held low and ready to
jab. But Greyface simply stroked his shade, his gaze on Jack.
Shade's own hands were inside the cloak, drawing the man
close to her as she nestled her head against his chest.

'She's given me some trouble, this one,' Greyface said.

Inside his cloak, Shade's fingers pinched him and he
winced, pulling her hair painfully. She stared up at him, a
meaningful smile on her face.

'More trouble to come,' she said in a loud whisper, 'if you
don't behave. You're not to hurt my father.'

Again, below the cloak her fingers must have been digging
into flesh. Greyface squirmed, looking pained, then reached
down to kiss her, jerking back in shock before his mouth
could make contact on hers and howling out.

'Yes. Yes! I understand what it is you're saying. Get your
claws out.'

Shade looked round at her father.

'Don't be sad, Jack. Don't be shocked.'

'I'm both,' he said truthfully. 'I can't help it.'

'I'm safe, Jack. I've chosen the life. This *scalp-cloak* won't hurt you. We understand each other now.'

Greyface silently agreed, watching Jack, watching him hard. He let Shade go and came over, so close, face to face, that each could smell the breath from the other.

'I dream of Nemet. I miss her. I miss her very much. I dream of you. I saw in my dream how you betrayed me.'

'Betrayed *you*? Don't make me laugh.'

'I sent you to fetch her back, instead you've made her run from me. She's begun to love you.'

'Then why not let her go?'

'You know why I can't let her go. You know why I need her here. And you know the consequences for your daughter if you don't fetch her. Soon!'

'I was frightened by that before, but I'm not frightened now. Shade seems to have you in control . . . and Natalie, the daughter you claim to be seducing, is fine. Yes, you get into her dreams occasionally. So what? I can't see that you've done her any harm.'

'Can't you?'

'No. I can't.'

Baalgor's gaze was almost amused; his breath was warm and foul as he breathed in a way that suggested he was holding back laughter. 'How many inches has her hair grown in the last season? How tall has she grown?'

'I don't know . . . a little, I'm sure.'

'Are you? How many new words has she learned? How many new songs has she learned? How much weight has she put on? How much have the seasons changed her? How much closer is she to being a woman and not a girl?'

'I don't . . .'

'Haven't you noticed the *absence* of those things? Haven't you seen how motionless she is, a child now, the same child, for ever a child? Haven't you seen the lack of growing?'

Baalgor's breath stank, but Jack was paralysed, standing before the leering man, limp and frightened.

'Oh, Jack. Jack! Look at your daughter, look at the life I've stolen from you. You'll be an old man, soon, with an infant daughter unchanged by time, a husk, a gabbling infant husk, a living ghost that will screech at you and paw you as the flesh shrinks from your bones and all you need is peace, but you'll have no peace, you'll have a *child* until you die.'

'My God . . . poor Nattie . . .'

'Do you get it now? I've stolen the *future* from her, all her later life sucked into this city, to be at my beck and call, no matter what *she* pretends.' He glanced at Shade. 'I've given her the illusion of independence. A fighting spirit. I find it helps. She thinks I won't hurt you. She thinks she can protect you.'

Suddenly angry, breaking from the horror of the image of his daughter that Baalgor had constructed, Jack said, 'And I believe that she can.'

'Believe what you want. But believe this: if I don't have Nemet, I'll have *all* the life you'd hoped for *Nattie*! And Shade can't stop me. She's growing older by the beating of her heart, faster than she knows, faster than you can imagine, and though she's strong now, she'll be weak soon. And *then* I'll use her. To be free from the hunt.'

As he spoke the last words, he turned, flinging Shade away from him, running towards the heart of the city. Hekut shouted at her friend, then loosed the dog. It bounded after the running man, Hekut in close pursuit, but after a while they both gave up.

Jack found woman and hound sitting on the steps of a small ziggurat, breathing hard. Beyond them, the sky whirled, a dark storm above the city's heart, faintly reflecting fire from below. For a while Jack sat with her, thinking of his daughter, holding back tears of fear and rage as he imagined the terror, the literal hell of the girl never ageing, a sweet, vital life denied to the one person in his life whom he truly adored.

After a while, drawn by the sense of familiarity in the maelstrom, Jack walked deeper into Glanum. Hekut jumped up and tried to stop him, her words a babble of urgency, her eyes narrowed with caution. The bone noselet rattled ludicrously across her face, but there was no denying that the woman was warning him away, that she cared for the danger he was courting.

'I want to see for myself,' he said, and gently removed Hekut's grip from his arm. She shook the clutch of thin javelins in her other hand, cursed him for a fool, then turned back, leashing the hound and calling for Shade.

He walked for an hour. The storm was almost above him. He stared at the cloud-swirl and became disorientated. He seemed to be falling upwards, plunging towards the Eye. Now that he was this close he could see how rain, earth and ruin were drawn up into the thunder-cloud, streaks and twists of shape that burst from beyond the walls and towers now barring his way, writhing like captured animals, he thought, as the maelstrom sucked them in.

'Yes,' he whispered. 'That's where it comes from. It surfaces in the Deep. I've watched it rise. I've camped in the shelter of its ruins. And Nemet is there. Above the storm . . .'

He could hear the sound of drumming, a frantic rhythm, many drums beyond the walls, beyond the towers. And the sound of creatures, the bellows, cries and growls of creatures, and he was reminded of his time in the Hinterland, where the primordial products of his own imagination stalked and thundered in pursuit of life and prey.

What's there? What's *there*?

And is this the place to which Nemet intends to return, descending from the storm like a green-masked angel?

He turned to find White Shade behind him, strangely solemn, eerily silent, watching him as a soft wind blew her hair, the shell dress rattling, glinting with mother-of-pearl, a shining luminescence, green and silver.

'What's beyond the walls?' he asked her. 'What's at the heart?'

'I don't know,' she said. 'A place that was abandoned. An old place. An angry place.'

That expression again; a place that was abandoned!

'I've heard it called the Place of Skins. But that's really all I know. Except that . . .'

'Except that . . . ?'

'Hekut knows of a legend from the far future of Glanum – she sees through the years sometimes; so does Sefonnie. She thinks that Glanum has many shadows, different cities on the same piece of ancient earth. One of them was destroyed by the Bull-roaring of metal horns. She dreams the scene, sometimes, and it frightens her.'

'The Bull-roaring of metal horns,' Jack echoed.

'That's all I know. Baalgor is watching you, by the way.'

Jack looked round. He could see nothing but the sheer walls, the storm-illuminated towers, the earth sucked into the night sky to beach in his own unconscious mind.

'If he's so close, why doesn't it kill him? If it hunted him for so long. Why does it tolerate him living so close?'

'It wants them both. They both did the deed. Baalgor is risking everything on Nemet coming back to him in the world he thinks of as the otherworld, the world you know as *real*. Once they're together he believes they can live for ever, and Glanum will never find them.'

'Is he right?'

'I don't know. It's what he's said to me. I live in the city; in my dreams I go to a heavenly place, I run and swim and dance with a girl called Natalie. I paint pictures with her. I watch her world through her eyes. I watch you through her eyes. It's the only life I have. I have to make sense of it in my own way. Baalgor told me very little and now that he has less control over me, I'm more alone than ever.'

'He says he still owns you.'

'He's a powerful man. We play a game together. I can't

escape him; but he doesn't own me any more. We live in the shadows of dead cities, and in the shadows of each other. But in my dreams I see the sunlight. It's very real when I see the world through Natalie. Without her, I'd sink into the moon pool and stay below the water.'

She suddenly swung her arm. Jack thought she was about to strike him and reacted by throwing up his hands to protect his face, but she had sent a slingshot into the shadows, aimed at Baalgor, he imagined. The stone clattered on rock and Shade had turned and was running. He followed, met Hekut and the hound, and returned with the women to the pool.

A place destroyed by the Bull-roaring of metal horns . . .

'You know the way from here,' Shade said to him. 'Goodbye. Daddy. . .'

'Goodbye,' he said to her. She was smiling, amused by something, but he felt sad, he felt he was abandoning her. 'Will you be all right?'

'Ask Natalie. I'm often there . . .' An hour later he crossed the stinking river and passed through the cave. The *Shimmering* shrank from him suddenly and he found himself standing on the open hillside, dew-drenched in the cold dawn, momentarily disorientated until he recognized the thatched roofs of the houses at Stinhall, beyond the trees, a few minutes' walk away.

A place destroyed by the Bull-roaring of metal horns . . .

Joshua . . . Bringing down the walls!

Was it ancient Jericho, then, that lay at the heart of Glanum?

31

In the stillness of the night, with Natalie soundly asleep in bed and, to his immense relief, apparently unharmed, Jack sipped brandy and read from one of the books in their hosts' extensive library: *The Mediterranean Region in Prehistory: A Re-assessment*, by Harold A. Knight. The information held Angela in thrall as more and more of a link with the Bull-runners was established.

The site on which the modern city of Jericho now stood, it seemed, had become a settled site at an astonishingly early date – 8000BC, or even earlier. Evidence for it having been a *town* at the time was disputed, but the settlement had covered four hectares, a very large settlement for this period in pre-history.

Four hectares . . . with round huts built of 'hog-backed' bricks, signs of walls within walls made of cut timber, and at *least* one watchtower built of white stone, occupying a prominent position against an inner wall, also of stone . . .

The white tower!

Nothing about this early Jericho made any sense – it could have supported a population of two thousand, ten times the population at other sites of this time in the Jordan Valley, such as that at Eynan – so if not a town, *what* had been its function?

At the site, the bones of gazelle, cattle, lion, rhino, bears, goats and boar had been found in abundance . . . probably from hunted animals because of their unusual size, some from species that became extinct in the next few thousand years, or moved east with the change in weather conditions.

The Jordan Valley had always been subject to alternating periods of intense drought and massive rainfall, semiforest and fertile river plain giving way to inhospitable desert.

There was no evidence for the domestication of animals at this time, though some herding must certainly have been practised. The staple grains were Emmer wheat, lentils, two-rowed hulled barley, and other crops in abundance, benefiting from the site's permanent spring.

The early site, then, was an enigma, its town-like nature an illusion; hunter-gathering from semi-permanent settlements was still the most common way of life.

The *precocity* of Jericho, however, was most dramatically evidenced by the fact that soon after its stone walls and tower were built it had been abruptly abandoned, standing vacant, perhaps demolished, for more than three hundred years!

Later settlers had re-occupied some of the structures, as well as using clay to coat the skulls of the dead and shells as decoration for those dead, especially in the eyes . . . but this was an echo, a more sophisticated application, of an earlier tradition . . .

The settlement, certainly by then a *town*, showed signs of having had a role in this early neolithic period that was unlike that of other towns of the time in the Near East, such as Çatal Hüyük in Anatolia, in Turkey, Tell Ramad near Damascus, Hacila and Çan Hassan to the north-east and north-west of the Euphrates river.

Only in the Bronze Age had Jericho shaken off its obscure past and become the city of legend familiar from the Old Testament.

'When the walls came down to the sound of Joshua's trumpet voluntary,' Angela said quietly.

'It would seem,' Jack said, closing the book, 'that the first walls had come down a long time before!'

*

The White Tower . . . the steaming forests . . . the simple *primitiveness* of the appearance of the hunted couple . . . and the red bull.

A red bull of enormous size had been painted on the walls of Çatal Hüyük in the seventh millennium BC. A creature of unusual shape, and obscure purpose, it supplied the earliest known evidence of a Bull cult in the lands around the Mediterranean Sea.

What had happened at Jericho?

What had Ahk'Nemet, Baalgor her brother, and the other five (*seven in all*, she had said) done to the Stone Place by the Great Spring to doom them to an eternity of being hunted?

Jack rested several days with his family, spending as much time with Natalie as she would tolerate, being an independent little thing who sometimes liked her own company. But they rode horses together, and rowed on the river, and picnicked on the hills where John Garth had stepped out of his life.

Natalie was happy and played noisily.

Jack could find no sign of stunted growth.

But she *was* more easily distracted, now, and there was an occasional vagueness in her eyes that made his stomach heave with fear. Angela encouraged him to think that this was nothing less than normal . . . but Angela hadn't been to the Moon Pool and encountered Baalgor.

Eventually he returned to the Institute where the Midax experiment was being run. He *had* to go back to the Deep again. The summoning voice – the urge to go felt just like that: a calling voice – was stronger than he had previously experienced; the need was greater.

Brightmore had been studying the latest accounts of Jack's experiences in the Deep and in the *Shimmering*. He was waiting in the Institute's small TV lounge, deep in thought, the pages of notes taken by Angela during Jack's latest debriefing spread on the coffee table before him.

'Curiouser and curiouser,' he said, watching Jack narrowly

through the curls of smoke from his cigarette. 'What a fertile mind you do have!'

'The experiences all seem so *real*,' Jack said as he sipped coffee and Brightmore laughed in that irritating, slightly mocking way of his.

'Of course.'

Jack ignored him. There were questions to which he needed answers, even if only half answers. 'Such real experiences,' he echoed. 'But I can't connect them. I can't understand a damned thing about where I *am* at any time, or how I got there, or what the hell's going to appear next . . .'

Brightmore glanced away for a moment, letting smoke trickle from his mouth. 'You mean the *Shimmering*, of course.'

'Yes. I mean the *Shimmering*.'

'The ghostly echo of Glanum in Exburgh . . .'

'Yes. And Glanum – the city – in *me*. The last time I went deep I saw it in the distance. This is what I don't understand. How can Glanum be . . . *here*, in this world, taking away a man called John Garth, travelling the *real* world, and also be . . . inside? In my *unconscious*? Is it the same place?'

Steven Brightmore gave the merest hint of a shrug, tapping the table with his pen. 'After all I've explained to you, Jack, I don't see what your problem is. Yes – it's the same place! The same place, but being experienced from two different perspectives. It makes sense if you accept that you *yourself* are a sort of Hinterland. You're a passing-through place to this strangely mobile *Glanum*. You asked me once: Why you? Why is it happening to you? I can't do better than think that you were in the right place at the right time. As simple as that.'

'That's what John Garth said to me, years ago.'

'He knew a lot more than he let on. Glanum, the supernatural entity, moves through the earth, God knows how. I should have taken your story more seriously when we began your Midax training—'

Yes. You should have!

'Angela was right, it seems. But to get to the point: Glanum was generated in pre-history when Jericho was abandoned, reading between the lines of your latest account. Now it exists both in the real world, but as a ghost, and in the human unconscious, buried as a shadow of memory.

'Imagine that like a *whale*, which blows as it surfaces, when Glanum surfaced below Exburgh years ago it *blew* – a spout of memory and emotion linked to its heart, the abandoned heart, memory of the deed perpetrated by your ghostly Bull-runners that caused it to be abandoned – an upsurge of memory that on this occasion *met* its own archetypal reflection, carried for hundreds of generations, and present in the newest, most vulnerable mind in the town. Namely *you* – minutes old. In the right place at the right time.'

Jack sat silently for a few seconds. 'So it was mere chance that involved me . . .'

'Mere chance. But at that chance moment you were *connected* – to the ghost city, and to the odd echo that it left behind in Exburgh, the *Shimmering*, like a shiny umbilical cord, holding you to its after-image.

'The entity you call Baalgor is hiding in that after-image. The second entity – Nemet – has returned to the buried world of archetypal landscape. Glanum, though, recognizes no boundary between our *earth* and your *mind*. Think of it as an animal whose boundaries are not physical fences but scent-marks – a different set of dimensions.'

'The Mallon Hills, the Frouden Moors, and my own unconscious – all part of a single road?'

'To Glanum as it moves, yes. And also: when you enter the *Shimmering*, you are entering a hinterland that exists both *inside* and *outside* your mind. You have characterized the connecting gate between inside and outside as a spiral storm, seen in the sky in the *Shimmering*, and swirling in the earth in the Deep, a beautiful use of imagination to symbolize both confusion and connection – just as your hinterland is a world of crumbling religion, rotting temples, broken icons, broken faith . . . *abandoned* faith, if you like. And when the *Shimmering* came for you near the Frouden Moors, like a mouth, it was simply shortening the umbilical cord that connects you.'

For a while Jack sat in silence, staring through the mist of cigarette smoke at the bright window.

Abandoned faith? I never had a faith to abandon! My parents gave it up when they were young.

It was an odd sensation, to be confronting for the first time the fact that his inner world was a graveyard of discarded dogma, unacknowledged belief, untried religion. He felt suddenly empty, which was strange – he had never needed churches; he had only ever needed family . . .

'What about the ruins below Exburgh?' His mind was unfocused. There were too many imponderables. 'What of John Garth – he climbed *aboard* the city!'

'My best guess is that the stone remains are petrified memory, as Garth, if I remember right, once suggested to you; memory *crystallizing* out in random form each time Glanum sheds a shadow of itself.'

'That sounds crazy . . . absolutely crazy . . .'

For a moment both men stared at each other, then both burst out laughing.

'Well . . . *crazier*!' Jack amended. After a moment he asked, 'But why does Glanum shed shadows?'

'Now we come to it,' Brightmore said, turning to a page of his notes – 'a honey trap perhaps? Each shadow a snare, a trap for the entities being hunted? And after ten thousand years, the trap has finally been sprung in Exburgh? One "Bull-runner" escaped, one is running back *in*, but Glanum is in both worlds, now, and its hunt is nearing its end.'

Jack just shook his head, staring at the other man, the words trying to nest in a mind that was reeling.

Glanum's hunt?

Brightmore said quietly, 'You saw a Bull chasing the runners. You saw white towers in most locations where they were fleeing. You have experienced a moving city – a city with a Bull-Gate – and that moving city may have at its heart prehistoric Jericho – which we know was a white-towered town ten thousand years ago!

'The question then is this: *is* it a Bull – or a *city* that is hunting your friends?'

Glanum itself?

Jack breathed deeply, remembering what he could of his childhood visions, re-living the dream-like encounter with stone walls and a grinning Bull-Gate on the sun-warmed Mallon Hills, a lifetime ago.

Glanum itself . . .

'So it will come back?' he said. 'To finish things?'

'I believe it will. You've already sensed its return, I think, when you saw it in the distance, in the Midax Deep.

'As for John Garth – I don't know. He stepped across the threshold with great ease.' Brightmore tapped the table again, then smiled. 'I have a feeling he belongs *there* not *here*. But I just don't know. Whatever happened in the Jordan Valley ten thousand years ago, Garth is involved in some way. But I just don't know.'

Brightmore's words echoed: *Glanum is in both worlds, now, and the hunt is nearing its end.*

So if it was inside as well as outside – then Ahk-Nemet was in danger.

Natalie threatened outside, Nemet inside . . . His real child and his . . . imaginary lover.

But the call *in*, for the moment, was the strongest and he scarcely dared think of the full consequences of the action he was about to take.

'This is the last trip,' he said to Angela. 'I promise.'

'Good. Steven thinks it's getting dangerous for you.'

'But I insist – don't bring me back until I *signal*. Don't interfere this time!'

'Then keep your hands off that bitch.'

For a moment he was stunned by the words, blushing with guilt. But Angela's smile was neither sardonic nor concerned; she was signalling that she was joking, and yet it had been her own anger that had pulled him from Nemet the last time he had been in the Deep.

We no longer know what we want, he thought.

Or do we?

There was a moment of awkwardness, of tension between them. Jack felt very distant from his wife, his fears focused entirely on Natalie, who was playing in the garden of the Institute. He wanted to go to her, to reassure himself that she was all right, to hold her in his arms, but Angela was blocking his way.

'Don't bring me back,' he insisted after a moment. 'Not even if it looks like my throat is being cut!'

'Then take care,' she said. 'There are two people here who need you.'

They kissed quickly, it was not intimate, then stood in each other's arms for a moment, more for reassurance than affection. All Jack could think of was Natalie, downstairs, and a distant warm breeze on a wooded ridge, where small horses grazed and dark, sensuous eyes entombed his own.

PART EIGHT
Abandoned Cities

32

I was running through woods, through a tunnel of trees, towards a growing and welcoming light.

For a while it was my father who chased me, a growling presence, menacing and furious, but as I came into the Hinterland, the irrational representation of the man dissolved into the mad stampede of horses, taller, streaked with red across their haunches, more powerfully flanked than the hippari from the Deep. They scattered across the broken piazza, stumbling on the disrupted earth, the shattered stones of the steps and the temples.

How and why my father, a man I had loved and joked with all my life, had become representative of fear I cannot imagine; except that there were other fathers at work in this zone, and Ahk'Nemet's was one of them, a man she had clearly trusted yet who had apparently betrayed her.

The horses took off again, like a flight of birds responding to a sudden shadow. They clattered through what had once been the Bull Temple, sucked into the maw of the cliff.

I watched them go, then tried to re-imagine this place of desolation, remembering it as I had experienced it previously. The cliffs were the same: high, infinite, curving out of sight, enclosing the place where once rich temples and churches had beckoned and enticed the curious mind.

All of those structures had been *eaten*; I can think of no better way to describe it. They had been cut back, bitten back to their cliffside walls, scoured away, leaving nothing but sad foundations.

The piazza itself, that wide, white space, had been broken upwards, as if shattered from below.

My instinct was to think that something massive had erupted from the earth and chewed away the familiar and potentially welcoming façades of saints and bulls, of magic and mystery. I thought, quite naturally, of Glanum, the city from the Deep.

But whatever the cause, there was nothing left for me here, now; this place was devastated. I was not wanted; there was no comfort.

I inspected my pack briefly, finding it to be an adequate representation of the supplies I had garnered before this third trip inwards, and turned back to the woodland. I walked back along the familiar hollow track to the roaring waterfall, passing through the honeycombed cavern behind the cliff and emerging onto the high mountain, to look again across the land and its distant lakes, where William and Ethne had loved, and where I hoped Greenface still waited.

At once I saw the rising bulk of a sinister dark structure, built, I was certain, on the site of the fishing village and the later defended town, which had fallen to the enemy from the Ice Age. It was hard to tell for the moment, but the new building seemed to be pyramidal. Small in the landscape now, it must nevertheless have been vast to have caught my eye across this great divide.

Two days later I stood in awe and in the shadow of the mausoleum. Built, or at least faced, with black obsidian, the tomb almost covered the shore and the woodland where Ethne's people had once lived. It gleamed in the pale sun; the waters of the lake broke against its flank with a melancholy sound. *Lakescrow*, or carrion birds of some description, stalked the edge of the flattened roof, flew down and into the echoing chamber through the tall, opened entrance.

I walked twice around the silent, eerie structure. Four sides for four seasons, each marked with a symbol of the time of the year: a snowflake of astonishing intricacy; a sunblaze; a reed pipe for the spring; a musk ox, bound and dying, for the autumn, the time of stockading.

And on each of the sloping walls, ten figures rose, twice the height of a man, icon-dressed, armed and watching the sky or the forest or the ground with long, lean-faced, blank expressions.

I remembered William's description of his function in the world: ten steps of the winter dance; waiting to be united with the dances of the other seasons.

I *knew* this was William's place, I could feel it in my blood.

I was shaking as I stepped into the inner sanctum, where shafts of light broke the gloom from slats in the ceiling, a towering distance above my head.

The tomb itself was in the centre of the space, dazzled by the light, crawling with crows which flapped and screeched as I approached, and took off, slow-winging, into the shadows. I watched them for a few moments, glad to delay the moment at which I would stare, I was sure, at the face in deepest repose of the man who had become my friend, and whom I had abandoned.

It was not William Finebeard, however, who lay in imperfect preservation in the glass-topped coffin.

She was dressed in shells and blue-green beads, her body swathed in this ornamentation; strands of the fine lace on which the shells were threaded drifted in the yellow liquid, for all the world, like anemones feeling for their prey. Ethne had been laid on her side, her knees drawn up, her hands tied together, palms together, as if in prayer. Her long hair drifted about a face reddened with ochre.

It was a vile sight. Whatever the preserving fluid, it was inadequate to the task, and the blotch and shrink of rot had begun to take its toll on the sweet corpse. The eyes were open, the lips drawn back, yellowing teeth bulging in the shrunken face. A cloud of fragments swirled in the tinted fluid, excited by the light from above, darting like living creatures among the drifting hairs and strands, in and out of the shell patina of the body.

Poor Ethne. Poor William.

Rose-pricked though she might have been, no princely kiss would bring *this* sleeping beauty back to life.

I walked the shore for days, searching for a boat, a hulk, something, anything that could get me to the farther side of the great lake. The jetties and harbour of the fishing city were all corrupt, shaped stone spread out below the water, sinking into the mud. Wildlife abounded; my hunting skills improved; my belly remained full. I slept, at night, in the mausoleum, curled into a corner, fire protecting me from the snarling beasts that roamed and searched the shadows, some even standing up to peer at the silent queen, biting and snapping at the glass before retiring to the growling, nervous night outside.

At last, a small boat beached, an old man entered the tomb and placed fresh flowers on the grave. As I watched from hiding, he walked about the hall, gathering the bones of the creatures which had been consumed here, brushing up the leaves, piling everything into a shallow pit and setting this rubbish-tip alight.

He crouched by the flames, stoking the fire, shifting the bones, throwing finger-fulls of powder on the conflagration, which roared and spat, filling the mausoleum with an acrid smoke.

He was aware of me; he had deliberately left my hiding place alone. When I rose and walked to the door he watched me, an old man, grizzle-bearded, sharp-eyed, his body frail, I thought, behind the robust swell of leather armour.

He followed me to the lake's edge, leaning on a thin harpoon, keeping the point ready. The boat, big enough for two, shifted on the swell as a fierce wind blew up from the direction of the maelstrom. I threw my pack into the boat and raised my hands, a question and an indication that I meant no harm.

He nodded, waved me in with the pointed stick, then clambered aboard himself, tossing me the rope that held the single sail, leaning hard on the rudder as the small craft sought the right angle of the breeze, dipped, swung and began to hop the waves towards the far white tower.

He watched me curiously, this greybeard, but never spoke, except to bark an order when the sail flapped, losing the wind, prompting me to tug the lines and secure them in the wooden cleats. I tried to remember if I had seen him on my previous Midax voyage, but only the gruesome face of Perendour came to mind. I was more exercised by the question of how many years had passed since I had last stepped on the land that circled the Eye.

From the rotten state of her hallowed corpse, it was impossible to say how old Ethne had been when fate or circumstance had intervened to cut her heart-strings. And for how long had she been entombed?

If the answer was centuries, then there would be no Greenface, waiting for me by the Watching Place. Or would there?

We came into the stone harbour, near the white tower, and the greybeard navigated the small boat between the half-sunk, rotting hulks of greater ships. This place, too, was long abandoned, though the smoke from fires further down the lake's edge suggested that the area was still inhabited, though by whom, and in what fashion, I couldn't tell.

With the boat tied securely, my captain led me to the shore, then turned and peered again; his breath was foul, his gaze close enough that we might have kissed. And then he grinned.

'Jack?' he murmured. 'Jackjack?'

'Yes. I'm Jack.'

'Jackjack,' he repeated, shaking his head, still half-smiling.

'I've come to find William.'

'William,' the man echoed and looked away, his brow

furrowing, the smile fading. A moment or two later he sighed and threw the harpoon towards the white tower.

'William,' he repeated, glancing at me. Then, quick as a wink, he had reached out and squeezed my ear before turning away, walking away, towards the distant fires.

I entered the city gate, pushing aside the tangling foliage with the sailor's discarded harpoon. The place was overgrown, ivy, rose and strangling creeper of luxuriant green, with flower trumpets of brilliant hue, forming a carpet, a wall and a barrier that only reluctantly gave way to my onslaught.

I cut and pushed my way to the entrance to the tower, snarled back at a feral cat, chattered in like manner to a red-crested, red-billed carrion bird that caught itself in the briar in its panic to escape my aggressive action as I stabbed at it with the spear, then entered the place I knew well, the dimly-lit chamber where William had painted images of his beloved. The dark designs, the ochred patches, were still visible, but time, condensation and the spread of lichen had made a mockery of Ethne's frail beauty.

On a pallet, covered in rough blankets, William Finebeard lay asleep below the icons of his passion. His body was entombed in briar, growing up from the floor, reaching down from the orifices in the tower, a web of forest, holding hard this winter warrior, growing into him through the pale skin.

From the slow rise and fall of his chest it was clear that *this* sleeping beauty was still alive, and I used a knife from my pack to 'prune' him, cutting away the thorns and ivy, aware that the stumps remained upon his skin, bleeding in a sluggish fashion.

He stayed asleep.

I walked up into the hills, searching for familiar paths, remembered ruins, but the world had changed beyond the lake and nothing encouraged me to think that Greenface was near, or had been close to the tower of ivory. I stood and watched the maelstrom, listened to the deep movement of the earth, the crash of rock, the loud and strident cries of the creatures that were spewed from the pit itself. I hunted for small game, gathered sharp fruit from a wide-branched, gnarled and twisted apple tree (I saw no serpents) and found a patch of the same mushrooms that Nemet had fed to me, those years in the past.

The world of my inner mind was rich with my favourite things, and perhaps I should not have been surprised.

Two days after I had cut the strands enmeshing my friend, a small flotilla of single-sailed ships passed close to the shore, cloaked figures on every prow, sharp cries carrying across the choppy water. They inspected the white tower, then caught the prevailing wind and turned like a flock to pass away to deeper water.

At dusk, hippari, brontotheria, bear-like megalotheria, brutish cynodontae and strutting aepyornithae filtered from the forest to wade, drink, feed, squabble and gallop along the twilight shore. They kept away from the sunken harbour, though the horses were curious and I entertained briefly the idea of trying to capture one. Their speed, their edgy energy, soon communicated the futility of the thought.

But if I had not been watching the evening feast, sitting on the stone wall which indicated the beginning of the jetty and surrounded by the cacophony of ancient voices, I might not have seen the city as it passed along the lake.

The sun had almost gone; the lake stirred, the waves came fast to the shore, spreading among the reeds, or breaking against the mudflats further down. The animals that were still watering became disturbed; the hippari bolted to the woodland. The cynodonts rose onto hindlegs, eight creatures standing like stooped, human grotesques, jaws gaping in the dog-like faces as they watched the lake. When they slowly backed away they set up an unearthly howling, then scattered as the great shape rose out of the water.

It was Glanum. The tower came first, the high walls, the tangle of trees and roots shedding water as they were thrust from the sub-aquatic world. It descended again, then broke the surface, turning towards the land, a mile distant. I could see the gaping gate, but other features were indistinct against its gloomy bulk in the deepening night.

The city ploughed the lake, then sank into the shore, and I felt the ground shudder and rumble, the woodland shaking as if a violent wind was whipping and coursing across the canopy.

Glanum was soon gone, below the high hills, travelling in the direction of the Eye. I stood on the jetty for several hours, reluctant to retire to the comfort of furs, matting and the fire that I had kindled inside William's broken stronghold. If the city returned, I wanted to see it. I wondered if John Garth had been standing on those shattered battlements, staring out across the Deep, perhaps searching for the boy he remembered from Exburgh.

Glanum was close now, and close for a reason; everything in my dreaming instinct suggested that I was soon to be reunited with the whale!

But . . . though the earth shook on two occasions, and wind took the trees, and a flock of carrion birds swooped low and angrily across the sunken jetty, the night remained quiet, and I went to bed.

In the morning, I examined the part of the shore where Glanum had passed, but found no trace, no cut, no gouge, no exploded earth, no sign as fierce and hard as that in the Hinterland, if indeed that scar in the piazza had been created by the whale.

Some time later, I returned to the bone tower, and as I entered the chamber where William lay in vegetative slumber, I heard his waking moan.

The cuts had ceased to bleed. I had left him on his side, but now he lay face up, his right arm above his head, his left draped across his belly.

Soon he sighed, shifted, turned on the wooden bed, letting the rags of the blankets fall from him, his fingers, in half-sleep, now brushing and fiddling with the cut ends of briar on his chin, his cheek, his shoulders and his belly.

Abruptly, like a man awakening from a dream, he sat up and stared at the open door.

He looked at me, blinked, frowned for a moment, then grinned with pleasure as he recognized me.

'Hello William, you romantic rogue!'

'Jack,' he whispered hoarsely. 'Jack! Came back! Came back!'

33

Older in years, William was still a boy at heart, and when he had recovered his strength he went down to the lake, marvelling at everything he saw, from the wild beasts of the forest to the shattered remnants of the harbour.

He was delighted with the sunken hulks of the bigger ships, wading out to peer into the broken hulls, clambering across the shattered masts, pulling lengths of sail and rope, nodding, talking, plotting, planning.

'It will take some work, but there's everything here I need to cross to Ethne again. And with your help . . . it will halve the time. I'll be afloat before the turn of the season. You came back! *Jack! Came back!*' he cried in English, tugging at my hair.

And he hugged me, rubbing a briar-bristled cheek against my own. He was bothered by the stubs, scratching and worrying at them, frowning as he tried to understand what had happened to him.

'I saw her,' I said softly.

'Ethne?'

'Yes. It came as a shock.'

There was sadness in his face, and a strange excitement. 'I haven't looked at her for so long. Has she changed?'

I felt awkward telling him the truth of her imperfect preservation, but since he seemed set on crossing to the tomb to view her again, it was better, I felt, that he should be forewarned. 'Time is taking its toll. But you honoured her beautifully. It's a wonderful monument.' I could see the dark rise of the mausoleum, across the lake, half-obscured by mist, but a looming, distracting presence just the same.

He stared at me for a moment, perhaps trying to understand me fully as we communicated in gesture, fragments of language and the movement of eyes. 'I'm going to bring her back,' he said. 'Bring her to this place. It's where she belongs.'

It seemed a strange idea. With a ship, water-safe and sturdy, he could cross the lake in a day. And why go to so much effort to build a monument to his 'princess' on the site of her birth, only to remove her?

What had happened to William Finebeard in the intervening years?

And when had he fallen into the rose and ivy slumber?

I could get little sense out of the man for most of the day; he had no appetite for food, seemed to need no water, and left me for hours, running the lake's edge, prowling the woodland, chasing hippari and laughing as they outdistanced him. He swam naked in the cold lake, dived to inspect the rubble foundations of the fallen harbour, rising from the murky, muddy water draped with weed, a monstrous image from the wild.

'This place is perfect,' he seemed to say. 'I can build on the ruins; make a city again. This place is perfect.'

'You should know. You built it in the first place.'

He stared at me, then shook his head, and the first inkling of what had happened to the tundra-dancer insinuated its unwelcome presence into my mind.

'Don't you remember building the harbour? Throwing up new walls around the tower? Taming horses to carry you inland, to forage for the best trees to build the great ships?'

'I remember the city,' he said. He looked darkly at the lake. 'It came out of the water and consumed everything that was here. I will never forget how it looked, a stone beast with a stone mouth and a stone heart, eating its way through the forest and the hill, leaving everything dead and broken.

329

Maybe it even ate the *maelstrom*. It took the sanctuaries, it took the temple, it took the trees where the armour of my friends was hung in honour . . . I remember that. I remember it clearly. But this place was here before me. You and I came ashore, you tended my wounds. It was here then . . . all we need do is salvage a ship . . . prepare for the crossing . . .'

He glanced at the lake, where the hulks and stumps of masts broke the surface, the playground of waterbirds. 'Have you ever salvaged a ship?' he asked with a thin, hopeful smile.

'Nothing as big as those.'

'Hmm. Well, we'll manage somehow. Now then!'

He turned abruptly to the forest and flung a piece of drift-wood, smiling as the clatter in the branches set up the sound of howling.

'Greenface!' he announced, and his look was one of curi-osity. 'Did you find her?'

'I've found her twice so far. This is my third attempt.'

He was surprised. 'You've been back? I didn't see you!'

'I couldn't find you.'

'But I was here. I've been here since you left . . .'

'I couldn't find you.' *Although I saw you* . . .

'How strange.'

He brightened suddenly. 'Elusive?' He meant Ahk'Nemet.

'Slippery.'

'Like a fish,' he mimed.

'Indeed. But I think she's waiting for me. It's just a ques-tion of knowing where. The last time I saw her, she was close to the maelstrom, by a gate shaped like a Bull's face. The Watching Place.'

'I've dreamed of it,' he said, scratching at the projection of a stub of ivy from his cheek. 'I've dreamed of it many times. I've dreamed of the Bull. A huge creature. It neither descends into the Eye, nor emerges from it. It walks the edge of the whirling pool . . . It's stronger than the earth, I think.'

'Did you dream it? Or have you seen it?'

'I'd know if I'd seen it. How long do you think you've been gone?' he asked with a laugh.

'I don't know. How long?'

'Not that long. A few months . . .'

A few months! He *was* deluded.

'You left me here, wounded. I've had very little opportunity to do anything other than think, and plan, and dream . . . But you're back, as you said you'd be. I'll help you find Greenface; you'll help me cross the lake. I shall resurrect Ethne from the hell of fish, gum and oil that embalms her. She belongs here, now. Here, with me . . .'

Embalms her? Had he truly said that? Or was this only my interpretation of his gesture and signal that meant no more than *entraps*, as in: take her away from the family who are holding her?

'What will you do with her, when you fetch her?' I asked tentatively, and he went dreamy, then excited, pointing to the hill behind us. 'Take her deep into the land. Find a place to spend our lives together. Dance with each child born. Avoid the ice at all costs, live only in the warmth!'

Dear God – he thought she was still alive! He had forgotten that his beloved Ethne had died years ago, and that he had buried her and built a tomb to her that now echoed with wind and wings.

I felt so sad for him. For a while I sat at the edge of the woods, watching him about his business, and my heart broke for him, since he was living in a state of such hope and such anticipation.

I went hunting, unsuccessfully as it transpired, seeking my own company, in a quandary as to what to do. At dusk, as I slipped down the hill towards the gleaming lake, I saw him standing knee-deep in the water, staring out across the distance towards the dark tomb. He was naked, his hands hanging limply by his sides. He remained motionless for nearly half an hour and I stayed quite still, crouched in cover, waiting to see what happened.

I believed, and was proved right, that he had begun to have an inkling of the truth about Ethne; that the past, drawn from him perhaps during sleep, was now seeping back, unwelcome days and nights, dark images obscuring the brief light that had set his face aglow on my return.

After a time he walked back to the shore, to the tower. I followed him as he pushed through the undergrowth, through gaps in the walls, a shadowy figure passing between the trees, soon discernible only by his rustling progress towards a deeper part of the ruined castle.

When I found him, he was asleep, wrapped in a tumble of ivy that spilled over a low wall and onto a carved stone bench. In the fading evening light, I realized that I was in a garden; small statues of children, carved in a blue-tinged granite, stood at the four corners of what had once been a deep pool. The fountain in the centre was shaped like the sturgeon from the lake that I had seen caught, a lifetime ago. Once, this garden had been covered with a roof of branches, open to the light, but casting shade in places; the wood was broken, rotting, overgrown with swelling, puffy fungus. But the blooms of flowers were still heavy with scent, and I could tell, just, that they were brightly coloured. They were closing to the night, but some of the trumpets were of enormous size.

I couldn't wake William, though I tried, concerned for him sleeping in the open and with nothing but leaves for a covering. 'Don't leave me,' I said to him, thinking that he might sink more deeply into sleep, and remain there.

Getting cold, I went back to the tower and for want of a better resting place curled up on his pallet, pushing aside the dangling vegetation, some fronds still dripping sap from the cut ends. The drops touched my skin like tears, and though I was tempted to move, I stayed where I was, thinking of William.

How long he had slept here I couldn't tell, but a long time, many years. As he had slept, the shadows had been drawn from him by the nurturing garden, which had spread from its small centre to encompass the tower. Now those shadows played briefly in my own dreaming mind, an echo of another's past, a heritage of war and anguish that would have to re-inhabit the fine-bearded man at some point, but perhaps not yet.

Such powerful dreams.

First, the anguish as he finally realized I was not coming back. He had waited on the shore for weeks, slowly healing, each wound a constant reminder of his feelings for Ethne, denied to him by the span of the lake. At dawn his crude defences were shattered by monsters. He starved for a while, then made a lucky strike, feeding on hipparion meat for several days before the flies discouraged him.

He was desolate, lonely, and frightened; the fear grew into rage; he stormed the hill, prowled the edge of the Eye, carved my name and called to me. I had never grasped the extent to which he had depended upon my help.

I had left him, and he soon decided that I was dead. He built a monument to me, a crude carving in wood. He blistered his fingers holding the knives with which he shaped the hard oak. When the icon was finished he took it up to the maelstrom and left it there, its blind eyes staring at the heart of the storm.

This memory had been taken from him, leaving him relieved to see me, as if only days had past.

I dreamed on: the lake crossing with a fleet of ships, low and sleek, rowed by a hundred men; hunters, mercenaries, knights, horsemen, raiders and rievers, all eager for battle.

I woke in the middle of the mayhem. The strong walls of the fishing city were broken down, the slaughter was complete, though Two Cuts escaped, badly wounded, into the forest. Ethne and her sisters were rescued, and as I passed back into sleep, trying to abandon the stink of guts and the sound of shrieking men, so I experienced the love that William and Ethne had known for several years . . .

And their children, twins, two boys of fair complexion, one thoughtful, one devil-may-care, both of them William's pride and joy.

And then the horror: of waking to Two Cuts' half-masked face, the dull bone that covered his eyes and nose giving him the look of a fish, the smile below unmistakable. He held the twins by their hair, two naked, limp bodies, red life still spurting from their throats where Two Cuts had brought grotesque meaning to his name.

Erhne was gone. The fort blazed. Out on the lake, the dark ships waited as Two Cuts' warriors abandoned the destruction, their quest achieved, the woman returned.

In the dream, William screamed, 'I killed you. I saw you killed!'

The spear sliced through him.

He was too quick for the hunter-fisher, though, and for a moment the face behind the fish-skull mask looked startled. Then Two Cuts was running for the shore, for the ships, William behind him, the spear raised although his body racked with pain from the wound.

Fire-shadow made the shore a confusion of movement. The air stank with burning. Ethne had slipped her captors and was running for the forest. As Two Cuts stumbled in the muddy water, screaming to his warriors, William killed him, a single strike to the back with the spear, a second strike to the neck, severing the masked head from its armoured corpse.

By dawn, the ships of the raiders had slipped away, dispersing across the lake, travelling further into the mountains, abandoning the fishing city for ever, now that Two Cuts lay mutilated in the mud.

Again I woke, but again, the sap dreams sent me back into William's memory . . .

Ethne, a pale-faced, beautiful figure, for ever to be found wandering naked and smiling along the lake, a primal creature among the brontotheria and hippari, bathing with them, drinking with them, chasing birds, fishing for the golden-scaled chubb and silver bream with a skill and a speed that was astonishing.

William made statues of the children and placed them in a garden, with statues of himself and Ethne making up the square around a fountain. Ethne loved the place. She slept here, danced here, bathed in the spring that one of William's discoveries in the hills – an architect, a dreamer, a man wandering the Deep aimlessly – had directed to the granite sturgeon whose jaws spouted the fresh and cleansing water.

Ethne roamed the castle. And after a while she began to sail across the lake, to the ruins of her city.

Since she always returned, William let her go; he was still lost in grief, for his twins and for the woman he had loved, who was now just a ghost in his fortress. She travelled with the builder, the man who could tame spring water, and he knew where to acquire a gleaming stone, black and hard.

Obsidian!

He woke one morning to the feeling of a kiss, but on opening his eyes he saw nothing but the room, the bed, the murals of Ethne and her sons that had been painted on the ivory walls of the tower.

He ran to the garden, then to the harbour. Her boat was gone. She had sailed, he learned, the night before, crossing the lake in darkness with the stone-shaper.

Intuitively, he knew that this was her final passage.

He followed her across the water, disembarking where her small vessel lay hauled up on the shore. The small, black monument had been built where once she had lived in her father's house. It was a stone coffin, crystal topped, shaped by the man who stood behind it, leaning on his staff, watching the distraught figure who stumbled to the mausoleum, to hold the stone, to kiss the glass that covered the gentle, peaceful body of his wife.

Ethne had built her own, small tomb. She had lain on

335

her side, wrists tied, legs tied, the poison taking her to her father's world. The stone-shaper had done the rest.

'It's what she wanted. To lie in peace, close to her mother's ashes.'

'But I want more. Build a hall to hold the coffin. You'll have all the labour you need, all the ships you need for the stone.'

'What would she think of what you're doing? She wanted something close to the heart.'

'Build it like I say. Build it so the roof is on the sky itself!'

'It's not what she would have wanted.'

'She's gone. She's in the world of lakes and forests. And it's what *I* want that matters now. When I come here, I want space to scream and hear the echo. Do what I tell you!'

And while the mausoleum was built, William stayed by the tomb, wrapped in furs against the cold when the winter blizzarded and silenced the whole land; draped in the same red ochre as his dead Ethne when summer made the land wilt with heat. He ate sparingly, slept a great deal, never walked outside the confines of the hall, standing and staring at the open sky, where the fragile scaffolding held the great blocks of polished stone as they were winched and eased into place.

His life was one of the sounds of carving, chipping, shouting, laughing, screams and music. The monument was built in a single cycle of seasons, and William sailed home again.

There was one more memory in the sap, but it was hazy, elusive. I began to wake, my awareness starting to wrestle with the sheer scale of the building that William had ordered, thinking in terms of pyramids, and the workforce, and the work hours involved, questioning how he had found labour on such a scale . . .

But the drip of sweet tears closed my eyes again . . .

A memory that had not been taken fully from him, now shaped and shimmered on the lake.

The Bull-Gate of Glanum, horns rising from the lake, the tower streaming water as it came above the surface. It moved through the dawn mist, ploughed through the harbour, into the mud, stone screaming as it cut the fortress right across, devouring the heart of the city. It threw down the statues that decorated Ethne's garden and engulfed the place where William had made a shrine to the lost dancers of his own land. Earth falling from its walls, the limbs of trees cracking from the trunks that grew from between the massive stones, Glanum entered the mountain, shaking the land as it turned towards the Eye . . .

I woke to the single, immediate thought:

Glanum was close and coming closer. It was circling this place, as if hunting an elusive prey. Greenface? Instinct told me differently.

It was seeking *me*. It knew I was here.

34

In the morning, I found the garden deserted, and though I called for William there was no answer. But I found the small hull of a boat hauled from the reeds beyond the harbour onto the higher bank, the mud around churned where the man had laboured in the dawn.

He was beginning his preparations to cross the water again.

Then at about midday the sound of equine protestations announced William's arrival from the hills. He was on foot, dressed in protective leather shirt and trousers, running towards the castle leading two of the hippari on short ropes. The creatures' hindquarters bucked and swayed as they ran awkwardly, and I realized that each had their hind-legs bound together at the hoof, allowing them to move, but frustrating their scythe-like, defensive kick.

He led them up to me, a breathless, grinning man, sweat pouring from his face.

'Watch!' he said, then turned and used his fist to hammer each of them solidly and stunningly on the muzzle. The beasts went down, eyes open, flanks heaving, totally subdued. The hunter drew his stone knife and went round each hipparion, severing the vestigial toes close to the hoof. Where the cuts oozed blood he spat on the wounds, rubbed them, then caked a little mud on the surface.

He tied the horses together by the neck and left them lying there, one of them, the larger, making faint sounds, somewhere between a whinny and a laugh, not at all happy, however.

'Leave them there for a few hours. They'll handle like old friends.'

'You've done this before,' I said and he frowned.

'Have I? Only in my dreams, then. It came naturally to me, a sort of instinct. Here, these are lucky.'

He passed me the sixteen stubs, some of them razor edged, some blunt and heavy. Was I supposed to make a necklace of them? An amulet?

William laughed, held up his arms and I realized that the sleeves of his shirt were stiffened from wrist to elbow with hipparion toes, a crude form of chain mail. To demonstrate their effectiveness he used his heavy knife to strike heavily at his own limb. The blade was turned aside harmlessly.

It had not occurred to him to question how the bones had come onto his sleeves if he had never tamed the creatures save in his dreams. He was a living contradiction, but I no longer felt inclined to confront him about it.

'Thank you. I'm sure they'll be very useful.'

I had assumed that he had acquired and (hopefully) tamed these creatures so that we would have one each to ride into the hills. But his unease at dusk, as he prepared grilled fish, giant periwinkles and a heavy cake made from wild grains and nuts, was more than obvious. When I politely refused the massive, tongue-like curls of the fresh-water molluscs, he was insistent that I ate them. 'For stamina. For the long ride!' he told me. I managed one and was nearly sick. A second, large though it was (it was impossible to bite into the half-cooked mass) sailed beyond the wall as I blew it from my mouth when William was away, urinating. Desperation had strengthened my lungs.

In the morning, one of the equines had been loaded with my pack, with poles to erect skins for a tent, and with strips of drying, salted, suspicious looking food.

He held the other hipparion by its bridle, stroking the striped muzzle, watching me with his shining blue eyes.

'Is this goodbye, then?' I asked him, and he handed me the crude reins.

'I think so. I've thought hard about it, and perhaps your path takes you away from me, now. I have a boat to build, a lake to cross, a heart to rescue. You have a Bull to find, a city to find, something I can't understand to resolve.'

'I have to find the woman,' I said with a shrug. 'Greenface. Beyond that, I have no idea what life holds.'

'She's close,' he said. 'The bull is close. The end is close.'

They were strange meanings, but they echoed my own feelings that I was at the centre, now, of a diminishing circle, that everything in this world of *mine* was coming together, coming to *me*, as if the wandering Midax spirit was at last taking charge of its own heaven and hell.

There remained a problem, and I pointed across the lake to the distant shadow of the mausoleum.

'Who built the black tower?'

He didn't look to where I pointed, simply tugged my ear and smiled. 'Things will have changed. I know that.'

'But *what* do you know? William . . . more time has passed than—'

He silenced me with a finger to my lips, a hand raised, palm towards me: quiet!

'I will find what is there for me to find. But Ethne belongs here, with me; I'll die unless I get her back.'

Did he know that she was dead? Were we talking at cross purposes? What should I say?

I said simply, 'Time has taken a terrible toll on the eldest daughter.'

But all he did was laugh!

'Jack,' he said with a sigh. 'Jack: I've fought and killed creatures as high as that ivory tower; I've battled against harpoon hunters and left them for the *lakescrow* to feed on.' He grinned meaningfully as he watched me. 'Do you think I can't make war upon that bloody tyrant *Time*?'

The image behind his words and gestures had a strange

resonance, a familiar feel, and I remembered school, the Sonnets ('*make war upon this bloody tyrant Time*') and I looked at William, saw myself again, saw the echo, the shadow of my childhood, embodied here in rose-torn, fine-haired beauty.

Though he probably knew he would find Ethne dead, nothing, it seemed, would dampen Finebeard's optimism. And I took a great strength from that. It seemed to affirm my own quest. I felt hopeful of finding Ahk'Nemet, and hopeful of releasing Natalie from Greyface's ghoulish grip.

And in any case: once out of sight, he would be out of my frame of reference, a cat allowed to play! In William's world, once I was no longer fixing it by observing it, perhaps Ethne was only sleeping after all.

And a kiss from his lips would indeed bring her out of the dark hall and onto the bright lake again, loving and laughing, and fishing in the Deep . . .

While in suburban Exburgh, I ate breakfast and went to work!

At the top of the hill, leading my pack-hipparion awkwardly through the crowded woodland, I blew three shrill blasts on the bone pipe.

From the shore came three imitations of the *lakescrow*, the carrion eater that plagued the water's edge. And then my name, bellowed three times and followed by the cry of Greenface!

And a laugh so suggestive that I will never forget it, loud enough to wake the dead.

'Goodbye, you rogue,' I whispered. 'And magic to your kissing!'

35

All my life I had been haunted by the Bull, but I had never felt endangered by it. It had threatened strangers in my dreams, and I had merely watched and witnessed.

It hunted me, now, and I ran before it, terrified, senses heightened, aware of the slightest shadow, the smallest path, the most concealing tree. The small horses had long-since been killed, one by the effort of the journey, the other by the predators which roamed the forest.

I had reached the edge of the maelstrom on the second day, sheltering from the rain and wind as a black storm raged across the swirling land. There was no sign of Greenface and I began the journey round the Eye, towards distant forests which, in the light-streaked gloom of the tempest, might have been the giant cedars that seemed to mark a place where she felt at home. I sought shelters of stone, the fragments of strong buildings, but the only walls I found were dissolving into mud and rotting wood; there was something older about the ghosts now spewing from the whirling pool of earth – all shadow of the mediaeval gone, replaced by crude and prehistoric dwellings.

When the rain cleared I entered deep forest, emerging occasionally on to the precipice that fell away to the deeps and divided the world of the shore from the maelstrom. Here, I lost the pack hipparion. It was ill, rather than overladen, struggling to breathe, and as I removed its burden it laughed in that odd way of the creatures and bolted towards the edge, plummeting instantly to its doom. Shortly after, I found the ruins of the Watching Place, the arch remaining full, but the decorated façade scarred by wind, rain and time, a dead place through which I passed and around which I found no recent trace of Ahk'Nemet. But she had made the place into a shrine, I thought: the broken walls of a wooden room revealed the smashed statue of a stooping man, the face sheared away, the arms broken. I kicked through the undergrowth and eventually found the features that had been destroyed; I stared at my own anguished face in stone, the hard, cold legacy of my previous visit. Who had smashed the idol, I wondered, and guessed that more of William's mercenaries had once passed this way.

The Watching Place, a dead place? So it had seemed. But as I walked on, Leading the second hipparion by the reins, so for the first time the earth shuddered in a less familiar way, like a beast stamping the ground. I turned in alarm.

The watery sun was behind the Watching Place. I thought I saw raised horns in silhouette, and though they seemed to move slightly, I imagined the whole effect was simply an illusion in the shifting light. Minutes later, the gate had disappeared from view as I hurried on.

I soon became aware of a strong, cooling wind blowing from behind me and of an odd restlessness in the forest and in the air. The hipparion became agitated, started to scream and buck against the restraining rope that was tied between its teeth. There was no calming the beast and I held it strongly as I stripped off the pack. Before I could disentangle the dried fish, it ripped away from me and ran ahead. The earth was shuddering dramatically and I began to follow the creature, glancing back, searching the trees and the skyline . . .

The bull's head rose suddenly and the bellow was deafening. It was higher than the trees, the horns scything the sky. Huge eyes stared at me. The red body shook, the saplings snapped as it stepped forward, shaking the foliage as it began to move towards me.

I ran for my life, half tempted to discard the pack, but clinging onto it with all my strength. I could feel the heavy breathing of the monster, and my memory threw up dreams of Greenface running just like this, the swaying bovine crashing through the trees behind her.

Abruptly, the woodland opened out into a steep defile, and I slipped on the slope and skidded in the mud, tumbling and rolling, aware that the monstrous shape had arrived above me, the head leaning out into space, the eyes watching as the muzzle gaped and moisture dripped.

I stumbled to my feet and followed the course of the stream and when hours had passed I huddled, pack to my chest, below a fallen trunk. It rained again and I was miserable. I hardly slept. At dawn I moved on, lost now, passing through a gorge that widened out, but rose more steeply on either side. The river deepened, grew faster. I felt watched at all points.

Soon I found the savaged remains of the frightened horse. Something, probably a smilodont, perhaps several, had killed it and dragged it into the fork of a tree, where half of it had been consumed, the other half still draped in tattered gore, the eyes open and watching me with a mournful gaze.

I began to recognize where I was; I had been here before, daydreaming in France, nearly losing Natalie by drowning. The day warmed, the sun brightened, the river wound away ahead of me, carrying spring blossom that was falling from wild cherry and rose in the forest, blown by the soft breeze. I cut through the woods and soon heard the sound of laughter and voices, and on approaching the river saw the four girls again, with their ring of flowers. It was strange to stand for the second time and watch them at their game. I looked around to see if some spirit echo of myself lurked here as well, some intrusion from my dreaming mind of long ago, but there was just the dappled light, the rustling leaves.

The girls fled suddenly, screaming, as the mastodons broke cover and thundered to the water, first drinking, then wading towards the village, where cooking fires scented the air with their aromatic smoke.

When I had watched this scene before, a shadow had darted

past me, ill-defined and unrevealed, perhaps Greyface, perhaps the woman. I waited for that same figure now, but this time she rose from the cover of tall grass among the scrubby trees, between the heavy wood and the river. She was watching me. Her face was the face of her sisters, green-lined, taut and beautiful, her hair braided and tied to the shoulder of her cloak, which was parted to reveal the glitter of cowrie-shell and brilliant lapis-lazuli that laced her tunic.

I broke cover and walked to her, aware that she carried a fistful of thin lances, a blow-pipe and wore a girdle of bone-blades. She seemed unmoved to see me, and waited unmoving as I approached.

'Nemet?'

She said nothing. The wind tugged her cloak, ruffled the grass. 'Nemet?'

I realized suddenly that her gaze was not on me at all but on the woodland behind me. Her breathing was shallow, almost resigned. I turned to follow her stare, but there was nothing to be seen, or at least . . . nothing as yet.

'Nemet?'

'Jack,' she whispered, and slowly turned to me. The lances fell from her hands and her fingers caressed my cheeks. She stepped into my arms and pressed her moist, sweet mouth against my own, breathing deeply as she kissed me as if drinking me.

'I missed you,' she said as she drew away. 'You became stone; your life was drawn from me, suddenly. I couldn't bear to see the statue, the face was so sad, so twisted in despair. Eventually, I smashed it. Perhaps somewhere you felt me end the pain for you.'

Had I? I couldn't remember.

'Yes,' I lied. 'I've missed you too. But I've failed again with Baalgor. He's just as hostile, just as determined that you should come to him.'

Amazingly, she smiled, then shook her head. 'I was frightened,' she said. 'I was alone, Baalgor had gone. I thought we

345

would be separated for ever. But Baalgor was like a goat on the end of a tether. The goat wanders away from the sleeping shepherd, far away, grazing and cropping, out of sight, down-wind, almost lost. But the shepherd wakes, and slowly draws in the rope, and the goat is brought home again. It had thought itself free, but it was never free, and like the braying goat he is, my brother-husband is returning to me, because Glanum is drawing him home.'

Baalgor here? In the Deep? Or was he still crossing the Hinterland? What did Greenface mean . . . where exactly was the man who tormented me; and where, then, was Shade?

I was being watched again and the skin on my neck crawled with apprehension. Greenface looked slowly to the woods and I saw the shape of the bull reflected in her dark eyes. It was standing inside the line of trees, head above the canopy, watching us silently save for the grumble of its breathing.

'Run . . .' I whispered urgently, but Greenface reached a hand to stay me.

'Too late,' she said. 'Jack. I'm going home. There is nowhere else to go, now. It's over. The hunt is up . . . You don't have to follow me. Just let me go.'

As she spoke, the giant bull shuddered, and from its maw came the sound of a dying breath. The great head turned slightly, then was still. The eyes glazed, the red hide began to lighten in colour, then turn grey. Cracks appeared, similar to the tracery that covered the clay face-mask of Greyface, but this bull had turned to stone, and the stone was being weathered as I watched it, becoming the gate again as I had seen it a few days before.

The ground shook suddenly and from behind us came the sound of the river exploding. Even as I turned in alarm, the city was rising from the water, the great span of its front wall dripping weed and branches, the white tower lost in the sky, the open gate below the dark bull's skull like a gaping mouth. As it came from the earth and the river it seemed to hesitate, watching, waiting, then moved swiftly and suddenly towards us, overwhelming us in moments. I had time only to grab for Greenface as Glanum swallowed our cowering forms, plunging on to consume the cracked stone bull at the edge of the forest. We fell into the city amidst earth and rocks and the severed trunks of the oaks and elms that had lined the river.

And moments later, as we scrambled for shelter, the city descended again, diving like a whale, and that same, strange darkness covered us which had covered me twice before, when I had followed Shade from the outside world of Exburgh.

36

I have no idea how long we huddled in the lee of the wall. We crushed our bodies together, clinging to a stone column among the shifting, sliding rubble of rock and wood that Glanum had ingested as it surfaced, two Jonahs in the throat of the beast. The city swayed as it moved through this chthonian realm; we felt it turn, plunge deeper, then rise again, but I couldn't tell how fast it travelled, only that it swam the deeps and that darkness swept above me.

Suddenly it broke the surface. Blinding sunlight illuminated the inner walls, the broken tower, the wasteland of stone, statue and reeking earth. We were travelling at tremendous speed, clouds streaking overhead, storms shadowing our frightened forms, vanishing as fast as they had cast their pall across the city.

Then down again, rocking to the side, our stomachs heaving, our arms tightly round the pillar and around each other as masonry bruised us, stone shards cut us.

It was imperative that we get away from this wasteland, deeper into the beast, closer to the heart of the city; closer to forgotten Jericho. Nemet agreed and we began to work our way along the wall, soon finding our feet. After a while, we left the mayhem of the gate behind, and though we were aware that the city moved, we sensed its swaying motion as it turned and dived as if distantly; we might have been walking on board a ship. We had found Glanum's equivalent of our sea-legs.

Now, as we walked the maze of narrow streets and empty squares, watched by wild or fabled beasts, or crouching men, figures from other worlds all shaped in gleaming stone or polished wood, now I thought of Garth.

John Garth had scaled the wall of Glanum; but was he now, like Ahab in Melville's tale, bound in his own ropes to the cold wall of the cold beast, dead eyes staring from a shattered skull? Or was he, too, at large among these ancient echoes?

I called for him, but my voice was swallowed by the city. Sometimes, when we came in sight again of the tall, white watchtower, I hailed him loudly, but only my echo returned to me, like a hollow laugh in the Stygian gloom.

Time and again, as we walked the passages in the city, we came back to the tower, and I realized that we were truly in a maze, following the intricate spirals of a labyrinth: at some moments, then, we would be close enough to the heart of Glanum to almost touch it, at others at the city's edge again.

Then abruptly we stepped from the stone streets onto a dark hillside, which sloped gently away towards a valley, thick with forest, bright with distant fires.

Nemet ran ahead of me. I was reminded powerfully of the drum-filled structure to which she had led me on my very first encounter with her, when she had – by magic – trapped me in the strangling briar.

I hadn't realized it then, but I knew it now: this was home to her. The wooden walls, the fires, the screeching of beasts . . .

Jericho of old.

The place of her birth.

As we stood below the walls, in darkness, the outer city glowing on the hill behind us, listening to the sounds of the heart itself . . . she started to cry.

She curled up against the gate, below the watching eyes that had been carved there. I sat down with her, put my arms around her, and after a while started to fall asleep. I remember she touched a finger to my mouth, tracing my lips, then leaned over to kiss my cheek.

She was going home. She seemed content.

I began to smell the fragrance of fruit trees, and the aromatic scent of herbs.

A warm wind was blowing.

I was following the woman . . . back . . . all the way back . . . to the time of the terrible deed.

Asleep against her, then, I shared her dream-memory of the time in childhood when she had been turned into hunter and hunted . . .

PART NINE

Remembering

37

(i)

A sudden wind had begun to blow along the valley, carrying the heady scent of cedar, balsam and wild rosemary; and the sounds of lions, probably moving down to the gleaming river to drink. Nemet was watching the stars, wishing one of them to fall to earth on this moonless night. She could hear her sisters chattering in the sprawling tent, behind the stockade. Beyond them, where the men gathered, her father's voice was a dull drone as he talked about his latest trip to Gl'Thaan Em. He had gone there with Jarmu, Nemet's elder brother. Baalgor, Nemet's twin, a year younger than his brother, had followed on the shore at dawn and was still not back.

Jarmu had stayed in the town, although quite why that should have been so, Nemet wasn't sure. Certainly, her father had been behaving very strangely on his return, and her mother, Kohara, had been sombre, painting her face in grey clay and rocking her body as she stood by the sparkling river.

Nervous of the animals moving from the forest, Nemet returned to the tent, where her sisters, Harikk and Hora, were making a shell dress for the youngest, Anat. Anat was performing a twirling dance round the small fire, sending the smoke curling wildly up to the wide hole, where the stars glittered. She was still sore from the bone needles that had punctured her skin, but wore her first green markings proudly, touching them as she danced and sang. She kept staring up to the sky.

'Look at me. Look at me!'

The lines were simple, two circling patterns around her cheeks, ready for the markings of the eye when another year had passed.

Nemet had a special affection for her youngest sister, who chattered non-stop, seemed always happy, and enchanted everyone who came to visit.

Only Hora refused to be charmed by the antics of the youngest, but a sense of foreboding, of caution, of detachment had been born into the cleverest sister.

Harikk had insight and pragmatism. She was beautiful, but old before her time. Sometimes when she and Kohara sat together, Nemet felt she was looking at a single person only, reflected in the surface of still water. But Harikk and Nemet often walked into the hills, or to the river, and Nemet felt at peace with this sibling.

'Look at me! Look at me!' the green bird chirruped as she flew around the tent.

Almost at once, the flap of the tent was flung back and Baalgor darted in from the night. Anat cried out, then quickly stifled the noise. She had been startled by the grey face and cowrie-shell eyes that had leered in at them, before realizing that it was her brother, teasing.

Baalgor laughed and popped the shells from his sockets, blinking. The clay mud cracked and he peeled it away, tossing the pieces onto the fire.

'It makes a good disguise. Nemet, you must come with me. It's safe. Truly. No one sees me through the clay. The sanctuary is wonderful. Rememberer of Beasts is such a strange looking man . . .'

'You'll get caught,' Nemet said grimly. Baalgor shrugged. He was almost a man, now, and dark hair stubbled his skin. He stank of animals and sweat, and Nemet suggested the river for a bath.

'I've got you something,' he said, and the girls crowded round as he emptied cowries from his pouch; they were perfect, painted, not yet bored for talismans, or shaped for the eyes of the dead. These were forbidden treasure and Hora, ever cautious, drew away.

'Don't touch them!'

Anat reached out and snatched a single shell, a blue one, running nervously round the tent. The wind gusted and dust blew in below the goatskins where they were loose on the ground. Harikk went to batten them down again and Nemet gathered the shell gifts into her hands, savouring their feel.

'I'll have to hide them.'

'I'll go with you,' Baalgor said. 'Look what I've got for my cloak!'

It was a cut piece of fresh animal skin, not yet cured, still sticky where it had been flayed. The fur was tough and sharp; the colours wildly red and green, not stripes but spots. The hide had been hanging, soon after the creature had been slaughtered and the carcase buried to clean the bones. While no one had been looking, Baalgor had scalped the hide and slipped away.

He led the way, then, up to the scented bushes where a tumble of rocks marked the fall from a cliff. Behind them was a wide clearing, where she and Baalgor had often come to play as children. The rocks were painted with hunting figures, and boats, and animals. Baalgor had once fashioned eyes in the trunk of a fallen tree and wedged it across the entrance to the clearing. They called it the Watching Place.

Here, now, he hauled away a boulder and reached into the space behind for his cloak. Nemet grimaced as the smelly garment was unfurled, but Baalgor stroked it.

There were feathers from birds he had never seen before; hide from giant beasts; leathery skin from fabulous creatures, soft hair from apes and monkeys; even a strip from the red and black mane of one of the bull-sized lions.

Quickly, using a hawk's-bone needle and goat-gut thread, he stitched the new piece onto the hem.

Half as much again, and the cloak would be full length for a man. Then he would dance among the animals as he had so often dreamed he would.

Gl'Thaan Em, the sacred town, lay beyond the hills, beyond cedar woodlands, close to a spring that had been known since the earliest stories that were told when the Watching Moon was at its fullest. Nemet had never seen the place, though she had heard of its towering walls of sun-baked mud, the stone tower where Rememberer of Beasts summoned his visions, calling wildly at dawn and dusk, his voice echoing and wailing across the plains. She had heard of the fires and the chanting and the drumming and the smells of the beasts that paraded through the centre of the place. She had heard of the skin-shrines and the skull rooms and the faces that watched from the mudbrick as the city grew.

And she knew that one day she would go there, and that her father would be proud of her as her animal spirit rose to inhabit her, making her full grown, giving her dreams of her own to dance to, as already Baalgor danced, though he had come prematurely to his own visions.

Baalgor gathered cuts of the skins, to make his cloak.

One day, shortly after Jarmu had gone to the sanctuary, he brought back a strip of scaly skin, which oozed on the surface and made him heady when he smelled the slime. The creature, long, low to the ground and very angry, had been driven from the river by torchlight in the middle of the night, and had been killed and skinned with the rising sun, the jaws, twice the length of a man, taken to the skull room. Baalgor touched his tongue to the sour and sticky fragment of skin and spat, but his head cleared and the world seemed to grow, to loom, to spin and dance around him. He laughed and licked again, then Nemet was tempted to try the poison, and for a while the Moon rushed towards her, filling the night sky, almost blinding her, though she could see every detail of the scars and skin of that great disc, and the movement of strange herds on the silver ground above her where she lay.

Baalgor rolled this piece of hide and kept it apart, ready to enhance his vision when the time came for him to meet his animal spirit.

'Paint your face to cover the green and come with me. There's no danger, Nem. Everything is mud grey at Gl'Thaan Em. And there are animals everywhere. Such strange beasts! Come and see the sanctuary!'

'I'm frightened. What happened to Jarmu? Why hasn't he come home?'

'I don't know. Come with me. We'll find out.'

'We should stay in the tents until we're called.'

'The earth itself is being shaped, Nem. Into a *town* dedicated to *beasts*. The mud and stone are being hardened by the hands of people like us. Ordinary people. The earth is being moulded to make the sanctuary. You *should* see it.'

'I'll see it when I'm called.'

'See it now. When we're called, we'll be grown, we'll be changed, we'll enter another life. See it now while our eyes are still young! Come *on*!'

His enthusiasm was persuasive. Nemet clung to him, clung to the heat from his mouth and his body. Her sisters watched, Hora alarmed and suspicious, Anat excited, intrigued by the idea, eager to come too and disappointed when her brother denied her; Harikk stitched clothes and thought hard, wondering how to cover for her eldest sister's actions to their father, when he returned.

Finally, Nemet agreed.

By the time she had caked her body with river clay, Baalgor had returned from the hills, wearing the half-finished cloak, the stink of animals forming an aura around him that was mesmerizing. They skirted the edge of the forest during the day, and crossed the hills by night. Before dawn they had come close enough to the sanctuary to smell the fresh water of the spring that bubbled from the deep earth within the mud walls. As the sun rose, Nemet stared for the first time at the city, amazed at how high the walls had been built, at the stone tower with its dark figure, the man whose voice called and echoed across the land, eerie cries that sometimes made her skin crawl. The air was filled with the stink of burning bitumen, and dark smoke coiled from a hundred fires where the black earth smouldered.

As if invisible, they ran swiftly between the tents, then through the narrow gates in the stockade walls of cedar, coming closer to the shaped earth where bricks of mud were drying in the sun, and the sound of stone being hammered and shaped rang unfamiliarly in their ears. Above the low gate was the skull of a bull; the road to that gate was lined with the curved horns of a hundred bulls, each point fluttering with coloured fabric. Baalgor led the way along this tunnel of ivory, rubbing the steaming droppings of beasts into his limbs and onto his cloak. Nemet did likewise, and the scents from the mud of the beasts were unfamiliar, heady, not at all like the smells of goat or lion or cow. Suddenly they were lost. Nemet flung herself into the darkness of a low doorway and when Baalgor came and crouched above her she almost shouted, 'Far enough! We don't belong here. I'm going home.'

'A little further. Just a little further. Come and see the creatures that are being summoned . . .'

'I'm frightened.'

'I'm *not!*'

'Then go on alone. I'm going home.'

Baalgor's fingers hurt her as he restrained her, then his arms were round her, embracing her intimately, a signal of his need and love for her. Clay lips touched clay lips, and Nemet felt secure again, though she was aware that her brother was confused.

'You've got us lost,' she said.

'Yes. I'm sorry. They've built a wall across the old street, and I've never been this way before.'

Nemet was aware of the path back; she also sensed the way

forward, deeper. She had never felt *lost* in this place, just frightened.

'Come on then.'

She led her twin through the maze of passages, and as Baalgor ran behind her, he re-iterated softly that she would *love* the sights that were soon to be seen.

Unerringly, she found the inner wall. The mudbrick was smoothed with clay: it seemed to grow from the ground like a tree, inseparable from the earth below. Beyond the wall, the world was loud with the cries and bellows, roars and screeching song of animals. Burning tar, burning wood, burning flesh, all tanged the air in their various ways. Smoke as dark as a travelling soul coiled and swirled into the moonbright sky.

Drums thundered. Voices wailed in song and ululation. 'Which way is the gate?'

Nemet saw fire and fervour in her brother's eyes. He would be like this, she knew, when for the first time he lay upon her. Her bowels thrilled and twisted in anticipation of the marriage. Would his breath smell so strong? Would his lips be as wet? Would the fire lick from eyes and mouth as it licked now?

'Which *way?*' he asked again, looking around anxiously.

She led him.

Invisible in their cloaks of river mud, they stepped into the heart of the town, where white stone rose taller than the cedar, and the dark Rememberer called and shrieked as he summoned the lost.

'Touch your tongue to this. Not too much!'

Baalgor had thrust the scaly skin below her nose, and obedient to her brother she dabbed her tongue to the cold, pungent surface. Baalgor did the same, then secreted the hide deeply inside his cloak.

At once, Nemet heard voices, mere whispers, from further away than she could see. The earth below her feet boomed and shuddered. Where the mudbrick was drying she could hear the sound of water, squeezing through the clay. The

359

thumping hearts and shivering flanks of beasts deafened her. The voice of the man on the tower dissolved into a thousand songs, each of them sweet to hear, haunting to the ear. They flowed and darted in the air like night creatures, and Nemet was momentarily mesmerized, seeing the notes, the melodies, as nightwings, trying to follow each of them as they drifted away across the walls, towards hills, and plains, deserts and the winding, distant river.

Outside the walls, the voice was harsh, meaningless. Now she could understand what an intricate web the man was weaving with the hundreds of strands of song and summoning. Her ear was being tugged. Baalgor was twisting the flesh, his face blank behind the clay, his eyes irritated. 'This way,' he snapped as Nemet came back to her body, leaving the song-strands floating away from her.

He was taking her deeper into the sanctuary and she tugged back.

'Home! It's not safe here. He's seen us, he knows we're here . . .'

She had sensed the eyes of the man on the tower, heard his breathing, the whispered names that told her he had detected their presence.

But Baalgor wouldn't be persuaded. 'I heard Jarmu. He's in pain. I heard him call.'

A mud wall barred their path, but Nemet saw a low door and they ducked through, coming nearer to the sounds of chaos beyond. They had entered a place where the shapes of animals had been erected on stilts, strange legs holding the bulging skins of the dead beasts. Grim muzzles lolled and sagged, eyes sunken, jaws gaping, strange colours striping the matted hide. The bones of these nightmares lay sewn inside the skins, bulging and sharp as Nemet brushed against them.

'What are these creatures?'

'Summoned from the mist,' Baalgor said. 'Brought here to be remembered.'

'The size of them. Like giants. I've never seen skins so hard and sharp . . .' she was touching the protuberances on a grey, leathery hide of an animal that had once been twice as high as her brother. Four horns grew from the wide brow; sand was spilling from the cavity inside the head.

A moment after she touched the flank, the flank heaved, sending her flying as she drew back in shock. She looked around at this place of ghosts, the stilt creatures all lined to the east, all watching the intruders.

A second belly writhed, then a third; and above the sound of drums, she heard the moan of a dying woman.

Frightened, she turned to find her brother again. Baalgor was standing by the bulging belly of a beast that had once been striped in black and yellow and whose mane flowed like a cloak about the snarling, skull-less head. As she watched, Baalgor used his stone knife to slit the skin. A length of bone slipped to the ground; a stench exuded that made Nemet gag. Then an arm draped out, the fingers moving helplessly. A moment later the whole upper body of a man, skinned from hairline to chest, flopped out of the belly and uttered a wail that came close to breaking Nemet's heart.

'Jarmu!' she cried, recognizing the sound of the voice. And the bleeding face whined, then murmured, 'Sister . . .'

Before she could think, before she could speak again, Baalgor had touched his knife to the red-raw throat and Jarmu had begun a longer journey, to the Fragrant Pasture.

Drenched with his brother's blood, Baalgor returned to the edge of the sanctuary and Nemet followed, sharing the tears and the sickness as the two of them reached the cold, clean air beyond the cedar gates.

They went to the river and washed, sitting in the shallows, their arms around each other, shuddering and sobbing as they tried to understand. It was still dark when Nemet heard the whisper-song of the summoner, reaching like a filament of gossamer across the plain of the river. Soon after, she watched as a reptilian figure reared from the water and stalked on its hindlegs onto the bank, looking up at the sky, then grumbling in its throat before sniffing the air and beginning a slow, weaving walk towards the fires beyond the hill.

Her brother was coming up the defile towards the Watching Place, aware of Nemet, glancing up at her, but trying to pretend that he hadn't seen her. She shrunk more deeply into a crevice in the sandy rock, clutching her treasured shells in her lap, no longer thinking of destroying them but rather holding them like a protective girdle.

Baalgor called out, begging her not to run. He was wearing a breechclout and had striped his chest with mud. He had cut his hair above each temple so that the scalp bled, no doubt explaining the act of self-defilement to his father as being for some small misdemeanour.

Nemet knew why he had defiled himself.

She felt frightened as he came close, aware that she was sweating now, and that her brother could scent the fear. As he stood before her he stripped the winding of rough cloth and tossed it on the ground, standing naked and humble before her. He held the knife loosely in his right hand, offering it to her.

'I did a terrible thing. I acted on the impulse of the animal. I heard his song of pain and heard the last dance of his heart before death. I sent him across the river, to the Fragrant Pasture, but I had no right to do that.'

'Why are you telling me?'

'If you forgive me, we can make him live again in our family's stories. And what other stories *are* there but the stories of our family? But if you accuse me, I'll die and he and I will remain always in the world of shadows. No one will speak about us. Alive yet abandoned. You *can't* want that?'

'There is a beast in you—'

'There is a beast in us all!'

'Yes. Our animal guides. I know that. But the beast in you is like a cat stung by a bee. It doesn't listen to the forest. It doesn't listen to its own heart! I can't forgive you.'

'I haven't committed the *terrible* deed.'

'I can't forgive you.'

'Then who can?'

'The forest. The river. The desert.'

He came closer, she shrank back further. His eyes blazed with urgency, not triumphant, not hostile, just need and hunger. 'Nem, I've scoured myself on the bark of the cedar; I've lain face down on the earth for a day; I've floated face up on the river, willing to be drowned, to be eaten. I'm still here. The earth hasn't taken me. Why can't *you* forgive me, then? You saw me kill him, only you. It's you alone who can release his song.'

He held the knife towards her. There was ochre red on the grey blade, but the blood was not Jarmu's – it was Baalgor's own. It had taken him a long time to make the blade, a year ago, under his father's guidance. It was his pride. But now he went to the rock where the heat of the sun had cracked the stone. He pushed the blade into the slit, worked at it, leaned on it, cried out with the effort until the whole of the cutting edge was buried and only the handle, goat horn and leather, jutted from the earth.

'There. No one will ever draw that blade. This is Jarmu's grave, and I will be content to come and remember him every year until I die.'

What did they say to their sisters?

Harikk especially was aware that something had happened, sensing Nemet's distress from the moment she and Baalgor had returned from their foray. She sat reflectively by the cooking fire while Anat chattered and laughed, anticipating the return of their father from a river trip.

At first light the next day, a wind blew through the tents, a hard wind, carrying a grey, stinging dust that swirled and billowed below the hides. While her sisters curled more deeply into their blankets, Nemet rose and went out into the storm. The sun on the horizon was a pallid, sickly disc.

Everything was shadowy as the desert storm gusted and raged at the flapping skins where the families huddled.

She became aware of the figure almost at once, a tall man, his cloak blowing about his body as he stood, staring through the dust. Nemet took a step or two towards him and became aware of his eyes, hooded and angry, watching her from the dark of his face.

Two days before, he had watched her from the white tower, although she had only sensed this probing gaze.

As abruptly as he had seemed to appear there, he had turned and vanished. Two loping hounds, lean-bodied and stilt-legged, their heads drooping as they walked, manifested in the dust storm, watched the woman for a moment or two, before stalking off behind their master.

When the Rememberer had gone, the dust storm cleared. The men went out into the hills to gather in the goats and pigs that had scattered, and the women tended to the season's plantings, where the wheat they had nurtured for so many years had been broken on the stem.

A premature cutting began at once, to save what could be used of barley, wheat and lentil.

Nemet looked for her brother, but Baalgor had gone again and she gazed at the valley through the hill, her head shaking as she fought feelings of anger and apprehension.

'We're in trouble,' she whispered to the haze of heat, 'and all you can do is go back and tempt the shadows!'

But he was back before their father returned, and had cleaned away his grey disguise, stitched purloined cat-skin to his cloak of scalps and feathers, and participated in the welcoming meal, the family sitting around three shallow stone dishes of meat and cheese, and baskets of fruit.

A day later, Arithon took Anat and Harikk on the river, and Nemet was surprised to feel envy, even a little resentment.

Until now, she had been the only one of the sisters to accompany their father on his short trips to the river settlements; her sisters hadn't noticed the change, too eager to sit in the shallow hull of the flimsy vessel as it bobbed and cut its way across the wind. But Hora was worried, and Nemet's mother too.

'What have you done?' Kohara asked.

'Nothing,' Nemet said, but the green lines on her face moved like snakes and her mother saw the lie. She sighed and turned away, saying, 'This will turn out badly.'

Hora, her face narrowed with concern though still sweet and young behind the lines and eyes that marked her status, hugged Nemet, then drew her away from the settlement.

'Last night I dreamed you were running, you and our brother. A great beast pursued you for the wrong you'd done. Nemet, don't go back to the sanctuary. There is something, a great shadow, hanging over that place.

'They're shaping the earth; they're making the earth itself into a town, filled with passages and shrine spaces, like treeless groves between clay walls. I knew you'd been there. I could tell . . . yesterday . . . Baalgor did this. He's a bad influence. Nem . . . I feel that the shadow is closing on you. I feel death, without the river journey to the pasture that follows.'

'We all go on the river, Hora. The flesh and the bones wait in the grave, but we all go on the river to the pasture until we come back to our flesh.'

'Not you. Not in my dream. Nor Baalgor. I'm frightened by what I dreamed . . .'

'You're frightening me too,' Nemet said testily. She tried to pull away from her sister, but Hora tugged at her dress.

'Why do I dream these things?'

'I don't know. Ask mother.'

'I can't. Each time I try to talk to her she turns away. Since Jarmu left us, she exists only for herself. I've heard her talking to the river. She whispers: *My daughters are gone; they are shadows with the beasts*. What does that mean? Why are we shadows with the beasts?'

Nemet remembered the flayed face of her immolated brother, flopping from the swollen belly of the creature, from the mist in which he'd been entombed.

More strongly, she remembered Baalgor's swift slice, the swift killing, the beast inside him acting with compassion.

'I don't know,' she murmured helplessly, then fled from her sister.

Baalgor found her by the marker for their brother. He stopped and kissed the horn handle where it jutted from the stone, then flung his stinking cloak across Nemet, huddling below it himself, though the day was warm. They were both shivering. They stared out across the trees and grasses of the river plain, watched the smoke from the fires of the community, thought of the earth sanctuary that was growing, stone-centred and strong where the spring rose from the Deep, beyond this line of hills.

'The earth is throwing up its ghosts,' Baalgor said.

'I didn't know it had any.'

'Do you remember the giant's bones? When we were children?'

'Yes. Very well.'

'They'd been carved in the red stone of a cliff and we made up stories about them.'

'I remember.'

'The stories were true.'

'All stories are true. How can a story be *not* true?'

'Exactly! No one *told* us the stories. We made them up, but we were simply remembering! Like the earth itself. The earth remembers beasts that once walked the forests and swam the rivers, but disappeared into the mist beyond the Fragrant Pasture. Not everything lives for ever. But nothing ever dies.'

'I remember a tale about a ten-legged goat, and a pig taller than a tree, and crocodiles with four heads.'

'Now just ghosts in the earth. Like Jarmu. Like Miat and Agathne . . .' Their grandparents. 'But they're coming back. To Gl'Thaan Em. The Rememberer of Beasts is calling them back!'

'Miat? Agathne?'

'The beasts! Do you think that river began to flow only at the moment of our birth?'

'Of course not. The river was always there, and these hills, and the grasslands . . .'

'Always there, always used! From before we were born. For *ever*, Nem! When a cloud passes overhead and vanishes into the distance, it takes its shadow with it. Nem, that cloud and its shadow come *back*. Time and again they pass across us, only by that time we've forgotten. All shadows live on, all ghosts live on, all the beasts are still alive, and they are coming back to Gl'Thaan Em, to be remembered.'

'Why? Why?'

'Because their bones are in the earth, and the earth is in the walls of the sanctuary. I've heard them talking in Gl'Thaan Em. This is not the only sanctuary that is being raised to the sky. There are *many* . . . very far away, further than the river.'

Nemet was astonished. How could her brother possibly have known?

'I've heard them talk. The builders. From the mud that's used to make the walls, the ghosts cry out to be remembered. That's why the Rememberer is here, to call them all, to call them from the mist. To honour them as we shape the mud with their bones into places that will hide us from the wind and rain, from the sun and snow, from the floodwater and locusts.'

Baalgor was alive with the idea; by whatever means he had managed to hear this talk, he had certainly entered deeply, very deeply, into the sanctuary of Gl'Thaan Em, and he knew things, now, that he should not have known. He huddled and shivered below the skins of beasts called from the mist. The feathers of forgotten hawks rose from the cloak, as if struggling to escape.

Floodwater! Locusts!

Echoing her mother's words, Nemet whispered, 'This will turn out badly.'

Now Hora was taken on the river, a two day journey that left Nemet standing on the river shore, frightened and abandoned, watching the small craft blur against the sun, sail dipping as the breeze took it and carried it to trade.

The other sisters were still talking about their own journey. Anat had come home decked with shells and flowers, the gift of fishers from the south who had been enchanted by her talk, her humour and her songs. Harikk had seen channels in the earth, ways deeper into the farther shore; and she had noticed the surfacing of strange animals, rising from the mud as they shook and shivered, at dawn, before beginning the walk towards Gl'Thaan Em.

When Hora came back, her hair was lank, her body scratched, her eyes unfocused. Her father stalked away from the shore, went to the rush-floor hut where the men sat, and refused to answer the call of his wife.

Hora bathed herself, then smeared healing wood-sap into her scratches. When Nemet knelt beside her Hora glanced at her sister sharply, then looked away.

A day later she had gone, her father too, and no amount of questioning could elicit the answer to where their sister had been taken. Kohara worked at the quern and at her sewing. Anat and Harikk talked about nonsense things, and creatures they had seen on the river with Arithon.

Only Baalgor scowled and growled in fury, running to Jarmu's stone and back, cutting himself across the scalp and above each breast, then rolling in the river clay until he was invisible.

He stalked the settlement at dusk, then stood like a tree at the edge of the water.

Nemet could see him and went out to him.

'How many sisters will I have in the morning?' he said stiffly, the air of his voice hissing through the small round hole in the clay mask.

'You'll have me. Anat and Harikk . . .' But even as she spoke, the figures of Arithon and Hora appeared at the edge of the camp, the girl huddled in her cloak, staring at the ground before she entered the family tent, her secret to be kept until her death.

'All of us,' Nemet added, and Baalgor nodded, then touched his brow and his breast in thanks.

'What do you dream, Nem? Tell me about your dreams.'

'Running . . .'

She had said the word before she had even thought. It was the only word that sprang to her lips. She had wanted to express the desire that was her life: to be passionate with her brother; to bear their children; to shout and be angry, probably with their mother, who would be old and infirm; to fish, to gather, to walk with the goats and sheep and pigs and dogs; to find deep valleys in the hills, with sweet spring water, where they could pitch their tents, then build their huts and gather bulrushes for the floor, and shells to clatter in the wind; to lie with the warm earth on her back, and combed sheep-skin on her belly; and the sun on her face, and the fragrant scents of bushes and trees making her drowsy as her husband stroked her.

This. This! What more IS there!

'Running!'

He tore the clay from his face and grabbed her by the hair. When their mouths met she stiffened, but relaxed to the fierce kiss, her fingers spreading across the seeping wounds above his breasts.

'Running,' he said as the clay peeled away. He looked at the tents, then at the hills.

'Running,' she whispered. 'Why do I dream that?'

'Why do *I*!'

She was stunned by the violence in his voice. He closed his eyes and sighed, then looked at her again.

'Nem! We're alone, you and I. We have to leave. We no longer belong here.'

'I can't leave them. Our sisters.'

'Too late. Too late. You're all that matters now.'

He was hurting her. She pushed him away, but held onto his clothing, her fingers digging into his flesh. He eased the grip, then took her into his arms again, reassuring her as she cried.

'I can't leave them,' she said again, and now he seemed to understand.

'I know. We'll take them with us. It's all right, Nem. If you follow me, we'll all go away together . . .'

'Yes!'

His mouth was on hers again. The night and its sounds gathered around them. They slipped down the muddy bank, feet and ankles in the water, laughing. There was singing from the settlement, and the bleating of goats left unmilked.

'Promise me that Anat—'

'I promise!' he insisted.

'That all of them: Anat, Harikk, Hora . . . they'll come with us!'

'I promise. How many times do I have to say it? My sister,' he added in a whisper, his fingers thrilling her.

'My brother,' she murmured, longing for him. She pulled his body over hers and said his name again, watching the bright moon over his shoulder, and the shadows of giant birds flying to the north, to Gl'Thaan Em.

A season had passed and they were still in the village; Baalgor's cloak, still wretched to smell, was now long and fully encompassed his tall body, although only Nemet knew this since he wore the cloak only at night, and only with his sister. Nemet's hoard of shells and the shining, colourful scales of reptiles was huge, now, and she had begun to make a dress, decorated with these purloined jewels from the sanctuary.

She had not returned with Baalgor to the labyrinth of mud and stone beyond the cedar walls. Her brother had ventured to the town alone. Nemet felt uneasy about his journeys, but it was her insightful sister Harikk who cast the strongest doubt.

'Arithon knows he goes there. He ignores it, that's all. I don't like the feel of this.'

'Only our father, though. No one else knows. He'd not betray his son.'

'*Everyone* knows,' Harikk whispered, but she was speaking through inner sight not real sight and shrugged and waved her hands to indicate her guesswork. 'If I was his sisterwife, I'd warn him that he isn't as clever as he thinks.'

I'm not his sisterwife. Not yet.

Harikk's warnings, her increasing gloom, began to irritate Nemet, who avoided the girl's company, concentrating instead on helping the chatterer, Anat, to prepare for the next tattoos, the next stage in her lengthening, blossoming growth. She would be tall, like Baalgor, and was willowy still, unlike Hora who was plump and rather slow on her feet. The chatterer was now her father's favourite too, or so it seemed, and Nemet seethed sometimes as the two of them sailed on the river, returning hand in hand with blades and polished stone, seeds, roots and on one occasion, odd little red clay icons – *zheen* – squatting figures and dancing shapes into which thoughts and dreams could be placed, or so it was claimed by the tribes who made them. Anat picked the *tekki*, enchanted by its closed eyes and pouting mouth, its sweet innocence. *Tekki was sweet voice, sweet words.* Harikk stared at the hoard for a while, then selected *etni*, the flaming face, the *watcher with other eyes*.

'I'll make sure to keep an eye on you lot!' she said with a smile as she strung the amulet.

Hora ignored the *zheen* for a long time, but eventually

flicked among them, discarding, scrutinizing, discarding, complaining, discarding . . .

She picked *bet – seeing over hills, finding paths*.

'*This* can't do me any harm.'

Finally, Nemet picked one of the figurines for herself, startled by her powerful response to the small, running figure, its swollen breasts indicating its sex. It was called *ahk*, meaning *running with beasts; the hunter*, and, like her sisters, Nemet attached the name to her own.

Ahk'Nemet; *bet*'Hora; Harikk'*etni*; Anat'*tekki*.

They called out their new names as they held hands in a circle and danced around the talismans, laughing and imagining the effects their new-found guides would have in life.

Baalgor waved the trinkets away, then changed his mind and picked out the smallest of the *zheen*, a hairless head, wide-eyed, heavy-browed, guileless. It was called *el*, meaning *the deepest thought; the first secret*. He used clay to shape a crude bull's muzzle around the face of innocence, and pushed the curving wishbone of a goose into the outer head to signify horns. He covered the clay with strips of skin from a bull that had been sag-bellied and stilted in the sanctuary, a red beast, impossibly large, the centre of the shrine as if it alone commanded the greatest respect.

It had been hard getting close to this monstrous puppet, and the belly had writhed with not one but two human shapes, being digested inside to hold the memory of the bovine in the shadow-world of the Fragrant Pasture.

He had succeeded, slicing a piece of skin from the throat, but had been aware as he slipped into the gloom of the alleys that the man on the tower had seen him, watching him without raising the alarm.

It had made the bull talisman stronger; it carried the seeds of inner strength, of secret purpose; and Baalgor hung it round his neck in triumph, though Hora was disgusted at his arrogance.

*

Anat had attained her full face, and though the scars from the fish-bone needle were still sore, she danced like a woman and teased like a woman, and chattered as the fires burned high, and the voices of the singers, and the melodious breathing of the pipes, filled the night with their celebration.

Arithon was close to Nemet during the feast, and in the morning shook her awake and passed her a bundle of nets and a bag of cheeses.

'Come on. Let's go fishing. The rains are coming from the north—'

Nemet had felt the cooling wind, the scent of moisture that always meant a rain-storm would swirl across the dry plain of the river in a week or so's time.

'—so the fish will be swelling in the shallows.'

Yes!

She dressed quickly, kissed her sisters on the cheeks, gentle with Anat who was still sore, still slightly swollen where the marks had greened her flesh.

Where was Baalgor?

'He's hunting.' Arithon was impatient with her. He wanted to go, to get onto the water before the shoals passed downriver.

For most of the day they fished, but the catch was poor. Arithon grumbled, but as dusk came he relaxed and lay back in the boat's prow, eyes to the sky, relaxed and content. Nemet joined him and for a while they drifted with the flow of the water.

Later, Nemet took the sail, her father the rudder, and the small craft skipped the waves, turning towards the fires on the shore.

For the brief time she had lain with Arithon, she had felt that something was wrong with her father; he had become solemn, agitated, his eyes on the faraway. Now, as the boat came close to the mud bank, Nemet felt her mouth go dry.

At least *one* of her sisters should have been there, to help them with the catch. But the shore was deserted, the tents flapping forlornly in the rising wind, the fires untended.

The village was deserted, even the goats had gone; even the two skinny boars that Baalgor had trapped in the forest and had brought back to fatten up.

Nemet ran between the tents shouting, half sobbing. Her father stood by the boat for a while and he seemed to be crying.

'You knew!' Nemet screamed at him, but he remained impassive.

She went into her house, searched through Harikk and Anat's clothes, found the small shells and polished stones that her sisters had so carefully gathered. She held the trinkets and wept, sensing that they had gone to the sanctuary, terrified at what this desertion meant.

'Baalgor too,' she whispered to her running spirit – the *ahk*. She went to his sleeping bench and touched the bulrushes, not knowing what she was looking for but suddenly seeing the green and silver feather that had fallen from his cloak. No! Not fallen. She picked it up and saw how the quill was *snapped*!

Arithon had come into the windy tent. His eyes were dead. The tight ringlets of his hair and beard, caked in river salt, seemed grey, ageing him dramatically. The skin on his face sagged, almost peeling from him. He held a rope and a club, and when he stepped towards his daughter, Nemet ran.

Tired though she was from the day on the river, she was still faster than her father, and she ran ahead of him into the hills, towards the gully in the rocks where she had hidden her hoard from the sanctuary. Breathless, she crouched behind yellow-flowering furze, watching the man labouring up the path, the sweat falling from him in shining droplets. He was still dead-eyed, but quite determined.

Nemet felt an overwhelming sadness. The man she had loved and respected had tricked her, knowing that she would fight to stop her sisters being taken. He had removed her from harm's way, leaving the girls and their brother to their fate. Now he was coming for his own, favoured daughter, to lead her like a beast into the mud-walled town.

He called for her, but the voice was that of a ghost, not of a parent. He spotted her and came towards her and she drew away, fleeing along the rough path until she came into the slight shadow of the rocks, where she and Baalgor had spent so many hours.

The knife was there, the handle jutting from the rock, feathery with grey wool where an animal had used it as a scratching post.

She wrestled with the handle, tugging, twisting, but the blade was embedded deeply and she couldn't move it.

Arithon stumbled into the rocks, breathing hard. The coil of rope snaked over her shoulder as he flung it, then fell to the ground. He stepped quickly towards her, swinging the brutal, polished wood.

His first blow missed her and she darted round him, flinging a stone which struck his cheek but didn't slow him.

'You *have* to come,' he whispered hoarsely.

'Not with you!'

'I've lived all my life for this time. The others have gone. I wanted a last few hours with you. To remember.'

She was too shocked by the words to respond. She saw, now, not a man who had loved her, an ordinary man, but a creature that had long since been gutted like the gutted beasts on stilts, the resurrected echoes in the sanctuary.

'Your brothers and sisters have made me proud. Make me proud too, Nem . . .'

'I'll kill you first!'

They circled the small clearing and again she reached the knife and tugged, screaming with frustrated effort. And again she flung herself aside as the club whooshed towards her. The wood struck the horn handle of Baalgor's knife and snapped it. The broken bone, with a slice of blade attached, fell at her feet. As her father stepped towards her, pushing her to the ground and hauling on the rope, she took the weapon and slashed across his throat.

For a second he looked startled, then stepped back, his hand red where he held the gash. Then he sat down heavily, a puzzled expression on his salt-bearded face. His eyes melted, filled with tears.

Nemet began to shake with fear.

She crouched before him, then made herself more comfortable, sitting cross-legged, the knife now cast aside. The dusk grew deeper as they waited, facing each other in silence.

I've killed my father. The terrible deed. I've killed my father . . .

After a while, Arithon sighed and slowly lay down on his side. His last words, no more than a ghostly whisper, sounded like *I was so proud.*

Nemet took her shawl and placed it over his shoulders, then wept over his body, her hands spread on him, her hair hanging loose across his peaceful face.

Later, she went back to the river and washed herself, holding her right hand away from her body as she did so, dipping and drinking as she remembered her father and cried for him. When she was too cold to continue she went back to the shore and picked up the *ahk*, crushing the fragile clay of the runner in hands that were suddenly strong, then smearing the gritty powder against her legs.

Yes! I did it. I have done it.

The terrible deed.

He was proud of me. I loved him.

But now I start running . . .

(ii)

She was halfway to the rock gully, where the stump of Baalgor's knife still marked the shrine to their eldest brother, when she realized that she was running in the wrong direction.

The camp had been deserted. They had all answered the call to the sanctuary. Who, then, was going to judge her for her father's murder?

She stood on the edge of the cliff, the wind in her hair, her mind clear, her senses heightened by the fragrance of the wild forest behind her. She had dressed herself in a linen tunic decorated with the shells from the sanctuary. She carried the club her father had used against her. She felt stronger, now, than at any time in her life, and one thought above all others made her turn her head towards the north.

I can stop what's happening. I can bring my sisters home . . .

And it occurred to her that Baalgor, too, was in the sanctuary, inside the earth walls, in the shadow of the white stone tower. He was among the beasts, and Nemet could not believe that he would have allowed himself to be trussed, to be made helpless, waiting to be skinned.

I we don't stop it now, there will be more sanctuaries, more skinning, more Arithons, living for nothing more than the deaths of their children as a price to pay for what belongs to all of us.

The thoughts were so clear. The horror of the subjugation of the people she loved as strong in her mind as the awareness of the heat on her limbs, and the subtle scent of balsam and olive blossom in her nostrils.

The earth is OURS to shape. We use it to hide from the wind, from the sun, from the rain. We use it to trap beasts, to trap water, to hold fires. The earth is OURS to shape!

It's wrong to let the earth shape US.

Such a clear thought, such a simple thought: that a price was already paid for the shaping of the world: in the lightning fires that consumed the tents; in the floods that swept down the valley, drowning men and goats and washing their flesh into the deep of the river; in the droughts when skins and minds shrivelled and decayed; in the beasts that flung themselves from rocks and branches to carry off the young.

This killing in skins, this skinning and living immolation, was a corruption of the way of life that had existed with the spirits in the earth since the flesh of the land had first folded into valleys and hills, and grown the forests, and moulded the creatures to inhabit them.

Wrong!

Nemet ran lightly, head low, the club strung across her back, her hair tied tightly in a single plait and pinned to her tunic. She had rolled in the dust and now was a red-grey ghost on the dry land as she moved through the hills, away from the shrinking river, towards the scent of fresher water from the springs where the sanctuary town was being raised.

Around her, the dust began to rise, to swirl as in a wind-storm. She tied a cloth around her mouth and pressed on, aware of the looming bulk of the sanctuary, a shadow in the sand ahead of her.

And then she heard the call, the strange song, the melodious summoning voice drifting like a searching snake from the tower that rose starkly above the walls and shelters in the town. She crouched as the sound entered her, feeling its rising, falling notes as spikes, impaling her, drawing her closer. But the song was not directed at the approaching woman. It was calling into a far-flung place, a long-gone place, and Nemet felt the earth shudder as the long-gone was drawn – fishes on a line – closer to the surface of the world she knew.

Behind her, the ground *bellowed* as if in pain, and she turned, shocked to see the great creature lumbering towards her. She darted away from it, recoiling from the faecal stink as it passed, its trunk slapping against its columnar leg, the shaggy hair on its body caked with black mud and glistening green slime. It walked towards the shadow town, dropping dung, bellowing its fear.

Again the earth shuddered.

Nemet watched as the ground folded down, then swelled, the scrub of trees and bushes rising as a second, monstrous head appeared, two dulled eyes buried in a face of bulging horn and flaring nose, a mouth gaping, teeth blunted and yellow. This thing stood on its hindlegs, stepping from the earth, shaking its hairless torso and scratching with curved claws as long as Nemet's arm. Its cry of pain was like a man dying, but sustained for a minute as its torso weaved and rocked, a child born into a strange world, gasping for breath.

This thing too began to follow the summoning song, and though it glanced and growled at Nemet, stooping to take its weight on its forearms, it stalked into the dust, shadowed and lost.

Again the earth flexed its muscles, and a pair of horns the girth of Arithon's river-boat punched up from the soil, and a bull's head followed, the muzzle snorting, the crimson body arching up behind it, hooves scrabbling to raise this forgotten monster.

Blood-red and massive, the Bull suddenly lay down as it passed Nemet, rolling over, legs kicking monstrously, its eyes never leaving the crouching, fearful woman.

When it stood again it was hesitant, aware of its small companion, almost uncertain in its actions.

Nemet approached the creature and it lowered its head. Its breath reeked of sweet grass. She touched its muzzle and its fleshy lips drew back from teeth like marker stones.

It bellowed in anguish.

Nemet soothed it.

The call from the white tower was still strong and the Bull became agitated, began to walk towards the summoning voice. Drawn out of a time when the earth was roamed by giants, now it carried a smaller creature, clinging to its underquarters, arms entwined with the matted hair that hung down from the grumbling bulk of its belly.

Swaying with the movement of the beast, limbs beginning to tire, Nemet was carried into the sanctuary, aware of the frantic beating of skin drums, the shrieking and chanting of female voices and the mournful, rising notes of great, bone horns. When she smelled the rot from the skins of the stilt creatures, and heard the faint cries of their human companions, shedding their lives into the Fragrant Pasture, she dropped away, scurrying into the shadows.

For a while she crouched in darkness, catching her breath, watching the irregular parade of nightmares stalk through the writhing skins, occasionally butting against the heads which swayed on the ends of their poles. The tower rose ahead of her, the shape of the summoner motionless as he uttered the eerie cry. When the breeze in the sanctuary changed, Nemet scented blood and fear and though her stomach heaved, she began to follow the stench, head low, moving from skinned creature to skinned creature as she strove to remain invisible to the watchful man on the edge of the white stone.

'Baalgor!' she whispered to the sanctuary. 'Where are you? Where are you hiding?'

Eventually she reached the slaughterhouse, passing unnoticed through the tall gate in the high wall of wood and clay, walking among the fires and drummers, stepping round the skins that were being cleaned, the bones that were being stripped of meat, aware of the strutting and circling flock of carrion birds, whose own cries added to the cacophony.

Whichever way she wandered through the noise and chaos of this arena of sacrifice, the white stone tower was always ahead of her, its base gaping where the unbarred entrance called to her . . .

She watched in silent horror as the first of the beasts she had seen summoned from the earth was brought to its belly by cuts to its legs, then beaten on the brow by clubs until it was still. The sawing and cutting began, the heat from its body manifesting as a writhing vapour above the carcase. The blood-red Bull bellowed and struggled against the leather ropes that now restrained it. And yet . . . suddenly it seemed to see Nemet and it calmed, as if recognizing an ally.

Nemet was shocked to feel a reciprocating sense of peace and understanding.

This beast is MINE. Its belly is my grave. Its bones are the forest grove where I'm to lie, skinned and travelling!

She turned from it, ignoring its angry cry, fleeing across the arena, stumbling suddenly to the base of the stone tower.

'Nemet!'

The call was distant. She couldn't tell which of her sisters had seen her and was crying for her, but again the voice sounded in her ears, distinct above the pulse of life, drums and wailing song behind her.

She stepped towards the open door, stepped towards the darkness. As she reached the threshold of the tower her mother appeared, hair awry, eyes wide, face sagging beneath the weight of horror.

'Nemet . . .' she managed, then thrust something sticky yet gossamer into her hands before suddenly running into the sanctuary, slipping on the wet pelts, sending fire and smoke swirling as she kicked through the burning wood. Flame took on her shawl, her dress, but she was lost in the smoke, in the confusion.

Nemet looked at the green-tinged fabric, spread the tissue slightly, recognized the marks of one of her sisters, then realized that she held two faces, and half a face . . .

'Anat,' she breathed, recognizing the eyes that marked the cheeks. She fumbled, shaking, to spread the faces. Whose was the second?

Then Harikk burst from the tower, one side of her face still burning where the flayed flesh had been sealed. Her good eye was wide and wild. She stared at Nemet, recognizing her, then screamed with pain before saying, slowly and angrily, 'Our brother has doomed us!'

'Baalgor?'

Still grimacing, her eye weeping as the scorched flesh smouldered, Harikk said, 'This has turned out badly. There will be no peace for us now . . .'

And she ran across the slaughter yard to the edge of the sanctuary, a naked shape glistening with oils, lithe and athletic despite her mutilation, hard like a creature, determined to escape.

Ahk'Nemet looked back, then – acting on instinct – looked up.

The grim sky was darkening. A man's shape was growing above her as it fell. The scream surrounded her, an alien sound. She stepped to one side a heart's beat before the opened body of the Rememberer broke and twisted on impact with the earth, a man's length from where she stood. Instinctively, she flung her spear at the body, striking it in the chest. The startling grey eyes, separated by a scar, watched her from the beginning of the forest path to the Fragrant Pasture. The long, grey hair blew in the breeze. The mouth chattered through the rictus of death, a nervous music that slowed, then stopped, and allowed the purple tip of a tongue to extrude and taste the air.

Everything in the sanctuary had gone silent. Glancing round, Nemet realized that the eyes of her tribe, and of the still-living animals, were set upon her.

A moment later there was mayhem, a panic that killed as the sanctuary was abandoned, a frantic escape to the outside world that left bodies broken and writhing beneath the feet of the untethered beasts.

A touch on her shoulder made her scream, but a finger on her lips silenced her and she was suddenly staring through the baked clay mask that covered her brother's face. He was shaking, but with triumph, not fear. He *stank* of triumph. The sweat on his body added to the glow of the kill that lit his eyes, fuelled his heart, powered his limbs.

He held a stone blade towards her, the stench of blood still strong on the cutting edge.

'They've killed Anat. Jarmu and Anat. There'll be no more, though. I've seen to that.'

'Hora is dead too. Kohara gave me her face . . . and half of

Harikk's. Harikk is alive and burning. She has started running.'

'Hora,' her brother whispered, then flung the knife to the ground, turning and spitting on the curved, cracked corpse of the Rememberer.

'Do you have the *ahk*?' he asked.

'It's on my body.'

'Then you can run for eternity. But sister: you'll have to carry me when my own legs go. I have this, though.'

He held up his clay talisman, the skin-covered bull, the clay-covered *el*.

'Inside the skin, the animal; inside the animal, the secret; inside the secret, the life itself; inside the life, the maker! I have woven my own needs into this small piece of the dead.'

'To do what?'

'To strip the inside from the outside of a beast. To take its essence, its power; to shape that essence, to make what I need.'

'New beasts.'

'New power.'

Ahk'Nemet smiled. 'I hope so.'

'I *know* so.'

'We're going to need that if we're to pass into the Fragrant Pasture at the end of our days, and not into oblivion.' Baalgor didn't seem to notice her warning words, and ignored, too, the way the sanctuary was beginning to shrink, to fold, to crowd in upon them. He was still fevered and shaking from the deed he had committed; the smell of hunting and lust was redolent on his lithe and towering form. He held Nemet in his arms and kissed her on the mouth. His right hand reached down to hold the muscle of her thigh, the fingers spreading, the thumb moving to intimate contact with her sex.

'Your legs are like the polished limbs of cedar; strong and beautiful . . . the scent between them as sharp and pleasant as the ripest olive . . .'

She pushed him away. 'Save the gossamer words for a time

when the forest conceals us. My legs may be like polished cedar, but my right hand took the life of our father.'

Astonished, her brother could do no more than echo her words.

'Arithon? You killed him?'

'Cut his throat. With my right hand.'

'Why? I loved him. We all loved him.'

'And he loved us. He truly did. So much so that he was prepared to have us skinned. He believed in something that only *he* understood. A voice told me to end him, and to escape.'

'The terrible deed,' Baalgor whispered, still shocked. Then he asked, 'What voice? Tell me what voice?'

Nemet smiled grimly.

'What voice?' he repeated.

Nemet said, 'In a city of lies, I lied about the voice. Unless, of course, my right hand whispered its needs to me . . .'

'My own right hand silenced the Rememberer. Silenced his song, his summoning . . .'

Nemet glanced at the twisted body. 'So I see. All things considered, brother, it would be better if we were somewhere else . . .'

'Our sisters are dead.'

'Not Harikk, remember? Her face is scorched, but she's alive. She's fled the sanctuary. The *etni* saved her.'

Baalgor's eyes widened as he thought further. 'And four others, all cut but not peeled. They held the Rememberer while I ended his song. I'd thought it finished. But it isn't finished at all! Which way, sister?'

'This way!' she said, and led him to the Bull-Gate in the high wall of cedar.

But as they stepped into the world beyond the sanctuary, they heard the echo of the song of summoning, felt it embrace them like a gossamer web.

'Which way, sister?' Baalgor asked again, his voice a whisper.

They stared at the land, which twisted and shifted like hills in the highest heat of summer, a vision not of the world they knew, but of worlds only the Rememberer had seen as he had sung through time.

Ahk'Nemet felt her heart sink and her mouth grow dry as she realized that after all they had not escaped the clutches of Gl'Thaan Em. She also felt her legs starting to move.

Running!

'This way,' she said. 'Trust me, brother.'

'I *do* trust you.'

Running.

(iii)

Silence and the stink of ghosts had come to the abandoned sanctuary. The fires guttered and failed, the wind began to stir the ashes. The bulging skins of the beasts, summoned and sacrificed, ceased to writhe, the hollow voices quietened.

Nothing moved except the Bull.

The Bull moved about the ruins. When the wind whipped up the dust from the plains, it became like a ghost itself, massive and slow, wandering the alleys and the chambers, stepping through the bones and hearths of those who had lived here during the long years of Remembering, of Summoning. It seemed to be searching.

Rains came, light at first, then heavy enough, year after year, to move the hills themselves. The mudbrick of the town walls dissolved and crumbled, burying the skins and bones of the beasts that had been called from time, burying the Bull as it lay dying, exhausted with searching and waiting for the eternal companion it had seen and recognized, burying the broken remains of the Rememberer, and the last echoes of his song and magic.

Times changed again and the rains eased. Under an unrelenting sun the land dried, the river dropped away, the mound of Gl'Thaan Em baked and hardened, the spring below its belly searching through the seeds of life for the way back to the surface. Trees grew, thick and vibrant on the hill, their roots tapping the hidden waters, tangling with the dead.

Travellers settled for a while, making a clearing on the hill, close to the crumbling tower of white stone, throwing up tents and letting their goats and pigs root and scavenge in the woods. They dug for water, but found only nightmares. Ululating songs and deathly screams rose from the hole at night, and spectres of giants stalked the wood, calling at the moon.

The travellers killed a goat, then killed a child, blood to the spring waters, a gesture of pacification before the nomads folded their tents and fled to the east, towards the distant river. They had strange stories to tell and stranger visions to interpret.

Blood to the spring! Life to the waters! And below the woods . . .

. . . life came back to the mound!

The spring rose and branched through the compacted earth, nourishing and renewing, touching the seeds of time, the echoes of the creatures that were carried in the sanctuary. Now the Rememberer's song returned, oozing from the remains of walls, circling inside the hill, vibrant and mournful. The hill of Gl'Thaan Em shimmered by night, visible to the nomadic peoples of the valley and beyond, tribes who arrived in their hundreds from the faraway, called and made curious by the stories of the burning forest on the burning hill.

Murdered and abandoned . . .

The notion flowed through the hill, carried on the spring waters that circulated like life-blood, carried on the spiralling song, reverberating through the network of skeletal remains that formed the matrix of the hill, pounding like drums off the hides of the beasts.

Murdered and abandoned . . .

This primal sentience began to form faces in its earthy mass, the faces of those who had murdered and abandoned it, this place of mud and brick, this shrine to the life in the earth, this uncompleted place.

It heard the sound of their running. They had gone into the song, the Rememberer's song, the song that touched the long-gone and the long-to-come. They were there, ducking and weaving through the worlds of wood and hill and shadow that the song encompassed. They were running through the ages, eternal in their terror, eternal in the knowledge of the deed they had committed.

Seven faces, seven lives, seven to be hunted down, seven to be brought back to fertilize the sanctuary . . .

The mound collapsed!

The shimmering light formed into the giant head of a bull, turning slowly to look across the camps, with their tents, fires and huddling figures. A voice echoed from the muzzle of the bull, or perhaps only in the minds of those who stared in terror at the spirit of the beast.

I AM RESURRECTED.

I AM LIFE.

I AM THE HUNTER.

I AM THE BLOODED CITY.

I AM ETERNAL.

The burning aura collapsed. The earth shook violently, and the fires of the camps roared, guttered and faded, their flame sucked away by the freezing wind that swirled about the hill.

Then something moved *downwards*, downwards to the earth, away through the mountains to the west, leaving only silence and desolation, and the smouldering trunks of cedar on the shattered knoll.

38

Nemet was calling to me, a dove's coo as she roused me from the inner journey, her hands gentle on my face as she turned my head to left and right. Her dark eyes showed that she was glad to see me surface, and her quick kiss conveyed relief.

'Jack,' she murmured. 'My Jack. Don't be frightened . . .'

'I saw what happened . . . Arithon . . . the remembering of creatures long extinct . . . one of your sisters, face burning, fleeing . . .'

'I wondered if you would go there.'

Ahk'Nemet had drawn away from me, standing and staring down. Behind her, the dark walls of prehistoric Jericho rose against the storm-swirl of the sky.

The elements of the encounter with her past were a similar swirl in my head: the sense of the fabled *ark* in the gathering of beasts, a place not just for continuity by the holding of the seeds of life – its *meaning* in mythology – but for *memory*, for holding the seeds of the life that had preceded the animals of the day. That strange function had been destroyed by Baalgor and his sister when they had killed the grey-haired summoner . . .

It had been John Garth's face that watched me emptily from the broken ground by the white tower.

And Harikk, the scorched face! The haunting image that I thought I had created in my childish stories, the watcher and guardian from the glades that I had embroidered around the glimpses of Greyface and Greenface, thinking this was fertile imagination; but she had been there too, part of the echo that did not belong to my own pre-conscious mind. Which meant that she, too, was loose and on the run!

How had Jandrok characterized the Midax Deep? The Hinterland giving way to marshes, savannahs, deserts, deeper layers – all of them with primal functions, all memories from the beast-times, all of them inhabited. From one inner world I had journeyed to a far deeper realm, to a place that had come into my mind by a means *other* than inheritance, hidden from even my deepest dreams by the barriers, the incorruptible walls, of the mind itself, walls which locked this intruder away at its heart.

Two . . . no, three, it seemed, Harikk too . . . three creatures had escaped that hidden Deep, and come through me into the world of flesh and consciousness; but how had the city itself, the sanctuary, the primal ark come to be there?

I had seen it in the real world, and John Garth had been in the real world . . .

What had Brightmore said? *Glanum recognizes no boundary between our earth and your mind – the same place being experienced from two different perspectives – a different set of dimensions . . .*

The storm turned, the sound of drums lulled me, hypnotized me. I could smell burning wood and flesh; in places, beyond the wooden walls, the brilliance of fires tinged the black clouds with red. I recognized this place; Nemet had led me here from the Hinterland, on my first Midax journey, trapping me by her own magic in a snare of roses, scarring me, stigmata that had surfaced on the flesh and shadow in the real world and so scared the watchers that they had hauled me back, dragged me back as if I had been a drowning man in deep water.

So the heart, this ark, had always been in the Midax Deep, and Nemet had come close to it once, almost 'home', but then abandoned the place for the second time, after trapping me in rose-thorn, to come and find me again.

Now she was at the gates of the shrine that had hunted her,

alone and unprotected, one of the seven of her tribe that Gl'Thaan Em had pursued through the earth and the minds of humankind. Baalgor was not here. And Nemet stood, shivering, staring at the sky, perhaps wondering whether to enter or run again.

I suspected that this was the moment when she would choose between life and death.

But the decision, it seemed, was no longer in her own hands; when Glanum had risen from the Deep and taken us, another spirit had controlled the movement, and he came now out of the shadows.

I sat up, then stood, watching as tall gates closed on the fires inside the heart of the sanctuary; by their flaring light, the tall, cloaked form of the Rememberer was silhouetted as he came towards me. Then the gates closed and only the grim light of the sky showed the grey eyes, and the deep scar between them.

Nemet had stepped away and dropped to a crouch, head bowed, arms across her breast, a posture of humiliation.

But John Garth was staring only at me, reaching out to touch my shoulders with skeletal but still strong hands. Below the cowl, he was smiling, a thin, grim gesture, that contained the merest hint of recognition and pleasure.

'Garth,' I said.

'I remember you,' he whispered.

'John Garth,' I said again, touching his fingers with my own.

'Yes. I remember you. I can still see the boy in your face . . . the boy who told stories . . . the boy who was born on the day I finally found where Gl'Thaan Em was hiding.'

'Mister Garth . . .'

'I remember you.'

'I've never forgotten you either. What happened to you changed my life. I've always lived in two worlds; neither has any real fear for me . . .'

John Garth was here, in the Midax Deep; and yet he had

been there, in Exburgh, and when I had stalked the ghostly streets of the city with him he had seemed not to understand everything that was happening, or that had happened. He hadn't known the past, or so he'd claimed.

'You must have known more than you told me. You must have known who my Greenface and Greyface were. You must have recognized the tower, and the Bull. Why did you pretend differently?'

Ahk'Nemet had begun to sing, her body rocking as she huddled. I thought she was in pain, perhaps in terror, but Garth ignored her.

'I remember you,' he repeated to me. 'But then, I remember many like you. It had been a long journey, searching for the city. Memory is like an echo, Jack. It fades each time it is reflected, but somehow, never dies. I had forgotten the city. The city had forgotten me . . .

'But when I saw your sketches, when I saw the crude faces in plaster in the ruins of ancient Glanum, I was looking at the last flicker of light on the faces of the two who had killed me – others had held me, but those two did the deed, drowning me in my own blood, watching me.'

He looked at Ahk'Nemet, who was silent and still, huddled and waiting for the end.

Garth went on, 'When I saw them in your own town, I began to remember. I knew they were close, whoever they were. And I started to realize that Glanum was close too. I was unaware of who or what had been born in me, but I knew I had to return to the city. When it finally came to me, as curious about me as I was about it, it didn't recognize me at first. I remember hauling myself up the city walls . . .'

'It was spectacular to watch!'

'It was terrifying to do. I hung there for days, wedged into the gap between a tree and the stone it grew from. I was like a bug on the city's skin, and it tried to scratch and scour me off; but I clung on, inching my way inside. I didn't know that I was coming home, but once inside, so much memory returned.'

I was a ghost, resurrected and adrift in my own song, passing through time, caught by that song as much as the city itself, and the beasts, and the seven who had done the deed. But I was insubstantial, surfacing at random in strange centuries, strange places in the world, only occasionally hearing the cries of the hunted, and the thunder of the sanctuary itself as it swam in pursuit of its killers.

I had been abandoned and had become lost; but I had never abandoned hope.

Garth was walking towards the gates, now open again to expose the fires beyond. Ahk'Nemet followed behind him. She had thrown down her weapons, cast off her robe. She was naked. Even the skins of her sisters lay on the ground, catching the grim light of the heart of Glanum.

At the gate, Garth stepped aside and Nemet passed through. The gates closed behind her, locking her in. She had not looked back.

The Rememberer watched me for a while, then looked at the hill, where the walls of the outer city glowed, shimmering in the moonlight from beyond the storm. He came back to me and passed me, saying, 'And now for the other one. The brother. Come on, Jack. My Jack. He'll come to you.'

I looked at the gates. *What would happen to her? She had gone so willingly, so compliantly.*

'Garth!'

He stopped and turned, shouting at me to hurry. I stood my ground. 'You were already dead when she put the spear in you. It's Baalgor you want, not Nemet.'

'Both of them. All of them,' he said.

'Let her go.'

John Garth stared at me for a few moments, his expression one of half concealed amusement, then said, 'I intend to, Jack.

Just as soon as her brother comes back to the sanctuary. I intend to let her go.'

He meant, of course: skinned and digested in a tent of bones and leather, fulfilling the role for which he believed she had been born.

'Let her go,' I urged. 'Let her live.'

'Why?' the Rememberer asked, his tone mocking; 'What is she to you?'

I struggled to say the words which would indicate my feelings; odd and inappropriate words, in their way; words of betrayal to my family; words I could scarcely believe would be so important to me. Something – perhaps the sense of being watched and monitored beyond the city walls (*turn the damned thing off! The machine. The Midax eye. Let me alone!*) – something stopped me expressing my love for Ahk'Nemet, my true passion for her.

I said only, 'She's been through enough. Can't you see that? She's been through enough.'

Garth watched me coldly.

'For her, it has hardly started.'

And he turned from me again.

I went quickly to the discarded faces on the ground, but on instinct picked up only the half-skin belonging to Harikk, the Scorched One. The thin gut-threads were still in place and I pulled the tissue over my head. It was cold, slightly greasy. I looked through the slit where her eye had once watched for warning omens, I looked at the man on the hill, his hair flowing, his cloak billowing, his stride as purposeful as I remembered from my childhood.

Help your sister, I said aloud, before pursuing the Rememberer. *Harikk. Help me.*

Like a great, rough ship of stone, the ark of Gl'Thaan Em ploughed the ages, a hulking, savage city, surfacing as the whale, sudden, vast and shocking, to hunt and gorge on the civilizations that had once covered the earth. No mindless beast, it was sentient, furious, a creature formed unnaturally from the earth, given hope, given meaning by its creator, then abandoned, now pursuing those who had betrayed it.

I watched from the white tower, braced against the chthonian swell, Garth beside me, monstrous in his coldness, singular in his own determination to scent and catch the man who'd killed him.

I watched as nations rose and fell, the proud pillars, the totems in grinning wood, the spires of marbled granite, all of this Herculean arrogance rising in the passing of a breath, all of it crumbling in the time it took to wonder at the beauty, their shards, their ruin, sucked into the white leviathan that was Glanum, a city built to remember all life, now a malevolent leveller of all hope, the eater of shrines to a system of belief that had *begun* within its first walls, perhaps consuming them to satisfy its own frustrated ambition.

And suddenly it surfaced into a place I knew well, into Exburgh, rising briefly among the shops and churches, the halls and arcades, swallowing back the haunting, snaring shadow it had left behind before, when it had passed this way. At once, Baalgor was thrown out of his hiding place and into the Rememberer's *song* again, at loose in time, and in the world of shadows, and on his own.

'He's running. Ahead of us,' Garth cried. 'I can almost smell him . . . there! Look there!'

As the city plunged into the dark, I glimpsed a forest, ages old, its canopy alive with birds of carrion. Somewhere in that swathe of green, Baalgor was fleeing the Bull, the gaping, staring Bull carved on the gate of Glanum, and which had manifested as the great beast itself in my crazy, childhood visions. Garth had sensed the feat of the running man, the anguish, and using that blind instinct had pinned him down.

We came up. I was giddy with the motion. We hovered, hanging in space, vertical to the world, the shrines like limpets on the body of the whale.

Down, then! And such a dive! Down into the earth through

a darkness that began to shimmer, and that shimmering illuminated corridors of bone and stone, of runes and marks, of the history of a world that had been swallowed by that greatest of tyrants, Time itself.

Up it came, rising from the Deep!

Like a shark, it chewed at the buried past.

Like a bull, it grazed the runes.

Like a cat, it clawed and played with the columns and façades of stone which had been decorated under the direction of a vision that had come from the earth itself. . .

From life itself!

Carved, shaped by the hands of the priests, put up to please the eye, subverted to please the soul, images of the life and the death of our prehistoric, wonderful and *sensual* awareness formed the ocean in which this most monstrous of all sanctuaries swam, in search of a man who had killed the first singer of the songs of *blind faith*.

Garth, beside me, exhilarated as Glanum plunged through the deserts of Egypt, the mountain valleys of the Hindu Kush, the monumental hills of Greece, the wind-swept, yellow grasslands of the New World, even biting at the bulking, ruddy, painted rocks of what I imagine was Australia at a time so long in the past that only a *whisper* of the songs we heard remained in my own age.

At last, Baalgor himself *gave up the ghost*, swallowed by the Bull-Gate, hunted through the world of my own preconscious and perhaps captured by my own *willingness* to have him caught, for this was partly a world of my own making, and surely by persistence I could make things happen! Yet strangely, I felt a moment's sadness as he tumbled among the earth and stone of his crude hiding place, which also had been consumed when he was *bitten* out of his wild running.

He recognized me at once, and came towards me. He stripped off his stinking cloak of scalps and feathers and threw it at my feet. His naked body bled from cuts. The clay had broken away from his body. Tattooed eyes gazed unblinking from his hard-boned flesh.

'I didn't kill my father.'

'I know you didn't.'

He seemed surprised, stepping forward. 'Nemet killed my father.'

'I know.'

'Then if you know . . . why are you hunting *me*?'

'I'm not. *He* is . . .'

Baalgor glanced contemptuously at Garth, but seemed confused as he looked back. 'But he's the skinner of souls! I killed him because he was taking something that didn't belong to him!'

'I know.'

'You *know*?'

'I have a good idea, at least. It all happened a long time in the past.'

'*What* past? It's now! He's come back. He's come back! And it will all start again . . .'

'He came back, Baalgor. A long time ago. He came *back*. And it *did* all start again. And in the words of the cliché: that's life! And life as we know it has been terrorized by the Great Lie ever since.'

'The Great Lie was this place of beasts. What do you mean . . . What do you mean by the Great Lie?'

Baalgor, young and raging, naked and bleeding, was a man doomed to die, but still violent in his defence of his philosophy.

'That there is something greater than you and I, an all-seeing eye . . . *a maker*.'

'But I *know* that's not true! That's why I killed the Rememberer! It all belongs to us! The life and death of even a single sprig of thyme. . . it *happens*. The flood that takes our dogs and donkeys, the rains that fill our wells . . . it happens. It belongs to *us*. When we go on, when we die, we have only the

Fragrant Pasture, a wonderful place. It's where we all go, the young who die in the womb, the old man who has been blind all his life, the strongest and the weakest of us. We all go there. It *belongs* to us.'

'I know.'

He was wild, frightened. Not at all the menacing figure who had taunted me from the *Shimmering*. 'You know! You keep saying you *know*.'

'Yes. And you're right. It's *now*. And right now, whatever you did, whatever you believed, whatever deed, terrible or wonderful you performed, is just a story! From the long-long-gone. Older than the Oldest Testament. *Forgotten*. It's of no importance. Only one thing matters to me.'

He had laughed inadvertently when I had talked about 'story'. Now, in an attempt to be brazen, he sneered at me. 'You. Yourself. Your precious daughter.'

I smiled at him, but my heart was racing. In this strange place, Natalie had suddenly called to me. I could imagine her at play, perhaps calling for her 'funny' friend, and I wanted to be with her, to be safe with her, to have her safely in my arms again.

'Yes. Me. Myself. My precious daughter. I *thought* you were lying. You know all about it. You *are* the same entity. *You* stole my daughter. And you certainly know why I will never let you go.'

He stared at me thoughtfully for a long time before speaking. 'Yes. Natalie. She was my only hope.'

He sounded defeated! My spirits soared. He'd lost!

'You still have her, then.'

'Some of her. I only ever had some of her. I took what I could, but mostly it was your love for her that helped me.' He smiled, staring me straight in the eye, a man lost, I realized. 'I enjoyed dancing with her . . . Jack. I told her funny stories; by return, she told me funny stories of her own. Childish stories . . . more charming than amusing . . . she is the daughter I would have wanted, funny, teasing, willing to listen . . . I took her into my hiding place . . .'

'Give her back to me.'

'Give back *what*? I took her there, but I kept only a shadow of her laughter, a shadow of her beauty, an echo of her life . . . she was just an echo . . . You can hardly have expected me to have told you that. Thin skins, stitched together like my cloak to make the illusion of a woman. My skill, if I had a skill, was not in stripping the soul from your daughter, but in making you believe that I had done so . . .'

'Give her back to me.'

'There's nothing to give back,' Baalgor said, and he had suddenly aged. 'And what I took is precious to me. You'll not miss it. She'll not miss it . . .'

'I want the shades. All of them.'

'You can't put spilled drink back in the beaker,' he said quietly, and added with a smile, 'You can't put piss back in the belly. But then – such loss hardly matters.'

Shaking his head he reached for his cloak, held it to his chest, his eyes closed, his fingers rubbing the feathers of the carrion crows whose scalped corpses had supplied the ruff that had once adorned his neck.

'I took nothing,' he said quietly. 'Nothing of consequence. Not from you. Not from Natalie. I tried only to stop the skinning, the burial with beasts, the sanctuary.'

'The first sacrifices . . .'

'Yes.'

'You failed.'

'Yes. I'm painfully aware of the fact.'

Throughout this long exchange, John Garth had stood silently, watching Baalgor with an impassive, unreadable expression. Now he turned to me and said bluntly, 'Enough talking. Go to the gate, Jack. Your journey is nearly finished. Your wife is waiting for you. Your life. Your daughter.'

He started to move away, Baalgor walking stiffly before

him. But I stepped between the two of them and shook my head. 'I won't let you take her. Not Nemet. I'll hunt you down, Garth; I'll pursue you with all the blind determination of Glanum itself if you destroy her now.'

'I know you will,' he whispered.

He came towards me and to my astonishment reached round to embrace me, holding me against his breast for a minute or so, silent but for his breathing. The odour of burnt tar and fresh mud was powerful on him. I could feel the heavy thump of his heart, the slow rise and fall of his chest.

When he drew back he quickly touched a finger to my cheek, to the false skin of Nemet's sister. The touch moved to my chin, then my mouth, and Garth watched me curiously as he marked out the shape of the scorched woman on my grizzled features.

'I haven't found this one yet. She is still hiding.'

'Then let her go too. Haven't you had your fill of death?' I could still smell the slaughterhouse around the white tower.

John Garth said, 'That's what you see, isn't it? That's all that has happened to your vision over the thousands of years – it sees death alone. Jack, Gl'Thaan Em wasn't built as a place of death, but as a place of life! You have the stories in your own age, of the Ark, the place of preservation. Why can't you accept that in the far-gone we did things differently? The infant sanctuary of what you call Jericho, the prehistoric place that was born with *me*, was about *keeping time still*. Everywhere, the earth was being hardened into walls, like sores on pristine skin. And the memories of the people were hardening too – what was once remembered naturally, now was being forgotten as the very pattern of life changed on the skin of the world.

'The Song came, a glorious song, eternal, all-encompassing . . . It sang at the oasis where Gl'Thaan Em began to grow. Both Land and Time, and all that had lived on that Land and in that Time, were marked and memorized so that their empowering spirit would not be lost—'

'By sacrifice. By the brutal mating of human with animal.'

'I have seen the world from the inside out, Jack. I can see what sacrifice *became* – the illusion of living-on in the shadow of invented Gods. But at Gl'Thaan Em, the dead were the gates by which the remembered life of the earth could continue to walk the valleys and the lakesides and the high hills. This was the deed the Song shaped us to perform. *You* make a judgement of right or wrong, of horrific, of brutal. But Gl'Thaan Em was built for a purpose that would have been wonderful – and that purpose was not fulfilled. Like any child abandoned, it has simply been doing what it needed to find its own way home!'

'And all to preserve the memory of extinct animals. To what end, Garth? To what end? We can dig up their bones, we can know them by their bones! To what end?'

'To an end that was in the hearts and minds of a people now remote to you, a people who had lived with ghosts, and couldn't bear to give them up.'

Exasperated, Jack shook his head, saying, 'And now? What now?'

Garth shrugged, glanced at the silent, brooding figure of Baalgor. 'And now it's almost over. Harikk can't be far. And then Gl'Thaan Em will dive one more time – and surface again somewhere in the world, and in the past, where it will complete its purpose.'

'But not at Jericho.'

John Garth shook his head. 'It doesn't seem so. Memory of Gl'Thaan Em haunted the people there until they invented reasons for the very sacrifice that you find so abhorrent. And with what relish the art was practised! I saw Ur in its heyday, a feast of death, ritual of astonishing beauty, incredible ruthlessness, a city like a mausoleum!'

'So where will you go?'

'I don't know. In my own time on this earth, before you were born, I looked for the final site of Glanum on every continent, a site ten thousand years old or more, but I couldn't find it. Maybe it's below the ice of Antarctica; more likely hidden in a mountain valley. All I have ever found, until Exburgh, was the occasional echo. So where we finish up will be as much a surprise to me as it will be to the explorer who one day finds our ruins!'

He glanced at Baalgor and I sensed impatience. Below my feet, the city shifted, a ship caught in strange winds, ready to cast off, to plough deep seas.

'Nemet . . .' I said again, and felt suddenly very frightened, very small. 'Let her go, Mister Garth. She has come to mean half the world to me.'

And Natalie the other half, I thought, but didn't say.

I was watching him through the half-face of Harikk. And suddenly I realized that through the eye of the scorched sister, Garth was smiling! Even though to my own, naked eye his face was hard and bruised, a man without compassion. Harikk was revealing to me the gleam of love in the heart of the Rememberer.

He moved past me and I stood my ground, shaking with an emotion I suppose was partly fear and partly hope.

'Go to the gate,' he said. 'Wait there. When you feel the city start to dive, go out. Go out no matter what! But wait there until that moment. Wait and watch.'

'Will you give her back to me?'

'Wait. And watch!' He marched away. For a while I stood my ground.

By the time he and Baalgor had disappeared from view, the white walls of Glanum were rising towards a summer sky.

39

One of the Brontotheria had blundered into the corral during the dawn hours, smashing the wooden fencing and freeing the wild hippari. The new animals were a bigger species than those he had caught with William, in another lifetime, and Jack was furious as he rode along the lake shore, assessing the best way to gather the kicking creatures back into the pens.

Nemet had circled round behind. He could see her, a dark shape on a dark horse, coming carefully through the trees, ready to turn the herd back if it began to stampede.

For the moment, the equines kicked and played in the lake water, snapping at the small birds that buzzed them, trying to land and peck at parasites.

At his signal, Nemet made her run, galloping down the shore, startling the creatures which began to bolt. But they turned away from the lake when Jack charged them, holding his long, red-flagged lance to the side.

Most of the hippari blundered back into the labyrinthine corral, and Jack hauled the gate closed, aware that Nemet was pursuing the three, ginger-maned misfits, the three largest of the herd, the three proudest.

There was a hailing cry from the harbour and Jack turned. For a second he thought it might be William Finebeard, and his heart skipped a beat; but it was not his lost friend who was summoning him. There remained no sign of William and Ethne, only of the mausoleum, the tomb broken, the contents gone.

It was his daughter Natalie who walked towards him, waving, a white shape against the white tower of ivory.

He called to Nemet, 'Can you manage now?'

'Yes. If we lose them we lose them. I'm fine.'

He rode through the lake water to his daughter, dismounted and hugged her.

'You'd forgotten. Hadn't you!'

It was a reprimand.

'The school play. Yes. I'm sorry. We've had some trouble with the big brontos. Nearly lost the new herd.'

'I guessed something was up. That's why I came to fetch you.'

She looked hungrily at the corralled animals, her eyes wide with the pleasure of what she saw. He knew what she was thinking and laughed, before wrapping his arms around her, calling to be drawn back from the Deep.

He surfaced on the frame, swung his legs off and stretched, plucking the sensors from the skin of his chest and scalp. Natalie stood before him, dressed in summer clothes, shoes polished, hair combed and ribboned. Angela was punching in the termination codes at the console.

She glanced at Jack and smiled briefly. 'I've got to pick up Steve. We'll see you there.'

'I only need a couple of minutes. Just to freshen up.'

'I'll go with Daddy,' Natalie said, and Angela shrugged. 'Okay. But don't be late.'

When Angela had gone, Natalie asked, 'What are you going to do with the horses?'

'Tame them, of course. Cut off their sharp little toes, then trade them.'

For anything but fish gum and icons, he added silently.

'Nemet said she doesn't like cutting off their toes.'

'Nemet has a five-inch scar on her leg which reminds her of the good sense in the . . . painless . . . operation.'

'Can I stay with you longer next time? I really like it by the lake. I'd like to help you look for William. Do you really think he's still alive?'

'I'm sure of it. He left me a picture: of "Greenface". And everything suggests that Ethne came back to him . . . The only thing that puzzles me is how.'

'And I'd like to ride one of the hipparions,' Natalie was persisting. 'With Harry.'

He leaned down and kissed the fresh-faced girl. 'Harry's too young yet. He's like his father . . . tall for his age, but very clumsy.'

'You're not clumsy!'

'You didn't see me rounding up the horses yesterday! Anyway, as far as I'm concerned, you can come and visit any time you like. You know how much I love you. And I *will* spend more time with you at home, just as soon as I've got the ranch working smoothly, back in the Deep. And then you can come and ride whatever you like. You can even ride a Brontotherium, if you want. But you'll have to ask Mummy. And Steve. They call the shots now. They have control of the inner eye.'

'I know,' Natalie said mischievously. 'She's always keeping her eye on you. Through the Midact-VR-Interact. Steve calls it MERV.'

'Does he indeed.'

'But that's silly. It should be MIVRI.'

'Not everyone has your perfect spelling. Off you go, now. Get your coat.'

As Natalie left the Midax room, at the top of the house, Jack went over to the console, irritated more by the fact that he'd had no previous knowledge of *Merv* than by Angela spying on his life with Ahk'Nemet.

Not knowing how to access the 'VR-Interact', as Natalie had called it, he used a red marker-pen to scrawl a simple message on the screen of his ex-wife's lap-top AppleMac.

'Mind your own bloody business! Keep your eyes to yourself!'

Author's Note

The spectral city of Glanum in this novel is an entirely fictional creation; but it was inspired by the site of the excavated sanctuary city of the same name that can be found near St Remy, Provence. The visible remains there are essentially Roman, but the site had been used for many thousands of years. The local museum contains a statue of the headless torso of CERNUNNOS, Lord of Animals of the early Celts, discovered during excavation. For me, that Glanum is a place of wonder.

Although the notion of M.I.D.A.C.S. in the book is my own, I am indebted to Dr Thierry Jandrok for his helpful discussions, enthusiasm and input on my proposed 'landscaping' of the unconscious mind. An article on this can be found at

Robertholdstock.com

RH
June 2009